Alan Gold... ...ng in the UK ... ...ed to Austral... ...fe Eva, whe... ...ng his action-packed thrillers and running his award-winning marketing consultancy.

ALAN GOLD

THE MARMARA CONTRACT

HarperCollins*Publishers*

HarperCollins*Publishers*
77–85 Fulham Palace Road,
Hammersmith, London W6 8JB

www.**fire**and**water**.com

This paperback edition 1999
1 3 5 7 9 8 6 4 2

First published in Australia by
HarperCollins*Publishers* 1998

ISBN 0 00 651271 2

Set in Bembo

Printed and bound in Great Britain by
Caledonian International Book Manufacturing Ltd, Glasgow

ACKNOWLEDGEMENTS

In order to research this novel I spent some time in Turkey. The recorded history of this wonderful land extends back ten thousand and more years. At the crossroads between Europe and Arabia, Asia and Africa, Turkey has known, and survived, almost every major ancient civilisation. But now, in the late twentieth century, Turkey is in severe danger of being conquered and destroyed by an enemy more deadly and devastating even than the Crusaders. Tourists!

Of course Turkey must welcome and benefit from tourists and the money they bring. But unless a proper tourist infrastructure is created, and the ancient sites better protected, a cultural tragedy will occur, and our children will wonder how we allowed such a thing to happen. At geological and religious wonders such as Cappadocia, guides walk up to unprotected wall paintings dating back fifteen hundred years and touch them with their bare hands; ancient mosaics, the produce of Roman genius, are trodden underfoot as thousands of visitors walk over them; sites which are archaeological wonders are left unkempt and barely examined; and the extraordinary mineral baths at Pamukkale are now denuded of water because of the avarice of nearby hotels.

This book could not have been written without the encouragement and support of Eva, Georgina, Jonathan and Raffe Gold, my long-suffering family who accepted with dignified resignation my long absences from their love and comfort during the many months of research and writing. As always, the wonderful people at HarperCollins were there with advice when needed and admonition when warranted. Special thanks to the wondrous Nicola O'Shea who edited the manuscript, and to Barrie Hitchon, Angelo Loukakis, Laura Harris, Darian Causby, Jim Demetriou and Karen-Maree Griffiths. Also to Amanda O'Connell who worked with me as a structural editor. Thanks to Jill Hickson, Sophie Lance and Gaby Naher of Hickson Associates, my literary agents and safety nets. Many people call themselves literary agents – few merit the term. Jill is one of the few. Thanks also to Helen Nicholson of Sydney University for her assistance on aspects of ancient Troy. And to my friends and colleagues in Writers' Bloc, especially Bryce Courtenay, Paul Wilson, Derek Hansen, Geoff Pike, John Newton and Gretel Killeen for years of congenial support.

WRITERS' BLOC

THE READER IS ALWAYS RIGHT

Alan Gold can be contacted via his web site at: http://www.cg.com.au

PROLOGUE

Berlin's Tiergarten, 20 April 1945

The afternoon of Adolf Hitler's fifty-sixth birthday was interrupted by the pandemonium of Berlin's concrete paving stones erupting like blazing rocks from a volcano, flying high into the air above the streets surrounding the Zoo. The distant boom of sewers exploding into flames could be heard clearly in the underground bunker. But nobody in his diminishing retinue of loyal servants and sycophants had the courage to explain to the Führer what the noise was.

The pavements exploded, slabs of concrete were ejected out of the ground atop roaring columns of fiery gas. As they crashed back to earth, many crushed the terrified residents who were scattering in panic from the advancing Red Army.

It was the end of the Reich which was supposed to have lasted a thousand years, the final drama for the residents of Berlin entrapped in the vice-like grip of the advancing American, British and Russian armies. Everyone knew it was the end, everyone except the madman and his mistress in the bunker. To the skeletal men and women of Berlin, reduced to frantically searching through the bombed-out rubble of shops and houses for scraps of edible garbage, it was now patently obvious that their messiah was insane.

But it wasn't only the starving men and women in the streets of Berlin who knew the truth. The thirty thousand privileged leaders of Nazi Germany, locked in the relative security of one of the vast anti-aircraft towers in the crumbling city, also knew that their days were numbered. Indeed, everybody's days were numbered in those last insane moments of the war. Even those of Adolf Hitler and his bride-to-be, Eva Braun. Ten days after sipping orange and carrot juice and nibbling *apfelstrudl* at his birthday party, the Führer would order his guards to shoot himself and Frau Hitler. Then his Prætorian guard would carry out their final assignment for their Master by siphoning precious petrol from the bottom of a near-empty tank, dousing them with it and setting fire to their bodies.

By the time Deputy Supreme Commander-in-Chief of the Red Army, General Georgi Konstantinovich Zhukov, broke through vicious resistance and conquered the city, he had a feeling that Hitler was already dead. It was a deadly race for Zhukov to capture the Führer before he was killed by his own people, or to take him prisoner before he killed himself. For the hero of Stalingrad, Adolf Hitler was the great treasure – more important than Berlin itself, more important than the whole of Germany. Bringing Adolf Hitler back in chains, parading him through the streets of Moscow in the same way that the Emperor Claudius had paraded Caratacus in the marketplace of ancient Rome, was to be Zhukov's greatest glory; it would ensure his survival. Because one thing was absolutely certain: that other madman, Stalin, was not to be trusted.

But it wasn't to be. In the end, despite murderous fighting for every street corner, every sewer, every attic, the ninety thousand soldiers who had been left behind to hold Berlin were incapable of the task. They were, in the main, young boys from the Hitler Youth or old men still dreaming their sad delusions of glory. As the war in Europe drew to an end, the devastation of the city was total. Few buildings were still standing, let alone damaged by bullets or tank shells. From within the rubble naked arms and hands and blue-tinged legs and feet reached up to the sky. Everywhere there was horror and death. Berlin had become a Hades. Except for the soldiers still shooting at each other on the streets, the city was deserted of life. Any survivors were cowering in cellars or deep in the bowels of the battered buildings. The only creatures prospering in the devastation were the dogs, cats and rats, which could be seen scurrying from bombsite to bombsite, feasting on the human corpses trapped in the rubble.

As the Russian Red Army laid waste to all buildings between the eastern perimeter of the city and the Reichstag, its defence was maintained in a half-hearted way by an elite group of protected strategists who were living in the massive Tiergarten flak tower. But gradually even they, the one-time glittering elite of Berlin's Unter den Linden nightlife, came to understand that the thousand guns of a thousand tanks were pointed directly at them. And so they gave in. They unbolted and opened up the massive steel doors of the flak tower, let in the dusty half-light of the day and emerged with their hands on their heads, smiling ingratiatingly at the Russian peasants in uniform like schoolchildren caught out in an act of mischief.

One of the group, however, didn't come out with his hands above his head. Nor was he wearing a uniform. He marched over to a Russian with the insignia of office on his breast and epaulettes on his shoulders who was standing on the front seat of his jeep, directing operations. The German demanded to be taken immediately to General Zhukov. The captain looked down at the diminutive German and laughed. He jumped out of the jeep, ordered his driver to shut off the engine and pushed the German viciously down onto the ground. Then he withdrew his gun and ordered the man to get back into line with the other prisoners.

The German stood, but he was in no way cowed. Instead of retreating, he shouted: 'Fool! You don't know who I am or what you're dealing with. I am custodian of the greatest and most priceless treasure in the world, in the whole history of humanity. Your peasant soldiers will destroy it if they get their filthy hands on it. How will General Zhukov react then?'

The captain looked at him coldly. He spoke reasonable German, learnt from a professor of languages during the nightmare that was the Battle of Stalingrad. 'You have ten seconds to explain what the hell you are talking about before I shoot you.'

The man swallowed. 'I am Wilhelm Unverzacht,' he said, 'director of the Pre- and Early Ethno-History Museum of Berlin. I was curator of the Heinrich Schliemann Wing which was devoted to the treasury of the city of Troy, to the gold jewellery and precious objects found by Heinrich Schliemann when he was excavating Troy in search of the riches of King Priam.' He swallowed again in fear, suddenly realising that his life depended on whether this man, this Russian peasant, had heard of Priam, the Trojan Wars or even of Schliemann. He repeated in a louder, more certain voice: 'I am custodian of the treasury of King Priam of Troy. Of Helen of Troy's diadem. They're here.' He pointed desperately to the massive building behind him. 'In there.'

The captain blinked. He remembered clearly what the professor of languages had told him about Greece and the stories of blind Homer. In amazement, he said: 'Helen of Troy's treasure is in there?'

The curator nodded.

'What's it doing in a zoo?' asked the captain.

The curator didn't answer. Instead he giggled. And then he thanked Almighty God that He had sent the one intelligent man in the Russian Army to rescue Priam's treasure for humankind.

CHAPTER 1

Istanbul, present day

Sarah Kaplan paid scant attention to the disembodied voice of the British Airways captain telling her that their flight would take them over Berlin and then south over the Czech Republic, Romania and Bulgaria before landing in Istanbul. She stretched her legs, kicked off her shoes and replaced them with the carpet socks offered to passengers in business and first class. Her weekend in London – two days of sleeping, visiting the theatre and art galleries, and relaxing after the pressures of being a war crimes prosecutor in Prague – had been nothing short of blissful. She'd had time to herself at last; long mornings and afternoons when she wasn't a prisoner of the telephone or impressed into the service of a colleague who needed somebody with a knowledge of English or, her particular area, the law of restoration of property stolen by the Nazis or the Stalinists.

But it had been the evenings when she had most joyously savoured her release from Prague. She had seen a play, attended a chamber concert, and walked along the banks of the Thames, smiling at almost every passer-by. Pleasant memories played in her imagination as the 747 lumbered over the east coast of England on its way to Turkey.

Sarah closed her eyes but the refined movements of the stewardesses in the cabin prevented her from luxuriating in her dreams. She opened the package of complimentary goodies the hostess had given her prior to take-off: it contained cologne, soap, make-up remover, eye shades, ear plugs and other paraphernalia to ensure her maximum comfort during the four-hour journey.

Sarah always admired the way the flight attendants managed to look so comfortable despite the length of the journey. Whenever she travelled, she always tried to do so with the maximum of comfort. A light cotton knit top and slacks were usually her chosen uniform to combat the inevitable stuffiness and claustrophobia of the cabin. Sarah was a tall woman, brown skinned with long chestnut hair; she usually chose clothes which accentuated her femininity yet caused her minimum fuss no matter what occasion she may be dressing for.

As an American lawyer, Sarah was used to going first class whenever she travelled for one of her clients. But that was usually within America. Travelling at the front of the plane on an international flight was still a novel experience – well, maybe not so novel since she'd been associated with Joshua Krantz. When she had flown to Prague with the Hollywood film director it had been first class all the way. But the nightmare of their discoveries, of the danger they had faced from men of malice and evil, had made those moments of luxury pale into distant memories.

Sarah had gone to Prague with Josh to negotiate the return of his grandparents' home from the Slovakian government. The simple act of demanding restitution had somehow disturbed a nest of criminal, amoral, power-crazed old Stalinist warlords. In the end, rather than attempt to regain Josh's family property, they had worked in great danger to expose the ancient crimes committed by these monsters. And their work had paid off: twenty old men and women, guilty of brutal crimes against humanity, had been arraigned and were currently being prosecuted.

The most terrifying part of Sarah's time in Prague had been those early weeks, when her very life had been in danger. But once the warlords were in prison the danger had passed, and the Czech government had asked her to join its prosecution team. Her life in Prague had improved dramatically then. She smiled as she thought about the past year, then noticed that the middle-aged woman sitting beside her was attempting to catch her eye. She looked as though she was ready to start up conversation, given the slightest encouragement. But Sarah didn't want to talk. For a whole year, she'd been conversing, advising, debating and cajoling her prosecuting colleagues, as well as standing before Czech government committees in the sumptuous Hradcany Castle once a month, baring her soul in an effort to convince them that the money they were spending on prosecuting the old Stalinists was money well invested in righting old wrongs, in raising the spirit of their people. Now Sarah just wanted to savour her excitement at the prospect of representing the Turkish government. She repeated the words to herself a few more times, rolling the cadences over her tongue like a delicious sweet: representing the Turkish government.

What an amazing irony. A year and a half ago she'd been a relatively unknown lawyer, working for a middle-sized Wall Street firm. Her last act before leaving America had been to represent a Holocaust denier, a hideous anti-Semite who had employed her purely to prove that he wasn't anti-anything, just a passionate striver after the truth of what really happened in German concentration camps. He claimed that they hadn't been used as killing machines, but simply for the purposes of hygiene, for burning victims of typhus and typhoid. Sarah had hated every minute of defending Frank Darman, but her defence of him had really been a defence of the First Amendment. She had used the argument that freedom of speech was more important than the damage caused by the obscene utterances of Darman and his cronies. Her defence and subsequent win had become front-page news; suddenly she was a cause célèbre. The media attention had brought her to the notice of Josh Krantz, the famous Hollywood director who was determined to get his grandparents' house back. Sarah's next job had been to begin an action for restitution against the Slovakian government on Josh's behalf.

And now this: a young Jewish lawyer suddenly catapulted to the forefront of international affairs because of her work in the restitution of property stolen by Josef Stalin and his loathsome cohorts. Sarah was being brought to Istanbul to advise the Turkish government in its appeal to the Russians for the return of Helen of Troy's treasure. What an amazing turnaround. What was that wonderful song from *Sweet Charity*? She thought, 'If my friends could see me now'.

'Are you going to Istanbul on business or pleasure?' the middle-aged woman asked.

Sarah smiled and said casually, 'My business is pleasure.' She burst out laughing, realising how that sounded. 'That came out the wrong way. I mean, I'm going there on business.'

The woman nodded, waiting for Sarah to respond with a reciprocal question. But Sarah turned away from her and reached for a copy of the airline magazine. She had already said too much; the woman had caught her in mid-fantasy. She would have to be much more circumspect in Istanbul, especially when dealing with a fundamentalist Islamic government. Boy, was she ever out of her depth! She hoped she was the only one who knew it.

Sarah glanced at her watch; the flight was proceeding slowly, but then international flights always did. It was still two hours before they landed. She would be met by a government car at the airport but she'd still have only one night to rest up and gather her thoughts before the meeting with Museum and Ministry officials to discuss the reclamation of Schliemann's treasure. Concern began to replace the euphoria she'd felt when she'd first opened the letter delivered to her Czech office by an under-secretary from the Turkish Embassy. She'd felt herself to be in a dream-world then; now she was in a world which would demand performance. What chance did she really have of recovering the treasure? She had spent her brief career as a trial lawyer, representing corporate clients: companies accused of pollution, of bias against stockholders, of breaching contractual terms. If it hadn't been for her work in Prague her name wouldn't have come to the attention of the Turkish government and none of this would have come about. What were the regular chances of a young New York lawyer with limited experience in international law being invited to advise a sovereign government? Especially in the area of reclaiming priceless works of art.

It was such a fraught topic. Society was only just coming to terms with the fact that many of the world's great museums were merely the custodians of the spoils of war. Growing up in New York, Sarah had thrilled at her school's visits to her city's major museums. Most of her schoolfriends had used the trips as a brief holiday from scholastic endeavour, but not Sarah. Entering a museum for her had been like entering a world of fantasy, a world of images. Staring through the glass of the cabinets she had fantasised about how people once lived, about who they were and what they dreamt. She had pored over the dioramas of Paleolithic societies and the statues of ancient fertility goddesses with their huge distended stomachs and wild child-like eyes, or the impish gods with massive penises which caused her classmates to giggle in hysterics. Sarah merely saw them as the innocent expression of early humankind coming to terms with itself. But these days society was beginning to look upon the ownership of priceless works of history with increasing concern. Many had been stolen from their rightful owners in the distant past, yet history had dulled the seriousness of the thefts, allowing the crime of the despoilers to be muted and diminished until the works came to be seen as valid acquisitions. Some were the spoils of war, stolen from a conquered people and carried off as booty in the creaking hulls of overladen ships. Other priceless works were stolen as a by-product of colonisation: treasure hunters, bounty hunters, colonists and overlords took the priceless works of their new land's history back to the mother country.

Not that this was a new phenomenon. The Romans had stolen thousands of Greek statues, friezes, vases and weaponry and called them the spoils of war. Every age and every part of the world had its history of this type of theft. Some were famous and still caused serious difficulties between nations: for example, the demands by Greece for Britain to return the Elgin Marbles which were stolen from the Parthenon along with two hundred and fifty-three sculptures. Now many nations which had suffered colonisation saw themselves as victims of imperialist aggression.

Which is why Sarah was flying to Turkey. She shook her head in wonder. How far she had come in only a year and a half. Turkey! Since she had received the letter from the Turkish government, and the attendant telephone calls from the Turkish Embassy in Prague making the arrangements, she had done a lot of reading about the country. It sounded so fascinating. Ten thousand years of history in which virtually every civilisation was represented: the Hittites, the Myceneans, the Greeks, the Romans, Byzantium, Christianity, the Ottomans. Each name rolled off her tongue, each conjuring up powerful images of ancient splendours.

She had discussed the assignment with a colleague in Prague. His reaction had surprised her. 'Aren't you concerned about going there, you being a Jew?' he had asked. She had explained that even though Turkey was an Islamic nation it enjoyed friendly relations with Israel, and, according to the histories she had read, it had offered sanctuary to Jews expelled from Spain. Consequently she expected there to be little anti-Semitism there.

Her colleague had shrugged. 'To me, it's still Islam versus Judaism, no matter what the country. Just be careful.'

Sarah had ignored his advice. There was virtually no anti-Semitism in Turkey, of that she was sure. But his comments had rankled and every so often when she woke up from the daydream of representing the Turkish government she wondered just what sort of an obstacle her Judaism might be.

At five o'clock in the morning the streets of Istanbul were silent. The sky was heavy with an oily humidity which owed its consistency and odour to the clouds of diesel smoke arising from the hundreds of ships that daily traversed the bottleneck separating Asian and European Istanbul; ships which shuttled through the Bosphorus, sailing from the Sea of Marmara into the Black Sea to deliver their cargoes into the underbelly of the old Soviet Union. The pollution hung like an ominous hand over Istanbul's mosques and their minarets and cupolas and added to the early morning gloom of the still-sleeping city.

Sarah had made a considered choice to stay in Sultanahmet, the old part of Istanbul. It was within a stone's throw of the Bosphorus and the Bosphorus was the centre of everything. The old hotel, the Turkoman, had originally been the home of a minor palace official of the eighteenth-century Ottoman Empire, and her window opened directly onto a breathtaking vista of the Blue Mosque. Sarah had gone to bed at nine o'clock the previous night, exhausted after the rush and bustle of the flight and the hysteria of the hair-raising journey from the airport into the city, but the continuous and cacophonous noise of Istanbul had kept her awake until the early hours of the morning when, finally, she had fallen into a deep sleep. She was still deeply asleep when an electronically amplified voice, pitched at an ear-piercing decibel level, boomed out of a bank of loudspeakers that Allah was great.

Sarah sat bolt upright, clawing at the sheets to protect herself from impending assault. Her mind reeled and she stared, bemused, around the pitch black room. Was it a nightmare? What was happening? Just as suddenly as the amplified banshee had dragged her from sleep, the city was plunged back into its eerie pre-dawn silence. But Sarah's ears were still ringing from the electronic assault. What the hell was going on? Was she going mad? As the wailing started up again she realised her stupidity. She burst out laughing. The tourist information leaflets she'd read in Prague had told her that the Hotel Turkoman was only a very short distance from the world famous Blue Mosque, right opposite the Hippodrome and close to the blissfully beautiful Hagia Sophia. In the refined peace and quiet of her apartment in Prague it had all seemed so obvious: stay right in the centre of town where the action was, enjoy the exotic pleasures of Istanbul, then fly down to Ankara to discuss matters with the government officials there. Then she would return to tempestuous Istanbul where she was to work with the experts.

But Sarah hadn't factored in the muezzins and their regular assaults on the sleep patterns and consciousness of the citizens of Turkey. She'd never been in an Islamic country before. She had read about the muezzins, the men whose job it was to climb to the tops of the minarets five times a day to call the faithful to prayer, starting at five in the morning and ending at ten at night. Last night, as she ate dinner in a restaurant close to her hotel, they had sounded Middle-Eastern in flavour and had fitted into the oriental tenor of the city. For the first time since she had landed, Sarah had realised she was truly out of Europe, virtually on another continent. But the music of ubiquitous wandering musicians and the ever-present din of the city had muffled and blunted the song of the priests. Now, as dawn was breaking, there was no barrier to the muezzins' piercing volume. The full fury of passionate Islam broke over her.

Sarah closed the window, which went some way towards reducing the decibel level. She went back to bed, her heart pounding from her sudden awakening and confusion. She'd had two hours sleep, three at the most, and this morning she was due to meet with an academic from one of Istanbul's major museums who had been appointed by the Minister for Antiquities and Archaeological Treasures to work with her on preparing the brief which would be presented to the Russian government. Sarah caught a glimpse of herself in the mirror: she looked like a harridan. God Almighty! How was she ever going to make herself look respectable by morning?

Sarah entered the grounds of the Topkapi Palace through the southernmost gate. Professor Mustafa Bengazi had given her explicit directions. It was summer, the height of Turkey's tourist season. Hundreds of men and women were already queuing for admission to the Ottoman sultans' seraglio. Most thought they were going to see the inside of the Harem, but in fact would merely be viewing family apartments; a misconception for which Mozart and his opera about abduction was partly responsible. And there were already thousands more people visiting the Topkapi, wandering the vast grounds of the huge palace and museum. The Topkapi was an extraordinary place with vast panoramic views over the Bosphorus,

Europe and Asia. It was built on a high promontory overlooking the junction of the Bosphorus and the Sea of Marmara at the Golden Horn. Driving around the outside, the palace had reminded Sarah of Hradcany Castle in Prague. That palace too had been built on a high promontory to dominate the city. Kafka had been overawed by the castle in Prague; Sarah wondered how he would have reacted to this Ottoman monolith.

She was shown up to Professor Bengazi's office. He was much younger than she'd expected, tall, athletic and not unattractive, though his teeth were tinged yellow with nicotine stains and the centre of his bushy moustache had a smoky hue. Perhaps it was the way he smiled at her, or momentarily bowed his head in a slight form of self-deprecation, but he reminded her of Laco. She fought back a smile as she shook his hand. Laco was the last person she would have expected to invade her thoughts at a moment like this. Laco, the Slovakian archaeologist. He had been an indiscretion, an affair, one so completely out of her character yet upon which she had embarked with gusto and in full flight. Laco was a man who was the antithesis of everything she was used to, yet he had filled a void for her in a moment of crisis.

Dr Bengazi smiled and welcomed her. Sarah immediately went into professional mode, curt and crisp. She'd done it a hundred times before: walked into a conference room full of strangers or walked out into the lobby to greet a new client. She knew how to be professional. Yet thoughts of last year's romantic involvement with Laco, as well as her intimate friendship with Josh Krantz, invaded her mind. In professional mode, Sarah the lawyer normally knew how to exclude all else; no thoughts of family, friends or personal involvements were ever allowed to intrude when she was one-on-one with a client or negotiating with the other side's legal people. Yet, as she looked at the gentle Mustafa Bengazi, unwelcome and unexpected images of Laco, Josh and David raced through her mind, dragging her back unwillingly to Prague and Slovakia and the hideous events of a year earlier.

She forced herself to clear her mind and think of nothing but the task at hand. But the association of Bengazi with Laco was too powerful. It was like meeting an old friend in an unfamiliar place. There was that indefinable moment of incomprehension, that second of other-worldness where she lost momentary track of who she was and why she was there. Turkey was still terribly new for her. Sarah's mind was still full of the Czech Republic and Slovakia and the Russians who had tried to kill her. Her time there had forced her to confront her deepest fears, to recognise her own history. And over the last twelve months any idea of her enjoying a personal life had been held in abeyance because of her commitment to the trial of the Stalinist henchmen and women. As it was, there were three men in her life – and she couldn't get one of them out of her mind.

There was David, her live-in lover in America, a passionate brilliant cellist who wanted to marry her. But something had happened to Sarah in the Czech Republic and the strength of her love for David had been mysteriously overwhelmed by her feelings for Laco, the very Bohemian archaeologist whose physical passion had opened up a part of her which still made her feel uncomfortable with herself – especially when she telephoned her mother and father. And then there was Josh! Dear sweet brilliant beautiful Joshua Krantz, Hollywood film director and the man whose passion to right the wrongs of the past had begun the whole thing.

Passion! It kept dominating her actions, counteracting the logical part of her mind which screamed silently at her whenever she did what she knew instinctively was misguided. And it was passion that she would have to control if she was going to do a solidly professional job for the Turkish government. Passion had clouded her judgements in Europe; Sarah was determined that she was not going to allow it to interfere with her decisions in Turkey.

She bit the inside of her lip. The pain drew her back to the present. Laco, Josh and David disappeared, enabling her to concentrate her mind on the formality of the moment. Bengazi led her to a cluster of sofas in his heavily ornate office. Its gold-hued walls were hung with pictures of sultans, their bushy beards, turbans and ostrich feathers showing the lifestyle they had once lived. Anyone looking at the pictures could easily imagine their great wealth. Sarah thought of the poem, 'Ozymandias of Egypt' by Shelley: 'Look on my works, ye Mighty, and despair!'

In the bookcase Sarah noticed jewel-encrusted daggers, as well as statues made of stone which to her untrained eye looked to be archetypes of the earth fertility mother. From her reading she thought they might be Hittite, or maybe even earlier. Bengazi noticed her looking at one particularly beautiful specimen. He picked it up and gave it to her to hold.

'Chalcolithic,' he told her. 'Copper Age. Before the dawn of the Bronze Age. Maybe six and a half thousand years old.'

'It's magnificent,' she told him.

He smiled and took it back from her. 'Many think of our earliest ancestors as nothing more than cave dwellers. Yet they had an amazingly sophisticated society, in many ways as sophisticated as some African and South American tribes today. The only difference between tribes today and back then is that our lucky primitives have Coca-Cola and monogrammed T-shirts.'

Sarah burst out laughing. She was going to enjoy working with Mustafa Bengazi. He had been given the job by the Ankara government of explaining the historical nature of Schliemann's treasure to Sarah, so that when she flew to Turkey's capital the following day she would be well versed in why the government wanted it back from the Russian authorities, who only recently had rediscovered it.

'Tell me,' Bengazi said, 'how much do you know about Heinrich Schliemann and the so-called treasure of King Priam which he discovered?'

Sarah shrugged her shoulders. 'Since I received that letter from the Turkish government, I've done a little reading. I know that he found the city of Troy, that he discovered Helen of Troy's treasure, and I know that he took the treasure to Berlin. In the closing days of the war it was lost, but now, somehow, it's been discovered in some museum in Russia.'

Professor Bengazi smiled. 'Then you already know more than most people. But what few seem to realise is that the greatest treasure of antiquity was stolen by Schliemann in the spring of 1875, two years after he uncovered it. He used fraud, trickery and lies to get the treasure. And pure and simple theft.'

As he began to tell the story, Sarah could sense that he was becoming agitated. Bengazi took a deep breath: 'Let me try to put Schliemann's crimes against the Turkish people, against the whole of humankind, into perspective. It was the closing chapter for the Ottoman Empire, although, at the time, the ruling classes were so blinkered that they simply didn't realise it. The sultans who ruled were weak effete men but, much more importantly, their eyes were turned towards Mecca. Although Turkey, north of the Bosphorus, had been part of the European continent since the time of the Hittites, the Ottomans – largely because of their Islamic faith – didn't consider themselves western. Quite the opposite. In dress, manner, aspirations, mentality and geography, the Ottomans considered themselves part of Asia in general and the Middle East in particular. Specifically they felt they held a kinship with the religion and customs of the nations of Arabia. Yet, oddly, they spent fortunes emulating the richness of Europe. You only have to look at that monstrosity which nearly bankrupted us, the Dolmabahce Palace.

'To understand why Schliemann was so able to rape Turkey, Sarah, you must understand more about Turkey itself at the time when he was digging into our ground. For centuries the whole of Europe had feared the mighty Ottoman Empire. We had conquered most of Arabia, the whole of North Africa, parts of Italy, had almost taken Budapest and were knocking on the gates of Vienna. Every king, every prince in Europe feared us. But by the middle of the last century we had grown weak from too much expansion and too little good government. We tried too hard to emulate the finest aspects of Europe: we based our army, our civil service, our diplomacy on European traditions. We welcomed Europeans like Schliemann with open arms.

'But we had no real understanding of European culture or history. And that meant that western archaeology's fascination with the buried treasures of Greece and Rome, and sites like Ephesus which have such a strong connection with early Christianity and much of the ancient history of humankind, was of little interest to these sultans. Of course they were as mercenary as everyone else and knew the value of gold and silver, but they had little interest in potsherds and what we now revere as the invaluable relics of humankind's earliest creativity and inventiveness, their expressions of themselves as civilised beings. They realised the artefacts had some value, and they were avaricious businessmen, but they had no passion for the role of custodians of one of the world's major historical repositories. In fact, it's hard to think of a country which has a greater wealth of history buried beneath its land than Turkey. Ten thousand years of civilisation and we've only just begun to realise its importance.'

Bengazi looked for Sarah's reaction. Her eyes widened. Good, he thought. Few men knew more about the history of their country or were more passionate advocates for it than Dr Bengazi was of his Turkey. He continued: 'Everybody's been here and made their mark. From the earliest humans grubbing an existence outside their caves to the glorious Hittites, Greeks, Romans, Christians, Ottomans ... You name it, they've been here, leaving behind the marvels of their culture.'

Sarah raised her cup, fascinated. But when she tasted its contents she had to do her best not to grimace. The coffee was thick and grainy. Not even the Turkish coffee she occasionally drank in restaurants in New York was as glutinous as this.

The professor was still talking. 'Heinrich Schliemann may be credited with beginning archaeology as a science, but he was little more than a merchant adventurer, a pirate whose sea was the landmass of the Middle East, a liar, a thief and a cheat. But he was also a genius. He was all these things and more, rolled into one enigma.'

Sarah was amazed. 'But he was the man who discovered Troy. All the books praise him to the skies, calling him the father of archaeology.'

'Ha!' laughed Bengazi. 'The discovery of Troy should be credited to the owner of the land at Hisarlik, just south of the mouth of the Dardanelles, a man called Frank Calvert, the US vice consul at Canakkale. Now there was an interesting man – and a real scholar. He, like Schliemann, was a knowledgeable scholar of Homer. But in every other respect Calvert was totally different from Schliemann. He was an unbelievably generous man who openly discussed the location of Troy with Schliemann in a spirit of academic quest. It was he who told Schliemann to dig on the hill at Hisarlik.

'And as for Schliemann being the father of archaeology, it's all nonsense. He was a wrecker, a vandal. Schliemann dug massive trenches this way and that across the land to get down to what he considered to be the site of the ancient battle between the Greeks and the Trojans. God only knows what that bastard destroyed digging through three thousand years of civilisation. Anyway, by luck – certainly not by judgement – he was digging at the bottom of a wall which was in imminent danger of collapse when, in one of the recesses he noticed something of interest, something which glistened. Knowing he could be about to make a discovery he sent away his Turkish workers so that he'd be alone. And that was when he found the great treasure of Troy. He called it Priam's treasure but of course it wasn't. It dated to a period which was very much earlier, probably a thousand years earlier. But that doesn't matter. What is important is not whether the headdress was worn by Helen of Troy but that we've found the artefacts, the very symbols of our ancestors. It's one of the greatest archaeological discoveries of all time. It ranks with the discoveries at Mycenae and at Knossos.'

Sarah interrupted. 'But if it's not Helen of Troy's treasure, how do we know that she existed?'

Bengazi paused a moment, trying to understand her question. 'Why does it matter?' he asked quizzically.

'But . . .'

'Helen of Troy may have existed or she may not. The Trojan war may have happened or it may not. Schliemann drove himself crazy trying to prove that it did happen.

But these things no longer interest archaeologists, only adventurers. Would you try to prove the story of Adam and Eve and the Garden of Eden? The important thing isn't whether or not these things happened. What's important is the stories that have come down to us, the myths. Through our myths, we understand where we've come from and what we are today. And you know something, Sarah, the world's greatest mythmakers lived right here, in Anatolia. In Turkey. The Hittites. They were the originators of the stories by which humankind came to understand itself. The Greeks took our legends. But we, we Turks, our Hittite ancestors were the creators! That's why myths are so important to us. So long as they *are* myths. In fact, I'll go further: we would be diminished as a society if Helen of Troy and the Trojan war *were* to be proven as historical fact. The gods would become smaller, less powerful. Some important element in humankind's imagination might very well be lost if we ever find the truth about Helen of Troy.'

Sarah nodded, wondering whether she agreed. When she was in Slovakia Laco's father, also an archaeologist, had said the same thing to her. She hadn't imagined then that one day she would be in the land of myth. She would have a lot to think about tonight.

'We're digressing,' he said. 'You see what happens when you get a Turk talking about myths. And there's much ground to cover. When you go to Ankara tomorrow you're going to be briefed about the Turkish government's claim on Priam's treasure. Let me tell you briefly what happened so you'll understand.'

Sarah took another sip of the acrid gritty coffee. Was it beginning to grow on her? She'd been in Turkey for less than a day. Surely not.

'Schliemann was an adventurer, a man who made a fortune by trading in Russia, another fortune trading in

America and a further fortune trading in antiquities he stole from Greece and Turkey. He was a citizen of Germany by birth and a citizen of Russia, America and Greece by adoption. All the stories he made up about reading Homer when he was a child are almost certainly nonsense. He was like a medieval knight on a quest for the Holy Grail. Anyway, eventually he was granted a firman by the Ottoman government – that's a right to dig. And after years of frustration and backbreaking work he found Priam's treasure on 31 May, 1873. The treasure consists of thousands of priceless items, most of them small, nearly all of them unparalleled in their exquisite beauty. They're some of the earliest and most astounding examples of craftsmanship we have. But amongst the wonders Schliemann found two artefacts which stand head and shoulders above almost any other ancient wonder: a gold death mask and an amazing diadem and headdress.'

Sarah put her hand to her chest and felt through her blouse. She grasped the edges of the amulet given to her by her mother, the amulet which her great-grandfather had dug out of the ground of Slovakia before he was murdered in a pogrom. The amulet which had caused her so many problems while she was in Eastern Europe with Joshua Krantz. 'Were any amulets found?' she asked.

Bengazi nodded. 'The whole of Hittite territory is rich in amulets. Anyway, Schliemann and his young Greek wife, Sophie, were beside themselves with joy when he uncovered the cache. But they knew they would have to give most of it away to the government. So when the treasure was taken secretively out of the ground Schliemann tried to hide it, but the Turkish inspectors were too clever for him and eventually he was forced to reveal to the authorities what he had discovered. Of course he never showed them the true amount, only a fraction was displayed on the table in the wooden examination hut

– the larger and more impressive pieces. Most he kept hidden somewhere in the camp. I'll cut a long and very dirty story short for you to say that Schliemann continued to lie and cheat and fool the Turkish authorities about his work until the spring of 1875 when his battle with the Turkish administrators was at last resolved. He agreed to pay the Imperial Museum in Constantinople two thousand English pounds against an undertaking that they would make no further claim against Priam's treasure.'

'Two thousand pounds!' Sarah exclaimed in shock. 'But that's . . .'

'It's a pittance, but it's not the money in itself which is important. It's the fact that the Turks allowed him to take the treasure out of the country.'

'Where did it go?' she asked.

'Well, Schliemann didn't live much longer. Only another fifteen years. But most of them were terrible years for him. He had recurring ear problems and life in those times, especially given the primitive conditions of digging in the Dardanelles region, was very tough. I think he knew in the middle of the 1880s that he would shortly die but even right to the very end he was travelling around Europe, examining archaeological sites and meeting with the great men of Europe. But he was faced with the decision of whom he could entrust his treasure to after his death. His wife, Sophie, and his children, Agamemnon and Andromache, as well as his children by his first wife, a woman he met in Russia named Ekaterina Petrovna, were all very well provided for. So Schliemann was more concerned with his eternal reputation as a scholar and archaeologist than making money out of his Trojan treasure.

'Right up to the end of his life, he didn't know whether to give it to the Greeks, because of his Greek wife Sophie, and the fact that he lived his last years in Greece, or to the Germans, because he was born there, or even to the

Americans, because they could pay him the most money. Truth to tell, very few countries who were offered it wanted it. Most rejected it because of the staggering amounts he was demanding. But eventually he gave the treasure to Berlin, on the condition that they build a special wing in the Pre- and Early Ethno-History Museum which he demanded be named after him. Arrogant to the last.' Dr Bengazi couldn't keep the venom out of his voice.

'And there it sat until 1939. At the beginning of World War II, it was moved for safekeeping into one of the huge anti-aircraft towers that Hitler had ordered built to protect the elite of the Third Reich. When General Zhukov conquered Berlin for the Red Army he learnt of the treasure and had it taken to Moscow, but by all accounts nobody there was particularly interested in it. They were still bleeding over their tens of millions killed during the war and archaeology came a very poor last to the need for bread and meat. And so, my poor beautiful treasure, which had enjoyed only seventy years of sunshine after four thousand years of burial, was again locked away from our sight. It was put into a series of archive crates and stored in the basement of the Pushkin Museum where it was forgotten.'

He laughed. 'Forgotten, Sarah! Can you believe it? Until it was finally tracked down in the early 1990s by a clever journalist. The Germans, of course, are making demands for its return but I've managed to persuade my masters in Ankara that Turkey has just as much claim as they do. Much more so, in fact.'

Sarah nodded. 'Was there a contract of sale or a document in which the Ottoman government agreed to allow Schliemann to keep his part of the treasure?'

'Certainly,' said Dr Bengazi. 'But I believe the terms of the contract were unreasonable and . . . what's the phrase they use?'

'Harsh and unconscionable,' she responded.

'That's what they were.'

'But there's an even stronger case against the contract, Dr Bengazi,' Sarah said. 'You see, the fact of the matter is that the then Turkish authorities entered the contract on the basis of a fraudulent understanding. I don't know for certain about Turkish law, but in the West contracts are only valid if both sides have full and reasonable access to a disclosure of knowledge about the terms and conditions of the deal they're signing. From what you tell me, Schliemann lied.' Dr Bengazi nodded enthusiastically. 'If what you say can be proven, that is.'

'Oh, it can be proven. His diaries. The records of people who worked with him. But even if we do prove it, where do we stand about getting the treasure back?'

Sarah shrugged her shoulders. 'You may have a watertight case, but when one country takes legal action against another proof is not the most important thing. Enforcement, I'm afraid, is where most of these problems fall down. If we do win in court – and God knows what court we're talking about – the only way you're going to get the treasure back is by imposing sanctions or by bringing the weight of moral force to bear against the Russian government. But after nearly a century of communism I'm not sure the Russians are particularly concerned about moral force. Not only that, but in April 1998 the then President of Russia went head to head against Russia's Constitutional Court. You see, the Dumas, the Russian Parliament, voted for Russia to keep all of the art treasures that had been appropriated from Nazi Germany during World War II. We're talking about millions of priceless archival documents, Monets, Goyas, Cezannes, Matisses, millions of books, as well as the Priam treasure. But Germany put pressure on Yeltsin and he refused to agree to the Parliament's decision. So the

Constitutional Court overruled him and told him that he had to agree to Russia keeping the stolen works. The Court and the Parliament looked on it as compensation for the cost of the war, both financial and in the lives of the people. They claim they're holding about sixty-five billion dollars worth of art and that it's going to stay in their country. There's no way they'll hand it back to Germany.'

Sarah smiled. 'Which of course is why I've been called over here. Because now Turkey's claim is so much stronger.'

'That's exactly right,' he said.

'Are you absolutely certain that the Russians won't simply give back the Schliemann treasure? With Germany's claim on hold, surely it would be good public relations for the Russians to give it to you? Let them hold on to the Mattises and Monets and things . . . but can't they see that this is in a different league?'

Bengazi smiled ruefully. 'No chance. We've had private conversations with them; I went over to Moscow and it was like trying to pull teeth. I could get almost no information. And then an official said that we had no claim at all and that there would be no reparation, not to Germany and not to Turkey. And worse, I don't think we've seen anything like the true treasure. I saw the big stuff – it's been on public exhibition. But there were thousands of smaller items. Why haven't they put them on show? What's going on over there?'

'So,' said Sarah, 'we have a bit of a fight on our hands.'

CHAPTER 2

Moscow, present day

Feyodor Mikailovich Meconski, deputy director of the Pushkin Museum in Moscow, took out a handkerchief and wiped the tears from his waterlogged eyes. For the past ten minutes he had been crying into a large tumbler which, apart from his tears, also held the last dregs of a bottle of vodka. His wife had been watching him in disgust for the past five minutes, wondering what had happened to the man she had once loved and respected. She stood up to leave the room. She could no longer bear to look at the wreck of the man in front of her, a man buffeted on the rocks of his own misery and of his own making. Ten minutes earlier she'd been forced to move his feet from the antimacassar covering the taboret, placing them instead on an ancient cracked leather footstool to prevent his ugly boots destroying more of the antique footstool's surface.

Meconski's body looked deflated as it sagged in the decrepit lounge chair, his head lolling close to the top of the table. He had never been pretty, not even in their early years of marriage would he have been considered handsome. But then he had had a brain which was startling; his knowledge of history, of archaeology, of Russian society was exciting. He had told stories in the tradition of the old storytellers: riveting, expansive and full of imagination. Now he was debauched and disgusting. His arm and his hand clutching the empty bottle of Stolichnaya prevented his head from tilting sideways onto the fading lacquer of their drinks table, but nothing could prevent his mouth from drooling like a baby.

He had been drunk now on and off for six weeks, sobering up to drag himself to the office, bleary-eyed and dishevelled, only to return an hour or two after lunch, having drowned his food in vodka.

His wife was totally indifferent to his suffering. She had been indifferent towards him for the past twelve of the twenty-four years of their marriage. She knew about his occasional flings with various busty research students from Moscow University, and whenever he came home from international conferences bearing gifts of lingerie and perfumes, she'd guessed that he'd probably enjoyed his evenings with some dried-up wasteland of a female archaeologist. Not only that, but for the past twelve years he had been so useless in bed that she had even thought he might be heading towards impotency. Anyway, she hadn't exactly lived an exemplary life herself. While he had been busy with his work, she had enjoyed herself with a string of young male students who were eager to curry favour with the wife of the deputy director of the Pushkin Museum. But throughout their twenty-four years together they had always managed to maintain the semblance of a relationship. They had gone to official receptions at the Kremlin together, arm in arm, walking down the long red-carpeted corridors beneath the massive crystal chandeliers, both glorying in their presence at whatever occasion they were being entertained for. Those had been the good times. Nobody at the receptions, however, had experienced the car journeys there or back to their desultory apartment, made in indifferent silence there and in an atmosphere of stringent criticism on the way back: why had he made that comment at the dinner table? or why had she laughed so stupidly at the remark made by that Kremlin official? Twenty-four years of growing isolation within marriage. Not complete unhappiness, not for the whole twenty-four years at least – but recently things had become unbearable.

Meconski watched his wife leave the room. Good! She was the last thing he wanted in his life at the moment. Recently something wonderful had happened to him, something he could only normally dream about. A sudden unexpected blissful moment which had awakened all the winter buds, which had made his face flush with warmth on a freezing Moscow morning, which had filled his life with colour and had obliterated the grey hues of his apartment, his job, his existence. That something was Natalie. He had met her while drinking in a bar with friends. He'd thought at first that she was one of the bar girls, the legions of housewives turned prostitutes who desperately eked out enough money for food and clothing. But she wasn't. She was an administrative assistant in an office. And she was beautiful and clever and witty.

During the evening, he and his friends had spied Natalie and a couple of other girls sitting at a table, talking and sipping their drinks. For an hour Natalie and he had exchanged glances across the room, occasionally smiling and nodding then pretending to ignore each other. But there was no ignoring her in the end. He had asked the waiter if he could buy the girls a drink. They'd refused at first, but he had persisted; in the end, they had accepted and he and his colleagues joined the girls' table. Feyodor took Natalie home that night. That was all, he just drove her home. She didn't invite him inside. She didn't kiss him or even shake his hand. She just got out of the car, thanked him for his courtesy and closed the door. He'd jumped out and asked whether he could phone her. She told him that he couldn't call her, that it had been a lovely night but it must remain just that — one evening of two people meeting, talking and parting. She had a life to lead and she knew just by looking at him that he was married.

The following day he sent her flowers. She didn't respond. Next day, more flowers; still no response. He tried one last time and she phoned him to thank him. She agreed to have dinner that night on condition that he send no more flowers. Feyodor Mikailovich phoned his shrew of a wife and told her that he had been ordered to dinner with the director and a visiting dignitary. Feyodor and Natalie spent the evening together, laughing and talking. He spoke extensively about his work; she was either flatteringly interested or genuinely keen on archaeology. She accepted his offer to visit the Pushkin Museum.

He had waited with almost overwhelming anxiety for the two days it took her to find time to visit during the evening. He had shown her downstairs into the bowels of the Museum, away from the view of the guards. She'd wanted to see the exhibits but he had convinced her that she could return at any time to see those, just like any tourist. The trip to the hidden parts of the Museum was a very special favour he was doing for her because he liked her. They had made love on the packing crates which housed the treasure of Helen of Troy, a treasure the whereabouts of which was known to only a handful of people.

Feyodor Mikailovich Meconski vaguely heard his wife banging around in the kitchen. There was a roaring in his ears but he could swear that she was angrily muttering threats and imprecations. He didn't care. His face was numb and his ears were ringing. An overwhelming feeling of sadness permeated even those crevices of his body normally hidden to the light. Every time he tried to lift his head, its oppressive weight somehow dragged it back down on his arm, and so he cried again. That was his life: cheer up, cry, cheer up, cry, when all he wanted to do was sleep. Sleep and get rid of the nightmares.

Feyodor somehow forced his head back into a vertical position, but was unable to hold it there — it lolled back onto the back of the old armchair. His stomach heaved with the vodka and an evil-tasting gorge rose up to strangle his throat. He swallowed it down and grimaced as he tasted its acrid biliousness. Somehow he lifted his hand, which was clutching his glass, and threw back more vodka, the oily aromatic taste washing the bile away.

Feyodor, in his position as deputy director of the Pushkin Museum had been decorated for services to Russian culture by Yeltsin himself. By Yeltsin! For popularising archaeology for schoolchildren. Those were his glory days, years ago. Before his crime. Feyodor closed his eyes. Within minutes he heard somebody snoring in the room; he listened as closely as the pounding in his ears would allow to the loud aggressive noise. He opened his eyes and through their slits tried to look around the room. Nobody. It was him snoring. Sleep!

The deputy director stayed asleep until a car backfiring outside his apartment woke him the next morning. His nasal passages had been blocked all night by the alcohol and he had been gulping air through his mouth. Now his throat was as dry as a mummy's shroud. He coughed but his head hurt too badly to make the sort of full-throated clearance he really needed. His feet were still crossed on the old leather footstool he'd stolen years ago from the Pushkin. What the hell. They had so much they didn't know about, he'd be dead and buried before someone did an inventory. Inventory! That word again. He tried to raise himself. The glass had somehow escaped his grip, slipped down and spilled its contents across the top of the lacquered drinks table. Fuck it!

Feyodor manoeuvred himself to his feet and staggered into the bathroom. He turned on the tap and splashed cold water onto his face, then gulped down ten mouthfuls to quell the raging of the desert sandstorm in his throat. He struggled out of his pants and sat heavily on the toilet. His head felt like shit. He tried to urinate but his head hurt too badly. He couldn't squeeze or put any pressure on his body. All he wanted to do was go back to sleep, or even to die. Yes! That was the solution to his problems. He would die. Throw himself out of the window of the Pushkin Museum. Write a note telling the world what he had done. Yes, that was the way out! But he was too much of a coward. He knew he would never be able to do it. He hated pain and suffering.

He tried to shave but he couldn't focus properly and his hands kept missing his cheek. He washed the lather off and squinted at his reflection: there were still large clumps of grey stubble poking out of his sallow skin. He was due to attend a meeting today with the Board of Management and the government officials. Just the usual time-wasting garbage. Yes, sir. No, sir. Unfortunately the Director is ill, sir, so I'm not in a position to answer your questions, sir, but if you think so, sir . . .

God Almighty, if only they knew! Yesterday, the Director, that lazy, artless, anti-intellectual careerist con, had made one of her appearances. The staff in the secretariat had actually applauded as she'd walked in through the door. She'd looked half-dead and had clutched her heart a couple of times while she was speaking to people. Good. Maybe she would die and leave him in charge. Then he could cover up his crimes. Somehow Feyodor managed to dress. His eyes were a mockery of his soul. Normally they were clear, unlike those of most of the middle-aged men whom he knew, but today they were swollen and blue-veined, like pieces of week-old steak.

How could he face his colleagues? Eventually he knew the moment of reckoning would come but every day he made an increased effort to put off its arrival. Every day he phoned Natalie, begging and begging, all to no avail. When the flow of presents had dried up, when the money from the illegal sales had stopped flowing in, the torrent of her love, her warmth, her sexuality, had suddenly trickled to nothing. It was as though she had been a figment of his erotic imagination, a diversion in his twenty-four years of marital hell. A fantasy, a beautiful exotic orgasmic fantasy. But now the fantasy had gone and he was left with the crime and the punishment. Who would believe that Natalie had been the instigator of his criminal actions, and who would care? The responsibility was his. He could have been covered in glory; he could have been the man who catalogued and gave the world the entire treasury of Troy.

He remembered so clearly his feelings as he had prised open one of the chests and ripped aside the old brown waxed packing paper. The markings on the inner wooden container were in German but he knew enough of the Teutonic alphabet to read it: Schliemann. König Priam. It was then that he should have told his colleagues, people he respected, who would have congratulated him. He had told his assistant but they had agreed on a strategy: catalogue the inventory and then surprise the world. Of course there had been speculation for years that Priam's treasure was in Moscow; journalists had been sniffing around for some time. But the bowels of the Pushkin Museum were so crammed with uncatalogued and unorganised crates that it took an archaeologist to trace and find it. He should have kept quiet. Instead he'd told a drinking friend when he was into his eighth vodka. And then he had told somebody else. And then Natalie had appeared, almost out of nowhere. Why hadn't he seen what was now so obvious? Why hadn't he realised who Natalie was? Fool! Stupid imbecilic fool of a man. But he had been flattered by her attention. And the lovemaking on top of Helen of Troy's treasure – that was something he would never forget! Even as he stood in the frozen wastes of Siberia, facing the firing squad, his body would be suffused by the memory of her warm lips sucking his mouth, his eyes, his ears and his nipples until she lowered herself and he exploded once and screamed his passion – as she had made him scream again later and again and then again.

He had never known love like it. It was more than sex. No woman could pretend like that. He knew enough about women to know that she was crazy for him. She had become insatiable. She had phoned him the day following their lovemaking on top of the treasure and begged him to make love to her again. Not in the Pushkin but in her apartment. He had felt like a god and she had behaved as though she were an acolyte. Even his relationship with his wife had improved when so many of his tensions and frustrations suddenly evaporated. But even then, he hadn't understood; he had been too naive to realise what was going on.

It was all too late now. He'd sold out for thirty pieces of silver. Silver which he'd spent like water in the early years. It had all been so easy then, and he'd thought it would never stop. A piece of the treasury placed in his pocket as he left the Museum for the night; he'd pass it on to her and she would sell it through her company to American buyers. Then another piece and another and so on. For months, he had lived like a king, spending a fortune on Natalie. The private collectors in America were insatiable for whatever he allowed to dribble in their direction. By now there must be hundreds of rings locked safely in the vaults of avaricious individuals, who thrilled at secretly telling their friends that this was the genuine treasure of King Priam. Feyodor had even committed the ultimate archaeological crime: he had written a certificate of verification for each object he had stolen.

And then the bombshell had come, except that it was more of a nuclear explosion. He had gone around to

Natalie's apartment one evening to make love. He had money in his pocket, expensive chocolates purchased on the black market for her, even French champagne. In the old days it would have cost him a week's salary, but salary meant nothing to him any more. The money was rolling in through her connections with overseas collectors. He never even questioned how a girl like Natalie, an administrative assistant for an import/export firm, was able to fence so much ancient jewellery. All she'd done was to give him a fistful of American dollars and he'd been hooked, his life transformed. But then the reckoning had come.

He had knocked on the door of her apartment but instead of Natalie a tall man with a gorilla-like physique smiled and beckoned him inside. His heart stood still. At first he'd thought it was the police, but then he saw three other gorillas in lounge suits and, in the middle of the apartment, sitting where Feyodor usually sat in a deep armchair while Natalie performed oral sex on him, was a man he had never seen before. He knew instantly that he was Mafia. There had been no raised voices, no threats, no nastiness at all. It had all been jovial, good-natured. Maxim Nikolaivich Lomonosov had greeted him like a long lost brother.

'I feel as if I've known you these past six months, Feyodor Mikailovich,' he had boomed.

Feyodor had realised he was looking at his executioner. Suddenly the whole picture, a picture he had denied for the last six months, focused to startling clarity. It had been a Mafia sting. He wasn't so unworldly, academic or naive that he didn't instantly realise what he'd got himself into.

'Come. Sit down,' said Maxim Nikolaivich. 'You know, I look upon you as my business partner. And what a privilege it is to have as my partner the deputy director of the Pushkin Museum. But what am I talking about? From what I hear, soon, if things go well, you are to be the director. Your current director is a sick woman and there's no reason on earth why you shouldn't take her position once her time is up and she departs to that great archaeological graveyard in the sky.'

He laughed. His laugh was menacing, there was no humour in it. Feyodor sat nervously. He said nothing.

'I believe that you are acquainted with one of my secretaries. A pretty little thing called Natalie. You and she have been making quite a killing selling trinkets from Helen of Troy's treasure. By my last reckoning it was over two thousand US dollars. That's a lot of money for a deputy director.'

All Feyodor could do was gulp. He felt as though he were in front of the very firing squad he had so feared.

'Of course, in order to convince you of the future viability of our little business partnership, I've had to fund it myself. No actual jewellery has left the country. It's safely stored in my office, along with your certificates of authentication.'

Feyodor was stunned. 'But the money . . .'

Maxim waved his hand in dismissal. 'Petty cash. Out of my own pocket. A little in advance to my future business partner. The reason I'm so glad you're here, my dear Feyodor Mikailovich, is to talk about some real money. Money for me. You've had your fun. Now I think it's time for me to earn back my investment in you. But don't worry, the money will be quite enough for you to keep living in the style to which you've become accustomed.'

He leant forward and smiled. 'If you understand my meaning.'

From then on it had all been increasingly easy. A new car, a bigger apartment, expensive clothes, dining out. He had answered his wife's constant questioning with the explanation that his salary had increased as he was doing the director's job while she was sick. She didn't question further. Natalie continued to sleep with him and would, she assured him, continue to do so, as long as he continued to supply them with rings and other jewellery and certificates of authentication from the thousands of objects which Schliemann had gathered from Troy.

But now all that had come to an abrupt end. Two journalists had got to hear about the treasure and the Minister for Antiquities had insisted that the Pushkin put on an exhibition. People had come from all over the world to view the exhibits, but still no-one had bothered to do an inventory. But now people were making noises; they wanted to check what was still undisplayed. The Berlin government had demanded that one of their experts be allowed to view the entire treasury and to check it with Schliemann's original list. There were rumours that the Turks wanted to see it as well. It would take an expert ten minutes to work out that someone had been stealing from the collection for years and since he was responsible for cataloguing the treasure, he was the obvious, the only suspect. God Almighty, how was he ever going to sort out this fucking mess?

CHAPTER 3

The woman stood naked before the entire village, her legs apart, straddling a newly made earthenware pot. Her ribs showed clearly beneath the fall of her breasts. She'd always looked so healthy but now she was thin. And thirsty, always thirsty. And in constant need of honey.

The Headman looked at the Man of Medicine, biding his time to see if any omens were present; but when he saw none, he nodded. The Medicine Man looked up at the distant mountain. Then at the clouds. Was there a message for him? No. Now was the time. He looked back at the Headman and shook his head sadly.

The Headman tapped the woman gently on her head with his wisdom staff. She closed her eyes. She knew it would not be difficult. She thought about gushing rivers and the water came out of her body in a strong stream. Small droplets splashed out of the pot. Some leapt back onto her legs but she didn't mind. When she'd finished, she looked at the Headman who smiled in encouragement and told her to move from the pot. The Medicine Man walked over and said an incantation over the urine. He knelt down and sniffed it. It seemed sweeter than the waters from other people. He cleared a space on the ground with his medicine stick, placed the stones he'd gathered that morning from the river in a circle around the small perimeter, and poured the contents of the pot onto the earth inside the circle.

He stood and announced in a portentous voice to the silent villagers, who were watching his every action: 'Tomorrow, when the sun is reborn, all will be revealed and the purpose of the Gods' will will be made known to us. If ants eat this woman's water, then she has the wasting sickness and the Gods will carry her to the land of the dead. If not, the Gods will allow her to live more of her time with her people.'

The woman, Mira, listened to the words of the Medicine Man. She already knew what he was going to say, just as she knew what was going to happen to her. It had happened to her mother and to many other people she had once known. She had consulted the Medicine Man when her thirst had become ravenous, her appetite for food had become too strong yet her weight continued to fall away, when her body had itched constantly and when she had desired the taste of honey more than the pleasures of her husband. She looked now at the people of the village; they looked back at her in sympathy. Everyone knew with awful certainty that in the morning an army of ants would be found eating the sweetness of her water. And that meant that within this or the next life and death of the Goddess of the Moon, her body would waste away until she looked like a skeleton, she would have no energy to walk or to eat, and her only relief would come from drinking sweet herb waters mixed with honey. By the time the Sun God grew weak and coldness crept over the earth, she would be dead.

The Medicine Man allowed Mira's husband, Hasga, to bring his wife an ox skin to keep her warm. It was already evening and although it had been a warm summer's day the sun's rays no longer lit the village and the cold of the shadows was beginning to dull the warmth of the mother earth.

Mira had given her water in front of all of her friends in the village. Everybody said a prayer. It was a good time of the year, the middle of summer, the growing season for fruits and for children. The half-light between day and night, the time of lengthening shadows, did not end suddenly as it did in winter or autumn but continued for

35

some time. The people of the village, all friends of Mira and Hasga, returned to their huts. Mira and Hasga also turned from the centre of the village and began the climb to the top of the hill where they had built their home. Most of the homes in the village comprised a single room where everybody lived, ate and slept. In the centre of the room there was usually a huge terracotta pot which contained all the family's valuable belongings. In most huts the belongings were removed at the beginning of each day and the pot was carried down to the river. There it was filled with water and carried by the man and woman of the family back to the house. It was then stationed outside the entrance during the day where its water was used for drinking or served as storage for washing, cooking and cleaning. But Mira and Hasga's family was different from most of the other eighty families in the village. Their house was similar to that of the Headman and the Medicine Man and had been built by villagers in return for Hasga's metalwork and forging. So they had a much bigger house, twice the size of the others, and their large central room was divided into four separate areas, each with its own doorway. When important people like traders or wandering priests came to the village, Hasga's house would be one of the places where the villagers encouraged the visitors to stay.

The two daughters of the family, Amra and Peta, slept in one of the rooms. Mira had given birth to three sons also, but two had died of fever before they could walk and one had been taken by raiders from far away who had come looking for slaves. Mira still cried herself to sleep, wondering where her son was. The largest room in the house was for Hasga and Mira. This was the room where they went when they wanted sex, or when they wanted to pray to one of their Gods for assistance. Amra, the eldest daughter, was allowed into her parents' room to change the straw of their mattress and to clean out any dead insects. The third room, the smallest, was where Hasga worked at night, hammering designs into jewellery, or sharpening the swords or daggers he was making for one of the villagers, or for someone in a nearby village. The fourth room was where the family met to eat after the meal had been cooked outside.

Hasga's room was always bright with light. There were four niches built into the walls where terracotta lamps burned brightly. A visiting trader had shown Hasga the technique of trimming the wicks in the oil so that they didn't smoke and dropping salt onto the burning wick and since then the room had become even lighter. Sometimes people would gather outside in the darkness, looking into the bright house and wondering at the miracle Hasga had created. He had shown them the secret of his lights, but they preferred to maintain the old ways.

Hasga knew that if the Gods smiled on Mira and she lived, he would soon need to build a new house. Amra was at the time in her life when she would start to bleed with the new moon. Unlike other girls of her age in the village, Hasga was intent on giving her a room of her own for her womanhood. He had looked around the village and chosen the site he wanted for his new house. The village was surrounded by a high wooden barricade made of logs felled from nearby woods and lashed together vertically. The barricade ran beyond the outer rim of huts and was there to repel attackers and allow the villagers to sleep safely at night. But closer to the river, lower than most of the houses in the village, was a large space which had once been occupied by the house owned by Wolfka, the maker of bread. It had burnt down when Wolfka left his ovens unattended early one morning. He had told everybody that he had been busy baking and hadn't noticed what was happening, but

Hasga suspected that he had his eye on a neighbour's daughter and had been enjoying himself by the river while his house was burning down. Nonetheless, the site was clear and on the day that Amra came to her mother and father and told them that the blood had arrived he would ask permission of the Headman to clear the ground and build two houses: a small one of three rooms for him and Mira and their daughter Peta, and a separate house of one room for Amra to use. This was preferable to the usual custom, where Amra would be sent to the house of the women over the river until the blood had stopped flowing. He didn't like the idea of being separated from his daughter so often, especially in these dangerous times.

But would the Headman allow him to have two houses? Nobody else in the village had two houses. But then Hasga was the metalworker; he could take rocks from the ground and from them make everlasting and always sharp arrowheads and daggers and spears, as well as amulets and rings and buttons and other jewellery which the men of the village were happy to take as presents for their wives in exchange for food and clothing.

Hasga and Mira arrived back at their home at the top of the hill. Mira was exhausted from the climb, she placed a hand on the door frame and rested there a moment. Her husband, his hand on her back, helped her to crouch below the low doorway. Flies buzzed in the room; it was the sound of life, and Mira said a small prayer under her breath to the God of Flying Animals to thank Him for sending His winged friends. She looked through the open doorway and saw her daughter Amra lying on her mattress, painting the image of a God which she had made late the previous evening. Mira sniffed. Soon the straw of Amra's mattress would need turning. It was already damp from the heat of the day and the wetness of the girl's body.

Amra sat up on her bed and looked expectantly at her mother. Mira smiled.

'Well?' asked Amra.

Hasga appeared through the doorway and shook his head gently. 'In the morning we'll know,' he told his daughter.

'Can I get you something to drink, Mother?' asked Amra.

The woman smiled and nodded. Amra grabbed a goatskin which hung on a peg and ran out of the house. Hasga and his family no longer filled their terracotta pot with water in the morning; they had decided that by the end of the day it tasted stale, so Amra's job was to fetch a new goatskin full of clean water each time the contents were used up. She didn't mind it, she enjoyed the freedom of running through the village and out of its large gate, smiling at the guards, who smiled back and waved at the mischievous child, then seeing the wonderful silver thread of the river down in the valley beyond. As she ran down the hill to the river, clouds of gnats and mosquitoes rose around her, disturbed by her footsteps. Transparent-winged flies and big slow old dragonflies flitted from leaf to leaf, flower to flower.

It was the fourth time that day that Amra had been down to the stream. Twice she had gone to take off her clothes to let the cooling meltwaters of the distant mountains refresh her body in the burning heat. It was so hot, so very hot. As she ran to the stream for her mother's drink, her mind wandered back to the excitement of her swim in the middle of the day. She had gone to the deeper part of the river where one of her friends had drowned in the sometimes violent currents. But Amra was a strong swimmer and knew the Gods would protect her. She had held her breath and swum down through the crystal-clear water to the stones and rocks at the bottom of the river. She'd held on to her favourite stone, the stone she called Old Man because it was gnarled and rutted, and had revelled in the refreshing coldness of the water, feeling like a fish as it rushed by her. She watched her long auburn hair streaming this way and that at the command of the currents as the water flowed past the rocks and eddied in miniature whirlpools.

Amra could hold her breath for a long while under water. She held herself anchored as rigidly as she could, clawing constantly as the rapid stream and the slime on Old Man kept dislodging the grip of her hands. She loved to be at the bottom of the water. She wondered if, when she went to the Gods at her appointed time, she would return to earth as a fish. It was as she was about to release her hold and float to the surface of the water that she spied the beautiful, sleek, mottled grey and brown trout lurking behind an upstream rock, gulping at anything which passed by its mouth. Her heart quickened. It was big, big enough for the whole family. She let go of Old Man Rock and allowed her body to be swept backwards so that she didn't frighten the trout and make it swim away. She rose to the surface of the water and floated without using her hands or legs so that she was a considerable distance from the fish when she swam to the bank.

She ran excitedly from the river to her home. She loved the taste of fish, especially the pink and delicate flesh of trout. She would make a small fire in the cooking grate outside their house long before nightfall, then she would find roots from the forest and bury them deep in the ashes of the fire. She would continue to heap wood on the fire so that the God of the fire would live and make the roots from the ground, roots like kumera and turnips and carrots, soft and delicious. She would clean and gut the fish and throw its body onto the ashes of the fire to seal it, then remove it before it had a chance to cook and rub its flesh with herbs like honeysuckle. Maybe she'd put some horehound into the fish's body cavity; it was bitter but it stimulated the appetite and might be good for her mother who didn't seem able to enjoy her food anymore. But first she had to catch the fish.

Amra took the reed net she had made just the other day and gathered the needle pole from inside the house. She ran back to the river. Her hair was already drying in the heat of the sun and she realised with a laugh that she had forgotten to dress, that she was completely without clothes. Her father had told her not to go without clothes in the village. There were men there who looked at her with eyes which should be reserved for their wives.

Amra wondered whether the trout would still be there. If the river hadn't been running so quickly, she could have gathered up handfuls of nettles and fennel, crushed them up and released them into the water upstream from the fish. The sap from the crushed plants would cloud the water and stun the fish long enough for her to scoop it up into the basket. But the river was too swift and the nettles would have no effect. So she walked back downstream from where she had seen the fish, hoping it would still be there, still facing up-river in the direction from which its food was travelling.

Slowly, without causing too many ripples, she lowered her body into the cold water. She broke a reed and blew the dust from its centre, put it in her mouth and gently bent it twice so that its end would remain above the water and she could breathe while slowly swimming upstream to spot the trout.

In her search for the trout, Amra became a fish herself in the sparkling clear stream, so cold and refreshing. It was there! Close to Old Man Rock. It hadn't noticed her and Amra strained against the current, swimming as gently as she could towards Old Man Rock. She found a handhold on the bottom so that she could remain stationary, but it wasn't easy. The stream was fast and

Amra was carrying the basket in one hand, the needle stick in the other and still had to keep the reed close to her head so she could breathe. But she was skilled; her father had taught her to be a good hunting woman. He had taught her how to fish without scaring the quarry.

Slowly, hand by hand, she pulled herself against the rush of the stream until she was within spearing distance of the trout. The lazy old thing was gently flicking its tail to remain in the same place so that the food came to him. It was no hunter! But then it began to move, slowly undulating against the speed of the current. Now and then it moved more energetically, darting to the top of the river to catch one of the flies which had landed on the surface. Amra was sorry she would have to kill the trout. Now that it was more active, she admired its skill in the water, its oneness with its home.

With imperceptible movements, Amra brought the spearing stick with its deadly bronze serrated needle close to the side of her body, then with her thumb and finger moved it forwards slowly, little by little, until it was positioned on the other side of Old Man Rock. The trout still hadn't noticed her.

She moved the basket in front of her face over to the other side of her body, again very slowly. But, despite her care, the movement dislodged some stones in a cloud from the river's bottom. Somehow, even though it was facing upstream, the old trout must have felt something because suddenly it turned and saw her. Amra's heart beat quickly as she realised that with one flick of its tail it would be away to the other side of the stream and her family might go hungry tonight.

She lunged her arm forward in a sudden movement, as quick as the fire in the sky, and caught the trout just above its tail, spearing straight through its body. It flapped and flipped, trying to dislodge itself from the spearing stick but the needle was embedded in its body and it was too well caught. Amra dropped the stick and, forgetting the reed which suddenly filled with water, pulled herself over the stones towards her captive, now flailing furiously on the river bed. She jammed the basket over the trout's body. It was hers. It wouldn't get away from her. She had it!

Her body was bursting for air and she knew the fish was safe, speared and trapped in the basket. Her legs gave a mighty push off the bottom of the river and she flew up to the surface where she gasped in a huge breath of the beautiful warm scented air. She swam back down again to the bottom of the river, took her basket and her stick, apologised to the God of the River for taking one of his creatures and resurfaced. She half-swam and half-paddled over to the bank, encumbered by the basket and the spear. She got out of the water, took the fish out of the basket and gently prised the needle of the spearing stick out of its body. It was still alive, still flapping. She picked up a stone from the bank and smashed it on the trout's head, not wanting to prolong its pain. Now it was no longer flapping and slapping in the bottom of her basket. It was big, bigger than she'd thought in the water. It would make her family a lovely dinner. Amra put on her flax skirt and the top she had made the other day. She was completely satisfied with the results of her hunt and had returned home.

But that been in the middle of the day, before her mother's ordeal. Now her mother was home and was thirsty. She was always thirsty, no matter how much she drank, and Amra was on her way to the river again, with her goatskin to collect water to slake her mother's thirst. She noticed with interest how the ground seemed to change with the falling of the light. At midday, when she had caught the fish, the sun had been directly overhead and the stones, rocks and the pathway were deep and certain. But now the God of the Sun was dying and was on his way to his eternal home. The only light was the half-light before the dark and stars. It was difficult for her to tell the difference between path and stones and grass.

As she ran she wondered what happened to the light when the Sun God went behind the mountain? Why did the light go? Was it as the Medicine Man said, that the heat of the sun and its light are drowned in the great sea beyond even the most distant mountains only to be reborn again after the God of the Moon has had sex with the stars? Were the shooting lights which sometimes flew across the sky at night really like the white foam from a man's penis when he had sex with a woman or on his own, or were the sky lights something else? And if the Sun God was reborn anew every morning after the God of the Moon had had sex with the stars, why on some nights were there no flashing lights in the sky and yet the sun was still reborn anew?

Amra stubbed her toe and fell heavily to the ground, grazing her hip. She let out a yelp of pain and anger. She was always dreaming. In the village she was often known as Amra the dreamer. But she had to stop dreaming. Her mother had a ravenous thirst and Amra had to concentrate on filling the goatskin so that she wouldn't feel sicker than she felt already. Tomorrow Amra would go out with her sister Peta and find wild honey. She had to cheer her mother up, because tomorrow her mother, and everyone else in the village, would look at her water on the ground and if the ants were there she would soon die. Amra and her sister, like all the other children of the village, had been banned from the ceremony by the Medicine Man, but she had watched from behind the large boulder on the outskirts of the village centre. She had seen her mother standing naked, surrounded by the adults of the village. And she was frightened that soon her mother would die.

When the meal was finished Peta took the baked clay plates outside and over to the pit. It had been built far away from the house because of its stench. Peta hated the job she now had to do, but she was of the age where she had to do it. She stood on the edge of the pit, holding her breath, and scraped the plates clean of bones and skin. A cloud of flies rose up, buzzing angrily as the remains of the meal dropped onto the stinking mass already rotting there. Standing by the pit was a dog who didn't belong to anybody in the village, but always hung around all the village rubbish pits, picking up scraps. It viewed her every action with hungry eyes and snarled when Peta spat at it. Nobody liked the dog, nobody owned it. Peta picked up a rock and threw it. It hit the animal hard on its flank. It yelped and slunk away, turning back to bark at her in anger. Peta smiled.

When she returned, Amra was sprinkling dried hyacinth petals into some oil. She reached over into a jar and took out a pinch of dried rosemary. With a spoon, she mixed the oil and spices. It was the evening ritual to make the house smell nice and to make her parents clean. Peta would soon have to do it and Amra was teaching her how. Peta knew that as soon as Amra bled and became a woman, she would leave their house, and Peta would have to take over most of the tasks which Amra now performed.

Their mother walked naked into the room and lay down on the straw mattress. Amra took a blunted bronze knife and wiped the blade free of the skin from the previous day. She rubbed the back of her mother's body with the oil then gently scraped her skin with the bronze knife. Peta watched, in awe of Amra's skills. She was so deft at the task. She knew each bend, each curve, each crevice of her mother's back, legs and buttocks. She manipulated the knife so that not even the smallest part of her mother's body missed being cleansed. Peta noted in sorrow how her mother's body was so thin now, so lacking in muscles. Her skin was dull where once it had been shining with life. Her skin had once been so smooth, her body so strong, yet now her bones were showing through her skin. How much more weight could she lose before . . .

Peta closed her mind to the thought and watched her mother turn onto her back. Again Amra's skill with the knife was awesome: she manipulated the blade around Mira's breasts, her stomach, and into the curves of the hair between her legs. Soon she was finished. Mira stood, kissed Amra and thanked her, then she called to her husband. Hasga walked in, his naked body covered with its mat of thick black hair. He lay down and Amra set to work, but the oil did different things to his body, making it glisten in a different way to their smooth-skinned mother. Amra's knife was not so deft on a man and her father winced occasionally as the tip pulled a black hair out of his skin. But soon he too was finished. Hasga and Mira returned to the central room of the house where the family sat together. The oil lamp in the niche in the wall was burning with a black smoke. Hasga took his knife and trimmed it, careful not to extinguish the flame. They lay on the woven cloths scattered over the ground and talked about the day. Amra particularly liked the cloth she was sitting on. She had watched some of the women in the village weaving it and they had altered the design to her specifications. In the middle of the cloth was a scene of a young woman hunting a deer. Amra thought it might bring her good luck. And in each of the four corners of the cloth was the symbol of a bee, Amra's totem. She liked her totem. A bee was brightly coloured, fast, clever, made beautiful things like honey, loved flowers, but had a vicious sting if it was annoyed. Hasga said that Amra was like a bee and so it had become her totem. Peta asked again how Amra had trapped the fish. It was the third time Amra had told the story but Peta could listen over and over again. One day she would be a hunter too. One day she would be like Amra.

During the night the ants came. The Medicine Man visited their house early in the morning, his expression sad and serious, and Amra knew even before her father told them, that their mother was soon to die. The two girls decided to go out on a special search to help their mother; it might be their last chance to do something for her.

Far away from the village they laid themselves down in the middle of the field, hidden beneath a pile of branches and twigs, brushing away the angry ants that tried to nip their skin. In front of them was a large cluster of flowers, growing in the space left by a tree which had fallen during the cold months and let the God of the Sun into the forest. But the God of the Forest hated the God of the Sun because when one of the trees died and fell the God of the Sun took over the darkness of the forest. So the God of the Forest had sex with the ground to make a new tree that would grow and block out the eyes of the Sun God, and the God of the Forest would plunge His home back into darkness. But for this season and next, and probably for the next five or more seasons, the dark forest was invaded by a shaft of light from the God of the Sun. Birds, butterflies, gnats, horseflies and other insects had gathered to dance in the sun's light, but Amra and Peta had no interest in these. Their interest was in something much slower, much more menacing. They waited, hardly moving a muscle, until they were rewarded for their patience.

In the silence of the forest they heard him from a long way off, a low steady buzz. Amra heard Peta gasp and moved her hand fractionally to pinch her sister on the thigh. Peta lay absolutely motionless. A sound, even the slightest crackle of a twig, could frighten off the bee, and from the sound of its flight this was the ideal bee, slow and old and easy for the girls to follow. The fat intruder found its way to the flowers, the other insects paid it no heed. The God of the Bees must have shown it the way. The Gods showed their followers everything and nothing happened without the Gods. The bumble bee settled on the head of one of the flowers, its weight caused the flower to bend slightly towards the ground. The bee disappeared inside and emerged a moment or two later, flew to another flower, disappeared and re-emerged. It continued its progress until it had taken its fill of the nectar of the Gods. Then it cleaned itself before flying off in the same direction that the sun would disappear later that day.

'Come on,' whispered Amra to her sister. They threw off the leaves and bracken and twigs and ran after the bee. Amra's deep blue eyes were wonderfully accurate, better even than her sister's, and she saw exactly where the bee was. One minute it flew high to the underside of the canopy of the trees, the next it changed direction and flew towards a dense and dark part of the forest. Then, for reasons only the God of the Bees would understand, it flew slowly and ponderously in the direction it had started from. Amra and Peta ran and ran to keep up with the bee. After a little while Peta began to drop behind.

'You go,' she gasped to Amra, 'can't run . . .'

'Come on,' said Amra. 'Not long now.'

'No. Leave me. You go.'

'Come on,' insisted her sister. 'I'm sure we'll be there soon.'

Grudgingly the younger girl continued to run, but eventually tarried further and further behind. Even Amra, swift of foot and strong with wonderful running lungs which she'd developed from her swimming, was beginning to tire and wonder when the bee would finally come to its home.

And then, suddenly, they were out of the forest — without warning, the gloom of the trees gave way to an open field. Amra had been here two, maybe three times before in her life. The bee settled on the branch of a dead tree and Amra fell to the ground, both to hide and to gather her breath. Her face was hot, her body aching with tiredness, her feet hurting from the twigs she had trodden on in the forest. She never wore her sandals when she was hunting, they made a noise and she couldn't run nearly as fast. A little while later her sister joined her, pitching onto the ground next to her, throwing her arm around her older sister's waist, heaving and panting.

When she'd got her breath back, Peta whispered, 'Where is he?'

Amra only had the strength to nod in the bee's direction but he was so tiny against the vastness of the meadow that Peta couldn't see him. When the bee had recovered its own strength, it took to the air again and flew across the meadow and into a further clump of wood. Amra had never been this far from her village before, beyond the mountain and into the hills. She looked at the sky: the Sun God was beginning to wane. It would take them until nightfall to return to the village. Her father would worry even though he knew they were out honey-gathering.

And her mother. Her poor dear mother who had only the strength to lie on her mattress and drink water. Any food she ate passed straight out of her body. All except honey. Honey, it seemed, was the one thing that gave her strength. Even the wonderful fish the previous night hadn't stayed long in her body.

Amra and Peta followed the bumble bee into the forest, worried that they were in for another long run. But suddenly their hearts leapt for joy at the sight they had been hoping for: in the dark air of the forest, in and around the many trees, they saw hundreds more bees, all circling around a big old dead tree. It appeared as though the tree itself was alive, its skin crawling with the tiny insects. And in the centre of the dead tree was a huge hole where a branch had once grown, but which had fallen down long ago. Amra smiled at her sister and nodded. Both girls understood what had to be done now.

Amra looked carefully at the hole in the trunk and saw the bees flying in and out of it. The hole was within reaching distance. Good! She wouldn't have to climb or pull over other branches to make herself taller. Amra looked up to the distant sky through the canopy of the trees and thanked the God of the Bees for making the honey accessible. Life would be easier for them all now. Amra and Peta gathered together bracken and twigs and wood and leaves and made them into a big pile on the ground. But Amra was concerned; they felt wrong. They were as dry as the bones of dead animals, much too dry for smoke. It had been a long and hot summer and none of the vegetation was damp any longer. The leaves and wood they had gathered would burn with a furious fire but without the white smoky breath they needed. She looked around for something to wet the leaves, but there was no river to dampen their dryness. She felt deeper into the undergrowth, but the leaves were still too dry.

She and Peta knew exactly what to do. Amra set aside a small bundle of dry leaves and twigs to start the fire then the girls straddled the large pile and wet the leaves and twigs with the water of their bodies. Amra took out her fire stones, said a small prayer and struck one against the other. It took her many tries before a big enough spark flew off the stones and caught hold of one of the dry leaves. Peta carefully blew on the glowing ember until it suddenly crackled into life. Amra put more leaves and small twigs on top until the God of Fire had taken control of the little bundle. Then the girls lifted the mass of urine-soaked leaves and twigs and placed it gently above the fire. They blew at the fire's bottom layer until white acrid smoke began to rise.

Once the mound was smoking heavily, they picked it up and carried it over to the tree. Heaving it into the hole where the bees flew in and out, the girls ran away and waited. They didn't have to wait long. The dense white smoke soon began to pour out of the hole. At first the bees buzzed noisily in anger, but it didn't take long for the smoke to make them drowsy and they fell away. Some settled on the ground, others flew away from the danger. Those who were still inside the hole crawled out and clung to the bark of the tree.

When the buzzing had quietened and the danger from bee sting had lessened, Amra and Peta ran towards the tree. They picked up green, still living leaves from the forest floor and rubbed them hard against their arms so that the sap covered them. Then they reached inside the hole, closing their eyes and nostrils to the white smoke, to find the hard gelatinous mass of the bees' honey.

Amra smiled. She couldn't open her eyes or talk as the smoke would get into her throat and make her choke. Instead she lifted her skirt, pulled out large handfuls of the honey and filled her makeshift bag with it. She said silent prayers of thanks, imagining her mother's delight when she come home with this nectar from the Gods. Her mother's strength would return.

It was while she was thinking of the joy on her mother's face that she heard the most terrifying noise that the forest had to offer. She opened her mouth in shock and fear and swallowed smoke. She forced herself not to cough, not to disclose her location. The noise wasn't as far distant as she had first thought; it was very close, so close that she knew she and her sister were in terrible danger. She heard the noise again, the guttural roar of a hungry brown bear. It had seen the smoke and come to investigate. By now it must have smelt the honey, which would have made its hunger worse. Amra knew from its growl that nothing would stop it until it had eaten and she realised with a horrible certainty that unless she and Peta ran away immediately both of them would soon be dead, torn to pieces by the fury of the gigantic beast. Amra withdrew the last handful of honey she could reach, threw it into her skirt, wiped her hand and grabbed her sister.

'Come on!' she shouted. 'We have to go.'

'But . . .' said Peta. She was young and had not fully understood the danger in the sound of the bear.

'Now!' shouted Amra.

The two girls, smoke blinding their eyes, turned and ran away from the tree, Amra still clutching her folded-up skirt with its treasure of honey. Blinking to clear the smoke from her eyes, Amra looked ahead to see where they were going. Her heart nearly stopped its furious beating when she saw the angry form of the huge brown bear loping quickly towards them, running on all fours. The bear stopped on the other side of the copse of trees and looked at the girls. Amra could see the fury in its eyes. Suddenly it reared up onto its hind legs, its huge paws clawing high in the air. It was twice Amra's size and many times her strength. Its paws almost reached the canopy of the trees. There was no escape. No matter how hard or fast they ran, they were already tired and would never outrun the bear. It would quickly catch them and then one of them, certainly, would not return home that night. One of them would be crushed by the giant bear's paws and torn to pieces by its salivating mouth.

The bear roared its anger to the sky. Amra didn't know what to do. She had never encountered a situation like this before. Her only thought was the safety of her sister. How could she return and tell her parents that little Peta . . . She couldn't even tolerate the thought. If the bear was to kill one of them, let it be her.

She turned to Peta who was staring at the huge animal in abject terror. 'Run that way. I'll run the other way. He can't chase us both.'

'But . . .' stuttered the girl.

'Run!' shouted Amra. 'Just run. Do what I say!'

Peta ran in the direction of the birthplace of the God of the Sun, back towards the village. Amra ran in the opposite direction. The bear's massive head moved from side to side, watching what both girls were doing. It was confused and fell onto four legs. Amra stopped and turned towards the bear while Peta raced away as quickly as she could. But Amra realised that speed alone would not beat the bear. She was Amra the hunter, she must beat him with her cunning. Even though her heart was racing, she knew that if she was to rely on running, she would be torn to death. So she reached into her skirt and showed the creature a handful of honey, hoping to distract him and stop him from running after Peta. At least she would live.

As soon as she had the bear's attention, Amra took off, running faster than she had ever run in her life. The delay had saved her sister's life; now she had to save herself. She was still tired from the long journey to the tree of honey but she knew that if she faltered in her steps, the bear, which could run at least as fast as a man, would be onto her and would kill her within seconds.

Amra ran up a hill and, panting, breasted its crown. The trees were thick in this part of the forest and she knew that if she were to stand a chance she would have to get out of the copse and into the open meadow. Maybe there would be somewhere there she could hide, or maybe she could jump down into a deep ravine in the hope that the bear would be too scared to follow. Sobbing and sweating, she looked behind her. She had somehow managed to outpace the bear which had spent precious moments investigating the honey in the tree, but she felt as though her heart might burst. The bear was ambling along, growling, sometimes roaring in fury, but all the time staring at her with its hate-filled hungry eyes. When she stopped because her legs were hurting too much to continue running, the bear quickened its pace. Amra's chest was heaving. It was as if a knife was sticking into her side. And she couldn't even run properly as one of her hands held her gathered skirt, encasing her mother's honey.

Suddenly an idea formed in her mind. She could see from the increase in light that soon she would be out of the woods, into open ground. A bear was much more dangerous out in the open. She took a daub of honey and smeared it onto a nearby tree, then ran to two other trees and smeared them also. She did this to other trees in the nearby area, as many as felt safe in case the diversion didn't work. The bear was drawing closer each time she delayed at another tree. As she turned she saw the animal crashing through the undergrowth; Amra ran as fast as her legs would carry her, down the other side of the hill. She didn't stop to look around, but kept running until she could run no more. She was crying with the exertion. She couldn't breathe. Her legs would no longer work. If she was to die, let it be now. Let it be quickly.

Amra fell headlong into the thick grass of the meadow, gasping for air, sweat pouring from her brow. Her legs were throbbing, her throat was parched with heat and exhaustion. Tentatively she lifted her head and looked towards the top of the slope she had just run down. With unimaginable delight she spied the bear in the far distance, licking the trunk of one of the trees high up on the hill. It dropped to all fours, ran over to another tree and began to lick that too. Amra lay on her back in the hot sun and laughed. She was safe. Safe at least for long enough to escape. She couldn't move, she was so tired, but she knew that she couldn't stay here long. Brown bears were clever. Soon it would realise that it had allowed a good meal to escape and it would come after her. She must lose herself and the smell of the honey. She must find her way to the river and walk in its water for a long distance, so that the bear would have nothing left to smell and would lose her scent. But first she had to skirt further around the hill in the direction that Peta had run. She had to make sure that Peta was safe and that her track ran off into the distance. Then, and only then, could she return home.

This would make a good story to tell to the villagers and her family around the fire. What would they call her, she wondered? Amra the bear tricker?

CHAPTER 4

The design of the building, circa 1950, defined both its use and its inhabitants: the antithesis of the high-tech skyscrapers of New York, it was built both for comfort and aesthetics. Instead of artificial air, piped through vents from an airconditioning tower, the building had windows that opened, and its glass and brick and painted exterior spoke of craftsmanship and care. It was amazingly different from the buildings Sarah had worked in in New York. This building was the ideal home for the Ministry, built because of the architect's desire to create a beautiful building, one which reflected a sense of aesthetics, not utilitarianism.

Sarah appreciated the building's beauty from the moment she saw it, but was sensible enough to realise that its old-fashioned beauty probably indicated that everything inside the Ministry of Antiquities was low-tech. And with low-tech came all the associated frustrations of the way business used to be conducted: the patronising, male-oriented stuffiness of old-fashioned business practices, the lack of recognition of women, of equity in the workforce, the impossible telecommunication system of one phone per office, the numbing slowness of correspondence without email. She shuddered as she pushed open the heavy glass front door and walked across the echoing reception area to the enquiry desk. The receptionists directed her to the lift. Sarah winced as she stepped inside; it stank of cigarette smoke. The lift operator smiled and nodded as he took her up to the seventh floor where the Director of the Ministry had his office. He pointed vaguely towards a door far down the corridor which was also heavy with cigarette smoke. For some reason the corridor reminded Sarah of pictures she'd seen of the inside of the Kremlin with its long dark passages, red carpeted hallways and massive chandeliers.

A secretary was seated in an antechamber off the corridor. When Sarah told her who she was the woman nodded, stood and opened a door for her. She walked into a large meeting room where seven people were seated around an ornate ebony table. Each stood up and introduced himself. There were no women in the room apart from Sarah. Pointedly they showed her to a seat at the lower left-hand side of the table, smiling and enquiring how she was enjoying herself. She answered politely but noticed that there was one seat left unoccupied. This presumably was for the Head of the Department.

A moment or two later the door opened and Dr Yussef Barrak walked in and introduced himself to Sarah. He was the image of the Ottoman Turk, his hair was slicked back with some form of pomade, he wore a conservative charcoal business suit, his fingers were adorned with several gold rings. He had an unctuous air about him. She disliked herself for it, but she immediately took a dislike to him.

After greeting her, Barrak took the seat at the top of the table. He immediately lit a pipe. All the others took out cigarettes, offering them to Sarah who declined. The man on Barrak's right opened a dossier and placed it in front of the director. Barrak looked cursorily at the pages, nodded, puffed on his pipe several times, cleared his throat and addressed the meeting, informing everybody of why Sarah was there and what he hoped to achieve.

Sarah felt herself catapulted right back to the 1950s, however she decided to bide her time. An hour later, her eyes were smarting and her throat was on the point of seizure; she hadn't experienced such a reaction to cigarette smoke since pot parties at Harvard. Yet she was determined not to complain; to do so would have shown weakness and cast her as a prissy American drama queen.

These men had been suspicious of her right from the beginning. They were only dealing with her because another woman, the Minister for Antiquities, had directed them to. But they made it plain that it was Dr Barrak who really directed proceedings in the Ministry offices.

Dr Barrak was seething at being forced to defer to the American lawyer; despite his courtesy towards her, his antipathy was obvious to his staff. He had been instructed to use the services of the girl sitting at the other end of the table. Instructed! Before the change of government, before the downfall of the Islamic Party and the rise of the army-backed Peoples Progressive Party, the arrival of a girl like this would never have been tolerated. It was an insult on all fronts: she was a woman, she was young, she wore provocative clothes, she was American and, worst of all, she was obviously Jewish. And here she was, preparing to hold forth about international law and the rights of countries in regards to treaties, holding forth to him! Yussef Barrak! Director of the Ministry! One of the Righteous of God! All Barrak's pleas, all his entreaties to use a Turkish doctor of law or someone from the university had fallen on deaf ears. The Minister had insisted on using this Sarah Kaplan girl to advise the government. When he had objected, he'd been told in no uncertain terms to follow instructions and do precisely as he was told. The Godless Minister had said that this girl lawyer was responsible for exposing major crimes committed in the time of Josef Stalin and she had worked in the international arena to recover some rich American's property. Furthermore she was an expert in the reclamation of property stolen in time of war and conflict, and if the Turkish government was to have any chance of reclaiming the treasures stolen from Troy by the German Heinrich Schliemann, this girl would have to show them the way. If he didn't like it, the Minister had added, there was always the prospect of him tendering his resignation. The former Minister would never have spoken to him in that way!

Barrak brought himself back to the meeting and prepared himself to squash the young American like some insect beneath his feet.

'Miss Kaplan,' Yussef Barrak said smoothly — a sign of his displeasure, 'to what extent are you familiar with Turkish law?'

'Why should I need to know details of Turkish law, Dr Barrak?' Sarah asked quietly.

'Because, my dear young lady, you have been brought to this country to advise us on a document signed between Schliemann and the Ottoman authorities. I would have thought that an expertise in Turkish law was mandatory. How otherwise can you comment on the prospects of our overthrowing the conditions of a document which has been legally binding on successive Turkish governments for well over a hundred years?'

Sarah had been waiting for an entire hour for Barrak to show his hand. The power play was about to start and she knew the game he was playing only too well. It was transparent. A lawyer had once tried this approach when she was an intern in a New York law firm. She hadn't caved in then, nor would she now when the stakes were infinitely higher.

'Firstly, Dr Barrak, you will address me as Counsellor or as Miss Kaplan. I am not your dear young lady. Secondly, before I came here I considered aspects of the Minister's problem from an international judicial perspective and concluded that it can be demonstrated in international courts of justice that the contract was entered into fraudulently, regardless of the place or time or law under which it was signed. And thirdly, I have been asked to come here at the personal invitation of the Minister. If you believe that my lack of expertise in Islamic, Ottomanic or

Turkish law precludes me from advising her, then I suggest you leave this meeting and write a detailed explanation to the Minister. If she agrees with your opinion no doubt she will exercise her authority and dismiss me.'

Her attack was made *sotto voce*, calmly and quietly, with complete self-confidence and control. The room descended into a shocked silence. Barrak's colleagues looked down at their hands in embarrassment; other experts in the room looked at either adversary, depending on which way their interests lay. Sarah noted that very few looked her way.

Barrak remained silent for a long moment. Then he smiled and deferred to her with a nod of the head. 'As you seem confident that you are able to assist us in this matter, I will leave this issue to my staff,' he said, standing and walking towards the door. Pausing, he delivered a Parthian shot: 'A small matter such as this need not involve someone of my level.'

With his departure the atmosphere in the room became frigid. Sarah realised that her next comment would be reported faithfully to Barrak, word for word. It would also determine how the people here would continue to deal with her.

'Well, now that Dr Barrak has left me in charge, let's get on with things, shall we?' Her voice showed no emotion whatsoever. Matter-of-factly, she asked the opinion of each of the experts at the table; within minutes, she had the group under her complete and genial control. Sarah wondered if this newly developed good humour would also be reported to Dr Barrak or if his minions would give him what he wanted to hear – that she had gone to pieces, stammered, made a fool of herself. No matter. Barrak had made his position clear; he was her enemy and would remain so until her departure. The important thing now was to keep him at a distance, to prevent him undermining her and her work with the Minister. A memo to the

Minister, advising her of the exchange, would be necessary. Sarah made a diary note of her decision.

The meeting proceeded without any further confrontation. Barrak's underlings had seen Sarah exercise her power and none of them wished to test it again. Sarah continued to ask pertinent questions and received detailed, almost sycophantic replies. What they didn't realise, and what Sarah was unwilling to admit to herself until the meeting broke up, was that she was quaking inside, suffering a mixture of anger, embarrassment and unease at the nasty exchange with Dr Barrak. She hoped her tension didn't show as she instructed her clients about matters of international law as they related to documents and treaties and discussed with them the difficulties they would face in getting a judgement in their favour.

The meeting lasted all morning, covering the judicial, political, social and financial aspects of the matter. When everything had been discussed, Sarah suggested that the government officials write a position paper for her to read, based upon their discussion and the advice she had given. Once she had seen it, she would add to it her expertise in international property law, then present it to the Minister so that she could take it to cabinet.

As the committee broke up and went to the dining room for lunch, two of the Ministry officials told Sarah of the plan to take her to Troy the following day. It hadn't even occurred to her that she would be seeing anything of Turkey, let alone the site of Schliemann's success. At first she was disappointed because she'd hoped to return to Istanbul, then realised she really wanted to see Troy! She agreed to meet up with her colleagues the following morning.

Her driver offered to take her directly back to the hotel but Sarah decided against it. Her head was so muzzy from the smoke-laden atmosphere that she preferred to walk the four blocks. She left the Ministry building and walked out into the main street. To her left was a large mosque crowded with tourists as well as Islamic faithful going in to pray. Sarah had made a cursory visit to the famous Blue Mosque in Istanbul but it had been so crowded that it was like being in Grand Central Station. She looked at her watch then smiled. It was a typical western thing to do. She had nothing in her schedule for the rest of the day. On impulse she decided to enter the mosque. From her observations since she'd been in Turkey, mosques were very different in every respect to Christian churches and Jewish synagogues. These were buildings used for a couple of hours at specific times of the week, but mosques seemed to be organic, a living part of the environment. They were crowded with people: little boys and girls running around in the courtyards, barefooted people performing their ablutions in the constantly running streams outside before padding in over carpets to the cool interiors – it was all so different to how religion was treated in the west. No wonder the Arabic world – not that Turkey considered itself in any way Arabic – constantly failed to understand the ethos of the west, and vice versa.

As Sarah turned from the main road into the avenue which led through the main gates, the building became increasingly imposing. It was brilliant white, gleaming in the afternoon sun. She knew from her guidebook that the mosque had been built by a student of the extraordinary Islamic architect Sinan. Its minarets looked aggressive from this angle, four needles jabbing at the blue sky. The aggression was something Sarah hadn't noticed before.

She stood, a rock in the stream of tourists, and stared upwards at the building's composition. Its huge dome sat squatly on solid walls, punctuated by central doors and windows on either side, and the entire edifice seemed to be protected by the four minarets standing like guards at its corners. Sarah was transfixed. Suddenly, through its architecture, Sarah began to perceive another aspect of Islam.

At Harvard, and throughout her working life, Sarah had been concerned with the principle of religious communion. She had strived to open dialogue with Islamic students so that Harvard's Jewish community could sit down with its Islamic community and talk about issues concerning both religions. Dialogue created understanding, understanding created tolerance, and tolerance created respect. And in respect was harmony. Her initiative had succeeded beyond her wildest expectations. In the many talks she'd conducted, Arabs, Israelis, American Jews and Christians had sat down and thrashed out workable solutions to the visceral hatreds which infected the Middle East. They'd talked and talked late into the night. Today Sarah still counted many American Moslems amongst her friends.

But that had all happened in America. Now she was outside of her secure territory, inside an Islamic Republic, face to face with living, organic Islam. This was the Islam of Mohammed, the Islam of government, law, politics, and empire; the Islam by which real people lived their lives. It wasn't an intellectual choice as it had seemed to be for some of her American friends. Sarah found the reality of Islam confronting, and frightening. In America, she'd been so convinced that she respected religious differences, but the differences here were overpowering.

The mosque itself was overpowering. It loomed menacingly above her as she walked towards it. But it was the needle-like minarets that frightened her the most; they could almost be rocket ships preparing to blast off from within the core of Islam and bring down all who didn't believe. Sarah shook her head. She was being ridiculous. This was an ancient mosque, a place of worship, home to tens of thousands of worshippers of God, people who worshipped the same God as she did, just in a different way. She walked closer towards the entrance but something about the blue light shining in through the distant windows, something about the minarets and their menace, unnerved her, and she turned and walked away. She hated her silliness. It was so unworthy. It would be different if David were here; he would talk through her fears with her, explain why her concerns were meaningless.

Sarah walked back to the hotel. It was only in her room, when she was completely alone, that she reached inside her blouse and took out the amulet which her great-grandfather had found on his farm in Slovakia at the beginning of the century. It had been handed down from mother to daughter since 1903. Maybe it was like the trinkets and amulets discovered by Schliemann. Her great-grandfather had discovered it just before he was killed in a vicious anti-Semitic pogrom. All his family's possessions had been destroyed in the attack, except for the amulet which her great-grandmother Serel had taken with her as she set out to trudge her way across Europe, intent on begging passage on board a New-York-bound steamer. But Serel had halted her journey in Berlin. Such a tragedy.

When Sarah received the amulet from her mother on her twenty-first birthday she'd been thrilled. But gradually it became a part of her everyday life and routine, and it had lost much of its significance. Then recently in Slovakia, where she'd gone to represent Josh Krantz, an archaeologist, Laco Plastov had noticed her amulet and had taken her to the place where it, and dozens of others like it, had been discovered. The place was a burial site of an ancient Bronze Age people. That in itself made the amulet extraordinary. But there was more. Laco had hypothesised that the maker of the amulet, or even the original wearer, must have had some connection with the Hittite people of ancient Anatolia because of the bull symbol on one side. What he'd found even more extraordinary was the symbol on the opposite side. To Sarah it looked like a couple of squiggles, simple lines, but Laco was certain that they represented the symbol of an owl. And the most famous owls in the ancient world, according to Homer, were at Troy. Could the original owner of the amulet have had some connection with that ancient, fabulous city, the centre of the epic poems which the blind bard had recited over seven hundred years before Christ?

Sarah's desire to know more about the amulet and its connection with the ancient past was one of the reasons that she'd agreed to take time off from the war crimes trial in Slovakia where she was acting as general counsel to come to Turkey.

Now, staring out of the hotel window, she could see the Anatolian landscape in the far distance, beyond the city. She felt the outer smooth edges of the heavy gold amulet and, with her forefinger, traced the outline of the bull image. It was small but it had been made distinct for her by Laco. These days, whenever she looked at it, the bull was the amulet's dominant feature. But she turned it over and smiled when she saw the owl. So childlike. So easy to mistake. Yet since Laco had lovingly explained the conjunction of the lines it had become so clear.

Now the amulet had grown in significance for Sarah. It had become a connection between her family and its past, giving her whole ancestry a new importance. It was a part of history, perhaps even the history of her people. And, in part – in large part – it was what drew her back to David. Before she left to fight Josh Krantz's case, David had been a part of her people, a part of her life, a part of her being, for several years. That history, that sense of continuity, was something the amulet symbolised for her.

David had been supportive of her working for Josh, had seen it as a wise career move. Sarah had agreed, but what she hadn't expected was for it to lead to a romantic entanglement with Laco, the archaeologist. The memory of her affair with him still pained her and it was partly because of her shock at her own behaviour that she'd delayed returning to America when the case in Prague had begun. Instead, she had accepted the offer from the Czech Ministry of Justice to act as an adviser. And every time she felt like packing up and going back to America, the thought of what she and Laco had done prevented her.

But David was ... Well! David. He had flown to Prague in between his concerts and had confronted the situation. Never once had he asked her to explain herself or to tell him what happened; he'd just accepted that whatever had happened had happened in the desires of the moment and that it had nothing at all to do with her love, her true, real and eternal love for him.

Sarah realised she was hugging herself. She wanted David so badly. He was in Athens, had gone there to replace the brilliant young cellist, Catherine Hewgill, who had fallen sick at the last minute. Fortunately David knew the concert piece, it was the Dvorak cello concerto with which he had made his debut in Carnegie Hall. Sarah looked at her watch; David had performed the previous night. She had meant to call him this morning but had been en route from Istanbul to Ankara. She walked away from the window, took out her pocket notebook and keyed the numbers into the phone. After some discussion with reception, she was eventually put through to David.

'It was terrific,' he told her. 'I got three encores. Catherine phoned me from her hotel and said the local concert promoter had been very complimentary. It's pretty gratifying.'

'David, you're wonderful,' Sarah told him.

'Yeah. I guess you're right,' he said. 'I'm also fabulously rich, phenomenally good looking and a great mountain climber.'

She sighed as she listened to his voice. 'When am I going to see you? Are you flying out of Athens tonight?'

David delayed a moment, just long enough for Sarah to realise something was going on. 'You really do know how to spoil a surprise, don't you,' he said.

'What do you mean?'

'The recording engineer at Philips has just had a coronary. He's the only one available for the next couple of weeks, even with rescheduling other recordings, so they've postponed my recording for a couple of months.'

'Oh, David, I'm so sorry,' she said. 'That recording was important to you.'

'No big deal. Other times. Other places.'

She remembered his word: surprise. 'Are you flying back to the States?'

'Not right away,' he said. 'Tell me Sarah, where will you be tomorrow morning?'

When she put the phone down Sarah discovered she couldn't remember the rest of the conversation. The thought of seeing her David again overwhelmed all her fears, all her insecurities. She was suffused with warmth and joy.

It was getting dark outside; Sarah could see her reflection in the window. Her hotel overlooked Atatürk Square and the massive mausoleum building which was the final resting place of Kemal Atatürk, the man who had made Turkey into a twentieth-century country. She smiled at the word, 'mausoleum'. So many of the thoughts and concepts, the words and ideas of modern man had originated not in Greece as most people thought, but in ancient Turkey. Even the simple word 'mausoleum' came from Mausolus, whose grave site at Halicarnassus was one of the wonders of the ancient world, as was the nearby Temple of Artemis at Ephesus. And just a few kilometres across the water had once stood another wonder of the ancient world, the

Colossus of Rhodes. Turkey! Such an extraordinary place. Sarah had expected to fly into meetings, advise the government and fly back to her work in the Czech Republic without seeing anything of the country. But tomorrow she was going to the site of ancient Troy. The thought brought with it a twinge of guilt; she'd been living life in such a frenetic state during the past couple of years that even thinking of taking time off for her own personal enjoyment and pleasure made her feel guilty.

Sarah realised that she was holding her amulet again. She peered beyond her own reflection, beyond the square, beyond the city, towards the distant mountains. She wondered about ancient times, about trade routes and bartering and men dressed in animal skins wandering hundreds of miles along unformed roads to bring rare tin to those who had an abundance of copper so they could make bronze spears and swords and jewellery. How had they travelled? Did they have pack animals? How had they communicated. Was there a universal language? How did they eat on the way? Did they have to pay a tithe to the owner of the lands they passed through? Had there been caravanserai in the ancient world? There were so many things Sarah didn't know about times long past. Before Jesus, before Homer, almost before time itself. And there was so much she would like to know, especially about that long-forgotten man who may have travelled from where her great-grandparents and their ancestors had lived for centuries to Troy, and who had brought back the amulet with the symbol of the bull and the owl.

She smiled. She was being silly. People hadn't travelled those fantastic distances in Hittite times, three thousand and more years ago. The amulet which her great-grandfather had dug out of the burial site was nothing to do with Troy. Its symbols were just happenstance. Just one of the millions of coincidences which made up history.

CHAPTER 5

Amra sensed that something bad was about to happen. She sensed it from the change in her father, the way he looked at her, the concern he expressed about her happiness, and even the fact that he was paying more attention to her than to her sister, Peta. He made sure that Amra ate the first slices of meat cooked on the fire, that she had the choicest of leaves from the cooking pot, and that the roots she ate from the embers of the fire were the softest and plumpest.

In the days following her mother's death it had been very different. Then Hasga had hardly looked at his daughters. Mira had died during the cold time, the time of the ice when the God of the Sun grew old and weak before being reborn anew in time to awaken the flowers and the buds of the trees. Amra's mother had wasted away until she was the weight of a little girl, and Hasga had been inconsolable. Nothing Amra or Peta or the other members of the village could do was sufficient to make him smile, to pull him from the grasp of the evil spirits. It was as if a demon from the Land of the Dead was in his head, confusing him and making him unhappy and morose.

But now, as the grip of winter lifted from the land, Hasga began to smile again. But it was a strange smile, a smile he only made when Amra was looking directly at him, when she caught his eye. It was a broad smile, too broad, as though she were one of the infants of the village and he a doting parent. He hadn't smiled like that at her for a long while. And there was no laugh to his smile. Amra missed her father's laugh. Sometimes she would hear it in her mind when she was alone. Whenever she was hunting she would hear it, no matter how far away she was from the village. It was a loud and resonant laugh, as though it was coming from deep inside his chest. His laughter gave her courage when she was afraid. But even though time carried away the pain of her mother's death and the Sun God grew in size and power, her father no longer laughed or welcomed the new warmth in the air. He didn't join in the village celebrations of the new season, he didn't join in the planting of the harvest or the cutting down of the first of the yearly trees to make room for more fields of crops. He didn't even participate in the celebration of the hunt in which Amra, because she was almost a woman, played the part of the deer stalked by three brave huntsmen. Nor did he greet the men from other villages who came up the river valley bringing presents of food and clothing to their relatives in Amra's village when the snow and ice had melted away. No, since Mira had died, Hasga hadn't participated in any of the village life, and people were noticing his absence.

But what frightened Amra most were the times she caught him staring at her sadly, smiling that strange smile. She had mentioned the idea that they should build their house closer to the river so that she could have a separate room as her body felt as though it was going to begin its bleeding. But Hasga had turned on her, saying that now she was the woman of the house she would have to be responsible for everything that Mira had done. She would get no separate room, Hasga had told her. She would stay in the home and cook, mend, gather and help him in his metalworking. Amra had fought back the tears. She felt her womanhood disappearing.

Lying on her straw mattress one night, Amra asked Peta whether she too had noticed any change in her father's behaviour.

'He seems to be sad all the time,' the younger girl answered.

Amra nodded. 'But why, if he is sad, does he smile at us? Every time he sees us, he smiles. As though he's done something wrong and is trying to say that he's sorry.'

Peta shrugged. 'He doesn't smile that way at me. He seems to be annoyed with me. He only smiles that way at you. I think he's still upset that Mother has gone to the Land of the Dead. Have you noticed how he just stays in the house at night and stares at her seat?'

Amra realised that Peta didn't understand, she was too young. Amra reached over, put her arm around her little sister, kissed her on the neck, and the two girls fell asleep in each other's arms.

The next morning Amra awoke before anyone else was stirring. It was still dark but she knew that it would take her until dawn to find what she wanted. Her father always woke to the first light, and it would be good for him to have his favourite drink when he got up. She took the fire stones from the small table and, as quietly as she could, hit one against the other. She had to repeat the process several times before a spark landed on the dry straw and set it alight. She took the burning stalk of straw over to the niche in the wall and lit the lamp which flared instantly. The room suddenly appeared, the God of Tricks making his shadow flicker and dance on the walls. Amra bade the God good morning and looked at the still-sleeping body of Peta, breathing rhythmically.

Amra took the lamp outside, shivering in the cold morning air. She opened the basket where the dry leaves and twigs were stored and made a mound. Then she used her lamp to light a fire. When the kindling was blazing and she could see part of the area surrounding her house, she put dry logs on top. Most of the light disappeared. One day she must ask the Medicine Man where the light went to. She looked around; there was one other fire much further away, but she couldn't make out whose house it was. Her fire caught. It was good. There would be hot embers to cook on when she returned.

Amra ran down the path. Although it was dark the guards recognised her footsteps. They were standing on the platform beside the entrance to the village. She called up a greeting.

'Did you sleep well, Amra?' asked one of the guards.

'I slept very well.' She could hardly make out his form in the darkness before the God of the Sun began His journey across the sky. 'May I open the gate?' she asked.

One of the guards climbed down the wooden ladder. 'I'll do it for you,' he said. 'There's nobody outside. Been no movement all night.'

Amra walked out of the gate and, as she did, the God of the Sun was suddenly born anew. She looked to His birthplace and saw that His light was burning the distant mountains. It was just enough for her to see the path which led down to the river. It had been a week since she'd gathered this particular herb and she hoped that the Medicine Man hadn't been there since her last visit and used it all up. Then she'd have to find a fresh clump. After walking the length of the village along the river bank, she traversed the water on the crossing stones and ran up the opposite bank, up the hill and out of the valley. At the top of the hill, she looked back. She could see tiny figures emerging from their huts, preparing to begin their day. Amra descended into another valley, this one smaller than her own. There was a marshy bog at the bottom. Animals often got stuck in the bog, especially after heavy rain, so she knew she had to be careful about where she trod. This place was where men from her village and men from a nearby village sometimes got together to hunt. After a heavy rainstorm, they would frighten a herd of cattle or deer down the steep sides of the valley until a number of them became mired in the bog. Then they would kill them with arrows or spears, rope them, and drag them out. The villages would have lots of meat for days and days.

But Amra wasn't after meat. She knew that it was on the edges of the bog that wonderful flowers and herbs grew. And this was where she had found the hyssop. She trod warily as she approached the morass. There were footprints in the still-soft mud, marks left by animals which had grazed there the previous night. She saw the paw marks of a small bear, the distinct prints of a large leopard or lion, and the hoofmarks of a herd of horses or cows. Her father would have been able to tell the difference; she still couldn't.

And there it was. Growing in a wet area in the inner part of the bog was a large clump of hyssop. There were about eight or nine of the small greyish bushes, standing as high as her knees. During the cold months, when the ground was dry, the people of her village gathered the herb to strew on the floors of their huts, so that when they walked upon it its delightful fresh smell filled their living spaces. But at the beginning of the warm months, when it was full of flavour, it was more useful for making a delicious drink.

Amra trod carefully over to the clump, testing each footstep for its security. She never put her full weight down until her foot had sunk into the mud and found a firm bottom. Fortunately there had been no rain for some time and she was able to reach the clump of hyssop easily. She gathered a handful of leaves, leaving many plants untouched so she could return in a few days. Then she backed away, avoiding her original footsteps which were already filling up with water.

By the time she reached the river again, Amra could see that people were already moving inside the huge wall of logs which protected the village. It looked so safe. At night the gates were closed and the great bar placed across them to protect everybody. There had been talk of building a large ditch around the outside of the village so that attackers would be slowed down as they tried to scramble up the steep ditch walls and the villagers would have time to shower them with arrows. But nobody was yet certain whether this should be done. Anyway, it wasn't Amra's problem.

By the time she entered the village, Peta was awake and stirring the red embers of the fire. Peta had put water into a pot to boil, and Amra could see that it was bubbling. She kissed her sister on the head, then plucked the leaves from the stalks of the hyssop. She tossed them into the pot and stirred them to break them up and release their delicious flavour. It was a strong taste which burnt the tongue, but her father said he could breathe easier when he had drunk the herb and he felt stronger and happier. Amra put the stalks into the basket where she kept her medicines. In there, they would dry and in the future she could use them to heal the ailments suffered by the people of her village. She had been watching the work of the Medicine Man and his wife, and she knew that the dry stalks were good to treat wounds and the weeping sores which came into people's eyes. It was also said that some of the young women put the stalks inside themselves after they'd had sex to stop themselves having a baby.

Her father emerged from the hut, rubbing his eyes in the still damp air of the morning. He looked at the two girls sitting by the embers of the fire. He saw the hyssop and smiled. This was the smile of pleasure, he knew that Amra had travelled a good distance to gather it and please him. He squatted on the ground beside the warm fire. Amra poured some of the liquid into a cup with the new ladle she had finished carving yesterday and handed it to him. He sipped it, nodded at Amra and thanked her. He began to speak, but then became taciturn.

Amra knew that something was seriously wrong with Hasga. She knew that once her mother had died, nothing would return to the way it had been. Her mother and father had been devoted to each other. And now her father behaved as if half of his own life had disappeared into the Land of the Dead. She knew that her father's mood had something to do with a conversation he'd recently had with the village chieftain. She had been in the house when the Headman had come to their home to speak to her father. The Headman had explained about the Land of the Dead and how people who left this life walked in eternal sunshine and warmth in the other land, accompanied on their journeys by the Gods, looking down on the doings of men and women below. He had given Hasga an idol of the God of the Dead and had explained that the land where the God Imka lived was beyond the clouds and could only be seen when lightning appeared in the sky. Even then, it was so light and glorious in the Land of the Dead, in the realm of the God Imka, that nobody on earth could look up into the sky when lightning lit up the heavens. He told Hasga that Mira, even now, was looking down on the family and smiling. If Amra's father didn't smile, then his wife would be upset and Imka would punish her. And all of the other Gods of the Land of the Dead would also be upset. Urged on by Imka, they would treat Hasga's condition as an insult and visit punishment on the village. Amra's father had forced himself to cheer up for a while after that, but eventually the evil spirits had returned to his head and he scowled at the world again. Amra thought that the evil spirits must hate the God Imka and be trying to upset him.

And so their father had remained like this for a long time. The cold days were slowly replaced by the warmer days but still Hasga didn't smile. He did only what was necessary for them to eat and to make enough jewellery and weapons to barter with the other villagers or the traders who passed through their village. Or so it had been until a few days ago. The Headman had again come to their house, but this time, after a whispered conversation between the two men, Amra and Peta had been sent down to the stream to gather water and leaves to eat with that night's meat. And ever since then their father had been smiling in a strange way.

Hasga finished his hot drink and shifted his position on the ground. Amra and Peta sat on the opposite side of the fire. In the days when their mother was alive, the four of them used to sit like this and talk about the day which had gone, and the day ahead, planning what each would be doing, finding out what was needed so that their meal in the middle of the day and their meal after dark could be taken care of without shortages. Their father would tell them what he was planning to make and for whom he was going to make it. Amra especially enjoyed it when he made jewellery. She loved to watch his fingers trace out intricate patterns in the metal and make an object of godlike beauty from something that had once looked like a lump of stone. But that was in the days when Mira was alive. Now her father didn't like Amra being near him.

She wondered what he would do today, but before she could ask him, he said: 'Have you heard talk in the village about the people beyond the mountains?'

Amra nodded. 'Last year, in the summer, there was talk of them. They were attacking villages on the other side. In the lands closer to where the Sun God is born.'

She looked at him in concern. Last year two young people had been sacrificed to the God of War as a way of persuading the Gods to ensure that the people beyond the mountains would not cross to their side and attack the villages in their region. There were ten or so villages running the length and breadth of the five valleys which lay beside the streams. Amra had been told that these streams all combined into one huge river many days' walk away, and that the river ran into the everlasting sea where the Gods of Fishes and Waves lived.

Her father continued softly. 'They have begun their march again. Word came seven days ago that the people from beyond the mountains have attacked and destroyed a village in one of the valleys which lies on the other side of the snow.'

Amra looked concerned. The village was a different place when these people, whoever they were, were attacking other villages. People became frightened and walked around with sullen looks. 'But we're safe,' she protested. 'Nobody can get across the mountains. They're too high. The ravines can't be climbed. Maybe by one or two men, but not many, especially with animals and weapons. Isn't that what people say? Anyway, inside our village we're safe. The barricade is too high. We have guards. And if we build the ditch, then if an army does manage to get across they'll be caught inside it and our arrows will kill them all.'

Her father looked at her and smiled. He reached over and touched her cheek. 'This army is different, Amra. It is vast and its soldiers use weapons made of iron. Each soldier has a weapon and there are more of them than there are flowers in the fields. They swarm like locusts.' He looked at his daughters, mystified. 'They all have weapons. I can't understand how they can *all* have weapons. It takes me three days to make a sword; I'd have to work for years to give every man in the village a dagger or sword or shield for him to defend himself.' He shook his head in desperation. 'Where do they get their weapons? How do they make so many of them? How do they make weapons of iron?'

He lapsed into silence, clutching the nearly empty cup in both hands. Peta was puzzled. All these questions. What did it matter? But Amra understood. And she was frightened. Every man had a weapon! That meant a large army which could destroy their village. Even combining with all the other villages, there weren't enough weapons for many men. The old people told of battles in the sky between rival Gods. They spoke of vast armies, hosts of people. Were the people from the other side of the mountains Gods? If so, how could the people of Amra's village protect themselves?

She spoke her thoughts aloud. 'Unless they're Gods, how can they travel beyond the mountains? We can't. Many have tried, but they get to the snow and can go no further, even in summer. The Snow God who lives there sends our people back.'

Her father shrugged. 'Perhaps the people from beyond the mountains were sent by the God of the Snow. Perhaps he's angry with us for trying to cross his mountains; or for not trying to cross them. How can anyone know what the Gods are doing, or why they do it?'

'So what does it mean, Father?' asked Amra. 'If they are going to come to our side of the mountains, are they going to attack us? Should we make more weapons and try to arm the strong men of the village? Should we gather the men from the other villages and go to attack the invaders?'

Hasga's look was rueful. 'These aren't men who can be attacked. There are too many of them. Even joining together all the men of the valleys, we wouldn't amount to anything like the numbers that are approaching us.'

'When will they be here?' asked Peta.

'Before summer. Maybe after the harvest. Who can tell?'

'Will we have to leave our village?' Peta asked.

Amra laughed and said, 'Of course not.' But her father didn't laugh. This worried Amra. Her village was her life, her security. When she was hunting, she knew the distance from her village by the faces of the mountains, the width of the river, the slope of the land. If the sun was just rising over the birth mountains, she knew how far and how long she could journey before she had to return, and she always walked into the village when the sun touched the tops of the death mountains before it plunged into the extinguishing sea. Leave her village? How could she? How would she know when to turn back? Where would she turn back to?

They withdrew into silence, each gripped by the fear of their knowledge. Then Hasga said, 'Amra . . . do you remember Henk and Annka?'

Amra nodded. She still remembered her feelings when her father had told her that her two best friends were to be sacrificed. It just didn't make sense. They were going to be killed to stop the iron men from crossing the mountains and entering the village. But how could the iron men cross the mountains when the Gods stopped her people from doing so? And how could they enter the village when it had such strong defences? When it had a wall around it which nobody could climb, when its logs were so thick that no weapon could possibly break them? It was all so unfair.

'Long ago Henk and Annka gave their lives for the village. Their sacrifices have kept the people from beyond the mountains away from us until now. Because of their bravery and sacrifice, Henk and Annka are walking with the Gods in the Land of the Dead. They live in eternal warmth and sunlight.'

Again Amra nodded. A feeling of doom was descending upon her. She had to remember to keep breathing. She closed her eyes, trying to understand the import of her father's words. She saw the ceremony again in her mind's eye. It was dark. There was a huge fire. She and Peta, as well as all the other children in the village, had been banned from watching but some of the older ones crept to the high wooden defence walls which surrounded the village and knelt on top where the guards stood. The fire was huge and brilliant even though it was far from them in the middle of the village. Its light was stronger than the light of the stars. All the adults of the village were there. The Medicine Man was wearing the head and the skin of a lion. The Headman was wearing the bones of power around his neck. They were singing a secret song, the words of which floated indistinctly on the air towards the mystified children who were crouching at the redoubt. One of the musicians beat a log drum, the other shook a skin-covered pot containing bones. The people standing around the huge fire were nervous – Amra could tell by the way they seemed to be moving in time to the beat of the drum. It was as if they had drunk too much and the spirits of the hops had entered their heads.

Then the chanting started. It was begun by the Headman, who sang loudly in a high-pitched voice above the music of the drum. The people took up the Headman's song, and then everybody seemed to be singing and moving and swaying and dancing around the fire. People began to throw things into the fire. Amra was too far away to see what they were, but the fire blazed into brilliant sparks like stars as each object cascaded into the flames.

When everybody was in a trance the Medicine Man stepped forward and barked a command to the guards. He was so close to the fire he should have been burnt, but he was oblivious to its heat and intensity. Amra knew enough to realise that both her parents, whom she could vaguely make out in the distance, as well as every other adult in the group, were drunk. To Amra's horror, her friends Henk and Annka were dragged out of a nearby house by two village guards. They were tied with their hands behind their backs. Annka, with whom Amra had been running in the fields just that day, fell, and the guard picked her up roughly and pulled her towards the fire. Amra could tell that her friends were terrified, but she couldn't hear their screams over the drums and the people's chanting.

Amra watched in horrified fascination as the Headman positioned Henk and Annka before the fire. The assembly of people shrank back as the ceremony proceeded, the music growing louder and louder, the musicians more and more frenzied, lost in the rhythm of their actions. Suddenly the Headman shouted out and the drums stopped, the people ended their chanting and the frenzied noise gave way to an overwhelming silence broken only by the crackling of the fire and the whimpering of the two children, muffled and indistinct. The Headman stepped forward and raised his hands high, crying out a prayer to the Gods. He took a huge knife from beneath his robes, raised his face again to the black sky and shouted out another prayer. The people of the village responded but Amra could no longer hear them for the pounding of terror in her ears. But she heard Annka screaming as the Headman plunged the knife into Henk's chest. The boy's body twitched while the Headman sawed the knife back and forward, concentrating on the task despite the huge river of blood which gushed over him. Henk's head drooped over the massive naked wound in his chest, his body slumped in death. Amra couldn't take her eyes off the horror. She felt vomit filling her throat but held it back. The Headman was still wielding his huge knife as though preparing to cut up a freshly killed animal. He was using the knife Amra's father had made not two summers earlier, the knife he had forbidden her to touch.

The guards were holding Henk's body to prevent it falling to the ground. Amra muffled her scream in her hands. Peta had closed her eyes in horror, refusing to look, and buried her head in Amra's enfolding arms.

The Headman put his hand inside Henk's chest and withdrew the boy's heart, bloody and glistening in the light of the fire. He held it aloft in his red hand, blood running down his arm, the firelight showing how proud he was of what he had done, how the people should respect him for his knowledge and bravery. Amra was desperate to close her eyes but she couldn't. Something, a hideous compulsion, forced her to keep them open, to try to understand what was happening. Why had her friend's heart been cut from his body? Why? And what would happen to Annka?

The Headman walked around to each and every person in the crowd, proffering the boy's heart as though it was the head of an enemy. Some of the people shrank back; others cheered and lifted their heads to the God of the Fire, shouting out prayers. The Headman returned to where Henk's crumpled body was now lying at the guards' feet. Annka was struggling hysterically in the guards' grasp, trying desperately to break free. Amra could hear her screaming for help. She could see Annka and Henk's parents crying in the firelight, being comforted by relatives. Amra wanted to jump down and save her friend but that would mean her own certain death.

The Headman again held Henk's heart aloft then, with a mighty action, threw it into the fire, shouting aloud a prayer to the stars. The drums began to beat wildly, the bones to sound, and the people chanted their songs and prayers. Annka screamed and screamed, her voice more and more hysterical as she realised that her heart was next to be plucked from her body. Annka's mother fainted.

The Headman crossed over to the child, put his bloodied hand on her head, whispered a silent prayer into her ears, then drew back his hand again. He turned his face to the sky and called out a prayer. Amra closed her eyes but was unable to shut out her friend's voice, screaming her anguish. The crowd of adults gasped and Amra opened her eyes to see that the Headman had cut out Annka's heart. Amra bit her lip hard to prevent herself from screaming her fear and her sorrow for her best friend. She pulled Peta away from the redoubt and the two horrified girls ran back to their house, where they spent the entire night, faces buried in the mattresses, sobbing for their dead friends. Amra woke many times during the night, the sight of her friends' hearts before her.

Amra's memory of those horrific events which had taken place two years earlier was interrupted by the low voice of her father. 'The Headman came to our house a few days ago, while you and Peta were away gathering wood. He came because he had something important to tell me. Some time ago he sent runners to the villages on the foothills of the far mountains where the Sun God is reborn each morning. When they return they will tell the story about the people from beyond the mountains. Then we will know whether this was just a raiding party, or whether the army is truly preparing to march over the mountains and attack us.'

Amra waited for her father to continue. Her heart was beating rapidly. He seemed reluctant to speak; instead he sipped his now-cold drink. Then he cleared his throat and said, 'If the runners tell us that the people from beyond the mountains are gathering to lay waste to these valleys, then you have been chosen by the village wise men to be the next sacrifice. To you has been given the honour of saving the village.'

Amra stared at him in horror. Peta turned white. But Hasga did not meet their eyes; he just stared at the dying embers of the once-warm fire.

They returned to the house with the wagon, dragging it over the rutted ground, its top overloaded with wood that threatened to tumble to the ground. Peta's job was to walk behind the wagon, picking up sticks which had fallen off as it bumped over rocks and other obstacles in its path. There was enough wood to last their father for six or seven days. It had been a good find, deep in the forest, but high on a hill so that when the old tree had died, it hadn't fallen into a swamp and the juices had drained out of its wood and the wind had dried it quickly. It was the best wood for their father's fire, old, thick and heavy. It would burn long and hot, and its heat would release the bright metals from the heavy earth which their father kept stored in an enclosure at the back of their house.

Nobody in the village – indeed nobody in most of the villages in the five valleys – could make metals as pure, as strong and as sharp as their father could make them. And nobody could make jewellery as fine or as glistening or as perfectly finished. The lines, the swirls and the indentations he delicately hammered into the gold and bronze jewellery were a wonder of beauty and craftsmanship.

The knowledge was in Hasga's head; he had been given the secrets by the God of Fire after much time spent praying for knowledge and sacrificing flawless animals in the secret grove deep in the woods. He was the best metalworker in all the valleys. But when he had first begun to make metals, even with all the skills he had learnt from his father, the jewellery and weapons he produced were never as perfect as those which traders brought to the village from far-off lands. Hasga had tried everything – different wood, different metals, different prayers – but he never managed to produce the gleaming hard metals which the traders brought on their visits to his village, jewellery and weapons made by craftsmen and priests of unbelievable skills who lived in lands far away, lands where the God of the Sun shone bright and long and where the winter snows never fell. One day, Hasga told his wife, he would visit these lands, learn their skills and improve his craft.

But then, perhaps because he had prayed particularly hard, the God of Fire had whispered into Hasga's ear. He had become a different man after that and from that time on his family had enjoyed prosperity. What had happened? What had been the source of Hasga's sudden knowledge? Amra didn't know. But when she watched him preparing the fire, she realised that the God had told him how to use different woods and how to blow air into the fire to make a brighter flame. There was something else as well. All the other metalworkers in the other villages of the five valleys who made metal had their furnaces above the ground, clay pots in which they burnt the metal-bearing rocks. But the metals that came out never shone the way her father's metals shone and the bronze arrow tips and spears and swords they made were never as hard or as sharp as those her father made. Because the God of Fire had given Hasga the secret, more and more people from their village and from other villages in the area came to him to barter for his jewellery and weapons. Throughout the length and breadth of the five valleys of the rivers, Amra's father Hasga was known as the man to whom the Gods spoke, the man who made the best weapons.

Into the furnace her father placed the hard earth which held the metals. He said prayers then, using a hammer, he broke up the earth which contained the metal. Depending on the metal, the stone became like dust or splintered into smaller bits of rock. Then he covered the furnace with a thick clay lid. He lit the fire, intoned more prayers, then took from his pouch the firemakers' amulet and waved it three times towards the place of the Sun God's birth and three times towards the place of the Sun God's death. More prayers were chanted as the fire grew hotter and bolder, then Hasga turned his attention to tending the fire, placing the wood first in one direction and then in another until the fire grew large and so hot that he had to stand back for fear of his skin burning. When the Fire God grew old and tired and the flames didn't leap so high, but the embers were reborn bright with every breath of wind, her father used bellows to fan the flames until they became white with anger and red with heat. Then he used his pushing stone to push the fire around the furnace before piling it with more wood which spat and sparked in anger. Finally he covered the conflagration with a funnel and its tall chimney.

Amra thought that this might make the fire go out but it didn't. Instead, after more prayers, her father used his knife to open a small vent in the chimney. There was a whistle as air was sucked into the hole. Amra watched in fear. The whistle was like the air which escaped from an animal's body when a knife was stuck into its lungs – the evil spirits leaving its body. Were there evil spirits in the fire? Was that why it whistled? Sparks shot up the funnel of the chimney high into the darkening sky. Her father took more wood and shaped it with a knife so that it was long and slender. He dropped the wood down the chimney, carefully withdrawing his hands so that he didn't burn himself.

Amra watched intently in utter fascination but never once did Hasga realise he was being observed. Sometimes he danced around the fire, as though imitating one of the flames which occasionally sprang up through the chimney to escape into the air. At other times he returned to the furnace and, despite its heat, thrust his head close to the fire and shouted. Then he would have to pour water from a goatskin over his red and angry face. He would take a mouthful of water from the same goatskin and spit it across the top of the funnel as though he were tempting the fire spirits to rise up and be quenched. And all the while he mumbled his prayers.

This, Amra realised, was why her father was the great metalmaker and metalworker of the five valleys which enclosed the five rivers – only her father knew the language of the Gods, only her father knew how to make a fire burn hotter and longer so that the earth gave up its metals to be formed into hard and sharp and beautiful bounty which the Gods let their friend take from them. But, even with all of his skills, Hasga still couldn't make iron. Try as he might whenever a trader brought him lumps of the red rock, all that ever emerged was a brittle and useless metal which looked dirty and broke when it was struck with a hard rock. Amra knew that Hasga was depressed because he couldn't make the metal, and because he knew that somewhere, in a far distant land, others could.

Amra stopped pulling the wagon as they approached their father's house. She waited for Peta to catch up. It had been a long hard road from deep in the mountains back to where they lived near the river but she knew her father would be well pleased with the wood. It was already getting dark; the village looked calm and peaceful, so different to the turmoil which her life had suddenly become. Entering the peacefulness, she could believe that the nightmare she had been living for the past few days didn't exist, or was just that – a bad dream from eating too many berries or too much meat. But then she realised that it was the calm before the storm, before the beginning of a horrible happening which was outside the control of the villagers, which was controlled by the Gods themselves. This was how it had been before Henk and Annka had been taken from their parents, put into the house of the Medicine Man and then sacrificed to appease the Gods. And now she was to be next.

She knew her father was in a state of deep distress. First he had lost his wife to the falling and wasting sickness and now he was to lose his elder daughter. Amra knew he loved her. She knew it because since her earliest times her hours with him had been times of joy. Swimming in the river with her arms around his neck as he dived to the bottom and then resurfaced to secure her; or taking her hunting and showing her how to weigh an arrow carefully so she knew how far to pull back the bow for maximum speed and power; or the times he took her deep into the forest to show her which woods were best for the heat of his fire.

Because of Hasga's love, Amra knew before any other girl or boy in the village how to make fire from the fire stones. When other children were still running around their house playing games, she and her little bow and arrow had trailed after her father, going out to kill the rabbits and hares, and even small deer, which he proudly called 'Amra's meal'.

So Amra knew he must have suffered a knife wound to his heart when the Headman told him that she must be sacrificed. She could envisage the scene: Hasga would have nodded and accepted it calmly, his outward appearance saying that it was the right decision, the decision of the Gods; but her real father, the interior man who was now hidden from Amra and Peta, was suffering intense grief. Amra ached for her father's distress. She knew that he despaired and feared the emptiness of a life without the people he loved. She wanted to tell him that she was happy with the decision. She wanted to make it easy for him, but she couldn't. She couldn't because she knew in her heart that it was wrong. In all of her life in the village, in all the days that she had lived, through all of the seasons of heat and cold, of wind and rain, of sun and snow, she had never been more sure of anything. Sacrificing her life to stop the men of iron from the other side of the mountains was wrong, and besides nothing would change with her death. The men of iron would still come. The only difference would be the fact that she was dead. Her certainty was based on her understanding of what had happened to her friends, Henk and Annka. To Amra, it was all so simple. If the iron men from the north and the east had not been stopped by the sacrifice of Henk and Annka, why would they now be stopped by Amra's death? They would still come. They would still come after the knife had been plunged into her heart.

Amra had been selected to be sacrificed because the God of War had whispered her name into the ear of the Headman. The Headman had told her father, and her father had told her. But the Headman had not asked the God of War why Amra's sacrifice would stop the men of iron if previous sacrifices had not stopped them. Why hadn't he asked the God of War how the men could still be coming even though Henk and Annka had given their lives to stop them? Amra had been pondering these thoughts ever since she had recovered from the shock of the news. She had gone to the river for a swim immediately after hearing her fate. Her mind worked better in the cold reality of the water. At first, she had accepted the Gods' decision. Yes, it was right that her life should be given up for the good of the village if it would save the others. But why should her life be given up if it *didn't* stop the iron men? It didn't make sense.

The next day Amra had been quiet and subdued. She'd asked Hasga a few pertinent questions: 'Will my death really stop the iron men?' and 'Where are Henk and Annka now?'. 'Why can't we find out how the iron men make their weapons so that we can arm ourselves with weapons like theirs and fight them?' 'Why aren't our bronze weapons good enough to beat off the iron men?'

To each question, and to the many more she asked him during the day, Hasga had given the same reply. A smile. A stroke of the hair. A kiss. And silence. To each question, except the last. Why couldn't he make weapons like those of the iron men? It was a question which had tortured him since a trader had first shown him an iron sword. The sword was as hard and as sharp as a bronze sword, though it didn't have the beauty of those which he spent days making, but it was so much stronger. According to the trader there were many such weapons where he had come from, and they could be made easily. The red stone of iron was found in many parts of the world and it could produce weapons which could equip more soldiers than the handful of men whose task it was to guard the village, or than the small army of men owned by the ruler of the city in the warm lands of the south. These small fighting forces were equipped only with minimal weapons because tin was so scarce and so expensive. And bronze only appeared when tin was mixed with copper. But with iron so plentiful, every person in the village could be given a sword, dagger and shield. Every village could have its own army. If only Hasga could learn the secret of making iron. He had tried so often. Every time a trader came through his village with some of the red earth, he had pounded it and mixed it with tin, with copper, with gold and silver, and said prayers, fasted and done everything he could think of to create the magical metal. But each time the cooled iron laughed at him: it was weak, puny, unworthy of a fighting man.

When Amra asked her questions Hasga looked at her in sorrow; he could give her no answers. He had not only let down the people of his village, he had failed the only person who reminded him of his dead wife, Mira. So he had remained silent, out of shame, and Amra stopped asking questions.

That morning Amra and Peta had left early before their father had risen. They had tended the fire, boiled the water for his herb drink, torn chunks of bread from the previous day's loaf and left it beside the fire to warm for when their father woke. They had been away for the whole day and had much to show for their labour. The girls left the wagon just outside the village wall. There was no reason to pull it inside, because their father would only have to pull it back again to take it into the lower part of the forest where he made his metal. They entered the house, their legs scratched from the briars in the forest, their arms dirty from carrying the wood. Amra was desperate to take off her clothes and go down to the river to cool her body. But the sight of her father stopped her in her tracks. He was sitting in a low chair in the corner of the room, her mother's favourite chair, where she always sat before going to bed. It had been her thinking chair, she had sat there and put the day's activities into order in her mind before sleeping for the night. It was the first time Amra had seen her father in the chair.

'Father?' she said quietly.

Hasga looked up slowly as though he was still part asleep. Peta came inside and whispered into Amra's ear, 'I don't think he has been outside. The breakfast is still there. The fire is dead.'

'Are you all right, Father?' Amra asked.

Hasga smiled, but it was a weak smile, a smile of apology, the sort of smile he had been giving her ever since the Headman had visited.

'What's the matter?' she asked.

Hasga looked at Peta then said gently, 'Peta, my love, go down to the river and swim. There's a matter I must discuss with your sister.'

The child did as she was told. Amra could feel her heart beating rapidly. Something terrible was going to happen. She knew it.

'Amra, I think the time has come for you to go from here. They want to sacrifice you. I can't bear the thought. I know that I must sacrifice one of you to the Gods, but Amra, you're young and strong and able to live outside of the village, outside of the valleys. You will find a good man. You will be his wife. You will have children. The Gods will smile.'

Amra stared in amazement. 'But if I go who will be sacrificed?'

'Another child,' he said, looking at the floor. She knew what he could not say.

'But they'll take Peta, Father! You know they will.'

He bit his lip, unable to meet her eyes.

'Father, you can't.'

'Peta is younger than you. For her, for me, the loss will not be so great.'

'Father!' Amra protested. 'I can't save myself, not when Peta . . .'

'Peta is too young to know what this means. She is a good and lovely child but she will not understand until it's too late.'

But Amra knew that wasn't true. Peta had already seen their friends sacrificed. Despite her age, she would know exactly what Amra's disappearance would mean for her.

'Father, the Gods have decided that I must be sacrificed. How can I live knowing that Peta has died in my place?'

Her father nodded. 'I knew you would say that.'

'Why can't we all go? We can carry the furnace and metal earth and some wood. We can go to another place, another village. Even beyond the sea where the sun dies. There must be somewhere we can go. All of us.'

Her father laughed. 'You really don't understand, do you, child? You can't defy the Gods. Nobody can. If we leave here the village will be destroyed, our lives will be made hard and we'll only live for a short time. The Gods won't allow us to escape. Where can we run where we won't be seen? Where can we hide? Everyone in the village knows what is to happen to us. The Headman has already told the others, and he's also told me that I can't escape their decision. The Headman said that wherever we go the Gods will see and make us suffer before we die.'

Amra was shocked. 'You told the Headman you were thinking of leaving?'

'Of course,' said her father. 'I've done everything to prevent your death. The only solution I can see is for Peta to be taken by the Headman in your place and for her to be sacrificed for the pleasure of the Gods.'

'But how can you? You love Peta as much as you love me.'

'I know,' said her father in despair. 'How can a father choose between two children he loves so much? But if you leave the village now, Peta will be sacrificed. Then you can return. You will become like your mother sooner than Peta will. You will marry and then your children, if they are boys, will learn from me the skills of fire making and how to get metal from the earth and mix it to make precious things. Maybe they will discover how to fight the iron men from beyond the mountains. But Peta is so young that I have no more time for her to grow up.'

Tears began to form in Amra's eyes. In the forest things had seemed much clearer. There she had worked out what to do, what to say. She had planned to tell her father that she would do anything necessary to avoid giving her life in sacrifice for the village: seek whatever information was needed, scout the bleak and dangerous mountains and spy on the villages and towns of the men of iron, capture one of their number and torture him to find out their plans. She would even go to the place where they knew the secret of making iron. The traders had told her people about these cities far away in the south, in the lands where it was always warm. Where the God of Snow never visited. In the woods, she had clearly remembered their names: Tarsus and Alalakh and Troy and Ugarit and Megiddo. Amra had listened in wonder as the traders described the size of the cities, their buildings, their temples and their streets. And when they had brought out the things these people had made, Amra had gasped in awe. The strange names of the cities defined their magic. She had memorised their names, repeating them over and over again in her mind, capturing their mystique, their wonder. What beautiful names. What beautiful things they made. What strange and mysterious skills the people there must possess. She had determined that somehow she would acquire those skills and help her father to save their people. She would bargain for her life. She would do anything.

Those were her plans in the woods. But now that she had returned, now her father had spoken, she realised that she must die. She could do nothing to save her own life if her beautiful little sister, her closest friend, was to die in her place.

CHAPTER 6

If Josef Stalin were still alive, thought Feyodor Mikailovich Meconski, he would have sent in the troops, arrested all the cosmopolitan degenerate scum and marched them off to Siberia; so would have Khrushchev, Breznev, Chernenko and Andropov. But not Gorbachev. He would have smiled benignly and thought what a marvellous thing it was, but then he'd started the whole thing with his damned *perestroika* and *glasnost*. Feyodor grimaced at the fury of the noise pounding out from the nightclub located in one of the darkened streets off Red Square. The music pulsated so loudly that the very air seemed to vibrate, as though trying to keep him away. Even from across the wide road he could smell the stench of stale liquor and tobacco fumes.

A guard stood there. Not a Red guard, a cavalryman or even a Kremlin guard in comic opera uniform, but a huge bear of a man. Broad-shouldered, impossibly tall, hair shaven down to his skull, he wore a blindingly white shirt beneath a grey suit which looked as if it had been spraypainted onto his muscular body. He had the flat wide Slavic features of a man whose ancestors had swung from the frozen trees in the north-east of Russia. But for all his apelike characteristics he was a man to be reckoned with, a man whose embryonic personality was imprisoned within the muscles of his body.

It was still early in the evening but people were already drinking, smoking, laughing and dancing to the thunderous music which erupted out of the basement.

Feyodor walked up to the guard. 'I would like to enter.'

The guard gave him a cursory glance, taking in his age, flaccid body and conservative clothes. He didn't look like a bum or a drunk, though his eyes were rheumy and his face florid. He just looked like a lonely old man. The only people the guard was instructed to keep out were the members of gangs who controlled other clubs, as well as certain police officers and city officials who had made it their business to close down all entertainment in Moscow.

The guard stood aside. Feyodor descended the steps into the claustrophobic heat, noise and vibrating tremors of the dance floor far below. A woman stationed behind a desk on a landing looked at him quizzically: his clothes were old-fashioned, his hair slicked back like a grandfather's – what the hell was he doing in a club for Moscow's glittering youth? Still, it was none of her business. She demanded the admission price. Feyodor took out his wallet and counted out the required number of notes. The woman gave him a ticket and a voucher for a free glass of Scotch, pressed a button on her desk and watched in profound antipathy as the door to her left clicked open. Feyodor walked through and was immediately engulfed in the hot, smoky, hell-like atmosphere of life below the pavements of Moscow.

He winced at the noise and the stroboscopic light which assaulted his eyes and his sense of balance. He stood at the top of the steps, enveloped by the surrounding cacophony, buffeted by the pounding music, desperate to orient himself for the further descent to the dance floor. Every few seconds his face was hit by a laser beam which reflected off a rotating silver mirrored globe. Intense beams of light arced at crazed angles across the ceiling and the floor, highlighting the gyrating bodies and bobbing heads that packed the over-crowded dance floor.

Steeling himself Feyodor prepared to walk down the stairs. The door clicked shut behind him with a menacing finality as though he were entering a prison cell. In the demi-light, he groped his way to the banister and moved slowly one step at a time until he reached the bottom. Here he had to negotiate his way around the entwined bodies of couples who had undulated into the periphery, pushing aside those patrons who sat at tables or stood at the bar. Feyodor managed to manoeuvre his way to the bar where he presented the token he had been given by the receptionist. The girl who served him was wearing a black diaphanous shirt which did nothing to hide her ample breasts. She pushed a tiny tumbler of whisky towards him. This was the reason the nightclub had taken off so rapidly in its early days: every other nightclub in town served vodka as the first free drink so the young had sought out Moscow Knights for its rare whisky.

Above the noise, Feyodor shouted to the barmaid, 'I want to speak to Maxim.'

The girl shook her head. 'No Maxim here,' she screamed back over the din, and turned away to serve other customers.

He waited until she approached his end of the bar again then interrupted her conversation with one of the obviously wealthy patrons. 'Maxim told me that if I had something important to discuss it was all right for me to come here. It is important. I must speak to him. Please find him.'

'I said there's no Maxim here,' the woman shouted, this time in a more cold and aggressive voice. She walked quickly to the opposite end of the bar where she picked up a phone and spoke a few urgent words.

And there Feyodor waited. Slowly he finished his whisky and asked the indifferent barmaid for another. This one came in a much bigger tumbler but the girl demanded an amount of money which staggered him. Almost a quarter of his weekly salary for a lousy glass of watered-down whisky. Under normal circumstances he would have objected to the price of the drink, but these circumstances were anything but normal. Sipping it sullenly, Feyodor felt a presence beside him. At first, despite the fug of cigarette smoke and perspiration, he smelt the perfume – rich, heady and aromatic. Curiosity made him turn. One of the most beautiful girls he had ever seen was standing beside him. Like the barmaid she was wearing a black diaphanous shirt but it was far more subtle and expensive than the other girl's, with pockets positioned carefully to show her cleavage but nothing else. She smiled at him and he smiled back. This was the type of beautiful woman whose face appeared in fashion magazines, blonde hair kissing her cheeks, her make-up subtle, her very stance alluring, energising. Feyodor wanted to stare at her forever but in middle–aged embarrassment he turned back to his drink.

'I'm Anna. I haven't seen you here before,' she said. Her voice was as sensual as her face and body.

'I've never been here before.' His voice was lower than he wanted, the voice of an older man.

'I'm a whore. Are you looking for a partner?' she asked.

He smiled. He wanted to tell her about Natalie, to boast that he enjoyed the pleasures of a mistress far more beautiful than she. But circumspection made him cautious. He said, 'Even if I was looking, I couldn't afford you.'

'But you don't know how much I cost.'

'Even if you were free, I still couldn't afford you,' he said. 'I'm not like these people.' He nodded towards the young men and women gyrating on the dance floor. 'I'm a government official on a government official's salary. I'm not an entrepreneur. Much as I'd like you to stay with me, we would both be wasting our time.'

She nodded indifferently. 'Have a nice day,' she said, imitating how she'd been told American whores behaved, and disappeared from his sight.

Feyodor turned back to his whisky and swirled it. He would have to make it last for hours at these prices. He began to conjure up fantasies of what he would do in bed with both the bewitching Natalie and the beautiful young Anna if only he had the money. He would take them to a hotel room, watch them both slowly undress each other, revel in how they both looked in their sexy underwear, smell the fragrances of their bodies, see their curves intermingle in liquid embraces, slowly flowing over his naked and engorged form with a warmth, an eroticism, a softness he had only ever dreamt about. Throughout his marriage he had relied on his fantasies on the rare occasions that his wife permitted him to enter her body. He closed his eyes tightly and imagined women like Natalie and Anna in his wife's place as he slowly ground his way to attempting to bring her to completion, they were the women who encouraged him, helped him to maintain his erection so that he didn't lose interest halfway through. But now Natalie and Anna were real. If only his life wasn't enmeshed in a web of vipers, he would revel in the experience.

A female voice interrupted his fantasy. Another woman, not as attractive as the first, but still very pleasing. She was wearing a business suit, a vibrant red jacket and a white shirt. 'Will you come with me, please?' she asked.

'My dear,' Feyodor repeated, 'unfortunately I don't have the income of the young men here.'

'I'm not a whore,' she interrupted. 'What's your name?'

'Why?' he asked.

'Just tell me your name.'

He told her. The woman pulled a two-way radio from her pocket and repeated what he'd told her. She put the instrument to her ear and nodded at the distant, disembodied voice.

'You wanted to speak to Maxim. Follow me.'

She turned and like a school boy he trotted after her. She knew the inside of the club well enough to execute a few subtle manoeuvres around tables which were so close they looked interlocked. Within seconds they were on the other side of the dance floor. A corridor appeared between two partitions, guarded by another of the ubiquitous gorillas. He ignored Feyodor because he was entering with someone in authority. Good!

The woman took him up a flight of stairs, down another corridor, down another flight of stairs, turned left, and finally came to a door guarded by two more burly clones. They nodded at her respectfully, pressed a number on a key pad and the door clicked open.

The room Feyodor now entered was the diametric opposite of the room he had just left. Here was an atmosphere of purity, permanence, refinement. Most noticeable was the quiet: the room was soundproofed against any intrusion by the outside world. Feyodor looked around in the muted light to orientate himself. There was a vast mahogany desk in the centre of the room with chairs surrounding it. Ottomans were placed strategically on rugs which looked like the finest Turkish double-knit. Before the desk, sitting on low chairs as if in supplication, were four men in expensive suits. They stared at Feyodor as though he were an exhibit which had just crept out of a museum case. Behind the desk, as imperious as Caesar at a meeting of the knights in ancient Rome, sat the man who was Feyodor's partner, the man who had surprised him in Natalie's apartment, the man who controlled Feyodor's fate.

Maxim Nikolaivich Lomonosov, businessman, entre-preneur, friend of the powerful in government, confidante of police, judges and politicians, paragon of the rapidly rising elite, the middle-class bourgeois whose ancestors had been eliminated three-quarters of a century earlier by the

Bolshevik Revolution, smiled as Feyodor walked towards him. Maxim Nikolaivich Lomonosov, fabulously wealthy boss of one of the major branches of the Russian Mafia, killer, fanatic, lunatic, the man who got things done in Moscow, motioned to Feyodor to take a seat.

Ironically, when the information first filtered up to him about the buried treasure in the bowels of the Pushkin Museum, Maxim Nikolaivich Lomonosov had been profoundly disinterested. It was Natalie, his long-term mistress and assistant, who saw the potential and suggested setting up a honey trap for the deputy director, with herself as bait.

'Antiques? Who gives a fuck about antiques?' Lomonosov had blustered. 'You make money out of drugs, currency and arms. Antiques? You're mad,' he told her.

'You're wrong,' Natalie had insisted. 'Listen to me for a minute before you say no. Drugs – sure, we're making lots of money but think about their real profitability. How much do we lose at the Bulgarian border? A fortune. It's the same coming in through Afghanistan and the Silk Route. And forget about Prague and Vienna. Weapons too. Again we're losing our pants in Bulgaria. We lose two shipments in every ten to the Kurds. I'm telling you, this Pushkin guy has found this buried treasure in the basement of the Museum. If we can get hold of it and sell it to antique collectors or wealthy Americans, we could make a fortune. From what he was saying it could be worth a billion American dollars.'

Lomonosov's jaw had dropped at the sum, but then he shook his head. 'Why would he give it to us?' he asked.

'He won't. He'll give it to me. I'll set up a honey trap. From the sound of it he's middle-aged, bored and bald. A perfect candidate for a honey trap.'

'Who will you use?'

'For something like this, only me,' she replied.

It had taken her just two weeks to close the trap. First she'd come away with a few trinkets, then rings, then more valuable stuff, and each time she went back with fistfuls of American dollars. That idiot Meconski started to walk around in expensive suits, he bought himself a new car, began dining out. It was all getting too dangerous. Some jealous Museum official would report his sudden wealth to the corruption police and then the whole game would collapse. He had to be stopped, and Maxim Nikolaivich Lomonosov was the man to stop him.

When Lomonosov had first confronted the little archaeologist in Natalie's apartment, he'd thought the little man was going to shit his pants. He had never seen anyone so frightened, so aware that he was completely trapped. Meconski realised quickly that his only hope was to keep putting more and more of this Helen of Troy treasure into Lomonosov's coffers. And what a gold mine it had proved to be. American collectors were paying hundreds of thousands of dollars for crappy gold rings with a certificate of authentication. Of course they had to sign an undertaking not to make their acquisition public for ten years, after which the shit would really hit the fan, but by then he would have distanced himself so completely that nobody would even think of looking his way.

Now suddenly Meconski had turned up on his doorstep. This he hadn't anticipated. And word was beginning to filter out from these two asshole journalists about the treasure. People were starting to realise what was down there in the basement of the Museum. It was time to look at damage control.

'I'm surprised to see you here,' said Lomonsov. His voice was deep, it resonated through his huge bulk. He wasn't tall but his body told the story of years of rich living. His weight seemed to have increased exponentially each year since the fall of the Berlin Wall.

'Believe me, I didn't want to come. I've left a dozen messages for you. Why haven't you responded? Where's Natalie? I've been phoning and phoning, but she never responds.' Feyodor's voice rose in pitch. He sounded timorous, as though trying not to show he was overawed by his surroundings.

Ignoring his question, Maxim said, 'What is it that you want? Why the sudden panic?'

'The director of the Pushkin is dying. The Minister is making noises about the Germans' demand for the return of Priam's treasury. There's going to be an audit any day, I'm sure of it. We have to get everything back. I have to be able to present him with the full inventory or we'll all go to the firing squad.'

The Mafia boss looked at him in astonishment; the little man's voice was stern and he was obviously restraining his emotions. Maxim burst out laughing, his jowls wobbling as he roared into the ceiling.

'I'm serious,' said Feyodor, raising his voice.

'And how do you propose to buy these things back? Your girlfriend Natalie is a very expensive proposition. You've spent a lot of money on her and on yourself. Do you have the money to buy back the treasure?'

Feyodor looked at him with contempt. 'You know as well as I do she works for you. Don't try and make a fool of me.' He looked down at his knees. 'I've already been made a fool of by Natalie.'

'Friend,' said Maxim in consolation, 'that's just not true. She's very fond of you.'

'Don't rub salt into my wounds,' said Feyodor. 'You used her to trap me. I'm not a complete idiot.'

'We used her as a way of developing our business relationship. Nothing more. She's gone beyond that. She genuinely likes you.'

'Then why haven't I seen her for a month?'

'She's been busy on other projects.'

'Other suckers, you mean.'

Maxim leant forward. 'Let me give you a word of advice. You're in my office. Many of my friends are here. It's not good policy to insult me. You see, I can take these insults on the chin. I'm a big man. But I have a certain reputation. These boys,' he said, pointing to the huge muscular phalanx surrounding him, 'they're like children to me. They look on me as a father. Now a father has to be held in respect by his children, and if you come in here insulting me and I let it pass then they won't respect me. That could be very damaging for me, so if you continue to insult me I'll have to kill you. Do you understand?'

Feyodor sat back in his chair, sweat breaking out on his forehead. He had gone too far. For a moment he'd forgotten he was dealing with a Mafioso. Maxim insisted that his relationship with Feyodor was a business partnership, but that was only a veneer. The menace, the cold, calculating, nonchalant way he threatened Feyodor chilled him to the bone. He had always known death was a likelihood but now the threat was in the open.

'What's the problem? So there'll be an audit – fix it. You're the deputy director. The director is on her death bed.'

'It's not that simple,' said Feyodor, beginning to regain his composure. 'If it was, I wouldn't be here. The problem is that the Germans are demanding to see the entire collection. We've shown them some pieces but have managed to keep most of the treasure hidden from view. We've put out the famous items – the diadem, hundreds of rings – but the stuff I've been slipping to you, archaeological curiosities which private collectors have been buying, that's still in packing cases. It's still buried in the vaults. I'm telling people in government we don't have the manpower to bring it up and catalogue it, but now the Germans are demanding it back. I've got pressure coming from the Kremlin which I can no longer ignore. It's really killing me. They're going to expose us.'

His voice was rising. Lomonosov knew a man on the edge of panic. The last thing he needed was to be exposed now; his business interests were very delicately balanced at the moment. He might have to sever his relationship with Feyodor; perhaps a suicide, the body found with a note in its pocket admitting to the theft would solve his problems, even though it would put an end to a very lucrative part of his business.

'What's your solution?' he asked quietly.

'I don't have one. If I did, I wouldn't be here. I had no idea when we began this thing that those fucking journalists would track down the treasure. How was I supposed to know it would be discovered? I couldn't have known that Germany would demand its return. I even had a note from the director who wants to exhibit it around the world to earn money! She wrote the bloody thing on her death bed. Suddenly everybody's interested, even the Greeks. I had an archaeologist from Athens phone me up to ask if he and his colleagues could come to Moscow on a private visit to look at the treasure. We have to get the stuff back. You have to buy it back. You have to!'

'You expect me to spend my money to buy it back? Me?'

Lomonosov looked around the room. Everyone, even the woman in the red suit, smiled in amusement. The idea of their boss shelling out money was too bizarre to contemplate.

'If you don't,' Feyodor insisted, 'the police will be called. Then the shit will really fly. Believe me, if the director gets better the first thing she's planning is to put the treasure on display. Even if she dies, nothing will stop the Minister from earning money from exhibiting it. He's not a fool. All just to prove that the Schliemann treasure belongs to Russia not to the Germans. That's why I'm certain there will be an audit; the government is counting seriously on it as a source of income. This isn't a joke, Maxim Nikolaivich, this is deadly earnest. We could all go to prison. We could all be shot.'

Lomonosov roared with laughter. 'Fool!' he shouted. 'Nobody is going to go to prison. First, I own the police. Half the people downstairs in the bar are in the anti-corruption squad. I fucking own them. Second, the only person in real trouble is you. Not me. So don't talk about us, talk about you. And third, you're making a big noise over nothing. So your boss wants to put on an exhibition. So when she recovers she'll want an inventory. She'll be dead before that happens. If Christ somehow makes an appearance and helps her to recover, one of my men will inject her with adrenalin and she'll be dead in an hour. As for the Minister, stall the stupid idiot. Delay him. That's what you bureaucrats are best at. Pretend. Lie. Do something. He'll forget soon enough.'

Feyodor shook his head vehemently. 'It's not like that. He's got a bee in his pants because of the pressure we're under from Athens and Berlin. It's gone all the way to the top, it's out of his hands now. Even the President is interested. The Ministry has been pushing us to get the collection together to tour Athens as a way of softening their demands. It won't go to Germany for political reasons – there were thousands of art treasures stolen from Germany at the end of the war, so it's still a political matter. But Berlin is saying that the Priam treasure is the spoils of war. Even Greece is saying that they're originally Mycenaen and belong to the Athens Museum.'

Lomonosov shrugged. 'So do an inventory and tell them some have gone missing over the past half century. Pretend the Russian art experts at the end of the Great

Patriotic War stole them. They're dead and buried. Nobody can prove it's you.'

'But an inventory was taken when they first came to the Pushkin then the boxes were resealed. Everything accords to the original German catalogue. What's missing sticks out like a sore thumb.'

Lomonosov nodded. The last thing he needed right now was an investigation. There was a new broom sweeping clean in the upper echelons of the anti-corruption department. Even the police gyrating on his dance floor knew that shortly they would be investigated. His Mafia unit, as well as a number of others which had once operated with complete impunity in Moscow, were now being seriously harassed because of local and international pressure. Many of the Sicilians had gone back home because things were getting too hot. An international scandal would be very bad for him. Very bad. And one thing he could guarantee was that if the pressure got too intense, this little runt, this nonentity of an assistant director, would be the first to crease up and blubber to the authorities.

Lomonosov studied the little man in the big chair opposite him. A couple of options ran through his mind. He could terminate him now, immediately. Take out a gun and pop him. His body would be found floating in the river, a suicide note stuck in his pocket admitting full liability. That would be the easiest option – but it wouldn't work. It would spark a major investigation and it was obvious that a little shit like him could never have smuggled the treasures overseas alone. Second option was to kill the director of the Pushkin Museum. But she was half dead anyway and would be replaced immediately, undoubtedly by somebody appointed by the Ministry to go in and clear up the suspicion. Third option was to eliminate the people from the Berlin Museum who were making the demands.

Lomonosov knew what was really going on, he had his ear close to the ground. The real problem was Berlin, not Greece. Those German bastards wanted their treasure back; that was why they were putting pressure on Moscow. Without that pressure, the Schliemann treasure would be put on exhibit somewhere in Russia and nobody would be any the wiser. Even if it went to Athens, Feyodor could say that only the catalogued stuff was leaving the country, that the rest was still being inspected. But the fucking Germans were meticulous about everything and they'd have documented precisely what was in the treasure. Yes, it was the Germans who were the problem. Settle them and the other problems would sort themselves out.

Lomonosov smiled and said to Feyodor, 'You know, once the pressure is off from Germany, I don't think that the Ministry will be as anxious about the treasure as they are at the moment. Your boss will soon cease to be a problem, and we can deal with the Minister. A swimming accident, or maybe a hit and run. That will give you all the time you need to cover your tracks. Don't worry, Feyodor.' Maxim reached over the desk and tapped the frightened little archaeologist on the cheek. 'You just leave it with me. I'll solve all your problems. Meantime why don't you go back outside and enjoy yourself. There's a whore called Anna who would like to meet you. I'll pay. You just have a good time.'

❋

The wooden horse dominated the entrance to the ancient city of Troy. As she stepped out of the minibus and saw it for the first time, Sarah winced. It was the epitome of crass and ugly commercialism, the denigration of the archaeological value of the site to the needs of tourism.

Handek Akbul saw the important visitor wince and suffered with her. As one of the official guides whose job it was to explain the wonders of ancient Troy to visitors, Handek both loved and hated his job. Troy was the greatest glory of the ancient world, yet to pander to British and American tourists the local Canakkale authorities had decided to dress it up like a child's birthday cake, prettifying it with this obscene gigantic horse in which visitors could have their photograph taken. He glanced at it for the tenth time that morning, his lip curling with contempt at Turkey's attempts to pander to the effete and incomprehensible tastes of the west.

But he had been informed that these people, especially the young woman, were very important people, not ordinary tourists. And since he had risen this morning to go to the mosque to say his prayers, Handek Akbul had been dreading their sight of the damnable wooden horse. He had been in a state of consternation ever since their ferry had docked on the Asian side of the Dardanelles. These were people of influence: three were from the Ministry of Antiquities in Istanbul, two others were academics from the university, and one was from the Museum. And then there was the woman, an American. In all the decades he had been treading the ancient mound of Troy, Handek Akbul had guided over a hundred thousand tourists; he knew by instinct which person in a party was most important, to whom he should defer, and instinct told him that the young and attractive American woman was the epicentre around whom everybody else gravitated.

As he waited to greet them, Handek reflected on the years of his life. Had he really been showing tourists around the site of ancient Troy for thirty years? Things had been slow for the first twenty and he had been forced to sell slides and articles to make a living, but over the last decade Turkey had become one of the key destinations for tourists seeking somewhere out of the way which wasn't too crowded. Now, to Handek's delight, tourists were flocking to Troy, desperate to see the wonders of the ancient world. It was both his business and his pleasure. He never became bored with showing people the genius of the men who had, over the millennia, built many-layered Troy. And it was profitable. Last year he had been able to afford a new television for his family.

The government was just as delighted. The moment the site became a real money-spinner, some genius – probably with a degree in tourism from some obscure American university – had instructed that a wooden horse be erected at the entrance. The Japanese, the Americans and the Germans all insisted on climbing the inner staircase, which looked like a giant penis between the structure's back legs, and waving to their camera-ready relatives on the ground below. Then would follow an inevitable ten minutes of confusion as one group came down while the other one went up for precisely the same photograph. Handek was only able to tolerate the antics and predictability of the visitors by turning his back on them and concentrating on the site of Troy, laid bare and vandalised by Schliemann, now being lovingly restored and repaired by dedicated archaeologists and scholars.

Handek was pleased when his important party ignored the wooden horse, walking straight past it to introduce themselves to him. He said the few words of welcome he had prepared that morning then asked them to follow him to the long entrance pathway which led from the tourist shops to the site of Troy.

'The lands which encompass the area between the Turkish Adriatic, the Dardanelles and the Sea of Marmara,' he said in his professorial voice, 'were originally called the Troas, or Troad, in ancient times. Of course you may know them better as Ilion or Ilios from Homer's classic *Iliad*. It's likely that they took their names from two kings, Tros and

Ilios. Tros was directly descended from Zeus and Electra, whose son Dardanus created the Dardan people who gave their name to the Straits a few miles north of here.'

One of the academics from the university spoke a few words into Handek's ear. He nodded and fell silent while the group climbed the short ascent to the site of Troy.

'What did he say?' whispered Sarah to Professor Bengazi who smiled and whispered back, 'He told him to stop acting like a bloody tourist guide and remember who he was dealing with.' Sarah fought back a smile of gratitude.

Although Troy was interesting, Sarah was tired. It had been a long journey down the European bank of the Sea of Marmara and the Dardanelles to Gallipoli, although both pleasant and full of interest. The bus had picked her up from her hotel at six o'clock that morning and they had arrived at eleven o'clock in the northern city from whose port the ferry crossed the narrow neck of the Marmara Sea from Eceabat over to the Asian shore. It was a stretch made famous in the ancient past by Leander's desperate swim, a feat emulated more recently by the passionate poet Lord Byron.

Sarah was fascinated by the way Turkey was split into two distinct entities: there was the northern part, whose capital city of Istanbul dominated the life and cultural times of the entire country and which gave the Turkish people their foothold in the sophistication of Europe; and the massive land to the south of the Sea of Marmara which was Anatolian Asia. The capital of the country, Ankara, was firmly positioned in the Asian part of the country, elevated to fame this century by the dictates of Kemal Atatürk and his dislike of the cosmopolitanism of Constantinople. He had even insisted the old name be changed to Istanbul to break away from the past.

This trip to Troy was more than the Turkish government paying deference to Sarah as an important visitor and more than a chance to impress her with the beauties and wonders of the ancient land whose civilisation had recorded its history for the past eight thousand years. It was also an orientation exercise so that when Sarah stood in front of the world's leading jurists to present the case for Turkey's reclamation of its crown jewels, she would be able to speak with knowledge, insight and passion. It was one thing for her to be dry and legalistic, a theoretician pleading a case, but the Minister for Antiquities hoped that once Turkey had ensnared Sarah with the magic of its antiquity, with its glories, she would fight tooth and nail to ensure the return of the stolen treasures of Troy.

A somewhat chastened Handek Akbul ventured to speak. 'Examine the walls of Troy from a distance, my dear friends. You are looking down on three thousand years of human habitation. Imagine, if you will, King Priam and the ancient people of Troy defending their city against the onslaught of the Greeks who sailed here to reclaim their legendary Helen and acquitted themselves proudly in the Trojan War. Imagine, if you will, the confidence of the people who lived inside these vast fortifications when they saw the sails of the Greek ships coming over the horizon. The sea in those days was much closer to the city, almost lapping at Troy's walls. The original harbour has since silted up, destroyed by the sediments carried in the rivers which run into the estuary, but in those days people would have stood upon the massively thick walls and looked out on the puny ships of the Greek navy, moored in their bay, tiny in comparison to the strength of their impregnable stone fortress.'

Sarah climbed to the top of the mound and looked down. The site was surprisingly small. She had imagined ruins spreading over a vast area within a huge landscape, an ancient city as far as the eye could see, in which hundreds of thousands of people had gathered and carried out their daily lives, buying bread and meat, learning philosophy and mathematics while sitting under olive trees, or standing in the agora listening to peripatetic Stoics and Epicurians and Platonists. But Troy was built on a small scale, almost laughably small.

The guide manoeuvred himself to stand beside her. 'Your first thoughts of course are that it's much smaller than you believed it would be.'

Sarah turned to him in surprise.

'It's a common misconception which people carry with them when they first come here. In fact much of Troy still remains buried; it was probably far bigger than the site before your eyes. But even so, it was a small and compact city, as were most of the other large cities whose fame has spread and come down to us through the millennia. Most of our understanding of ancient times has come from the monumental architecture of ancient Egypt. We see the pyramids and the Sphinx and Abu Simbel and we think that people of ancient times built cities the size of today's Athens or Istanbul. In fact the primary need in those ancient days was for defence. Houses were built within very large walled enclosures, often at the foot of palace walls; the marketplaces and communal meeting rooms such as temples or bathhouses were the largest of the public buildings. The residences were very modest by today's standards.

'And you mustn't forget that in Troy we're dealing with a Bronze Age city, much earlier than an Iron Age city. Architects were able to build much bigger cities in the days of the Romans. Don't forget, also, that even though some of the buildings were massive, it wasn't until the invention of the arch by the Romans that buildings became truly monumental. So when we walk around this ancient site, we must forget Greece and Rome, which were very much later civilisations. We must constantly remind ourselves that Troy owes its greatness to the Hittites and to the Bronze Age, whose zenith was reached between two thousand and one thousand BC. As you'll appreciate, we have to imagine a far older city with a smaller population than anything the Romans built. In fact it was the coming of the Iron Age, with its better and more easily affordable agricultural equipment, which allowed more food to be produced, a higher standard of living, more wealth and hence a greater population.'

Sarah was surprised. 'I don't follow. You're saying that this was a fairly small place. What about the huge armies? From what I remember of Homer, I imagined that thousands of men fought for the city.' She felt herself instinctively clutching her golden amulet nestled securely between her breasts. She always reached for it whenever something touched her emotions. She had done so from the time her mother had given it to her.

'It's very unlikely that there were large armies before the coming of the Iron Age, which began very late in the life of Troy,' said Handek Akbul. 'Once it began, in about 1200BC, most of the great Bronze Age civilisations were destroyed in a very short period of time. Troy, like Mycenae and Knossos and many other great cities, went into decline. It was still here when Alexander the Great came through but almost accidentally. Next the Romans tramped through the area. By then the city was severely degraded; it never again achieved the same glory as when the Bronze Age people controlled its existence.'

Handek Akbul pointed down to the ancient ruins. 'Can you see the ancient walls down there? They used to encompass the whole of the plain of Troy.'

Sarah looked again as he swept his hand across the ruins before her. She could pick out squares and the remains of round towers and walls which seemed to rise up from the earth. To her untrained eye, the site had no symmetry; she realised with some embarrassment that she was searching for something akin to the grid system of Manhattan.

Handek Akbul continued: 'The people who lived within these walls used to farm, fish, hunt and breed animals. We know from ancient stories that they were horse tamers. We also know that they traded with neighbours in Anatolia, to the north, the south and also across the ancient sea to Mycenae, Sparta and other Greek cities. They became very rich through their produce and their trade and they enjoyed an extraordinarily high standard of living. As legend has it, it was as a result of this trade that King Priam's son, Paris, sailed to Greece where he fell in love with Helen of Troy, and it was when he brought her to this land by force that all the troubles for the Trojan people began.'

Handek Akbul turned to Sarah with a line he had practised a thousand times in the past, a line which never failed. 'And you, madam,' he said raising her hand and kissing it gently, 'are as beautiful as Helen herself.'

Everyone in Sarah's group, including Sarah herself, winced with acute embarrassment.

CHAPTER 7

The moment Amra saw her father leave the meeting hall, she knew her life was to be sacrificed. She could tell by his defeated walk, the look on his face as he climbed the hill which led to their home. Amra squatted at the front entrance, poking the fire, cleaning a cup, doing anything to avoid the pain of waiting, waiting for the most important decision of her life. She pretended not to see her father until he was standing beside her. Then she looked up and smiled. Hasga didn't smile in return. He shook his head.

'Why?' she asked.

'They say that the Gods have decreed it. The Headman said that he dreamed your face and that the great God of the Mountains wants you to be with him. He wants you because you're brave and skilled and resourceful. The message was clear.'

Amra nodded. 'May I address the council?'

Her father shook his head. 'Girls cannot address the council. You know that.'

'Why not?' she asked.

Her father frowned. 'Why not?' he repeated.

'Yes, Father. Why can't girls address the council?'

'Because they can't,' he said quietly.

'And who made the law which said that they can't?'

'They have never been able to. It's against the law. You cannot disobey the laws, Amra. They are made to be followed.'

'Why?' she asked again, her voice determined yet quiet.

'Amra, you must not ask these questions,' her father said simply. He went inside to sit on the low seat her mother had favoured.

Amra was left alone. The village was quiet. It was the middle of the day when people were hunting or tending the soil to ensure the crops would be large and plenty, or they were out gathering herbs and leaves for the evening meal. Amra looked around at the familiar surroundings. She would be sacrificed tonight or tomorrow night. That was the decision of the elders. But a thought had entered her mind as she had watched her father walk across the village, returning in defeat after having pleaded for her life. It was a thought which nagged at her and made her wonder. She felt her heart begin to pound with excitement.

She was trapped in the village as surely as if she was secured by ropes to a tree. If she ran away, Peta would die and that she could never allow. The thought grew and grew in its insistence. The anger inside her began to swell. She was to be sacrificed yet the law refused her access to the meeting place of the elders. It was wrong. There was no justice in what was going to happen to her. Why was this different from the other ways in which things were decided? If somebody stole something, then the thief was brought before the Headman and the victims had to prove that the accused man had taken their property. The Headman made his decision then announced to a village meeting what punishment the thief must suffer. Death, banishment or replacement of the stolen property. There was a hearing; the facts became known.

When one person killed another, the victim's family had a right to kill a member of the killer's family. That was just, it was right. Yet Amra was about to be killed to satisfy the Gods without being able to ask why. It was especially unjust when she had already seen Henk and Annka sacrificed and still the iron men threatened to come from over the other side of the mountain. Amra bit her lip, thinking back to the image of her friends being sacrificed.

They had screamed in terror but their lives had been extinguished as easily as throwing dust onto a fire. Amra thought it was the most unfair thing she had ever seen, and now that same injustice was about to be perpetrated on her.

She stood. Her legs were stiff from crouching. Her heart was pounding with fear. But something in her mind said that she couldn't just be sacrificed. She had to fight. She had always been a fighter. She fought other children in the village when they called her names. She had always been more adult than the others. Well, if she was adult then she should talk to the council of elders.

Amra walked down the hill to the centre of the village where the large meeting hall stood. The meeting was coming to an end and the guard outside the door was already walking away to tell the women to prepare the meal for the elders. Amra peered inside the hall. The old men were standing around and talking. She had only ever been in there twice, both times as a dare from the other children. It was always locked and barred and guarded, but she had climbed in through the hole in the ceiling. The hall had terrified her. She remembered clearly the heads it contained; they reminded her of her nightmares. It also contained the magic stones and wisdom sticks which the Headman and Medicine Man used when the whole village came together. More frightening still, Amra had heard that somewhere in the meeting hall were the frozen tears of the Goddess Athna, whose child had exploded from her womb and whose body had formed the earth and the mountains and whose blood was the sea. All of these fears came back to her as she stood in the entrance of the meeting hall. The five elders of the village, all of whom she knew by sight, were talking animatedly. One of them, Haka, noticed her and turned around. He shouted at her aggressively, 'Go away! Children are not allowed in this hall.'

The others immediately stopped their conversation and stared at her. Amra could feel the waves of hostility washing towards her.

'I've come to talk to you,' she said, trying to control the fear in her voice.

One of the village elders stepped forward. She could see his face clearly in the light, she knew him. She had sometimes spoken to him when she presented one of her kills for sacrifice. He stepped forward to block her entry and told her to go home. 'Leave before you get into serious trouble,' he said.

The Medicine Man, resplendent in his lion's head and shawl, shook his stick at her. But the Headman said, 'You are Amra, aren't you?' She nodded. 'You must go away from here, Amra. Only village elders are allowed in the meeting hall. You know this.'

'I want to talk to you,' she said again.

'Then you must talk outside. Now go immediately.'

'No,' she said. It was as if they had just jumped naked into a freezing river so profound was their shock. 'I will not go away,' said Amra. 'I am to be sacrificed to stop the wild men coming from over the mountains with their iron swords.'

'Yes,' said the Headman. 'To you goes the honour of being sacrificed.'

'Then nothing you can do to me now frightens me. If I am to be sacrificed, I will stay here and talk to you whether you allow me to or not. If I am to die, you can't hurt me more.'

'Go, child, or we'll call the guards to force you away.'

Amra had expected this. 'If you force me away then you will not hear my dream.'

'Dream?' said the Headman.

But the Medicine Man was getting angry. 'You are breaking the law,' he snapped. 'Terrible things will happen to you and your family if you stay here. Not only will we call the guards to throw you out, but we'll harm your father. Children, girls, are not allowed in the meeting hall. This is the law. This is as it has always been.'

'I don't want to break our laws,' said Amra. 'I just want to know why my life is to be sacrificed.'

'Because your face came to me in a dream,' said the Headman.

'And how do you know that the dream tells you to sacrifice me? Maybe the face you dreamed has a different purpose.'

The Medicine Man interrupted. 'When one of the elders dreams of a face, that face is to be the next victim of sacrifice. This is the law. This is the way it has always been. This is the way it is. Now go before you get yourself into more trouble.'

'Tell me this,' said Amra, standing her ground, gaining in confidence. 'Have any of you ever dreamed of the faces of your own children? Of your wives?' There was silence. She knew she had struck a blow. 'Then why have you not sacrificed them?'

'That is different,' said the Headman. 'You are a child. You don't understand.'

'I do understand,' said Amra, raising her voice. 'I understand that something has to be done to stop the men from the other side of the mountains. But I also understand that we've already sacrificed valuable children of our village in the past. And even though Annka and Henk died, still the mountain men come with their iron swords. If you sacrifice me, they will still come.'

'No, they won't!' shouted the Headman. 'The Gods say that if your life is given to them, then the Gods will stop them.'

'Then why didn't they stop them when Henk and Annka were sacrificed?' Amra demanded, her own voice rising now in anger as the injustice of the situation clarified in her mind.

'Amra,' said the Headman, 'you are too young to understand these things.'

'No, I'm not,' she insisted again. 'I understand very well. You sacrificed my friends because the Gods told you to. You will sacrifice me because the Gods tell you to, but maybe you are wrong.'

It was the wrong thing to say. The five village elders shouted at her in anger. But Amra had nothing to lose. She shouted back. 'Prove to me that you're right. Prove to me that this is what the Gods want!'

The Medicine Man struck her across the face, knocking her to the floor. He shouted down at her, 'We have nothing to prove to you. Our decision is law.'

'Then let me tell you something,' she said, her face stinging from his blow, 'I also had a dream. You know what they call me? Amra the dreamer. Amra who hears the voice of the Gods. My dream said that if I die then the mountain men will sweep down with their iron weapons and they will kill everyone here.'

'Your dreams are not law,' said the Medicine Man.

'But they have come true in the past. They always come true,' she said hurriedly, inventing her story as she went along. 'Every dream I have had has come true. Before she even became sick, I dreamed that my mother would die of the wasting disease. Before the Headman had his dream, I also had a dream. I was too frightened to tell anybody. The Goddess Athna came to me in a dream. She said that a false god would put a false dream into the sleep of the Headman. He would do it to weaken the village so that there were fewer and fewer people left to defend us against the mountain men. She said that this god wasn't one of our Gods but was a god who lived with the iron men and gave them the secrets of iron.'

The Headman looked at her in fury and was about to crush her when the Medicine Man stopped him. 'What did the Goddess look like?' he asked.

'She was on a cloud. There was light. I couldn't look straight at her because she was too bright.'

'What did her voice sound like?'

'Like the voice of a stream as it falls over stones.'

The Medicine Man nodded. The other elders listened to Amra's words in consternation.

'Who calls you Amra the dreamer?' the Medicine Man asked simply.

'Everybody who knows me. I have dreams on many nights and these dreams lead me to where animals play or where honey is to be found. Even though I am young I am a skilled hunter. You know this. But it's not my skill that lets me kill more animals than the others. It's not what I've been taught by my father and the other hunters. The Gods show me where the animals are to be found. The Gods make their tracks which I follow. The Gods speak to me and through me.'

The Medicine Man helped Amra up from the ground. 'What else did the Goddess Athna tell you?'

'She told me that she will destroy the iron men by showing me the secret of making iron. They are protected by their own god and have their own totems, but with my help she will show us how to overcome them and drive them back. She will show me where the men of iron get their secrets from. She will give me the knowledge and I will tell my father and he will make iron weapons for the five valleys and for the men who live by the rivers. And when the men of iron come over the mountains next year, Athna will be ready, our men will be armed, and Athna's armies will fight the men of iron and will beat them back. Then we will climb the mountains and we will go over to where the men of iron live and destroy their villages. Then Athna will rule over all the land on both sides of the mountain.'

Amra fell silent. She looked at each of the five men. Her heart was pounding so hard it felt as if it would burst. They had been cruel and angry when she had first entered the meeting place but now they were silent and confused.

She prayed to her own totem, the totem of the bee, that her lies would be believed. Finally the Medicine Man said, 'Wait outside, Amra. We elders will consider what you have said. We will talk to you later.'

'When will you go?' Hasga asked his daughter.

'Tomorrow.'

'Where will you go?'

'To where the sun is warm in the winter. I will follow the river down to the great sea and there follow the route of the traders into the land of the Hittites.'

'And do the Hittites know how to make iron?'

'They have iron. I will get the secret.'

'How did you convince the council of elders?'

'I told them of my dreams, Father.'

'Dreams?'

'I've been too scared to tell you. I am Amra the dreamer.' Her father nodded. 'And Peta?'

'Peta will not be touched. I have until the first snowfalls to return. When the night is the longest and the day is the shortest, I must return with the secret of making iron. I must give this secret to you.'

'And if you don't return?' asked Hasga.

'I will return.' Amra threw her arms around her father's neck. 'Trust me, Father. I know what I'm doing. For Peta's sake, I have to return.'

Her father understood. He kissed her tenderly. She was so like her mother, the strength, the determination, the honesty. He knew that his wife would be looking down from the seats of the Gods and smiling in pleasure at the way her daughter had broken the taboos and convinced the Headman to give her a chance of finding the secret of iron. He reached over and opened a chest. He rummaged in the bottom and took out a beautifully carved dagger with a golden handle and an exquisitely carved bronze blade. It was as sharp as flint and as true as a ray of the sun.

'Take this. You'll need it. Take the cooking pot and the oven as well. They're not heavy to carry. And take this also.' He pulled out an exquisite amulet which he had made for one of the women in the village.

'But . . .' Amra began.

'Take it. I can make another one. This you will carry as your totem around your neck. I will bless it with prayers and it will protect you from animals and the cold and from the spirits of the night.' He kissed her on the forehead and on the cheek. 'Sleep now, Amra. Tomorrow you must find the secret of iron.'

Amra knew she must begin her journey with a show of great enthusiasm and a strong sense of purpose, but deep in her heart she harboured great fears. The journey was so long. Would she be able to return before the first snows? How would she deal with the many dangers she would encounter so far from her home?

But her mission was clear. Since the council of elders had given her permission to go, Amra had discussed her route with the traders from her village who knew the lands far away. In the past, Amra had often sat around the evening fires, listening to the tales they told of their adventures, of the strange lands they had encountered, the people with fascinating customs, the beasts and flowers which sounded too odd to be believed. And now Amra was about to tread these very paths. She was destined to go much further though than any of the village traders had travelled. They only went to the Eternal Sea to bring back pearl and amethyst and the great conch sea shells. Amra would have to travel around or over the sea in order to reach the lands where the sun was warm in winter: the lands of the Hittites. Other traders, those passing through her village, who had travelled across the sea told of people who lived in vast cities where the streets were smooth and the buildings were made of stone cut up into massive blocks, where the men and women wore clothes of the finest materials, not the skins of animals or flax or wool from the backs of goats and sheep, but fabrics which were somehow made from the flowers of strange plants with white clouds attached. But, most important of all, the traders who came to their village said that these people, these Hittites, had the secret of making iron.

It was the middle of the morning by the time Amra had collected what she needed for her long journey. On her back she carried the cooking oven and in a basket over one shoulder she carried leather shoes to replace the ones she now walked on when they wore out. She carried the knife her father had given her, a digging tool to hunt for roots along the way, medicines which she knew she would need if she developed a fever or cut herself, and herbs and spices to make her meals tasty. There were plenty of rivers along the way so she didn't carry with her a waterskin. She was concerned when she stood and felt how heavy and uncomfortable her pack was.

Could she walk a long distance with this pack on her back? Amra had no idea how far it was to the land of the Hittites. The men who occasionally came through the village to trade their goods had told her it took them a full passage of the birth to death of the moon for their caravan to travel from there to the valleys of the rivers, but these men had horses and carts. Amra knew that the heavy weight on her back would make her horribly tired after just a few days on the road and her speed would naturally decline. The council of elders had only allowed her three full cycles of the moon to return, but she was determined to do it. She had to do it to save Peta.

Hasga looked at her in concern. 'These things are heavy, Amra,' he said. 'Are you sure . . .'

Amra interrupted him. 'Of course. I can carry them easily.'

As she spoke her eyes caught a movement on the far side of the square. The Medicine Man was walking towards them, leading his horse. She smiled as she saw the huge beast; Amra had often played with the gentle giant when it was tethered to a tree in a field. She had whispered into its ear and had felt a communication with the animal. The horse had nuzzled up to her in friendship and she had responded by giving it the juicy tips of the hay she gathered.

'Greetings,' said the Medicine Man. 'Amra, you have undertaken to go on a perilous journey, one which is very long. Longer than you can understand. You have never been to the great sea. Neither have I, but I know people who have and they say it is very far. But you have to go beyond the great sea to the land of the Hittites. To walk and still return in time for the first snowfall would not be possible. Take my horse. I have seen you handle him. He is wild and often difficult, but your way with him is gentle. He likes you.'

Amra looked at the Medicine Man in utter bewilderment. A man's horse was his most valuable possession. The horse was worth more jewellery and weapons than her father could make in an entire year. And yet he was giving it to her. She looked at her father whose face registered an equally deep surprise.

'Amra,' said the Medicine Man, 'you showed great courage when you came to the meeting hall of the council of elders. If you truly are Amra the dreamer, and if the Gods do talk through your mouth, then the loan of this horse will be a sign to the Gods that I have helped you. Take the horse and return it to me before the snows and together we will save the village from the iron men.'

Amra nodded, still overcome by surprise. The Medicine Man turned and walked back to his house. Her father said softly, 'I'll strap baskets to the horse so you need carry nothing.'

The young woman nodded, still speechless. Her father fetched two panniers and a rope, which he threw over the horse's neck. It reared in surprise but Amra sprang over and held her arms around its neck, whispering into its ear, 'Hush, friend. Hush. We are going on a great journey together, a great adventure. These baskets are nothing for you to carry but for me they would make the journey so hard. We are going to see wonderful sights together. When you return you will run to tell all the other horses what you have seen. Then you will be king of your herd.'

The horse snorted and whinnied, shook its head to try to throw off the irritating rope and the bulk of the panniers, but gradually began to calm down as she continued to cling on to its powerfully muscled neck, stroking the mound between its ears and whispering to it with her lilting, calming voice.

'This horse isn't tame, Amra,' Hasga said, his voice failing to mask his concern. 'You must be careful. Don't race until you're sure of each other, hold on tightly to its mane. Tether it well to a tree when you stop or it might bolt and you'll never see it again.'

Amra smiled at her father. 'This horse is my friend. His name is Wind, for that is how fast he runs. It's why the

Medicine Man doesn't like him. It's why the Medicine Man sometimes beats him to try to break his spirit.'

'Have you ridden him? Has anybody ridden him? *Is* his spirit broken?' her father asked.

'Of course he's been ridden. But he still has a lot of spirit left. That's why he'll be fast. I've often wanted to ride him but he's always seemed so big.'

'How do you know that you'll be able to ride him?'

'He's spoken to me,' she said. 'I've whispered in his ear and he's spoken back to me.'

'The horse spoke?' her father laughed.

'He didn't use words but I know what he means. He doesn't want to be beaten. He wants to ride to places he's never been. He wants a mate. Maybe on the journey he will find a mare to couple with.'

Hasga nodded. 'Be careful, Amra. If anything happens to you I'll lose both you and Peta. In your hands are all the things that are precious to me.'

Amra nodded and kissed her father. She loaded the oven and her other precious possessions into the left pannier. She left the right pannier empty for all the things she would gather along the journey.

'Now you have Wind to carry your goods, take food for the journey.'

Amra shook her head. 'No, Father. I'll find food on the way. I have my bow and arrows. I'll trap or kill what I need.'

Peta was waiting, half-hidden by the shadows of the doorway. Amra walked back into the house and picked the child up. 'You are the woman now, Peta. You must look after Father. Remember where the herbs are that I showed you? He likes hyssop in his hot water in the morning. And you must give him fresh fennel for him to clean his teeth and cleanse his mouth in the evening. Remember I showed you where to find it? And also remember how I showed you to gut and scale a fish and to skin rabbits? Everything else is too heavy; Father will do that.'

The child nodded. She threw her arms around Amra's neck and held her tightly. 'When will you be back?' she asked.

'Soon,' said Amra.

'Tonight?'

'No. Not for many nights.'

'But you've never been away. We've always . . .'

'I know,' said Amra. 'That's why you must be a woman now.'

Peta started to cry. Amra licked a salty tear from the little girl's eyes and smiled. 'I'll carry the taste of your tears with me until I return. And then I'll taste your tears of joy.'

She put the child down, kissed her father again and walked Wind out of the village onto the rutted road which led to where the rivers ran until they joined with the vast roaring river that emptied into the great endless sea.

In nervousness, knowing that the village and her security were disappearing behind her, Amra put her hand to her breast to feel the heavy gold amulet her father had given her. It brought her a sense of comfort and security, it was her totem. Whenever she wore it she knew that the bees would warn her of impending danger and protect her from the other gods and totems along the way. Above her, flying in the trees or sucking the juices of the flowers, were her totems, accompanying her on her way. Beside her she had the strength and power of Wind, and strapped to her side she had the bronze dagger her father had given her. She smiled and turned to watch the village recede into the distance. No-one could defeat her now. Especially if the lies she had told the Medicine Man and the Headman all came true.

Soon she would be in the land of the Hittites. She would go to the great cities she had been told about, to Hattusha, the city of the people who were called the Hattis, and to the great city of Troy where, according to the merchants, the houses were made of gold.

Wind must have sensed her excitement because he raised his huge head and whinnied into the canopy of trees which hung across the river. Amra looked up at the giant horse; she had been too scared to climb on him in the village in case people saw and laughed at her silliness. But now was the time. She threw her arms around his neck and whispered into his ear. The horse rotated his head to try to shake her off but she held on. Her weight pulled the horse's neck down. Amra sprang off the ground and hooked her right leg over the back of the horse, pushing the panniers askew. The horse's body shuddered, he neighed in anger and then began to canter.

Amra lost her grip and immediately fell off the huge beast, painfully hitting the ground. She lay there stunned, shaken and hurt. Wind was cantering away down the path. Her heart fell. Was her journey to end before it had even begun? Wind turned away from the river and galloped up the hill. At the top, he stopped; his body was silhouetted against the sky atop the steep bank. Amra could see the beautiful muscles taut under his skin. He lifted his head and neighed with the delight of his freedom. Amra had heard other wild horses neigh like this before. It was a cry of joy.

She lay breathless. Her elbow hurt, so did her thigh, but she didn't dare move. She felt an overwhelming sadness wash across her. All her hopes had rested on Wind. With him she could find the secret of iron, she could save the village, she could save her sister's life. Without him . . . she didn't want to think.

And then the horse slowly, arrogantly, began to trot down the hill, his head high, master of the valley. He picked up speed and cantered back to where she was lying. Amra felt an ineffable joy, a thrill greater than any she had felt in her young life. Wind was returning to her. The horse reached her in the space of a moment and nudged her gently with his head. She rolled and nearly fell into the river. The horse stood over her. She was sure there was a look of humour in his eyes.

Amra stood up and threw her arms around his neck and whispered into his ear. She knew she would be safe from now on. She threw her body over Wind's massive back and clung on tightly around his neck. He straightened with her on top of him, pushing his head back to enable her to sit higher. And then, as if he knew precisely which road to follow, he trotted off in the direction of the flow of the river. Amra held onto his mane for fear of falling off but the wonderful horse carried her at a speed faster than she had ever run in all her life. It was as if she was the wind herself, as if she and the beautiful horse were one. All the while she whispered encouraging words into his ear. She had seen the Medicine Man ride him in the fields and had envied his freedom, but had never for one moment imagined that she would experience such a feeling. It was as if she was a cloud floating in the sky. She was, indeed, wind.

Amra looked up into the deep blue sky and shouted her thanks to her mother whom she knew had caused Wind to return.

CHAPTER 8

Sarah Kaplan smiled and nodded robotically as the eighth person she had interviewed that day expressed his inordinate gratitude for her consideration and the amount of time she had spent listening, and his ineffable regard for her undoubted brilliance and competence. The continual and unrelenting sycophancy was starting to grate on her nerves and she had to keep reminding herself that the adjustments she had needed to make when entering Turkey were not only to her watch but also to her way of doing business. As a Wall Street lawyer Sarah had dealt with every client in a matter-of-fact way; as the chief prosecutor's assistant in the Prague war crimes trials during the past year she had played the part of the diplomat, as well as being one step ahead in her knowledge of law. But nothing in her previous experience had prepared her for the Byzantine ways of Turkey.

Her head was pounding. The muscles in the back of her neck were aching. Her fingers were stiff from the reams of notes she had taken. In Turkey it was the duty of the lawyer to take the notes; there were no such animals as paralegals, nor were secretaries considered worthy to be admitted to the august presence of the interview room, even to do some shorthand to relieve her numb fingers. Were it not for the fact that a number of people were expecting her to make a fuss and act like an American drama queen, she would have said something about the appalling conditions she was expected to work in. But at least the people on her team were terrific. They made it all worthwhile.

She looked across at Professor Mustafa Bengazi and Dr Satap, whose volumes of notes were as copious as her own. She could tell that Bengazi felt far less comfortable in this conference room in the Ministry of Antiquities in Ankara than he did in his comfortable office with its familiar artefacts buried underground in the Topkapi Palace in Istanbul. Satap on the other hand was a typical bureaucrat, easily accommodating the routine.

Sarah smiled at her choice of words. What she was doing was anything but routine, taking evidence from dozens of experts about speculations which were over a hundred years old. She hadn't done this sort of elementary evidence-taking since she was fresh out of Harvard Law School. How could she possibly tell her Turkish colleagues that in wealthy America, in her middle-sized law firm in New York, secretaries and assistants would have dealt with the note-taking? Would they believe her when she told them that paralegals did all the crap work, all the running around? But the Minister had made it very clear that this matter must be treated with great confidentiality. She had told Sarah that various government departments were leaking like sieves, so the fewer people that knew what was going on the better.

The three of them stood as the last witness bowed in deference and walked out the door. Dr Satap, a local expert coopted from the Department of Justice, smiled at Sarah. 'I'm privileged to be working with you,' he said. 'I've always hoped to work with an American lawyer.'

Oh God, Sarah thought. Not him too! She shrugged indifferently, her mind still numb after a full day of interviewing. 'It's no big deal,' she told him. 'Lawyers are lawyers no matter which country they come from.'

'But it's the system of law,' he said. 'To see the way your mind works. Your cross-examination technique is very revealing.'

She decided to let the comment go.

'Coffee?' asked Dr Bengazi.

'Not another one,' Sarah moaned. 'I need a stiff drink.'

'Me too,' he replied. Dr Satap nodded in agreement. Sarah looked at him in surprise. She'd assumed he was an orthodox Moslem.

'How many more experts to give depositions?' she asked.

Bengazi flipped over the list. 'None today. Four or five tomorrow, maybe six if Professor Akman comes. He's quite important. He's a historian who knows all about the private life of Schliemann. In fact his great-grandfather was one of the men who negotiated the contract on behalf of the Ottoman government. They say he has personal papers that relate to events at the time of the contract.'

'Good,' said Sarah, regaining a little bit of enthusiasm.

All the witnesses they had interviewed had told virtually the same story. Schliemann the liar. Schliemann the fraud. Schliemann the trickster. All of it was good emotional background stuff but nothing that got to the heart of the matter. Would an international court be capable of viewing the contract that Schliemann had written with the Ottoman government in such a way that Sarah could convince even the most sceptical of jurists to overthrow it and return full ownership of the treasury of King Priam to the Turks? It was becoming an increasingly important field of law. These days many nations of the colonised world had similar claims against the colonisers. Apart from the Greeks and their Elgin Marbles, there were now claims by the Punjabis for the return of the Kohinoor diamond, presently adorning the crown of the Queen of England; by the Cypriots for numerous mosaics purchased by American art dealers; for bronzes stolen from Benin; for priceless jewellery and works of art stolen by the Nazis from the Jews; for antiquities from Peru and for American Indian art, now in the hands of private collectors. Aborigines in Australia were claiming the skeletons of their ancestors from imperialistic Britain, as well as laying claim to half the continent as sacred to their people. Junk bonds had been the mother-lode of lawyers' incomes in the seventies, consumer rights in the eighties, and now land and property rights, as well as the intensification of the move to obliterate the colonialism of the nineteenth and twentieth centuries, looked as though they would keep lawyers in fast cars for the rest of the nineties and into the first years of the new millennium.

Sarah stood and stretched her spine. 'I'm so tired,' she said. 'I haven't worked as hard as this on evidentiary material since I was a trainee lawyer on Wall Street.'

Dr Satap was surprised. 'Not even when you were preparing a case against the Stalinist killers?'

She took a sip of water. 'Oh, it was hard work but I had a lot of people to help me. The Prague government really threw some serious resources at the issue.' Too late she realised she had inadvertently insulted her two colleagues. 'Of course I know the Turkish government is doing what it can, but . . .'

'Don't worry, Sarah,' said Professor Bengazi. 'We're a poor nation. We're grateful to have you working with us and advising us. Tell me, are you going straight back to your hotel?'

'That's what I was thinking of,' she said. 'Why?'

'Since you arrived you've seen very little of our country. Taking you to Troy the other day was important, but I particularly wanted to show you the Blue Mosque and Aya Sofya. They're wondrous buildings.'

'But they're back in Istanbul.'

He smiled and nodded. 'Just an hour's plane ride away. Frankly I'd like to go there overnight. Any extra time I spend in Ankara is a day out of my life. I need Istanbul to recharge my batteries.'

There *was* a particular reason Sarah would like to return to Istanbul, even overnight. She was missing David terribly. He had arrived the day before she flew to

Ankara. They had made love, eaten in a wonderful restaurant by the shores of the Sea of Marmara, returned to their hotel room and made love again, slept long and deeply in each other's arms and then made love a third time before she caught the flight to Ankara. Since then she had been ensconced in meeting rooms taking notes. She wanted to go back, to hold David again, and also to see some of the wondrous sights Istanbul had to offer.

She readily agreed. 'I've already been into the Blue Mosque. I went in there briefly. But I'd love to see it with you.'

Bengazi smiled. So did Satap. 'Believe me,' said Dr Satap, 'there are more wonders in these buildings than you could ever begin to understand as a tourist. I hope you'll enjoy seeing them as much as we're going to enjoy showing them to you.'

'I'll ring down for a car to take us to the airport,' Dr Bengazi said. He looked at his watch. 'By the time we get there it'll be getting a little bit late in the day. There will be far fewer tourists. I'll be able to take you around in peace and quiet and explain the wonders of our heritage.'

In the car Sarah began to feel what was becoming a familiar sense of disquiet. David had told her not to be so silly when she'd discussed her fears with him, but the feelings kept coming back. Dr Satap and Professor Bengazi were both young men, very intelligent, cultured. But they were Islamic. They were different from the Moslems with whom Sarah had worked to build bridges when she was a student. Those young men and women had been American too, in fact almost completely enculturated in the American ethos. For all their westernism, Bengazi and Satap were so inherently Turkish and Moslem and that made Sarah feel uncomfortable.

She couldn't rationally explain her edginess, her growing insecurity. She knew she would just be a tourist, gawking up at the ancient wonders of Islamic Ottoman architecture – at worst, she would feel culturally indifferent, looking at an artefact with no relationship to her or her life – yet she still felt an overwhelming sense of something threatening her, alienating her. Everywhere around her, in every street, on every corner, were mosques with their minarets pointing angrily to the sky. It was all so alien to her and everything she believed in.

Two hours and twenty minutes later, after the usual frenetic rush through some of the world's heaviest traffic navigated by the world's worst drivers, Sarah alighted from the government car with her two companions. They were at the ancient Hippodrome, near the entrance to the world-famous Blue Mosque. She looked back and saw the Hotel Turkoman, where she would be staying for the duration of her visit, standing proud and imperialistic halfway up the hill.

As she stepped from the car, poverty crowded around her. If she was accorded respect by her colleagues or within government circles, the dozens of half-dressed and badly nourished urchins who tackled her as she tried to walk along the street didn't care one iota about her status or her position. They thrust their hands into her face and inveigled her to buy maps or postcards or scarves or counterfeit watches or a dozen other touristic items. Professor Bengazi shouted at the children to leave her alone but it made no difference. Two adult peddlars had recognised the importance of the three well-dressed visitors stepping from their government car, but the children held them in no such awe. Three of them grabbed Sarah's legs, accosting her with postcards until she was forced to brush them aside. She felt guilty. The hungry eyes of the children demanded her sympathy, yet it was a bottomless barrel. Once she gave to one, a thousand more would swarm around her like bees. For her own sake she had to be indifferent, but that was something she found hard with children so young. They reminded Sarah of the pictures she had seen of starving children staring at the American troops who had arrived to relieve the misery of the German concentration camps. She told herself she was being hysterical. She had experienced much the same in Athens, and in Hong Kong where she had spent three days on her way to Australia. Although there was a strong undercurrent of menace here; the children were more grown-up, less innocent, despite their age. They were experienced in the ways of beggars. Where had their childhood gone?

Sarah turned to Professor Bengazi. She knew she mustn't show any weakness as her hosts were embarrassed enough by this show of the underside of Turkish life. To have exhibited sympathy might have seemed condemnatory. Sarah said, 'For God's sake, Mustafa, get these kids off me!' There was a harshness to her tone which she suddenly regretted. Tourists were supposed to be enamoured of the cuteness of the street urchins, yet she felt tainted by the whole thing. Bengazi pushed the children away from her, snapping at them again in Turkish to leave her alone or he would call the police. The children dislodged themselves from her, rising like vultures who had finished their feeding frenzy, and took themselves off to find another well-dressed tourist to attach themselves to.

'I'm sorry,' he said. 'It's one of the facts of life in Istanbul.'

'They're so young,' Sarah remarked as they walked down the length of the Hippodrome to the entrance of the mosque. 'Do they go to school?'

'No,' he said. 'These children are from the east of the country. From the Armenian, Georgian, Iranian border area. Their parents come over here because they think it's a Mecca. Over there, there's no work at all and no tourists. They're starving. Turkish governments since Atatürk's time have spent a fortune on the west of the country, where most of the people live. They've developed it for tourism so that it lives up to its greatest potential as a source of income. But the east of the country has far less potential so it's been sadly neglected. Indeed, there's usually a civil war going on over there. It's terrible. We in Europe, and especially in the west of the country, feel nothing but contempt for the people who come from there. We treat them like lepers. Yet still they come, just to escape the barrenness of life in the east. Here at least they make enough to live.'

'But their childhood?' she wondered.

'You have a very romantic understanding of childhood, Sarah. In America children have a childhood. Here we see things very differently. For us childhood isn't a state of grace or innocence; it's merely a time when people slowly grow to learn the techniques needed for work and survival.'

Sarah remained silent as they walked along the crude pavement alongside the massive mosque. Anything she said would sound patronising. It was all too easy to sound like a rich American comparing your standard of living with those of a country whose quality of life was so dramatically lower.

Outside the mosque, they took off their shoes and placed them in bags which they were given to carry inside. Dr Satap began to explain the history of the building as they walked along its portico towards the huge wooden door which led into the entry vestibule.

'Once there were palaces where this mosque now stands, Byzantine palaces from the days before Constantine moved the Roman Empire to Byzantium and changed its name to Constantinople. Sultan Ahmet I, who lived during the seventeenth century, looked at the Church of Holy Wisdom, the Aya Sofya, over the road, the biggest building within Christendom, and determined to build a mosque which would be even greater and surpass the genius of the Church's builder, the Roman emperor Justinian. This mosque is a wonder of proportion and lightness of touch and harmony. Its layout follows classical Ottoman style. You'll see what I mean when we go inside.'

They entered through the portico. The heat and clamour of the outside world were instantly stilled by the cool, quiet, reverential air of the mosque. Sarah held her breath in amazement as she gazed around the edifice. It was the light which amazed her, a blue surreal haze. It was as though she was standing beneath the surface of a warm ocean. The walls of the vast building were dominated by blue tiles, all of them different. They were everywhere, on the four massive pillars which supported the dome, on the subordinate pillars which carried the arches, all the way up the walls into the very ceiling dome itself.

Dr Satap smiled. Hers was a common reaction. He whispered, 'The tiles are Iznik. The story has it that when the young Sultan Ahmet was deciding upon which tiles to use for his mosque, tilemakers from all over brought their most beautiful designs to show him. He couldn't make up his mind and so he said, "Let every one be on the walls".'

They walked further into the building, up to the rails which prevented all but the faithful from proceeding. Sarah stared up at the extraordinary cupola; she felt giddy at its height and grandeur. A few feet above her head were massive iron wheels supported on chains which disappeared into the roof. They held lights which illuminated the mosque so that the faithful could see the Imams praying in the early morning and late at night, when it was dark. She looked down at the glorious carpets over which hundreds of thousands of feet trod each year. Inside the railings, in the vast centre of the building, the Moslem faithful were kneeling and silently praying.

'Sarah,' said Mustafa Bengazi. 'Look over there.' He was pointing to a raised area covered with a marble lattice. 'That contains a piece of the sacred black stone, the meteorite from the Kaaba in Mecca. It's very precious to us, though I don't think the Saudis are very happy that our Sultan took a piece of one of their holiest objects.'

They stayed inside the Mosque for ten minutes, Sarah hardly speaking, but listening to the lilting sounds of the prayers in the cool blue light of the late afternoon. Eventually Mustafa touched her on the arm, and suggested that they cross the road to Aya Sofya, which had begun its life as the greatest church in Christendom and had remained so for a thousand years until Pope Julius gave the world St Peter's in Rome.

Even as she left the glorious Blue Mosque, Sarah was still imbued with its ancient beauty. The massive mosque dominated Istanbul's Golden Horn, and as the sun began to fade it touched the top of its minarets, making them look like huge candles surrounding a glorious cake. The moment they emerged into the hot noisy fume-laden air, the twentieth century returned with a stark and unforgiving force. They walked along the broad pathway which led from the mosque across the busy road to the far older and far more austere Church of Aya Sofya. Again beggars approached, but Mustafa's growling threats made them retreat.

They entered the Church of Divine Wisdom – Sancta Sophia in Latin, Hagia Sophia in Greek and Aya Sofya in Turkish – from the south-west side. Since arriving in Istanbul, Sarah had been anxious to visit the church; she had heard so much about its glories. Unaccountably, just as she was about to enter, Mustafa took hold of her elbow to prevent her walking any further.

'One must be very cautious and circumspect about entering Aya Sofya. You actually have to delay your passage, as though you're about to relish an exquisite meal. You must *experience* the entry to fully appreciate the awesome magic of the building.'

Sarah smiled. There was more of the showman in Mustafa than she had realised. It was endearing. As they approached the building proper, he said, 'It was originally constructed by the Emperor Justinian in the sixth century AD to show how great the Roman Empire was. He had it built over the original Byzantine acropolis and on the site of another church which had been destroyed in riots. It only took fifteen years to build and yet it was the greatest church in the world until the Barbarians destroyed Constantinople in 1453.'

They began to walk slowly up the steps, like pilgrims about to enter a holy site. Mustafa set the slow and deliberate pace, whispering as they ascended, 'Its two architects, Anthemius of Tralles and Isidorus of Miletus, intended the building to be a part of the experience of Godhood for pilgrims. Just watch what happens as you walk up the steps.'

Having escorted many important visitors, Mustafa and Dr Satap knew what to do. They each gently grasped an elbow and guided Sarah up the steps, leaving her free to lift her head back to look at the ceiling. At first there was darkness in the dim entryway, barely illuminated by a dull rainbow of colours from the stained glass window, but as her eyes adjusted Sarah saw two huge doorways inside. Through the doorways she quickly perceived the glory of Aya Sofya: a dome emblazoned with the most exquisite gold mosaics of the Madonna and Child.

They continued walking slowly up into the building and stopped at the threshold of the first door. Mustafa restrained from smiling. He knew what was going through Sarah's mind. She thought she had seen the entire building, and even now, even on its very periphery she was awestruck by its height, its mastery of space and light, its subtle grandeur. But the ancient building was one gigantic optical illusion and soon she would be overawed by the genius of its architects.

Sarah gazed at the mosaics and the apse at the far end of the building and was amazed by its symmetry and scale. Bangazi encouraged her to look up at the mosaic of Christ Pantocrator, the ruler of all. He and Satap gently assisted her to climb further inside the building, her head straining upwards to comprehend its vastness, until the face of Christ slowly became visible to her. It was then that Sarah began to realise that the dome of the Madonna and Child, the dome which she thought marked the epicentre and zenith of the church, was in fact merely the top of yet another dome, above which soared the gigantic main dome of the church.

She shook her head in amazement as she walked a few steps further into the centre of the church, in order to encompass the enormity, the sheer overwhelming physicality of the building. It was humbling, awesome, majestic. Unlike the Blue Mosque across the road, whose huge dome was held up by four massive pillars, the successive domes of the Aya Sofya appeared to be floating, supported only by air. She had never been in a building as complex and glorious, yet so unified and harmonious, as the Church of Divine Wisdom.

But the surprises were not yet over. The two men walked her further into the church and what she had thought was the huge main dome was in fact only another semi-dome. Rows of windows were visible in the upper levels, hiding the real secret of the church. As they approached the imperial threshold, Sarah saw the vast main dome soaring above her. And there her hosts stopped, allowing Sarah to stand in the centre of the church, staring upwards, a tiny woman lost in the enormity of the building's genius.

When he considered the moment appropriate to interrupt the thoughts swelling in Sarah's mind, Mustafa whispered, 'When Justinian first entered this church fifteen hundred years ago, he fell down on his knees and said, "Glory to God that I have been judged worthy of such a work. Oh Solomon, I have outdone you."'

Sarah felt her eyes brimming with tears at the sheer joy of a work of art. The blazing gold mosaics bordering the Madonna and Child, the ornate mosaic of Christ as the ruler of all, the sheer immensity and overwhelming volume contained within walls so light that they seemed almost incapable of supporting the roof, took her beyond her ability to control emotions. Tears coursed down her cheeks.

Exhaustion had sapped both her strength and her hunger. Four days of heavy work in Ankara, relieved only by the quick trip to Istanbul had exhausted her. Now she had returned to what, for her, was the real capital of Turkey. Sarah opened the door to her hotel room and fell onto the ornate double bed with its heavy damask and brocaded counterpane. She closed her eyes as the relief of sleep rapidly overtook her. It was only seven in the evening but the accumulation of a year's exhausting legal work in Prague, the sudden dislocation to her routine by the trip to Turkey, the tensions she had experienced with the Ministry officials, and the enervating experience of interviewing expert after expert about Schliemann's theft of the Trojan treasury finally culminated in an overwhelming need to sleep. Her body, her mind, her resources were spent.

When she eventually awoke it was to the sound of the phone ringing. She had no idea what time of day or night it was. All she knew was that she had lain down on the bed in the muted light of early evening and now it was pitch black outside. She strained her body across the bed and pulled the phone off its cradle. She mumbled something incomprehensible into the receiver and felt herself slipping back into sleep.

'Sarah?' The voice was familiar.

Her eyes snapped open. 'David?' All her tiredness suddenly evaporated. 'Jesus, I must have been asleep. Where are you?'

'I phoned the number you gave me in Ankara. They told me you'd come back, so I phoned the hotel. Right now I'm at the Conservatoire. A guy I studied with in New York is one of the teachers here so I thought I'd pop in and see him while you were in Ankara. Why didn't you tell me you were coming back?'

'I tried to,' she insisted, now fully awake. 'I left a message with reception. You obviously didn't get it.'

'You sound tired, Sarah.'

'I am. It's been an exhausting couple of days, but I'm here. What shall we do tonight?'

'I'll be there in half an hour. We'll discuss it then.'

She put the phone down and smiled at the thought of seeing him again. How wrong she'd been to behave the way she did in Prague. And how typical of David not to want to know the details, to prefer to put it behind him and get on with their life. She would marry him. She realised now that life without him could be exciting, but life with him would be just as stimulating but with a depth of security, warmth and love that was missing from her current existence.

She lay back on the bed. Half an hour before he arrived. Should she sleep a while longer? No, she would go into the tiny cubicle that was the bathroom and have a shower, wash away the stale smoke, the pollution, the crowds, the alien environment, the anger in the streets, the filth and dirt of Istanbul, and return to the Sarah David had always known: clean, fresh, bright, happy and perceptive. A good hot shower with plenty of rich shampoo, some delicate body oil, a crisp new outfit just back from the dry cleaners. That would do her very nicely. She took off her clothes and walked naked to the window where the curtain prevented anybody seeing inside. She pulled it aside a fraction and looked through the gathering dusk at the Blue Mosque across the road. Then she looked eastwards towards Aya Sofya. They were both monumental yet delicate structures, extraordinarily brilliantly beautiful. But despite the best efforts of Dr Satap and Mustafa Bengazi, despite their pride and joy in the wonders of ancient architecture, Sarah still had some misgivings. It was the exterior of the buildings which overwhelmed her, which caused her strange insecure feelings.

Thousands of Istanbul residents were in the streets below. Most were dressed in western clothes but there were many wearing Islamic dress. The muezzin began his call again and the faithful turned towards the Mosque. There was something confronting about the sight of so many people responding unquestioningly to the beckoning of the electronic voice which shouted God's greatness above the traffic noise.

It was the relationship between these people and their religion which made her feel threatened. They were so sure of their beliefs, so certain of their traditions and customs. Sarah had always felt alienated from the mainstream by her own religion. She'd spent her life working that little bit harder just to prove that her Jewishness wasn't a handicap, that she was as good as anyone in the American WASP establishment. Strike one: she was a woman. Strike two: she was Jewish. Strike three: she was smart as a whip. Three strikes and she was out. But she had worked her guts out to be in. She was a damn good lawyer and she'd taken on cases which other lawyers preferred to turn down. She'd put herself out on a limb and as a result had made front-page headlines day after day. She'd been on Oprah and Jay Leno, she'd been interviewed by CNN and NBC and ABC. Her face was well known, her reputation high. She had arrived. She was an important member of her society.

But the streetscape she was looking down on wasn't her society. It was Turkish society: Islamic, foreign, alien. It was a place which didn't recognise her. She was starting off at the bottom again, having to prove herself. Even though she'd been brought in as a high-level consultant by the Minister and was treated with a degree of regard, the powerbrokers, those with real authority – people like Yussef Barrak and the small coterie that surrounded him – just saw her as a smart Jewish woman: a threat. Three strikes and she was out again. Out in Turkish society.

But when she examined her insecurity further, Sarah discovered it went deeper still. In America, and especially in New York, her Jewishness was something she could feel proud about. There was some residual anti-Semitism, of course, there always was, but there were so many Jews in New York that the anti-Semites were a pitiful minority. She could stand in the middle of Fifth Avenue and shout out, 'I'm Jewish!' and ten thousand people wouldn't pay her any attention. If she did the same on the street down there people would look at her with hostility and suspicion. This was Islam versus Judaism. This was east versus west. It went much deeper than Sarah Kaplan and her own personal fears.

Sarah shivered despite the warmth of the room. She couldn't wait for David to return and hold her in his arms.

CHAPTER 9

Wind was more than a horse, more than just a fast way of travelling to the land of the Hittites. In the two days since Amra had been riding him, Wind had become her friend. He seemed to have an instinctive understanding of her needs. When the way ahead was clear, Wind would speed up to a canter, enjoying the freedom. At these times Amra was forced to lie flat along his back and neck, her head close to Wind's, her arms firm around him to prevent her from falling, her warm legs straddling his body. But when the trees became thicker and Wind was forced to negotiate a more complex path around them to continue following the river track, Amra sat up higher on his back. It was then that Amra sensed a change in him, as though he was missing the contact with her and her gentle soothing words.

As the Sun God descended to his death behind the mountains, Amra realised that, after two days of riding, her legs were beginning to feel numb. They ached with pains which didn't vanish overnight like the aches she'd experienced after running or hunting. This was different; she had no experience of riding astride such a giant beast, even one as friendly and powerful as Wind. She had blue patches of skin and brown bruises on her calves as well as inside her thighs. She'd noticed them the previous night as she was tending to Wind. Her first duty was always to him. She could eat when he was properly looked after. Amra had led him down to the river where he had drunk deeply, and she had splashed his sweating body with cooling water. Then she took an armful of bracken and grasses and rubbed his coat all over, scratching to give him relief where she could see his skin had been bitten by fleas.

Once she'd finished looking after Wind, Amra had realised that she was too tired even to prepare the food she had brought with her. Instead she had abated her hunger with the nuts and berries she had collected along the way and placed in one of Wind's panniers. This morning, the second morning of her journey, she had awoken stiff and sore, intending to feast on the rabbits she would trap as the sun rose. But when she'd tried to rise from her bed, her legs felt as though they were made of wood and she looked with concern at the blue weals on her skin. Again, she had foraged through the panniers to satisfy her aching hunger, and had decided to ride Wind into the distance to put as much of the journey behind her in the early stages while she was still strong.

They had rested in the middle of the day when the sun was at its height, Wind drinking hungrily from the river, munching grass by the riverside and biting at the juicy parts of pine cones from the lower branches of the fir trees. Amra had whispered to Wind to stay where he was while she went in search of game with her bow and arrow. She'd seen a deer in the distance, but the twig she broke as she stole towards it frightened it off. She had returned and eaten yet more of the food out of the pannier before remounting Wind and riding along the river as it flowed towards the great sea.

Now it was beginning to get dark and she knew that there was only enough food for that day and probably the day after before she would have to hunt in order to eat and stay alive. She had no idea how far she had travelled but she knew it was a long way from her village. Everything was strange here. The trees and plants were the same but the landscape was completely different. How far had she ridden already? She had no idea. She had deliberately avoided the other villages in the five valleys, knowing that they would only hold her up by asking her questions. Her only experience of distance was the distance she could travel on foot from her village in the early morning until the sun was at its zenith before having to turn back to be safely in her village again before nightfall. That was when she was hunting on foot. But things were different with Wind. Did he travel in a morning as far as Amra could run in a day? Or two days – or even ten days? How fast did the giant horse gallop along? Certainly she couldn't hope to keep up with him on foot when he was cantering or galloping, but often he slowed down for long periods and trotted happily along, looking around at the trees and the rocks and sometimes up at the sky, flaring his nostrils and whinnying with happiness.

But Amra's most immediate problem was not distance but food. She had looked in the pannier many times since she had woken that day and nothing was different now. There were still the same scraps of a smoked rabbit which would last her for only one meal. There was a hen which she had cooked and wrapped in leaves to retain its moisture and there were cooked roots and tubers which she had already nibbled on while Wind walked slowly through the shallows of the river in order to cool his sweating legs. But once these were gone, certainly by tomorrow night, there was nothing more. Amra knew what it was like to run out of food. Once on a hunt with her father, they had been away for four days and the Gods had caused luck to be against them. There had been no rain so the earth was dry and it was hard to follow the tracks or spores of the animals. By the time they got back to the village empty-handed, they were ravenous and had to trade precious goods cheaply with a neighbour for that night's food.

But food was something Amra would have to deal with in the morning; first she had to address the problem of her bruised legs. They were painful to touch. She had been gripping onto Wind too tightly. Maybe she would have to kill a deer and skin it to protect her legs, but then she realised this wasn't possible because the deer's skin would have to dry and cure before she could use it and that could take days. Amra understood now how ill-prepared she was for the hardships of the journey. She saw that she had been dangerously silly. She had thought that she would meet people along the way, that she would sit down at their fires and talk to them about where they had come from and where she was going, that they would offer her hot food and a safe place to sleep. But she had seen nobody in the three whole days that she and Wind had travelled towards the Hittites. Indeed she had gone out of her way to avoid being seen. Despite what she had thought before she set out, once she was on her journey she had realised that the last thing she wanted was the company of strangers.

Wind slowed to a halt high above the bank of the river. No matter what Amra said, he would not continue, he was too strong willed. His body shook with tiredness and he stepped away from the trail and walked down the steep bank which led to the river. He lowered his head, which nearly made Amra pitch forward over it and plunge into the water, and drank greedily, his hooves clacking over the stones at the river's edge. Amra slid off Wind's back into the shallows. The water was cold but immensely refreshing. After three days as his constant companion, Amra was confident that Wind wouldn't run off, so she removed the baskets which straddled the horse, pulled her dress over her head and walked naked into the deeper part of the river. She lay down and let the cold water race around her body; it seemed to leach the tiredness from her arms and legs, sweeping it down to the eternal sea. Amra came back up for air and noticed with amusement that she had floated past Wind who was looking at her curiously. He followed her, wading deep into the river, his elegant head the only thing visible as he swam into the middle and was carried along in the current.

The giant beast and the young woman were revelling in the river's refreshment but enough was enough. Amra swam over to the bank and scrambled out, walking back upriver to reclaim her dress, the panniers and her weapons. Wind, she knew, could look after himself. Her job was to hunt. She took a rabbit trap from the pannier and lay it just above the riverbank where the tree line began. She found a young sapling about her own height and bent it over until it formed an arc. Then she searched for a stone big enough to hold the sapling in place and stop it from springing back. The first stone she took from the riverbed was too heavy and would require too much weight to move it. But the second was just right, only the slightest movement would dislodge it and the sapling would spring back into the upright position. She tied some twine to the top of the sapling where it bent over and nearly touched the earth, then unrolled it some distance and used a twig to support it in the air. She looped it into a slip knot and placed a tender piece of cooked vegetable within the slip. Any rabbit coming along would nibble at the vegetable, loosening the string from the upright twig which would then fall and loop firmly around the animal's neck. The rabbit would try to escape the knot, pulling the twine which would dislodge the stone holding down the sapling. The small tree would spring back vertically and the rabbit would be hung by its neck, trapped there until she came back to collect it. Amra returned to the river and filled a jar with water to wash away all traces of her presence from the twine and the area. As the twine dried it would tauten and strengthen, making it more difficult for the rabbit to escape.

Amra then took a spear from the pannier and waded into the shallow part of the river to wait for a fish. She prayed that Wind wouldn't return too quickly and disturb her. As she stood there motionless, feeling the cold water flowing around her knees, desperately peering into the river for the welcome appearance of a fish, the tiredness returned. She felt completely exhausted. Her mind began to wander. Would she be able to sustain a journey as long as this if she was already exhausted when she had only just started? She was afraid of what she had committed herself to, yet she also felt a sudden pang of desperation in case she failed in her mission and Peta was sacrificed to the Gods.

It was while she was thinking about Peta that Amra realised a fish, a large pike, had swum close to her then back out to the middle of the river. She bit her lip in anger. Her father had taught her that she must always be alert while hunting, must never lose her concentration. Her father's words were true; while she had been distracted, food for two days had come and gone in the blinking of an eye. But then, because she was Amra the dreamer as well as Amra the hunter, the Gods smiled upon her and the fish returned, its ugly mouth snapping at anything that moved. It was a big fish, about half as big as her. It was strange that it was swimming about in the open; normally they skulked in a clump of weeds and grasses and only dashed out when prey swam by. That's why she didn't like pikes – they were ugly hunters. Too cunning. They didn't seem to have any daring. And she didn't like the flavour of pike either. It tasted of mud. But in her hungry state she would eat anything.

As the huge pike swam towards her again Amra stood like a rock. She didn't blink. Her hands were motionless. She could feel her breathing become shallow and her heart beat faster at the thought of her spear shafting the fish. It swam towards her then swam away, disappearing into the centre of the river again. Had it seen her? Who could tell? But she remained motionless. She was part of the river. The pike could see only two grey trunk-like legs, it wouldn't recognise them as those of a hunter. Why *was* everything grey in the water? No! She would not be distracted again. Like trout, pikes were quite clever. But trout were honest fish whereas pikes were mean. That was why she didn't like them. They were easier to hunt than trout. But she didn't want a challenge right now, she just wanted food.

Again the Gods smiled at her and the pike came back to within spearing distance. Amra held the spear rigid, judging the distance accurately. Her mind instinctively determined where to throw the spear. She had learnt from an early age not to throw it *at* the prey because the God of the Water tricked inexperienced hunters. She knew instead to throw it just before and slightly below where she thought the fish was. She hated the trickster God of Water, who made you slip on stones and misjudge distances. The pike seemed to stop in mid–swim as though considering whether or not to move forward. Its long tail weaved in the water, holding it motionless as it considered where to swim next. Amra heard her heart beating loudly, her stomach rumbling. And then she heard the noise she least wanted to hear: Wind whinnying in the distance, happily trotting back upriver towards her. He would scare the fish away. It was now or never.

With the speed of lightning she jerked her hand back and threw the spear forwards with a mighty movement. It cleft the water and its ripples obliterated the view. But Amra's heart leapt as the stick appeared to dance around, flipping and flopping – she had speared the pike. She shouted with joy and ran over to reclaim the spear. It was a big fish; she needed two hands to hold it still. She smashed its head against a river stone before pulling it out of the river. The barb had passed clean through the animal's body close to its head. She made sure the pike was dead then carried it and the spear to the bank where she threw them both down.

Amra danced around the fish, shouting and clapping. She heard Wind whinny in fright at her antics; he turned and cantered up the riverbank away from her. But Amra didn't care. She had food. She was overjoyed. Before the God of the Night had grown old, she would smell the delicious aromas of cooked fish. She would eat and her stomach would stop rumbling. Amra withdrew the barb and cut off the fish's head with her knife, slit its gut open and hollowed out the body cavity. The fish was as long as her legs and she knew she would only be able to eat half, maybe not even that. It would make good picking for days to come.

She foraged in the undergrowth for some sticks which she gathered together over a bundle of dry leaves. She took out her fire stones and banged one against the other. It took her many tries before a spark flew out and landed on a leaf. Amra gently blew on the leaf and watched with joy as the smoke began to curl and the heat of the spark spread around the leaf and a tiny yellow tongue of flame began to rise. When it had properly caught, she pulled the other dry leaves on top then the twigs. Once the fire was well established she ran quickly to collect more pieces of wood, carrying them down to the fire and throwing them on top.

Then she made a cradle from some smaller, pliant sticks, threaded another stick through the fish and suspended it above the fire until the wet flesh began to hiss. She stood over the fire, breathing in the divine aroma. She said a quick prayer of thanks to her totem, the bee, for providing food for her. Now her job was to find roots to go with the fish.

She saw Wind trotting towards her from the distant bank of the river and smiled. Had he smelt the fish? She didn't know whether horses ate fish or meat or anything except leaves and grass and pinecones. She would give him some just in case.

Amra looked at the lay of the forest. She was a skilled gatherer; her mother had taken her many times into the forest and so she knew what to look for. She found an old dead tree which had fallen many years ago and searched in the vines covering it for the wet part of the tree. There, as she'd expected, she found mushrooms. She picked a few and put them into her skirt. In a clearing she found the telltale stalks of turnips. They would be delicious once they had been peeled, cut into small chunks, and softened in her cooking pot. She dug with her small spade until she had plucked four from the earth's grip. She would use the tops of the turnip to flavour the fish. Shortly afterwards she found wild carrots which she also pulled from the earth and gathered into her skirt. On her way back to the fire she came across a clump of lemon balm growing in a clearing. She smiled. It would taste wonderful steeped in hot water, especially if she could also combine it with orrisroot which was wonderful for assisting the breathing. She silently blessed her mother for showing her the bounties the forest had to offer.

As she was walking back to the fish, which was cooking gently as the fire died down and the coals continued their heating, Amra noticed some unusual bushes. They were covered with red and black berries. There were also some delicious-looking raspberries; she particularly loved to eat them. She gathered them all, eating a handful as she walked back to the fire, partially satisfying her nagging hunger. Wind was already back at the camp site, pulling grass up by its roots, and occasionally trotting back down to the water to drink his fill.

Amra also went down to the river with her cooking oven. She removed the detachable upper cauldron and half filled it with water, then fixed it above the space where she would place the hot coals, and returned to her camp. She examined the fish. It was ready for her to remove from the heat until the vegetables had cooked. Its outer flesh was seared nicely but its inner flesh was still raw. She went in search of some large leaves and found a plant she had never seen before. It was strange, similar to a huge lettuce or the top of a rhubarb. She cut off the largest of the leaves, wrapped the fish inside and put it back on the fire.

She took some more dried leaves and put them in the space in the round bottom of the cauldron. She took a flaming brand from the camp fire and set the leaves alight, pushing them deep into the oven. She added more twigs until there was a hot and noisy fire crackling in the fire space. Soon steam began to rise from the water in the top section. Amra used her knife to peel the turnips, carrots and mushrooms then she cut the roots into small pieces and threw them into the boiling water. She turned the large leaf the fish was cooking in onto its other side, brushing away the coals which had adhered to it.

Then she sat back and waited for the cooking to finish. The fish would be ready soon; already her mouth was watering in anticipation of its delicious flesh. That thought made her smile. In her village she would probably refuse to eat a pike. Here she hungered for it. The turnip and carrots would shortly be soft and just before they were ready she would throw in the mushrooms. Then she would find another large leaf to use as a plate and her meal would be complete. She missed the refinements of her home, the lovely pot or bronze plates that they ate from, the pot of water always outside the door to wash her hands and face in, and to clean the pots when they were dirty. The water was kept suspended over the fire and was always warm. Life was much harder when you were travelling alone.

Amra lay back and smiled up at the sky. She closed her eyes as the delicious smells of cooking enveloped her, then started as she heard a snapping of wood behind her. She grabbed her knife and turned to look up the hill. There she saw that a rabbit had sprung the trap. It was hanging by its neck and kicking furiously, suspended from the top of the sapling. Her day was complete! The Gods were smiling upon her. She had food enough to last her many days. Maybe things would be well after all. She ran up the hill and snapped the petrified rabbit's neck then carried its warm body back to the fire. She would gut it and skin it, then cook it over the fire so that tomorrow morning she would have fresh rabbit to break the hunger of the night. Life was beginning to be good again.

Amra took out the map the Headman had drawn for her. Although the Headman had never before travelled outside the lands of the five valleys, he had spoken many times to traders who came into the area, men who knew the routes to the warm lands, and so was able to give her directions. The map, he had confidently informed her, would show her where to go and what to expect on the journey. She unfolded it. It was painted onto a piece of deer hide with black dye made from dried fish scales mixed with dust and a black mud found in a waterhole at the foot of one of the nearby hills. It made a liquid which, when used on skin, never came off.

Amra had studied the map when the Headman had drawn it up for her. She knew that the dark line which threaded its way from the top to the middle of the skin was the large river she had been following for three days. And she knew that further down, beyond the centre of the skin, the river crossed mountains because here the Headman had drawn a series of hills and peaks. How did a river travel uphill and over a mountain? She would soon find out. Then she saw that the giant river turned back to join the Eternal Sea. But before it did so, Amra had to leave its course and follow a path which took her in the direction of the Sun God's evening dying place. Then she would be in the lands of the Hittites.

But she was confused. She looked at the map carefully. She had been travelling for two days yet she had no idea where on the map she was. She hadn't yet come to the mountains, and even when she did that didn't take her to the bottom of the map. How much further was it, she wondered. And would she ever make it back in time to save Peta's life?

The days blended into each other. Amra wondered if there really was any difference between yesterday and tomorrow. Wind had developed his own momentum. When the ground was clear he covered large distances, galloping over the tree-bare hills, but when the land became rocky and potholed he stepped slowly and carefully.

He seemed to know how to pace himself and when he was tired would refuse Amra's urgings, instead trotting down to the river. There he would stand immobile until Amra dismounted and removed the panniers, then he would whinny and bathe and frolic in the water like a little child . . . like Amra when she was younger.

It was ten days since Amra had left the village; the moon which had been full when she began her quest was now thin and dying and would soon disappear back into the belly of the God of Night. But she had no idea how far she had travelled in that time. She felt as if she'd travelled further than any other human being, further than the traders who came lumbering into the village with their horses laden with exotic goods, their wagons creaking with statues of gods and goddesses and idols made from smooth white stone or woods the like of which she had never seen before. Amra had loved the excitement of the arrival of a trader's wagon. The whole village would buzz, waiting to examine its wares and hear news from the faraway lands.

Amra would always be the first to the wagon, the most excited, the one whose curiosity was most aroused by the traders' stories of strange people and stranger places. And now she was like the traders. But it wasn't as nice to be out in the world as it was to hear news of it in her village. Suddenly Amra felt lonely. She'd been so busy gathering nuts and fruits, or hunting deer or rabbit or fish, or glorying in the joys of travelling the world on the back of Wind, seeing valleys and distant mountains which she'd never known had existed before. Her mind had been full of new smells and sights, new horizons and new experiences, and she had hardly thought about home at all. But now she began to feel homesick. What was she doing? Why was she risking her life riding to the warm lands when she had been so happy in her home, where she knew the forests and the meadows, and where people would come running to help her if she was in trouble? Who would help her if she was in trouble in this country? And where were the people? She'd seen traces of villages in the distance, farmers tilling the earth, a hunting party which had stopped in its tracks as she cantered across their path. Amra had been tempted to climb down from Wind to greet them, but her courage had failed her and she'd kicked Wind in the flanks so that he'd raced away, leaving the men far behind. In her valley there were many villages along the banks of the river, yet this was a far wider, much more important river and there were hardly any villages or encampments to be found. If there were few people in the wide world, why was the Headman so worried about the iron men coming from over the mountains? How many of them could there be that Amra had to leave home to search for the secret of making iron weapons so that the peoples of the valleys could defend themselves?

As she was thinking, Amra noticed Wind had carried her to the top of a steep incline. They had deliberately ridden away from the river because its banks had suddenly become very steep, cutting a narrow path through the hills and the river itself had become very swift and angry. Wind had been forced to walk over wet stones in the shallows, unable to find a suitable path at the river's edge, and the noise of the river's voice had frightened him. So Amra had guided him away from the river but their route had become steeper and steeper. The river had cut a gorge through a steep ravine, and Wind and Amra had had to negotiate their way uphill to continue their journey. Amra had intended to return to the river banks when they'd crossed the hill and the river had calmed down, but she saw now that the hill did not end. Instead it rose and rose, gradually blending with a huge and seemingly impassable range of mountains, their distant tops snow-covered. Amra knew that the God of the Snow wouldn't allow her to pass. Yet the river now lay far below and Wind would find it impossible to travel along its course.

She spied a track which seemed to be in regular use – probably by hunters or traders – and urged Wind to follow it. The path led up and up. Even when she'd climbed to the top of the nearby hills from the valley where she lived, Amra had never been this high above a river. At every twist and turn in the track she could see further into the distant lands below. She looked back to where she had come from. The trees lay far below her. They seemed to stretch to the very ends of the earth. Looking ahead again she could make out the way the land lay. She could see the deep indentations of the valleys, the path of the river, the distant mountains which looked forbidding. And far below, dotted throughout the landscape, Amra could see many columns of smoke rising into the cloud-covered sky. She tried to count them but gave up when she ran out of fingers and toes. So this is where the people were! They were so spread out throughout the large world. And they lived so low on the ground, unlike Amra who now appeared to be climbing into the very clouds themselves. To the seats of the Gods.

Her heart missed a beat when she realised what she had just thought. Was this high place to which she and Wind had ridden visible to the God of Snow in his perilous kingdom? Her lightness of spirit suddenly gave way to a feeling of dread. She longed to talk to her father who knew so much, to be reassured that she would be safe, to seek the wisdom of the Headman who would tell her a story about people who had climbed a mountain and returned safely. But she couldn't. She was alone.

Wind seemed to sense the change in Amra's mood and slowed his stride, as though he too was weighted down by the crushing spirits of the mountain. The air grew colder the higher they climbed. The path blended more and more into the rocks and scrubby grass. Amra could sense that Wind was straining to climb, each footfall more difficult than the last. It was as though the mountain was draining him of his power, just as the heat of a summer's day drained Amra of her ability to run long and fast. Finally they reached a plateau where there was sparse vegetation, but enough grass for Wind to feed. The air was definitely colder than it was in the trees far below. There was a bite to it; it gave Amra the same feeling on her skin that she got at the start of the cold winter months. Again she cursed her lack of preparation. She had simply jumped onto the back of a horse and ridden off without considering the lands she might traverse on the way. Because she was travelling to the lands of the warm sun she hadn't thought that she might need warm clothes for the cold land she would pass through along the way. And now she was cold too. She craved a hot meal.

Amra slowed Wind down to a walking pace, patted his knotted neck and thanked him for the hard work he'd put into helping her climb the mountain. Wind stopped where the grass grew between the rocks, lowered his head and ate hungrily. Amra climbed off his back and wandered around the plateau. The rocks were cold; she could feel the cold rising through her sandals. She walked to the edge of the plateau. Suddenly, without warning, the ground disappeared. Had Amra been walking faster she might very well have plummeted to her death. She drew back and sat down quickly on the ground. With trepidation she crawled to the edge of the rock and again looked down. The drop was precipitous. Biting her lip in fear, she crawled forward bit by bit until her head was over the very edge of the rock, hanging in space. She saw the river far below. It was nothing more than a silver ribbon, a thread of light weaving its way between the faces of the cliffs on either side. It looked as though a God had painted it on the ground, just as the potters in her village painted thin red and black and yellow lines on the plates and vases they made. She crawled back and lay full length on the ground. The sky was closer than normal. Normal? What was that? It was normal for the sky to be far above her head. It was normal for the weather in summer to be warm. It was normal for her to finish the day with her family and to plan exciting things to do the next day.

Amra could feel tears welling in her eyes. She hadn't cried since the sacrifice of Henk and Annka. Even when her mother had died her eyes had remained dry of tears. She had nursed her mother to the stage where Mira couldn't even raise her head above her pillow. Her death had come as a relief to all except Hasga. Yet now, alone, close to the Gods, cold and hungry with nobody to talk to except a horse who couldn't answer back, Amra felt more lonely than she had ever felt in her life. She blinked away the tears, feeling ashamed of her weakness. Children cried. She was no longer a child, far from it.

She lay there, staring up at the close-knit clouds scudding across the sky, feeling as if she could reach up and touch them, when suddenly Wind whinnied furiously. Amra sat up and saw the horse rearing on his hind legs, looking terrified. Instinct made her grab for the knife strapped to her belt. She looked around but could see nothing. She ran over to a large boulder and hid behind it, her mind racing, her fear rising in her throat. Wind had done this once before, when they had been riding through a forest and a large wild dog had jumped out barking at them. Initially Wind had raced off, but then had gathered his courage and had turned to chase the dog away, rearing onto his hind legs as if to crush the cowering beast beneath his hooves.

Perhaps it was another dog. But up here, so high? Amra felt the security of the knife in her cold hands; she grasped it tighter. Wind was skittering across the narrow plateau, leaping as if he had a fire beneath his feet. Amra suddenly realised that in his fear he might go too near the edge and plunge to his death into the deep gorge. Suddenly she heard the source of his fear: the roar of a lion. There were lions near her village but they lived high in the mountains where it was cold throughout the year. She had heard stories about them, and had even seen one once in the distance.

She looked around for the source of the roar and let out a cry of anguish when she saw the animal high on a rock a long way above her, its gaze focused on Wind. It would take the beast no time at all to run down the hill and throw itself at the horse. And once it had tasted Wind's blood, there was no doubt that it would also kill her. There was nowhere she could run, nowhere she could go. Death stared her in the face. She would join her mother. And Peta would follow her shortly afterwards. The stark reality of the moment made all thoughts of loneliness disappear. No longer did Amra pine for home; all she thought of was extricating herself and Wind from this terrible situation. Perhaps she could jump on Wind's back and ride down the mountain? But no, the lion would race after her. Perhaps she could light a fire and scare the lion away. But that would take too long and there was not enough dead wood and leaves around for her to light.

All she had was her knife, her bow and arrow and the spear which she used for fishing. She ran across to where she had left the panniers and pulled out her bow and arrow, her heart thumping in her chest. Wind calmed momentarily when he saw her emerge from the rock but he was obviously still terrified, his nostrils flaring wide as the lion jumped down from its rock and moved towards them, closer and closer. Amra threw her arms around Wind's neck, pulling the huge beast's head towards her face. She could smell his fear. She whispered in his ear, 'Wind, don't be nervous. We can beat him. Come on. Join me. Don't be frightened. Please.'

Her lilting voice calmed the horse, but then the lion roared again. Wind flung back his head, lifting Amra off the ground. She clung on desperately, saying, 'Wind, I'm here. I'll help you. Don't be afraid.'

She let go of his neck and fed an arrow from the sheath into her bow. She was a good shot for her age and could kill a deer across a large gap in the trees. But you could creep up on deer. They weren't fierce and would run away rather than attack. Amra had never shot at anything which might attack her like a bear, or the wild dogs or the ferocious wild boars. But she felt better now, calmer. Her mind was racing but her heart was becoming still. Amra knew how lions fought. She had been told by her father. They circle behind their prey and as the prey runs to escape they follow it from behind. Then they spring upon its neck. As long as Amra kept behind Wind she had a chance of wounding the lion. Holding her bow and arrow firm she ran behind the rock. Suddenly the lion appeared at the opposite end of the plateau. It stood there, stock still, summing up the situation. There was a large stone on the ground by Amra's feet. She picked it up and threw it at the lion. It bounced a long way short of it but she had let the lion know that she wasn't scared. Its eyes found her and it growled.

It was a mistake. Amra realised too late how stupid she was. The lion's shoulders were suddenly raised as if it was about to strike. It raised a paw and clawed the air in front of it, telling her that if she was closer it would tear her apart. Her throat caught and she found she could not breathe. She was so frightened. The lion had not really been interested in her until then. Wind had been its target but now it had found her. She was a small prey but she would do.

The lion flared its nostrils and bared its teeth. Saliva dripped from its hungry mouth. Again it opened its vast jaws and snarled in her direction. And then it began to move towards her, stalking, crawling, one foot menacingly in front of another. Amra wanted to turn and run but she would be dead if she did. That was certain.

A cry of terror escaped her. It goaded the lion into snarling again. She picked up an arrow and fed it into her bow. The lion presented a small target, face on; if only he would turn, then she could hit him in the side. Her hand was shaking so badly she knew the arrow would fall far from its target. But it was her only chance. If she missed she would die. She began to mumble a prayer. She would soon see her mother.

But the lion turned as Wind whinnied again. It was now facing two enemies, one of them a huge beast, much bigger than he'd looked from up on the rock. The lion's massive head moved from one to the other. Wind seemed to have calmed a little when Amra threw the rock at the lion. He was still showing the whites of his eyes, still foaming at the mouth in fear, but she could tell from his stance that he was not as panicked. Perhaps because he could see how small the lion was compared to his own bulk.

The lion growled from deep in its belly and began to circle back to the opposite end of the plateau. Amra realised then that she might live. She wanted the lion close to the dangerous edge so he would have another enemy at his back. She fired a warning shot from her bow, hitting a boulder in front of the beast. The lion started and retreated to the path it had used to approach the plateau.

Wind moved across opposite Amra so the lion was between them and began to slowly edge it towards the precipice. Did Wind understand what was in Amra's mind? He was standing firm though she knew he was still terrified. He had confused the lion; it was used to its prey running away in terror.

The hunter had become the hunted. The lion crouched down, growling ominously in this unfamiliar situation. Suddenly Wind reared up, his enormous body high in the air above the lion, his legs kicking. He came down with an enormous crash right where the lion had been standing only moments before. The animal cowered back towards the edge of the plateau. While it was distracted, Amra took another arrow and fired it at the beast. It was far too long and disappeared into the air over the precipice. Amra bit her lip in anger. She picked up another arrow and threaded it into her bow. Her hands were no longer shaking. She was no longer Amra the prey. She was Amra the hunter. She fired another arrow – it hit the lion in the throat. It reared up, roaring in agony. Amra quickly let off another arrow which found its chest. The smell of the lion's blood drove Wind into a frenzy. He raced over to the beast and reared above it. The lion lashed out but Wind's teeth were bared and he rose up again, almost kicking the lion in the head and crushing its skull. But the lion retaliated, springing from his crouching position, sinking its teeth into Wind's shoulder, clawing at the horse's skin.

Amra's third arrow hit the lion in its flanks. It released its grip on Wind and fell back to the ground, one leg kicking in an attempt to dislodge the arrow. Wind, bleeding from the shoulder, turned his back to the lion and viciously kicked it, accurately and mercilessly, in the head. The lion fell to the ground, roaring in agony. Amra fired another arrow, this one flying straight to the beast's heart. It shuddered and lay still.

Wind continued kicking the lion even though Amra knew it was dead. She dropped her bow and arrow and ran over to Wind, throwing her arms around his neck and whispering to him that it was all over, that he should come with her away from the plateau. But nothing she said could soothe him. He was wounded from the lion's claws and its savage teeth; he didn't want comfort, just relief from the pain.

Amra had herbs in her pannier which would help him if only she could still him. She returned to the lion. Close up she saw how beautiful it was, even punctured by four arrows. She tore them out of its body and returned them to her sheath, intending to clean them later. Then, with all her might, she rolled the animal over the edge of the plateau. It plunged through the air, crashing down into the gorge below.

Amra sat on the ground and realised how near to death she had come, and how much depended upon her living. She understood how vulnerable she had been; only her skill as a hunter had saved her. Now her hunting experience told her that she and Wind must leave this area immediately. She had killed a male lion. A female lion and perhaps cubs would be close by. Females were known to be even more vicious than males when it came to protecting their cubs. But suddenly she felt like a little girl again. She wanted her father, her mother and her friends. She began to cry and her tears did not stop for a long while.

CHAPTER 10

Amra descended into the light and warmth on the other side of the mountain. It had taken her three days from the time she had killed the lion to climb to the peak of the mountain, passing the snow line, and following the ridges to the top of the world. As she'd breasted the final ridge Amra had seen the mountain side fall away from her and the trail outlined clearly against the stark browns and greys of the land below. She let out a joyous cry. She felt as though hope had been returned to her and the way ahead was clear again.

After the killing of the lion, Amra had built a small cairn and burnt some food for the God of the Mountain, offering him thanks for saving her life. And as she had climbed onto Wind's back she'd continued to mouth prayers and paeans of gratitude. But the next two days had been the hardest of her life. She was always freezing cold, and had to rely on Wind's warmth and the size of his body to shelter her from his howling namesake. There were no caves for her to shelter in, no wood for her to light a fire, no people to offer her comfort. She was approaching the top of the world and she was completely alone. And so she and Wind continued onwards and upwards, through clouds, through misery, through loneliness.

But now the struggle uphill had come to an end, and from the vantage point of the eagles, Amra's world took form again. Wind seemed to understand the excitement which had gripped her; he trotted faster and faster down the mountain track. Amra looked at the land below them. It was criss-crossed with copses of trees, rivers which ran into and away from each other, villages in clearings, with smoke from their fires rising up towards her, but dissipating long before it reached her level. As Wind descended, the air itself seemed to be more welcoming and Amra's spirits soared.

Halfway down the mountain, Amra discovered a rook's nest with eggs in it. She cracked one open and drank the liquid greedily. She'd eaten food at the top of the mountain but it had been old, stale and cold. This egg's juices were warmed by the sun. She also found edible flowers, some herbs which refreshed her mouth, and berries which grew in abundance below the snow line. By the time she reached the foot of the mountains, and had rejoined the path of the great river, she was no longer hungry or thirsty and was feeling positive about her trip and its outcome. Her feelings of joy lasted only until the evening.

She made camp that night on the banks of the great river. Where it emerged from the gorges of the mountains it was narrow, angry and furious, but once back on the level plains, the path of the river widened and it became calm and gentle once more. Amra used its bountiful waters to provide her with food. This time she caught a fish she had never seen before, its scales a breathtaking combination of gold, silver and red. She cooked it with mushrooms and herbs then swam in the freezing water to refresh herself before going to bed. She settled down beside her fire to think about her journey, as she did every night. She rehearsed in her mind the numerous stories she would tell first to her sister Peta, then to her father, and then to all the people who lived in her village.

As she was thinking about the mountain lion, Amra thought she heard the snap of twigs deep in the forest. She sprang up, grabbed her knife and a flaming brand from the fire, and stood stock-still, listening, her acute ears picking up every sound the trees made. The noise didn't come again; but still Amra didn't move. She was too experienced in the ways of hunting. Animals only moved when there was silence, when they were confident. The only sound was her heart beating in her ears.

And then it came again, further down the river bank this time. Amra whirled in fright, catching her breath. Were there two of them? How could an animal possibly have moved from one place so far to the other without snapping twigs or making any other sound? Amra wheeled again as she heard a moan from the opposite direction, upriver. A moan? Like a wounded animal. Then a whistle in imitation of a bird, like an owl. It was a human whistle, Amra knew that for certain. What was going on?

Then she saw a movement out of the corner of her eye, in the forest where she had first heard the noise. A large shape. It was hidden behind a tree, but she saw it distinctly. It stepped out: a large man wearing a crude animal skin and leggings. On his wide leather belt he carried a large dagger. Over his shoulder was a quiver of arrows, but he had no bow.

Amra gasped. He was brutish-looking and unshaven, and even in the dim evening light Amra could see that he had a huge scar along the left side of his face. But it was the look in his eyes which caused her the most fear. It was the look of the hunter who has seen his quarry and is about to strike. Instinct made her tighten her grip on her knife, it was the look in his eyes that made Amra realise that she must run. Wind was in the forest somewhere, eating flowers and cones, so she would have to outrun the man then circle back to find the horse. Amra was a fast runner and although scared she was confident that the man wasn't as fast or as young as she was. She turned to run down the bank of the river, but her heart turned to stone when another man, as big as the one in the forest, strode up the embankment. He was as ugly as the first man and as tall and powerful. He carried a huge spear with a metal tip which he brandished as though to bar her way. Amra stopped in fear and raised her knife. There was a laugh behind her. She turned to see yet another man, this one running towards her along the embankment. Now Amra knew she was dead. With skill she could outrun one, maybe two. But to escape three large hunters was impossible. She called out loudly for Wind; perhaps he would come running and she could escape on his back. But as silence descended, broken only by the voice of the river and the footsteps of the three men walking menacingly towards her, Wind's hooves were nowhere to be heard. Perhaps she could run into the river and swim to the other side. No. They would surely kill her with their spears and bows and arrows. Amra mumbled a prayer to her totem, the bee, and to the Gods. But the overwhelming vision in her mind was Peta's face, who would now surely die in her place.

The three men continued to move towards her slowly, as though she were an animal to be herded into a pen. The man downstream poked his spear towards her, daring her to run towards him. Amra looked at the others; they were grinning at her fear. They were old men but powerful. As they came closer she saw that it wasn't only the scar-faced one who carried hunting wounds; the man upstream had a long raw gash in his leg. Yes, these men were definitely hunters – and she was their quarry.

Instinct took over. If she was going to die, Amra thought then she would take at least one of the men with her. She'd left her bow and arrow in the pannier but she did have her knife. She'd make sure that it found its way into at least one and hopefully two hearts. The three men stopped. They surrounded her standing about the length of two spears away from her. She scanned the men with her knife, letting them know she would make a dangerous victim. She asked them what they wanted.

They replied with grunts. Did they understand her words? How could she communicate with them?

Suddenly the man downriver screamed. He dropped his spear and hopped around as if he had been bitten on the foot by a snake. Amra turned in shock at his screams. As she did the other two men rushed her from the side and behind. She smelt them before they grabbed her. She smelt the woods and the dankness which came with sleeping outdoors for days. They grabbed her viciously around the waist and throat, one man twisting her slender arm and forcing her to drop her knife. Her wrist felt as though she'd plunged it into fire. She screamed at the pain but stopped quickly when the men threw her like a dead animal to the ground. They stared down at her, all three of them. Grinning.

Two of the men bent down and held her arms and head. They were so strong that she was pinned to the riverbank, unable to move. The third man undid the knot in his trousers and they dropped to the ground. She saw his penis; it was erect, huge, ugly. He knelt down and forced her legs open while the other men laughed. The pain as he entered her was the worst Amra had ever known. It filled the whole of her body. It was as though somebody was thrusting a knife into her. He plunged inside her, withdrew then plunged again. She screamed and screamed but the man didn't stop. Neither did the pain. As he got more and more excited by her fear and pain, the man shuddered, shouted out and collapsed on top of her. Then he rolled off, laughing.

The other two let go of Amra; they sensed that she was too weak to fight. Her body was burning. All she wanted to do was to roll down the embankment into the river and let its icy waters wash away the pain. But it wasn't to be. Another man towered above her. His penis, like the first man's, was massive, engorged. He fell to his knees, forcing her now flaccid legs open and thrust himself inside her. If the pain Amra had felt from the first man had in part been from shock, the agony she felt now was because her insides were raw. There was nothing human about what he was doing to her. She had seen her father and mother doing this, people in the fields too. The women often laughed and the men made funny noises. But there was no pleasure here. Amra was in so much pain that her mind ceased to process what was happening. Instead it filled with images of her mother, her sister, to obliterate the horror and pain.

The third man raped her too. By the time he had finished Amra wanted to die. Her agony encompassed every part of her body; there was no part of her which was free of it, or which retained the spirit of girlhood. Her muscles, her insides, her head, all ached with an unbearable pain. But slowly a form of relief came over her. She lay there on the soft loam of the riverbank, breathing gently, willing the pain away, her body settling into a state of dormancy like the halfworld before sleep. She saw the three men kneeling at the riverbank, washing their faces and bodies. She should stand and stab them in the back with her knife, but she was too tired. She heard them talking, laughing. They looked back at her and nudged one another in the ribs, comrades in the hunt, joint victors of the prey. She heard them walking to where she had left her possessions in the pannier. One of the men, the one with the scar on his face, bent down and took her knife which was lying close to her. She heard them empty her pannier on the ground and in her mind's eye Amra saw them take her amulet, her bow and arrow, her food and her blanket which had saved her life on the mountain. Her heart sank. If only she could move she would fight. But her whole body was numb.

She could hear them quarrelling now, voices raised in anger. They surrounded her, talking over her body. What would be her fate? Would they kill her? One of the men shook his spear. Another nodded. But the third, who was now wearing Amra's amulet, pointed to the bee symbol then to her. The amulet prevented them from killing her. Amra had no idea why. They were hunters and she lay prone before them, a wounded animal.

Instead of driving the spear through her body they pulled her roughly to her feet and marched her down to the river. The man with the hideous leg wound picked up a large rock and brought it crashing down onto Amra's skull. It glanced off her head and landed heavily on her shoulder. But Amra felt nothing. She saw only blackness.

Dreams came to her out of the blackness, as if she was being called by her mother who sat with the Gods. Voices so distant she had to strain to hear their words. Images floated in her mind. Images of fish and of her in a sunny stream, swimming with them. A large fish, a type she'd never seen before, swam into her mouth, preventing her from breathing. She swallowed huge draughts of water with the fish. But she needed to breathe, not to drink. So she breathed. And then she coughed, so loudly that the very air around her exploded into bubbles and violence.

Amra floated to the surface of the river, her head just above water. Had she surfaced in front of the rocks, the men would have seen her and returned to kill her properly, but luckily she drifted behind them, her body slowly turning in the current. She moved her shoulder fractionally and floated onto her back. The light hurt her eyes but her instinct for survival forced her nose and mouth out of the water to gulp in air.

Then the pain returned. This time the agony throbbed at the back of her head. It felt as if somebody had torn open her skull and was twisting a knife inside her brain. The pain spread down into her shoulders then into her chest and back. She tried to move her hands but they felt cold and numb. Slowly Amra returned to full consciousness. She had seen people hit hard on the head in her village; some had been forced to spend the rest of their lives sitting uselessly in their houses; others had found that their arms and legs would no longer work. Was this happening to her? She desperately tried to move her fingers but they refused to respond.

Amra let her wounded body float free of the rock island and drift lazily on the surface of the river. Drifting until she became one with the water, like a branch which had fallen from an overhanging tree, to be carried by the will of the river until it reached the everlasting sea. She breathed heavily to stay aware because if she let herself drift into the blessed relief of sleep her body became heavy and sank towards the river bottom. Then the water would close over her face and enter her mouth and her nose, making her choke and splutter, and she had to kick her way back to the surface and precious air.

Two thoughts struck her as she drifted along. The first was that if she was kicking with her legs then she couldn't have lost the use of her arms and legs; and the second was the danger she was still in from the men. If they saw her moving, even breathing, they would surely run downstream after her, haul her body from the water and drive a spear through her. Why hadn't they done that in the first place? Why had they tried to kill her by hitting her on the head and drowning her instead of driving the spear through her body? It had something to do with the amulet. But now she was so tired, in so much pain, that the questions seemed of no importance. She was floating away from her hunters. She was escaping quietly, slowly; the longer the river ran the further away she would be from them.

The river meandered around a bend and the scenery changed. Amra could no longer see overhanging trees.

She turned her head fractionally and looked at the bank. The forest seemed to have retreated and she could see thorn trees and clumps of berry bushes near the water's edge. Now Amra turned herself over and floated on her stomach. The men were far away, over on the other bank. She swam painfully to the shallows and clawed her way onto the bank. Lying half in and half out of the water, Amra put her hand up to her head. She touched the wound and winced in pain. Her head felt twice the size and the bump was enormous. But that was something she would have to deal with later. Now all that she wanted was the relief of sleep.

It was Wind who woke her. She had no idea how long she had been asleep, but when she felt the shock of cold water her eyes opened slowly and she realised that she was alive. She didn't feel happy though; instead a great depression swept over her. She hurt so badly she longed for the relief of death. She rolled back down the embankment and the last thing she heard before she plunged back into the water was Wind's surprised neigh.

Amra sat up in the shallows, soaked to the skin, and put her hand to the enormous ache in her head. Her shoulder pinched fiercely as though there was a knife deep inside it. She stood, her legs wobbling, and fell to her knees again, as if praying to the River God. She crawled her way back up the bank. Wind was watching her. If horses were able to show consternation, then there was a definite look of worry on his face.

Wind spread his hind legs and shifted his flanks forward, urine streaming from his body. Amra stood and held out her hand to him. She was in so much pain she didn't know which hurt most, her head, her chest, her shoulder or the very centre of her being where the men had entered into places no person had ever been before. Her body was hot with pain and yet freezing from the cold water. Her dress was torn and filthy. She painfully raised her arms around Wind's lowered neck and began to sob. The horse nuzzled her neck and gently pulled her away from the thorn bushes and the berry bank towards the trees, back towards the place where she had last enjoyed a meal before she had become a hunted animal.

The tiredness infused her bones. She was desperate for more sleep. She massaged her shoulder and again felt the lump on her head where the men had crashed the rock onto her skull. Thank the Gods she had moved her head fractionally so that the rock had deflected and hit her back and shoulders instead. Had she not been so young and fit, her shoulder would have been smashed by the weight of the rock and she would surely have drowned when the men threw her into the river.

Amra could move her fingers, arms and legs and bend her back so she knew there were no bones broken. She tried to look at her shoulder to see the bruising but could hardly bend her neck. Wind half carried her, half led her back to the remnants of her fire. Amra judged that she had probably been asleep for the entire night and early morning. From the position of the sun in the sky, it was now late morning. Her legs had been immersed in the water all that time. She looked down to see the damage. The motion was painful but she grinned to see the big black leeches attached to her skin.

She picked a blade of grass and tickled one of the leeches close to where its sucker was biting into her flesh. The irritation of the grass made it momentarily withdraw its mouth and she quickly lifted it off her leg. A drop of blood ran down her leg. She put the leech onto the wound on her head, hoping that it would suck up the blood which had gathered there. It was a trick she had learnt from the Medicine Man's wife. Leeches kept wounds clean and stopped the smelly green flesh from developing. It took her some time to persuade all the other leeches on her legs to let go. When there were four on her head she threw the others back into the river to enable them to find other food.

Amra lay back. Despite the heat of the day Wind lay down beside her, nuzzling up to her as if to protect her from the elements and any further danger. She was grateful and patted his huge flanks.

The next time she woke it was dark. Her head still hurt her horribly. She lifted her hands and felt for the leeches. Two had dropped off. She found them close by in grass, fully engorged. Two were still there. She left them, knowing that they would drop off when they had filled themselves with the blood of the wound. She stood and immediately felt giddy. She had to steady herself against Wind who was munching at some grass nearby. Amra knew she had to eat or she would become so weak she might die. She walked unsteadily down to the berry patch by the river and pulled off both ripe and sour berries. Her mouth exploded with their taste and she vomited. She washed her face in the river then drank in huge gulps of the refreshing life-giving water. Slowly she ate some more berries, more cautiously this time. She was still famished but the taste of food in her mouth made her feel better. She found some green apples on a tree close by, then some mushrooms growing on a stump. She had never tasted flavours so rich nor experienced food as so delicious before. She ate until she could eat no more, walking unsteadily from mushrooms to apples to berries and then some wild damsons which she found in the forest. Then she returned to the river and drank even more, washing her face and her body, stepping out of her dress and trying to force water into the place where the men had been. She needed to clean away what they had done to her.

Returning to her panniers, Amra put her arms around Wind. 'We have to delay our journey, dear friend. They have taken everything. I have nothing and I don't even have the ability to hunt without a bow and arrow. We must follow them. Somehow I have to get my things back.'

Amra put her arms around the huge horse's neck and pulled herself up onto his back. As she spread her legs to straddle him, she felt a pain searing through her. She put her hand between her legs to staunch the agony and saw that she was still bleeding. It was the blood of her youth passing away forever. But it was a pain which would keep her going, the pain of remembrance of what the men had done to her. It would drive her on until she had taken possession again of her amulet, her dagger and her bow and arrow. Only then would the pain stop.

Amra searched for the tracks of the three men. The ground was a confusion of tracks and footsteps, but eventually further upstream she found the three sets of prints. She urged Wind on, inspecting the trodden-down grass and broken twigs where the men had passed. Their trail stretched towards the mountains, from where she had come, as well back into the low lands. If they were travelling up into the mountains then it would be difficult and dangerous to follow them. She knew from having crossed the peaks that there were few hiding places and that she and Wind would be visible from far off. So, with a prayer to the Gods of the trail, she turned towards the low lands and followed the trail deep into the woods. The track was fast and easy and she and Wind made excellent time. If the men had come this way, then she would easily catch up with them. The danger was that she might ride too quickly around a bend and suddenly confront them face to face. Then she would surely die.

After travelling some time Amra saw that the trail led

up a small hill. She slowed Wind down and dismounted then walked him slowly to the top of the hill, crouching as she reached its apex. The way ahead was completely clear, no smoke, no sign of human beings. She remounted Wind and rode quickly, covering more distance, feeling safe in her quest.

Much later in the day, as the sun was beginning to descend, Amra came to a bend in the road. Again she dismounted from Wind. It was the fifth time since they had started their journey together to follow the men. She whispered into his ear to be patient. Her stomach was rumbling, the berries, mushrooms and fruit having been finished up long ago. Amra crept slowly around the bend in the trail. Her heart jolted when she saw a telltale column of smoke in the distance ahead. It spelled danger.

Amra told Wind to remain where he was. 'I'll come back for you soon, old friend,' she said. 'Don't worry. Just stay here.'

Then she set off along the track as fast as her aching body would allow her. By now she had got used to the pain between her legs, her head wasn't throbbing as much as it once had and her shoulder and arm, even though they still ached, no longer hurt as viciously. She left the trail for the safety of the woods, still moving in the general direction of the smoke. Even though she felt safer hidden by the trees, Amra knew there was still the danger of snapping a dry twig and alerting the men to her presence. She crept forward as cautiously as she could, praying that Wind wouldn't follow her. The closer she got, the more softly she walked.

Gradually, as she neared the smoke, Amra realised how unbelievably stupid she was. How could she possibly attack three huge men, without a knife or a bow and arrow? Only an idiot would even contemplate such a thing. And yet hatred impelled her forwards. She had never felt such hatred before. She longed to see them suffer, to see them hurt as badly as they had hurt her. With frustrating slowness, she crept ever forwards. The anger made her want to race towards the smoke, to scream into the hideous faces of her tormentors. But her skill as a hunter controlled her fury, her need for revenge.

When she was close enough to smell the smoke and to hear the men talking, Amra fell from a crouching to a crawling position. The ground was covered with the soft leaves of summer. She moved her arms and legs like a lizard until she came to the breast of the small hill. She looked down. Down by the bank of the river sat the three men. The gorge rose in Amra's throat. She felt like vomiting. But she restrained the agony in her body, lying above them like a stalking lioness, hardly breathing, waiting for an opportunity to kill.

The men sat around a fire, watching the hind of a deer cooking on some sticks. The rest of the butchered animal lay downwind to attract the flies away from the roasting meat. As the cooking smells came to her nose Amra realised she was starving. The gnawing pain of hunger augmented the pain in her head and body. But strangely that was good. Pain kept her mind focused, her anger sharp and her need for revenge the most pressing thing in her life. She watched the men with growing frustration. They were foolish. They never looked around them, so confident that they were in control.

Amra kept watch until the light faded. When it was almost dark she carefully crept down further until she could see the encampment more clearly. She saw her knife in a sheath, hanging over the stump of a fallen branch at the edge of the men's camp site. Her bow and arrows were close by, thrown casually on the ground. Her fury grew when she spotted the man with the scarred face wearing her amulet. His filthy greasy fingers fondled it as though he were fondling her breasts. The leering grin on his lips made her feel sick again.

Amra saw that the men were drinking beer with their meat. She could smell it clearly but she could also tell from their movements. The more they drank the more they laughed and shouted, and punched each other like the children from her village did when they were playing in the fields. They drank long into the evening. Sometimes one would get up and walk around to unstiffen his legs, or to urinate in the river. Eventually sleep overtook them. The beer had affected their wits so they forgot to tend the fire to ensure that it continued to burn through the night. But Amra wasn't ready to move. Not yet. She knew that sleep had many faces. Early in the night the slightest noise can waken somebody up, but wait until they are in the grasp of the God of Dreams and then almost nothing will bring them back to the land of the living.

Amra listened for the snoring. She knew they would snore; her father always snored after drinking beer. When the snoring gained in volume Amra picked up a small stone and tossed it into the middle of their camp. She heard it clatter on the ground, roll and hit one of the men on the leg. But it didn't disturb him ... or the others. She smiled. She stood and cautiously walked down the hill. The closer she got the louder their snoring. She could smell them too; her nose wrinkled in disgust. Thoughts of their violation of her body flashed in her mind but she forced them to subside. She would allow nothing to distract her. Nothing!

Her first goal was the knife. She crept over to the tree and unhooked it, fastened the belt around her waist and took out the blade. Confidence flooded back into her. She was the hunter again, not the quarry. She bent over the first man, the one who had been upstream when she'd first seen her attackers. Now she could see him clearly she realised how young he was, maybe only ten or so years older than her. But she felt no compassion. She placed her hand over his mouth and pushed his head down into the ground. His eyes shot open in shock. Good! She wanted her face to be the last thing he saw before the Gods took him and cursed him for ever for what he'd done. His eyes narrowed, they were bloodshot. He started to twist his head to free himself from her grip but she was strong and had the advantage of the pressure of height. She smiled and slit his throat. His body jerked violently and his arms shot up to try to dislodge her hands, but Amra held firm. Nothing would dislodge her now. Her tormentor died, fighting for breath as the lifeblood drained out of him.

The other two men were still sound asleep. Amra smiled at her proficiency as a hunter. She had killed silently and swiftly as her father had taught her. She turned to her other two quarry. These she hated even more than the younger man because they had led the attack on her.

Killing the second man was as easy as the first. Again she pressed her hand over his nose and mouth. As soon as he recognised her she drove her blade upwards through his stomach into his heart. He too died noiselessly.

But a quiet death was too good for the scar-faced man. For him Amra had been saving a special death. Now she was completely confident that she had control of the situation. Stealthily she searched the camp for rope. Hunters always carried rope to tie their prey onto branches so they could transport them home. She found what she was looking for. She uncoiled the length and moved quietly over to where the third man was sleeping blissfully, completely unaware of his fate. Patiently Amra tied one end of the rope around the man's wrist. She was terrified of waking him. If he did wake she would kill him quickly with her knife, but that would deprive her of much of the pleasure she had been anticipating ever since she had become the hunter rather than the quarry. With infinite care she looped one end of the rope through the other once then twice until it was knotted firmly around his wrist. The moment he jerked the knot it would tighten, and then she would have him secure like a trapped animal. She unwound the rest of the rope and tied it to a nearby tree, allowing him only a short length.

Then, almost casually, with complete confidence, Amra wandered to her bow and arrows. She picked them up and returned to her enemy. With all her strength she kicked him viciously in his groin. His body jerked crazily and he sat bolt upright, roaring in agony, clutching at his crotch. The movement tugged the rope around his wrist, tightening the knot and capturing his arm. Struggling to release his arm, the man forced open his eyes and looked around. Standing at his feet was his nemesis.

He roared again, in anger as much as in pain. Scrambling to his feet, he reached instinctively for his spear. But Amra had already removed it, as she had removed anything else which he might use against her. He ran towards her but the rope securing his arm prevented him from taking more than three steps. Again he let out a bellow of rage. Amra stood her ground, smiling. Slowly she took an arrow out of her quiver and placed it in her bow.

The man struggled to untie the fast knot. Amra called out, 'Don't bother. That was taught to me by my father. The harder you pull it the tighter it becomes.' Her calm voice made the man stop and look at her. Recognition dawned on him and his drunken stupor began to recede. He blinked and shook his heavy head. It *was* the same girl. But how could she be standing so confidently before him, pointing an arrow at him? She was supposed to be dead.

Amra shot her arrow. It flew straight into the man's thigh. He screamed and fell to the ground, clutching his leg, rolling around in pain. He screamed out to his friends for help. This pleased Amra. She walked over to her enemy and grasped his head by the hair, pulling him into a sitting position so he could see his companions' corpses. Realising that he was trapped, he began to claw frantically at the knot but untying it was impossible with only one hand. He scrabbled around the small area the rope allowed him to cover, searching desperately for a weapon, a stick, a stone, anything to defend himself. There was nothing.

The man realised that he was dead. Amra calmly placed another arrow in her bow. This one she aimed at his heart. The man began to cry and to mumble prayers. Amra smiled.

A fraction of a second before Amra let the arrow fly, she changed its course. It hit the man in his other thigh. Again he roared in pain and clutched his leg. But he only had one free hand to tend to his two wounds and so gave up his attempts at relief. He stared at Amra, waiting for her next move.

Amra motioned to the man to sit up. With the utmost difficulty he did so, the arrows in his legs sending shocks of white heat through his body. Amra aimed her third arrow at his heart but again changed direction at the moment of release. It pierced his groin. The man's body jerked and he fainted with the pain, falling back so that he was lying full length on the ground, the three arrows standing vertically. Amra took a flask of beer and poured its contents over the man's face. Consciousness returned to his grey features and he opened his mouth and muttered a plea.

Amra helped him sit up. Then she took out her knife and sawed off his penis. Again the man fainted. This time when Amra doused him with beer he didn't move. Satisfied that nothing more was to be gained she forced her knife through his ribs into his heart and let him slip into death.

Amra looked around the scene of her revenge. She was hungry. She tore chunks off the haunch of venison to abate her hunger, chewing on them ravenously. Then she gathered her possessions, removed the amulet from the scarred man's neck and searched the other men to see if they were carrying anything of value. Finally she took her knife and cut the testicles off each of the three men. She threaded them onto a piece of twine and washed off the blood in the river. She placed the victory necklace over her head; it rested on her breast next to her precious amulet. Amra surveyed her work: there lay the bodies of her tormentors, she had their manhood around her neck, she had some of their possessions and she had eaten the meal they had killed. She was Amra. She was the hunter. She raised her arms, and shouted her thanks to the God of the Hunt and the God of the River.

Amra rode towards the village with confidence. The confidence of a hunter, a woman who had been blooded. The rape, the beating, the men who had tried to murder her were a part of another life now, another world. She imagined that these incidents belonged to the other side of the mountains, not this side. Not the side where the forests had been tamed and cleared to make fields, where crops grew in abundance, where men and women worked in the fields and didn't look at her strangely when she passed them on Wind's back.

The village was large, at least twice the size of her own village. Like her own it had a high wooden wall built around it. From the top of the hill Amra could see inside. There were houses built around the perimeter but they were different to those of her village. They were made from stone instead of wattle and daub with thatched roofs. Some, the bigger ones, had an unusual red material on the roof. She had never seen thatch that colour. Within the outer perimeter was another group of houses; these were separated by large rows which appeared to run into the epicentre of the circle where a large building – Amra assumed it was the meeting hall – was situated. She had never seen so many houses crowded together. How, she wondered, could all the people in this large village possibly know each other?

She halted Wind at the top of the hill. Beyond the village, stretching into the distance and all around, was nature as Amra had never seen it before. The trees had been cut down and in their places fields of crops had been planted on a huge scale, much larger than the small crops area in her own village. The fields were divided by the colour of the crops: corn, wheat and various vegetables. In the fields, men and women were bent, tilling the rows, removing weeds and driving oxen to and from the river to bring water to the plants. It was an amazing feat of organisation. These people must be so clever, Amra thought. How could she compare?

For a brief moment, she felt cowed. But then she remembered who she was. She was Amra the hunter. As soon as she told the people what she had done to the three evil men who had tried to kill her they would respect her. Instinctively she reached up to the amulet to touch it and say a silent prayer of luck, but her hand brushed against another necklace, the newer one which she wore just as proudly as the amulet, the manhood of the beasts who had raped her. She wondered what would happen to their bodies. Perhaps lions from the mountain would smell them and come down to eat them. Yes, she thought, she would like them to be eaten by lions. Or maybe carrion birds were pecking out their eyes and their tongues, or the humble ants and beetles were taking tiny bites out of their decaying flesh and carrying it back underground to their nests so that the bodies eventually would blend with the earth.

Amra rode down to the village. Before she became Amra the hunter of men she had avoided villages. She had pretended to herself that they were too far away or that she was in too much of a hurry to stop. But she knew the truth: she had been too scared. But that was before she was violated. Now she was no longer frightened of anything. She had been through the worst and had won. And so Amra rode confidently down the hill and onto the path between two of the fields. The sensation she created made her smile and feel even more proud. People straightened up from their labours when they saw the extraordinary sight of a young girl riding towards them, seated like a headman or a king on a big black horse.

Amra pulled the hair on the nape of Wind's neck to slow him down, whispering for him not to be scared. She felt more confident than she had ever felt before. She was higher than the people, looking down on them. She knew she was young but she had the body and strength of a warrior. Even the wounds on her head and the blue rawness of her arm and shoulder gave her authority. The wounded hunter who had survived was a storyteller. She would be welcome around the fire that night to tell of her adventures.

A man stepped forward and spoke to her. Amra didn't understand what he said.

'I speak the language from the other side of the mountain,' she explained. The man nodded. He understood some of her words. He had learnt some of this language from traders, and her tongue was in many ways similar to his.

'Where are you from?' he asked.

Amra told him the name of her village.

'Where are you going?'

She explained she was going to the land of the Hittites. The man nodded and smiled. He pointed in the direction of the Eternal Sea. 'Soon you must leave the river,' he said, 'for it travels around to the north.'

Amra shook her head. She didn't understand the word 'north'.

'Beyond where the sun comes from,' he explained, 'where it rises in the winter. In the north.'

'North,' she thought. But she still didn't understand what he meant, despite his hand pointing in the direction from which she'd travelled.

Hearing the conversation and recognising that Amra wasn't a threat, a woman stepped forward. 'I am Pak,' she said. 'Have you eaten?'

Amra smiled and shook her head. Pak looked up at the sun nearly vertical above her. 'Come. Join us. Tell us who you are.'

The other people in the field put down their farming tools and gathered around Amra. She jumped off Wind's back and patted him, kissing him on the side of his face. The others introduced themselves but she forgot their names; they were harsh, alien names, different from hers and those that she knew from her own village. She remembered the name Pak and Stal but the other names were longer. She told them she was Amra. She said she had come from the other side of the mountains and was travelling to the land of the Hittites.

'Is it far?' she asked.

Stal shrugged his shoulders. 'I went there many years ago. It took me a month. But on your horse,' he said, pointing to Wind who was pulling up vegetables by their roots, 'it won't take long. Maybe five days. And the journey isn't difficult now you're through the mountains.'

'Are there more mountains between here and there?' Amra asked.

'Some' said Stal, 'but the journey isn't difficult. There are trails leading along the foothills.'

They took out bread from their baskets, roasted meats and fruits and berries, which they spread out on a large cloth on the ground. One of the women, Bria, looked at Amra and at her necklace. She pointed to it. 'That looks strange,' she said. 'They look like they were taken from men.'

Amra flushed. 'We take them from our enemies when we kill them,' she said. 'I made it before I began my journey across the mountains. There was an attack on my village and I killed many men myself. This is their manhood.'

She covered her untruth by holding up the necklace. Bria looked at her in consternation.

'It was very hard travelling over the mountains,' Amra continued. 'It was good to cross to this side and see the flat lands ahead of me.'

'My husband and two brothers are hunting up there,' Bria said, pointing in the direction Amra had come from. 'They are due back in a few days. Did you see them?'

A cold fear went through Amra's body. For the past day she had wondered where the men might be from, assuming that their village must be nearby. But the sight of so many people had closed her eyes to the possibility that these kind people, who were offering her food, were the same tribe as those who had raped her.

The woman continued, 'My husband has a scar on his face where he was clawed by a bear. Maybe you saw him?'

Amra shook her head. 'No,' she said firmly. 'I have seen nobody.'

She looked down at the food, her appetite gone. The people continued to press her for details of her adventures, as well as which gods she worshipped, how her village traded and many other questions. When she didn't understand the man Stal found a way of explaining it. He also explained to the others things which Amra said that they too didn't understand.

Amra made little of their questions, explaining that almost nothing had happened from the time she had left her village. She mentioned the lion but dismissed it, saying that she had been lucky to kill it. The people of the village wouldn't accept her luck and lauded her for her skill but she couldn't accept their praise or respect. She was overwhelmed by feelings of rage, the same sense of violation she had felt when the men had attacked her. These people were related to her attackers, her killers, they had grown up with them, eaten with them, loved them. Even though Amra felt sorrow and guilt towards Bria for killing her husband and her brothers, her anger outweighed everything else. She wanted to be away. She stood. 'Thank you for the food. I must go.'

Pak stood also and touched her face. She explained that Amra must follow the course of the river until it turned back on itself, northwards, and then she would find a trail which would lead down towards the sea which she called the Sea of the Dardans. There she would find a crossing at its mouth and then she would be in the land of the Hittites.

Amra thanked her and whistled for Wind who came trotting over. She jumped on top of him and rode off, feeling the eyes of the villagers on her back as she left their village behind. She felt tears welling up in her eyes. All her pride at revenging herself on her attackers had faded away. She swung Wind around and headed back towards the river. On its banks she took off her new necklace, the six testicles threaded with twine, and swung it around her head, throwing it with a mighty arc. She no longer wanted their manhood. She had what strength she needed. She hated them and she hated the people of the village, even though they had shown her kindness. The necklace landed in the middle of the river, disappeared for a moment then resurfaced. It looked like a ring of flowers she used to make and place on Peta's head, calling her the queen of the village. The ring floated downriver and Amra watched until it disappeared around a bend.

She was still Amra the hunter. She put her hand to her amulet and felt its rough edges, its indentations, its solidity. This was all she needed. Her totem had saved her life. It had protected her and she drew strength from it. She wheeled Wind back to the path and detoured around the village, heading south towards the land of the Hittites.

CHAPTER 11

It was the middle of the morning when Sarah realised that she had cracked the case. She'd finally found the pathway to an appeal for the return of Schliemann's Trojan treasury to the land where it had originally been discovered. An aspect of law relating to fraud suddenly became relevant when associated with one of the terms of the contract Schliemann had signed with the Ottoman government. It would be impossible to prove that Schliemann had deliberately lied to the government about the value of Priam's treasure; the man had been dead for decades. That had been Sarah's difficulty all along. But associating Schliemann's actions with the clause of undertakings in the contract effectively ruled out the need to prove that the archaeologist had actual knowledge of the value of the items found. His intent during the negotiations was now no longer the issue, it was whether his actions had robbed the Turkish people of their heritage. Sarah was convinced that with this new approach, the international courts which would rule on the case would rule in favour of the rightful owners – Turkey.

The difference between her reading now and when she'd read the original transcription of the agreement was the translation by a new expert in the language of the Ottoman court, an eager young man whom Mustafa Bengazi had called in. He had gone into an extremely detailed explanation of the meaning of the words which lay behind the clauses, revealing much of the intent obscured by the lawyers' original translation. Sarah had been working on those translations since the day she'd arrived and had always felt they contained some hidden and almost intangible reference just outside her grasp.

When she discussed it with Mustafa he had called in the linguistics expert from the university who had retranslated the contract into more modern English. And when Sarah read this new translation for the tenth time, she suddenly came across the loophole which would break down the contract and nullify its terms.

Mustafa Bengazi had been watching Sarah with interest. She had been silent for nearly an hour; for somebody as garrulous as Sarah this was unusual. He was sure something important was about to happen. She looked up at him when she had completed a fourth page of notes in her foolscap folder, shaking her hand to restore its circulation. She smiled and he knew she was there.

'You've got it, haven't you?' he said.

She nodded confidently. 'This contract is null and void. If you associate Clause 5, Sub-clause 2A with a section in the Law of Fraudulent Dealing you'll find the concept of intent associated with the nature of disclosure. Now Ottoman law differs from western law in many respects. One of the most significant differences is that in Ottoman law, as I understand it from the experts we've been meeting with, once the contract is signed then the deal is done, regardless of the circumstances. *Caveat emptor*, let the buyer beware, seems to apply. Recent western law overturns this principle and offers far greater protection to buyers. However in the Ottoman Law of Fraudulent Dealings, especially in relation to . . .'

Mustafa interrupted. 'But as I understand it that law was only meant to apply to the Sultan and his family. It was specifically introduced for those times when people tried to trick the ruling families in land deals, or when traders came through the region peddling valueless junk which they said had great worth.'

'I know,' said Sarah, 'but it can be read to apply to the government as well as the Sultan's family. You see the

Sultan *is* the government via the National Assembly of tribal leaders and the beys who ruled in the Sultan's place in the far-flung districts of the Ottoman Empire. And so it can be read that an assault against him or his family is an assault against the government, and it was the government that was screwed by Schliemann.'

Bengazi shook his head. 'It's not going to wash, Sarah. It won't be accepted.'

She smiled. 'By whom? Where is there a representative of the Ottoman government or of Schliemann's family who is going to stand up in a court and defend the contract on the basis of its morality or its application to ancient laws?'

'No representative then, but now we have to fight the Russian government. And as if that's not serious, if we win against them we'll have to fight the Germans who claim to be the rightful owners.'

Sarah shook her head. 'This approach will nullify any claim Russia or Germany can make. They can't claim what was never rightfully theirs.'

'But if you overthrow this law,' said Mustafa, 'then every other law . . .'

'You have no expression of common law. These sorts of things don't apply. Not until modern Turkey and Atatürk. We've got him, Mustafa. We've got that bastard Schliemann by the short and curlies!' Bengazi frowned. He didn't understand.

'Look, let me try to explain this a bit better . . .' she started.

But Bengazi held up his hand. 'Enough! Sarah, I've heard nothing but legal talk for the last week. For God's sake, no more. I'm an archaeologist, not a lawyer. I've hardly understood a word you've said for days. Just tell me that breaking this contract means we can now officially make a bona fide claim against the Russians?'

Sarah nodded confidently again. 'Totally. Absolutely. One hundred per cent. We don't have to prove Schliemann was a liar, which was the difficulty from the very beginning.'

'And there's enough here to show . . .'

Again she nodded. 'I'll write a position paper for the Minister for Antiquities, which she can give to the Minister for Justice, which he can then present to Cabinet. The Prime Minister can then officially declare the terms of the contract null and void. Turkey will own King Priam's treasure. But like I've said all along, Mustafa, the problem isn't ownership, it's getting it back from the Russians. Your chances aren't great.'

Bengazi crossed the room and sat down beside Sarah. He put his hand on hers. She was surprised at his touch. He had been so circumspect about propriety; he had offered no contract except to shake her hand, despite the fact that they had been working together for so long. But the look in his eyes surprised her even more. It was one of wonderment.

'You know, I liked you from the very minute I saw you and now I realise why. You're a genius!'

Sarah burst out laughing. 'Don't be silly. I'm a lawyer. I'm trained to . . .'

'No. No, this is more than lawyer stuff. This is a real insight into the understanding of laws which we haven't thought about for a hundred years. You're an historian, a lawyer, an archaeologist digging up the past, a sociologist. You're a bloody genius.'

Again she laughed. She had never heard him swear, not once. Even so mild an epithet was strange coming from his mouth.

'Mustafa!' she said.

'I mean it, Sarah. I think you're marvellous.'

'Well, I hope the Minister thinks so.'

'She will,' he said confidently.

He reached over and gave her a big kiss on the cheek. He stood up. 'That was from me and from Turkey.'

'I've never been kissed by a country before.'

'Well now you have.'

'Unfortunately, much as I appreciate your generous compliments, the problem isn't going to go away. Sure, I can make a strong case for legal rights on our side but there's still Russia to deal with.'

'We know that,' he said. 'We've known that all along. But what this approach seems to do is to knock Germany out of the race. Their claim is based on Schliemann's gift. If he didn't have the right to give then they have no right to take back. Which means that we only have to convince Russia that, for the sake of international relationships, they should return the treasure to us.'

Before Sarah could answer there was a knock on the door. It was Fatima, the young woman who was acting as her secretary. 'There's somebody to see you, Sarah.'

She was surprised. She had no more appointments that day. 'Who is it?'

'He calls himself David.'

Fatima stood aside and allowed a dark young man into the office.

Sarah introduced Bengazi to her fiancé. The word sounded good coming from her lips. In America, they were lovers; they never described each other as engaged. And in Prague Sarah had always described David as her friend. But now she was very happy to tell people he was her fiancé.

Bengazi greeted him warmly and the two men shook hands. Bengazi hid his surprise. Sarah had told him about David, his gentleness, his calm, his inner beauty, his perception. She was quite obviously in love with him. In his mind, Bengazi had built a picture of a tall rugged young man, something like a woodsman in the Appalachian Mountains, masculine yet sensitive. David was so very different from what he'd expected. He was tall and thin, with a delicacy more that of a woman than man. Yet his standing and bearing showed strength and inner resolve. He had dark ringlets, unkempt and somewhat untidy, and his eyes were a vision from Omar Khayyam, black, deep and introspective, revealing nothing yet radiating a depth of understanding. But it was his hands which drew Bengazi's attention. His fingers were long and delicate, they were fingers made for caressing a cello or a woman's breast. Bengazi had always been attracted to beautiful young men, something his wife had come to terms with in the early years of their marriage. Now he smiled at David, the forbidden fruit.

They sat, but before Bengazi could ask any questions Sarah said: 'David's the most brilliant cellist in America. He was on the August cover last year of *Classical Music Monthly* after he played the Dvorak cello concerto at Carnegie Hall. "An interpretation even Dvorak himself would have applauded" the critic said. "A marvellous amalgam of the circumspection of intellect and the abandon of youthful passion".'

David smiled, somewhat embarrassed at the tributes flowing from his overexcited girlfriend. 'Do you like western music, Professor Bengazi?'

The other man shrugged. 'Our radio stations tend to play Arabic and Turkish music, which I listen to. But I was a student in London for many years and the Albert Hall was my second home.'

Fatima brought in a tray of apple tea and mineral water.

David turned back to Sarah. 'Honey, I'm sure you're very busy at the moment. When will you be free?'

Sarah glanced at her four pages of notes which needed to be transcribed by her secretary then formulated into a paper she could deliver to the Minister by the end of next week. There was at least four hours work ahead of her today if she was going to keep to schedule. But Bengazi intervened. 'You've had the big breakthrough, Sarah. Rest on your laurels. Take your young man and show him a bit of Istanbul while you still have the best part of the day. One thing I've meant to do, but failed because of time pressure, is to take you to lunch at Topkapi. Let him have the privilege.'

Duty told Sarah to send David to the hotel where she would see him later. But she closed her notebook with a flourish and said, 'I'll be in early tomorrow. If anybody wants me . . .' She stood and shrugged her shoulders.

They emerged from the Ministry building into the blinding midday sun of Istanbul and the yellow strata of pollution which hung in the air above the streets. They followed a meandering route around the ancient walls of the Palace then walked in through the massive ornate doors where they paid the entrance fee. Inside David was astounded by the size and magnificence of the grounds. One extraordinary pavilion after another enchanted the eye, a conflation of styles and architectural grandeur. He especially wanted to see the harem, the world-famous seraglio and the treasury palaces where the ostentatious wealth of the nation was displayed, but Sarah pulled him onwards through and in between the buildings, telling him that she was starving and that they would return when she had more time.

As they began to descend from the upper level of the Topkapi Palace to a lower terrace where the public restaurants were situated, David stopped and looked at the sight before him, lost in awe at the breathtaking magnificence of the city. Istanbul was cut into three distinct parts by vast stretches of water. Topkapi Palace was built on a huge pinnacle jutting out into the Golden Horn and the Bosphorus. He turned to speak to Sarah but stopped. Anything he could say would sound banal. And there was no need, she knew exactly what he was thinking. She had felt the same way on her first and every subsequent visit to the Topkapi. The thrill of being in one of the world's most romantic cities still wasn't wearing thin.

Sitting in a restaurant overlooking the very point of the Golden Horn, the Asian continent visible across the narrow waterway and the Black Sea and the Sea of Marmara on either side, they relaxed in each other's company. Sarah reached across and took David's hand.

'You can never begin to know how much I've missed you.'

He smiled. 'All you had to do was call . . .'

'David, let's not do the guilt thing. You're sounding like my mother! Let's not talk about the past until we've had more time together in the present. Let's just enjoy what we have.'

He nodded. They ordered a light Turkish meal. As soon as the waiter had disappeared, she continued, 'You're still hurt, aren't you?'

David remained silent.

'You're hurt because I stayed a year in Prague prosecuting those murderers instead of flying back to you and getting married.'

Still no response.

'David, I know you think I'm selfish. Career first and that stuff. But it wasn't like that.'

'I thought you said no guilt trips. We've haven't been back together all that long. Isn't a bit early to . . .'

'It has to be said,' she told him, squeezing his hand. 'I was going to say it as soon as you arrived, but there was never the opportunity. And I'd rather say it sooner than later. Sure, let's not have recriminations, but we need to clear the air.'

He nodded.

'Is there anything you need to ask me? Is there anything you want to bring out into the open? Speak now or forever hold your peace.' She attempted a joke but the tension was there in her voice.

'Sarah, why are you doing this? We've put it behind us. I don't think it's necessarily good to clear the air, in fact, you're getting distressed. It's not good to dwell on the past. You're an adult. I have no right to question or even demand to know about your behaviour. Let's enjoy this holiday together, go back to the States, start again and take it from there. Provided we can both answer to our consciences for what we've done in the year we've been separated, then what the hell.'

Sarah smiled at him, squeezing his hand even harder. He was such a good man, so kind and tolerant and understanding. An ocean of emotions swept over her: her suppressed fear from living a year of hell in Slovakia and the Czech Republic, the pressure of work in preparing the case against the legion of evil old Stalinists, the feelings of guilt at the way she had excluded David from her life because of her overwhelming professional responsibilities, her mortification at the thought of what she'd done with Laco, how close she'd come to sleeping with Josh, and the pressure of the past week and a half of working day and night for the Turkish government in a place where she was respected by a few and had unwittingly made enemies. All of it suddenly erupted in the calming presence of the one man in her life who loved her for who she was and accepted her with all her faults and failings. To David's surprise, and the complete incomprehension of the waiter who brought over their snacks, Sarah burst into tears. She buried her head in her hands and wept.

Mortified, the waiter asked, 'You don't like the food?'

It was the Minister herself who left the message saying that as she would be in a planning meeting for at least a week, the report wasn't urgent and could be presented to her later in the week. In the meantime, she suggested, Sarah and her young man should try to see something of Turkey. She even instructed that bookings for their flights and accommodation at the best hotels should be charged back to the Ministry's account. Sarah was gratified by the Minister's generosity but knew that it was the wonderful Mustafa who had put the wheels into motion to organise it. She thanked him profusely but he denied all knowledge. Nonetheless she kissed him as she left the office, assuring him that she would ring in at every arrival point so that if anything urgent happened he could let her know and she would return immediately.

They had decided to travel to Cappadocia. Their flight was due to leave early the following morning and so they spent their last evening in Kumkapi, the beachside suburb of Istanbul famous for its garish nightlife and fish restaurants. It was a warm night, filled with the subtle perfumes of myrtle, balsam and carob trees, their scents blending with the aroma of fish cooking in spicy olive oil and the pungent aniseed of *raki*.

As they walked from the main road north of the Sea of Marmara and turned into Kumkapi, they linked arms. It had been a long time since Sarah had enjoyed the pleasure and warmth of close physical contact, and David's arrival a couple of days ago had unleashed long-suppressed feelings in her. The linking of her arm through David's brought the joy of physical intimacy flooding back into her mind. She had consciously turned off her body when she was alone in Prague and feeling terrible guilt after the relationship with Laco fizzled out and her powerful attraction to Josh was put on hold. Now, with David here beside her, all those emotions welled to the fore again. She wanted to ask David whether he had been intimate with anybody but it would be inappropriate and unwise, especially after his escape clause stipulated during their lunch at the Topkapi. Anyway, she knew the answer. David wasn't interested in casual relationships, he believed in the bonds forged by a long and passionate romance, the type of romance they had enjoyed together in New York.

David put his arm around her shoulder, hugging her close to him. 'You know,' he said, whispering into her ear, 'I've spent so many nights remembering your body. It's been one of the joys of my life. When I'm alone at night in our apartment I close my eyes and I visualise your breasts, your waist, your legs, your eyes and your lips, even your toes and fingers. Remember when I used to clip your toenails in the bath? Remember . . .'

Sarah held up her hand to stop him. She pulled his body towards her, holding him close. 'David, you're making me regret my decision to stay in Prague instead of coming back to the States.'

'It's not what I wanted to do,' he interrupted. 'I just wanted to tell you what a terrific memory I've got. Now I'm holding you my hands remember every curve of your body, every beautiful line I used to love so much. Which I still love.'

Suddenly four men surrounded them, aggressively waving plastic-coated menus at them and shouting at them to enter their fish restaurants.

'Best fish. Come please.'

'We have good menu. Fresh fish.'

'Where you from? You English? American? Visit my inside, please.'

'I am proprietor. I give you special price.'

Sarah whispered to David, 'How do they know we're tourists?'

'You don't think we stand out like sore thumbs? It's our clothes, they're different, expensive. All we need are cameras around our necks to make the picture complete.'

Despite the entreaties they chose a small, slightly out-of-the-way restaurant and delighted in the freshness of the mezze entrees and then the astonishingly rich, bursting flavour of the fish. The proprietor, who fawned upon them like an acolyte before a priest, explained, 'I pick this fish up myself two hours ago. Is no finer fresher fish in Kumkapi.'

They drank *raki* and wine and ordered more food and then more alcohol. As the night wore on wandering musicians came into the restaurant and played a song Sarah hadn't heard since her childhood. It was 'Mustafa', a tune more closely associated with Egypt than Turkey. She found herself singing, 'Cherie, je t'aime. Cherie, je t'adore . . .', much to David's amusement and the approval of the other diners. As the evening wore on, they grew headier with the alcohol and were swept up in the musicians' warm exuberance. Men and women wandered the streets outside the café window, shouting, laughing and talking in the warm aromatic atmosphere. It was wonderful, just what Sarah needed to unwind and make the year she'd spent away from David vanish like a guilty secret.

It was David who finally looked at his watch and said, 'We have to get up early in the morning to catch our flight.' Sarah nodded. The café owner took them back to Sultanahmet in his own car. David was surprised at his generosity and wondered about his motive, but after nearly two weeks' experience of Turkey Sarah assured him that it was normal practice. It was a way of ensuring that when they returned to Kumkapi they would go back to his restaurant.

In the elevator up to their room, Sarah's mind flashed back to the first time she and David had met in New York. It had been at a party. She was holding forth, talking about the law; he had been standing in the circle around her, listening to her views. The others had nodded but David had merely smiled. Sarah thought he was being patronising and asked him later why he found her views so amusing. David had replied that he wondered how vehement she would be about the law under different circumstances, say if she were sitting in the splendour of a Baroque salon listening to Vivaldi conducting one of his concerts. David explained that while he obviously recognised the importance of law, only music was capable of transporting him into realms of passion similar to those Sarah had shown when talking about law. He told her that when he was playing music he was transported to a realm where the rule of law had no meaning, where people were kinder, where those listening were uplifted by the beauty of the music into a different strata of morality, even if only for an hour or so. Sarah had accepted his challenge and he'd taken her the following night to a Bach recital. He spent time beforehand advising her what she should be listening for and Sarah opened both her mind and her heart and heard things in the familiar piece that she had never heard before, that she'd never even contemplated.

Two weeks later they had moved in together. Their relationship was the most satisfying time Sarah had ever known. She still believed passionately in the rule of law but now, unlike many of her colleagues, she recognised that there were other important things in life. Since she left David a year before to work for Josh Krantz, Sarah had had a brief and passionate affair with the Slovakian archaeologist, Laco Plastov, and had developed strong feelings for Josh himself. But the depth of her love, she had realised, was only for David. She hoped, as they entered her room, that she would continue to be worthy of him.

The landing strip in Kayseri was a kilometre of tarmac with small private planes on one side and military transporters on the other. The flight from Istabul took nearly an hour over a landscape which appeared deserted, as though Turkish life removed from its capital cities was devoid of towns, villages and civilisation, seemingly unaffected by the hand of human intervention. The air strip and the tin shed which served as an arrival hall looked completely misplaced in the emptiness, a scar on an otherwise perfect body.

Sarah and David descended from the plane along with the other passengers and filed past groups of profoundly disinterested machine-gun-toting soldiers, talking laconically amongst themselves, grudgingly there to protect what little the army considered important. They were young men, little more than boys wearing soldiers' uniforms. Sarah and David waited in the blistering mid-morning heat for their bags to be thrown from the belly of the aircraft onto trolleys which were hauled by tractors to the side of the arrivals shed for identification. When they had retrieved their luggage, they saw a toothless wizened old man, his head shaved and nut brown from the sun, holding a placard on which was scrawled, 'Kiplen'.

Sarah walked over to him. 'I'm Sarah Kaplan. Are you here for me?'

The old man grinned. He had no teeth and reeked of body odour. He collected their cases and put them into the back of his Toyota then motioned them into the back seat. There were no other passengers.

The countryside seemed more like a lunar than an earthly landscape. They left the town of Kayseri with its half a dozen mosques, countless featureless huts and houses, and long main street, dusty shops and a gaudy travel agency, and ended up on a country road bordered by fields of crops wilting in the heat of the sun. This was no prairie land of middle America, nor a breadbasket of European fields; here the sun made even the hardiest crops thirst for water.

Sarah's experiences of Turkey so far – Istanbul, Ankara and Troy – had given her a false impression of what the rest of the vast country was like. She had expected it to follow the same colourful pattern, but one look out the window was dramatic proof of her misconceptions. Even travelling at speed, both Sarah and David recognised what they could only call a biblical landscape. The herds of goats, the impoverished shanty dwellings and huts which littered the hills, the squalid villages their Toyota roared through, the bemused semi-naked children, were a stark contrast to the fabulously gaudy wealth of the palaces of Istanbul where pampered Sultans had demanded the obeisance of sycophantic underlings. Here was real poverty, a depth of penury which angered David and made Sarah wonder if men like Dr Yussef Barrak and his Minister had any real idea of the struggles of their countrymen to survive.

But their growing fascination with the countryside gradually overcame their anger. It was as though the lessons they had learnt in Sunday school were being enacted before their eyes. Neither would have been surprised to see a biblical patriarch wandering along the road, crook in hand, leading goats to a well. For mile after mile they passed through tiny villages where adults and children lived similar lives to those of their ancestors stretching back across the centuries. The villages sprawled over the bare hills, baked in sunshine. Each contained as its epicentre a number of mosques, their minarets pointing angrily to the sky. Sarah shivered at the constant reminder of her alienation from this Islam-based society.

Just as suddenly as their world had changed from bustling Istanbul to the rural emptiness of village life, so again the landscape altered. The last village disappeared and the road cut through an isolated mountain range. Sarah felt as if they were leaving the real world behind them, as though there were a clear dividing line between the rest of the world and the phenomenon known as Cappadocia.

Sarah recognised the name from her knowledge of early Christianity, but beyond that she knew it only as a tourist destination. The few conversations she'd had in cafés in Turkey had been with American or other tourists. They had told her that she simply had to visit Cappadocia and the cotton castle of Pamukkale. Whenever she'd asked why Cappadocia was so spectacular all she'd got were knowing grins and the advice: 'Go and see for yourself. You can't put into words what you'll see there.' This alone made Sarah curious; she had never had problems putting her thoughts into words. But nothing, not the pictures in the brochures nor the knowing silence of the tourists, could have prepared her for the experience of Cappadocia.

The Toyota struggled to the top of the mountain range, rounding the last hairpin bend to pull into a parking area. Their guide invited them to step out of the car and view the panorama set out before them. Sarah and David complied, walking over to the edge of the precipice which looked out over the valley floor below. Now they saw what made this area one of the wonders of the geological world. It was true, Sarah thought, words simply couldn't define what they saw. It was beyond beauty, beyond mysticism, beyond the phatic nonsense of tourist brochures.

Stretching for miles into the misty distance were the most extraordinary geological structures Sarah had ever seen, thousands of tall thin chimneys of rock dotting the valley floor in a pattern of military precision. They looked like gigantic mushroom stalks with their caps trimmed. Or, as David whispered into her ear, 'I'm sure that you know what they remind me of, but I'm too much of a gentleman to say it.' Sarah dug him in the ribs.

Their driver grinned toothlessly and pointed to his crotch, mumbling a Turkish word, the meaning of which wasn't difficult to guess.

'How?' Sarah asked simply. 'How were structures like this ever formed? What caused them?' It was a rhetorical question born of wonderment. She knew the answers. She had read the guidebooks. The giant structures, the fairy chimneys, were the remnants of an eroded landscape. Once, thousands of years earlier, the valley had been filled with lava from volcanic explosions. Over the millennia erosion had worn away most of the tufa, but faults had left standing these tall structures which had caused the eternal rainwater and melting snows to fail in their mission.

David was equally muted by the scene. They stared in silence as the hot wind from the valley floor rose up towards them. A thought occurred to him. 'While you were in Prague, I went to Ivan's fortieth birthday party in Greenwich Village,' he said.

'Ivan?' Sarah asked. She was puzzled by the sudden switch.

'You met him once. He's an ophthalmic surgeon. He operated on my dad's eyes. Anyway, halfway through the night his wife wheeled in one of those theme birthday cakes. This one was designed specially for him; it was huge, shaped in the form of an eye. As his wife was placing it on the dining room table someone from the back of the room shouted out, "Thank God you didn't become a gynaeocologist, Ivan".'

Sarah burst out laughing.

'My point is, if there's a whole valley full of these penis structures then somewhere there's got to be a female equivalent. And wouldn't that be a dangerous place to walk!'

The driver, his body odour warning them of his presence before his actual arrival, came up behind them and pointed to a settlement far in the distance. 'Urgup,' he said. His stench was so overwhelming that Sarah had to move forward to put some distance between them. The driver thought she was stepping forward for a better view. 'Goreme,' he continued, stepping closer and pointing to a collection of houses even further away.

He ushered them back to the Toyota and drove them along more precarious roads and around hairpin bends down the escarpment onto the single road which bisected the town of Urgup. The hotel they had been booked into was billed as five star by the travel agent who had also booked a tour for them. But Sarah felt despondent the moment she entered. It would have been rejected even by the cheapest American chains. Its outward appearance, including the ornate marble reception area, was geared more towards effect than function and may very well have impressed the unsophisticated Turks, but both Sarah and David were experienced travellers and reserved judgement on the luxury levels until they reached their room. The sparse double bed, broken furniture and leaking bathroom plumbing were what they had anticipated.

'Let's book in somewhere else,' said David. 'There must be something better than this.'

But Sarah shook her head. 'We're only going to be here for a couple of days and, let's face it, this is as good as it gets in Turkey. Once you get outside the big cities the hotels are crap.'

'How do you know?' he asked.

'Trust me. You talk to tourists long enough you get to know the country without having to have first-hand experience. With no-one to talk to at night I've been doing the rounds of cafés. It's amazing what you pick up.'

That afternoon, after a desultory lunch of stodgy mass-produced food in the cafeteria, they took a tour of the district. Their mood of keen anticipation suddenly plummeted when the same smelly toothless driver pulled up in front of the hotel and ushered them into his car.

A few kilometres out of town the driver turned off the main road, stopped the car and encouraged his passengers to get out and walk.

Sarah and David looked up in amazement at the monolithic chimneys towering above their heads. Some were only a few feet taller than they were, others were fifty feet or more tall. They moved away from the main road, deeper and deeper into the rocky forest, wandering between the amazing structures.

Gradually Sarah's mood began to change. As she moved deeper and deeper into the woodless forest she realised that her head was reeling and she felt shaky, ungrounded. She remembered feeling this way once before, when her mother told her that her aunt had died. Sarah had been on that peculiar cusp between childhood and adolescence, a time when nothing bad ever happened, when death was something she read about in books. Suddenly she had to cope with an altogether new reality. She had gone to her room crying, knowing that she would never see her favourite aunt again. But in the middle of her grief she realised that she had moved beyond crying for her aunt and was now crying for her lost innocence, for the fact that she had suddenly grown up.

Those same feelings came flooding back now as she walked between the massive fairy chimneys. She felt strange, as though she had somehow been taken out of herself. She shuddered in the brilliance of the sun and put her hand up to the amulet around her neck. Sarah had been told that her great-grandfather made the amulet before he was killed in a pogrom in eastern Europe in 1903. But when she had travelled to Europe to represent Joshua Krantz, her archaeologist lover had proved to her that the amulet was not one hundred years old but nearly four thousand years old and had been made by a Bronze Age craftsman. Laco told her that her great-grandfather might have dug the amulet up from a Bronze Age site in Slovakia, but the markings on the amulet – a bull on the front and an owl on the reverse – almost certainly indicated that the original owner had some connection with, or had even possibly travelled to, the Anatolian city of Troy in the days of the Hittites. Despite Laco's pleas that the amulet was essential to his museum to help gain a better understanding of the links between ancient central Europe and the Hittite kingdom of Anatolia, Sarah had steadfastly refused to give up her treasure to him.

Now, as she wandered among the fairy chimneys, Sarah tried to envisage the Bronze Age man or woman who had travelled the long and perilous road across the Carpathian Mountains, where her great-grandfather had found the amulet, through Anatolia to the city of Troy. Today the journey took only a couple of hours by plane. How long had it taken back then? What dangers had the traveller on the way? How had people communicated with each other? How had they carried food? What weapons or strategies did they have to protect themselves from danger? How did they escape parties of hunters who wouldn't appreciate strangers coming into their area? Or would they? Perhaps Bronze Age society, fifteen hundred years before the birth of Christ, was much warmer and friendlier than society today. In those days there were no borders or passports or barriers. Life was much simpler. She got carried away by her imagination, taken into another world far from David and their guide.

David was sensitive to Sarah's introspection, but was concerned at how deep it seemed to be taking her. 'What's happening?' he asked softly.

'What do you mean?' Sarah didn't want to be disturbed.

'Something's happening to you, like you're not here. You're miles away.'

'Don't you feel it?' she asked. 'It's awesome. The geological structures are unbelievable in themselves, but don't you feel something else?'

David looked around and thought for a moment. 'Like what, Sarah?'

'A presence. A connection. As if we've been here before.'

'Sarah,' he said gently, 'déjà vu is a fairly well-understood phenomenon. It's a powerful feeling but it has a relationship to information which the brain receives . . .'

'David, don't give me the scientific crap. I know what I feel. I feel some ancient recognition of this place.'

'Maybe your ancestors came from Turkey. Your family history in Eastern Europe doesn't go back much beyond this century. Who knows how they got there. Let's face it Sarah, if you go back more than three or four generations so much becomes speculative. Very few families know where their ancestors came from.'

'Is it possible that my ancestors came from here? You've read the guidebooks. There's no Jewish connection here.'

'No,' said David, 'but there's a Christian connection. A strong link to the time of the Bible. Ephesus isn't all that far away and it was a fantastically busy port city, one of the hubs of the ancient world. Jews would have been all over there. Traders, merchants, religious leaders – they could have travelled here. Some could have converted to

Christianity. That's how Saint Paul got the first congregations, from the Jewish community.'

Sarah nodded. 'And you don't feel anything at all?' she asked.

'I feel no sense of . . .' he searched for the word, 'proprietorship, no sense of previous history. Nothing personal. I'm overcome by the chimneys, by the wonder of the geography, but I see it as a tourist. I'm sorry if you're disappointed, Sarah.'

She smiled and put her arms around his waist. 'Am I being silly?' she asked.

'You're being yourself. You're being normal and natural. You feel a link, whether it's true or not doesn't matter. The feeling is there.'

'And you've never felt anything similar?' she asked.

He thought for a moment, stroking her hair and kissed her on the forehead. 'Yeah,' he said reflectively. 'Yes, a few times. Usually when I'm playing eighteenth-century music. Sometimes, when I'm in a small ensemble and I'm playing to a small audience, I lose myself and imagine I'm part of an orchestra in Beethoven and Bach's time. And I imagine that I'm not holding my cello but a beautiful woman and the whole process of playing becomes organic. It's a huge, powerful, overwhelming feeling. And I know it's happening because there's a different vibrancy to my music, a different passion and intensity. Then I catapult back into the twentieth century and snap out of it. Does that compare in any way with your feelings?'

'A bit,' she said, ' but it's much more . . .' She wanted to say 'magical' but felt that David might laugh, so left her sentence unfinished, hanging in the air between them.

They returned to the car. David was keen to talk, but instinct and an intimate knowledge of Sarah which not even a year of separation had blunted, told him to remain quiet. Their driver took them to several more valleys populated with only the beautiful, silent, awe-inspiring fairy chimneys, and throughout Sarah maintained her introspective silence.

It was at their next destination, the sites of early Christendom, that Sarah's feelings threatened to overwhelm her. From time immemorial the men and women who had inhabited this area had carved out their homes and places of worship from the very rock itself. Entire mountainsides were honeycombed with man-made caves, dwelling places and churches – an entire town built inside a cliff. As far as the eye could see, stretching along the entire length of the valley, thousands, perhaps hundreds of thousands of people had carved their homes and had lived the simple worshipful life of the early Christian church. The caves were adorned with frescoes and paintings depicting scenes from the Christian faith.

David, too, was moved by the history of the place and its simplicity which stood in stark contrast to the grand edifices to religion in the western world. He could almost feel the people who had lived here; their presence was everywhere, still living in the caves they'd hollowed out from the soft tufa, the paths their countless feet had worn into the rock, the drawings inside their homes. He was quietly examining his own feelings, when he noticed that Sarah had become even more contemplative than she had been among the fairy chimneys. She wandered away from the guide and up to the higher caves, scrambling up an ancient and eroded path and David realised that she was experiencing something beyond her everyday existence, some sort of personal insight. Her movements had become trancelike, reminding him of how he sometimes felt before a performance.

Recognising the importance of the moment to Sarah, David told the guide to wait below. Then he climbed the path to join her.

He found her in a cave, sitting at a rock table which was probably thousands of years old. He wanted to ask her to explain her feelings, but was reluctant to interrupt her rapturous state.

Sarah was fascinated by the wall drawings, childlike yet passionate. She felt as though she were seeing again something familiar from some ancient mystical past.

'It's all so hauntingly beautiful,' she said quietly. 'You know, I've visited lots of ancient buildings and monuments and I've read up on their history and it's been interesting but in the end the stories are removed from my experience, they have no direct relevance. The Romans, the Greeks, the ancient Hebrews, the Saracens – they're just people from another age, people from a history which isn't mine. But this . . .' she gestured around the cave, 'I recognise the people who lived here. People like you and me. They had children, hopes and emotions, they had to hunt their food and rug up against the fierce winter winds. They were real flesh and blood.'

David nodded.

'I told you about Laco Plastov, the archaeologist in Slovakia, the man I became very friendly with. Well, he had a theory which I found fascinating at the time but never got the chance to explore further. He believed that it was the people of the Bronze Age – the age before the discovery of iron – who were the mythmakers, the creators of the great stories of life, death, renewal and hope which we've carried down to our culture today. Laco thinks that when man discovered iron and went on the great migrations a thousand years before the birth of Christ, he not only destroyed the Bronze Age but in the process also put an end to his childhood, his innocence.'

Sarah took out her amulet and held it towards David. 'The people who were here, David, the people who inhabited this whole plateau of Anatolia were the

Hittites. They were a Bronze Age people, the people who created some of the great myths, stories of the spirit, to explain the inexplicable which we accept today as part of our own cultural mythology.'

David smiled and kissed her on the cheek. Sarah smiled back at him. They stared at each other for a moment then left the cave to return to the guide.

'David, what's happening to me?' Sarah asked. 'I've travelled all over the world. I'm used to different things, different cultures. But this place. It's . . . I can't adequately describe it. It's a feeling, an emotion, in part a fear, in part alienation. It was what I was talking to you about the first day you arrived when you told me not to be so silly. I feel strange here, unusual things are happening to me. I love Istanbul but there are parts of it which frighten me. The mosques and minarets, the ancient markets. I feel completely disassociated from the real culture here. I thought I could come here as a tourist and lap up the differences, snap off a hundred photographs, gasp at the Blue Mosque and the Topkapi Palace and Hagia Sofia then leave, having accommodated the differences and expanded my experience. But it's not happening that way. Instead I feel overwhelmed by Islam, threatened by it. I feel as if I'm an alien here.'

'That's a very strong word to use.'

'I don't know what else to say.'

'Is it just that things are different? That you're out of Europe, away from the security of the west?'

'I think it's more than that,' she said quietly.

'What?'

'I feel the pain of my people here.'

'But they weren't your people, Sarah. It was the Christians not the Jews who suffered in these caves.'

'I know that, David and that's what I don't understand. Maybe I just feel the suffering of humanity here. Maybe

I'm wearing everybody's problems on my shoulders. I don't know. If I did I would feel a hell of a lot happier. All I can tell you is that I feel as though I've been here before. And that . . .'

'What?'

'You'll laugh. It doesn't matter.'

'Tell me.'

'I feel that there's danger here. A danger to me personally.'

'Sarah!'

'I told you you'd laugh.'

'I'm not laughing. I think what's happening is that you're overwhelmed by something which is strange and disturbing. This place has struck a chord within you, maybe opened up some part of your memory that you don't want to revisit. But honey, I really think you're going a bit overboard. There's no menace here. You're a representative of the Turkish government and you have the whole of the power structure of America behind you, for God's sake. More than that, I'm here to look after you.'

'Mm. Just put it down to me being dumb.'

'No,' David said, putting his arm around her and walking her out of the cave towards their guide, 'you're not dumb, Sarah. You're just a bit more sensitive than the rest of us.'

CHAPTER 12

Feyodor Mikailovich Meconski sat back in his ancient armchair, deeply satisfied. Gently he increased the pressure against the rusty springs. The chair grudgingly fell backwards into a horizontal position and Meconski looked up towards the ceiling and sighed. The springs creaked in agony as they bore the full weight of his body. He put his feet up on the desk. For over a year he had requisitioned for another chair, one befitting his status as deputy director of the Pushkin Museum. But nothing had come up from stores. Bureaucracy was rampant even in the Pushkin. But he didn't care anymore. There was a self-satisfied smile on his face as his head rested on the back of the chair and he stared at the ceiling. One wall of his office was filled with books, papers, archaeological exhibits, trophies and photographs of him shaking hands with visiting archaeologists or dignitaries. On the other side was a phalanx of display cabinets whose glass shelves and doors were as filthy as the glass in his office windows. Piled on top of the cabinets were books which he had appropriated from the director's office in her absence.

But none of this mattered now. Not this morning. Not in the wondrous mood he was in. His job, his endangered career, his torturous relationship with his wife, all were trivialities compared to the joy which still surged around his body. He had spent the best part of the night in bed with Natalie, only leaving her when she forced him out after midnight and told him he had to go home to his wife. She was a wonder to behold. Perfumed, veiled in the most sensuous of silk lingerie, hot and warm and willing. And she knew just when to withdraw her special favours in order to prolong his joy. A subtle application of cold towels to mop his brow and sweating body, an invitation to leave the bedroom and join her in the dining room for chilled champagne and caviar on ice. And then returning to restoke his fires, to rekindle his lusts until he finally climaxed in a volcanic eruption, a crescendo the like of which he had never experienced before.

Natalie was the perfect partner for him – loving, generous and uncomplicated. Of course he knew she was a sop given to him by Lomonosov to keep him in line, the bait Lomonosov let dangle in the pool of his avarice. Feyodor knew he was being used, but it didn't make any difference. He still snapped her up, ingested her, swallowed her whole and loved every delicious mouthful. Yes, he was being a fool. He knew that one day he would have to face a firing squad for what he had done. There was no getting away from it. Eventually the truth would come out, the audit would be done, the accusing finger pointed. Whatever means of escape he conjured up simply wouldn't work. He was spending all the money he was making from the sale of the Schliemann treasure, but even if he saved it all into a nest egg for his escape, the security services would find him no matter where in the world he went. And when they found him they would kill him.

Even if he turned State's evidence and informed against his Mafia boss, he would still be professionally ruined. And his life would still be at risk; the Mafia would ensure that he didn't live longer than forty-eight hours after the trial. He thought about running away with Natalie, changing his identity and becoming an American citizen. But she would never go with him. Why should she spend the rest of her life as a Russian truck driver's wife in America?

There was always suicide, but that would be the end of everything. He couldn't voluntarily give up the chance to enjoy Natalie as long as she was on offer. He put his hands behind his head and stared at the cobwebs in the corners of the room. He was in love. There was no question about it. There was of course something of a question about whether Natalie was in love with him. He hadn't lost all his ability to reason. She was a young, incredibly beautiful, hungry young woman. He was so far below what she could expect of life that he quickly dismissed any thoughts of his love being reciprocated. But that didn't negate his love. And God, did he love her! He could think of nobody but Natalie. His wife, suddenly attracted by his recovered virility, had approached him one night, to his surprise. He had been drunk and asleep, snoring loudly, but she had shaken him awake and asked him to make love to her. And he had, boldly, manfully, as he hadn't made love to her in years. She should have been pleased. Instead she knew he'd been fantasising about another woman. He hadn't been that hard for that long since she was a girl. The next morning she treated him with utter disdain.

Feyodor jumped as the phone rang. Like a guilty schoolboy he took his feet off the desk and the chair sprang back angrily to correct itself. He snatched the phone off the cradle. He had instructed his secretary not to put through any calls as he was compiling a report for the Moscow Institute of Sciences asking for additional funding for the Museum.

'Yes?' he barked.

'Meconski?' A man's voice, deep, authoritative.

'Yes,' said Feyodor, curious now.

'It's Vardian.'

'Who?' The name registered somewhere deep in his mind.

'Mikhail Gregorovich Vardian. The Federal Minister for Antiquities. You may recall my name,' he said, his voice oozing sarcasm.

'Yes, Minister. Forgive me, Minister, I'm in the middle of writing a report about . . .'

Cutting across his babble, Vardian said, 'Get over to the Kremlin immediately. There's something I have to show you.'

'But . . .'

'When is the director back? Is she still sick?'

'Yes, sir. That's why I'm in the middle of . . .'

'Drop everything and come here. I've made room in my schedule to see you in an hour.'

The phone clicked in his ear. Feyodor replaced the receiver cautiously as though it was a deadly weapon. He had met Vardian six or seven times in the last two years but always as an underling. Suddenly the Minister himself had phoned. God Almighty, had somebody done a secret audit? Was he going to be exposed? Was this the day of reckoning? He stood on shaking legs, his whole world suddenly in a state of collapse. All his bravado about enjoying his time with Natalie before his ultimate descent into hell evaporated as he realised this was the beginning of the descent.

The journey to the Kremlin was terrible. Feyodor felt like a convicted man being taken to face the firing squad. His mind raced as the car drew nearer its destination. The only avenue of escape left to him was suicide. He would have to take his wife with him. He became distracted by a fantasy of the look on her face as he pulled out a gun and shot her through the head. But the closer he got to the Kremlin the more desperate he became to save his own skin. He conceived of a better plan: he could leave a note blaming everything on his wife and let her face a lifetime in Siberia. Yes! That would be the ideal solution, leaving him free to continue his relationship with Natalie.

By the time his car transported him through the main gate, Feyodor had a desperate need to go to the toilet. He quickly relieved himself in one of the cheerless disinfected latrines in the damnable rabbit warren of corridors that comprised the Kremlin. But he needed to go again as he waited on an uncomfortable chair outside the Minister's office, suffering the severe gaze of a sixty-year-old grey-haired harridan of a secretary who told him that the Minister was dealing with 'an important matter'. As if his matter wasn't important! Didn't the old fool realise it was a matter of life and death? His life. His death.

The light above the Minister's door changed from red to green. The secretary raised her eyebrows and Feyodor stood on uneasy legs and walked in. The Minister's office was larger than he had imagined. Never had he been in such an august place. It was like something out of Tolstoy, ornate, heavy, imposing.

The Minister continued to sign letters. Without deigning to look at Feyodor, he said, 'Sit down, Meconski.' He continued to write for another few minutes then put his pen down and rang a bell beneath his desk. A secretary responded immediately, collecting the letters and soundlessly leaving the room again. Vardian waited until she had closed the door behind her before he began to speak. Feyodor's heart was thumping so badly, he thought he would faint right there on the floor.

'It's the Turks,' said the Minister.

Feyodor leaned forward and strained to understand. It didn't make sense. He had been preparing himself for a series of allegations and threats. What was he talking about? Turks?

'I'm sorry, Minister?' Feyodor said in a high-pitched voice.

'The Turks are making demands. It's not just the Germans now, not just the Greeks, now it's the fucking Turks as well. Soon it will be the Americans, then the fucking Jews. It's got to stop. These are our treasures!' he shouted. 'Zhukov brought them back here for us, they are the spoils of war. We can make millions out of the treasure every year just by showing it around. But the fucking Turks are about to inform us that they're going to make a claim for ownership. Somebody spilled the beans to our embassy in Ankara. How likely is it that their claim will succeed in a court of law?'

'I . . . I . . .' To his horror Feyodor burst out laughing. Relief coursed through his veins and life took on an entirely new perspective.

'What the hell is so funny?' demanded the Minister.

The deputy director shook his head, biting the inner part of his cheek to stop his hysterics. 'Nothing, sir. I apologise. I've been under a massive strain ever since this whole matter with the Germans began. This is just another example of the injustices perpetrated against the peace-loving peoples of the mother country by those antidemocratic forces which . . .'

'Shut up, idiot! This isn't the Soviet Union anymore and I'm not Brezhnev. Don't you understand, fool? Now we're not just fighting the fucking Krauts; the fucking Turks also want our treasure back. Our people in Ankara tell us that some smart bitch American lawyer, some expert on international property rights, has advised them that Schliemann's contract with the Ottoman government is null and void because he lied. She's arguing that Germany has no rightful claim on the treasure which means that neither do we. And Turkey is demanding it back. Now, what's the situation? We've put some of the treasure on exhibition, but if we have to give back the Trojan stuff then Germany will make claims on all the other treasures Zhukov and everyone else took from the fucking Krauts at the end of the Great Patriotic War. It will denude the Pushkin and the Hermitage and every other fucking museum in Russia. And the compensation bill will bankrupt us.

'I want a full account of what's what. I want you to build a case from an archaeological point of view saying that the treasure is ours. Cite the Elgin Marbles in the British Museum as precedent. Say that it wasn't Turks or Hittites who made the treasure but Russians. Say it's Cossak or Siberian. Say anything. We have to stop this claim from the Turks before it runs too far. It's not just a case of fighting the Germans for the third time this century, now we've got another serious legal battle on our hands. Tell me, do you have any archaeological contacts in Turkey who can find out what's behind all this and advise us what to do to make it go away? Bribery built the Ottoman Empire. See if any of your archaeology friends can tell you whose pocket needs filling.'

The Minister dismissed him with a flick of the hand. Feyodor walked out into the sunlight of a Moscow day. He hadn't noticed before, but the trees in the Kremlin courtyard were in bud.

His euphoria faded that night as he sat in the noisy smoky nightclub explaining to Lomonosov how the Turkish demand would affect the decision taken at their last meeting. Lomonosov had organised the termination of the entire German team dedicated to getting Helen of Troy's treasure back to Berlin. Now Feyodor could get the Germans a reprieve and direct Lomonosov to concentrate his efforts on bribing someone in Istanbul. But the Mafia don had reacted with disinterest to the wonderful news that the mass killing was now unnecessary. Feyodor's joy changed to the depths of despair when he realised that the German archaeologists could not be saved.

'You don't understand, do you?' he repeated. 'We don't need to kill the German archaeologists anymore, they're no longer the real threat. This American lawyer in Istanbul is the problem, her and the Turkish government. We have to do something about them. We can leave the Germans alone.'

Lomonosov looked at his watch and regretfully shook his head.

Feyodor's wife looked at him across the dinner table. Even she was concerned at the state he was in and she had ignored him for the last few months. His face was white, bloodless, as though he had just been told of a death in the family. She asked him several times what was wrong but each time he snapped, 'Nothing. Leave me alone.'

She was planning to do just that, hopefully forever. One day soon he would come home from work, barking for food and drink, and the apartment would be cold and empty. Serve the bastard right.

But Feyodor's thoughts were miles away from Moscow and his wife. One thousand miles away, to be precise. He kept glancing at his watch even though he had no idea when the massacre would take place. Lomonosov had convinced him that the mass destruction of the Berlin archaeologists was absolutely essential. There was no way around it. It would be staged as an accident, or a terrorist attack by the neo-Nazis. Feyodor had begged and pleaded but to no avail. Lomonosov could not understand why he should be concerned at the taking of so many lives. Do you know how many Russians the Germans killed in the last war? he questioned. Do you know how many of our countrymen were tortured in concentration camps, starved to death? Why would you have any feelings for Germans?

In the end, all pleading for humanitarian compassion had been useless. The Mafia don was more concerned about protecting his own empire than he was about human life and, to his eternal shame, Feyodor had given in to Lomonosov's point of view. He had gone home meekly and tried to close his mind to the horror that the archaeological museum in Berlin would soon become but his fears came to the surface in his nightmares. Each night visions of twisted bodies, blood flowing down gutters, men and women trapped under wooden beams and massive masonry blocks, screaming as life was extinguished from their bodies woke him in a cold sweat. He *had* to stop the horror, even if it meant his own destruction. How could he trade mass murder for the pleasures he enjoyed with Natalie and protection of his own criminal activities? Yes! He would put a stop to it. Tomorrow. Or the day after.

Berlin Archaeological Museum

It was a Wednesday morning, unseasonably cold for the middle of summer. A rain squall and the frozen wind that blew in high over the city from the Urals made the temperature drop from the previous day's twenty-eight degrees to twelve. People who had been sunbaking on the beaches of Berlin's Grunewald, Wannsee and Muggelsee lakes now dragged out their winter woollies again.

The curator of the Museum shivered in his office while maintenance staff urgently tried to refire the boilers deep in the basement and get some heat up into the radiators. Nobody had expected such a cold day in the middle of summer.

The meeting had been scheduled for ten o'clock. It wasn't a particularly important meeting nor was there anything private about it, which is why the curator's secretary had been quite happy to tell the journalist who telephoned that her boss would be tied up in conference with his archaeological team in the east wing of the building on the second floor for most of the morning. Yes, she explained to the journalist, the whole team would be there. She made an appointment for the journalist to see the curator at four o'clock the same day to discuss Germany's involvement with archaeology in Iraq now that Saddam Hussein was no longer president.

She forgot the conversation as soon as she had recorded the appointment in the curator's schedule and turned her attention to collating the material required for the meeting. She made ten copies for all the Museum staff who would be present. The office was icy. She took a cardigan from the cupboard and took the notes down to the conference room, two floors below. The corridors were even colder than her room. One day she and her husband would sell up everything and move to a warmer climate. South America perhaps, or Australia, or even Florida. She had heard Florida welcomed German migrants.

She turned on the conference room light and distributed the papers around the seats. She checked that the carafes of water were full, that there were enough glasses, that the slide projector was working and that the laser pointer which the curator particularly enjoyed using – a present from the staff to celebrate his ten years in the position – was fully operative. She walked to the radiator; it was still cold. When would those idiots in the basement get the boiler working properly?

There were four people working down there. The problem was that the oil supply had been allowed to run down over the summer months and now there was insufficient to heat the boilers for the three or four days the weather bureau estimated the sudden cold weather would last. It was all very well to just turn on the machinery and let it run, but turning it off wasn't that simple. If the machinery stopped too rapidly the contraction could cause the metal joints to fracture – and all hell would break loose. Steam gushing out of pipes, water dripping out of fractured joints and damaging exhibits!

So far the maintenance workers had received seven irate phone calls from freezing people at the top of the building. At first, they had explained politely; now they were rude and caustic. Two engineers were checking the dials and ensuring that flow patterns were working properly. Two others were working against the clock to ensure that the pumps would supply a steady flow of oil to the burners. They had been working since six-thirty that morning and the only thanks they got was abuse. They were so busy that they didn't notice the seven young men slowly filing into the antechamber of the boiler rooms at ten o'clock. The first anybody knew about intruders was when a black spectral shape loomed out of nowhere and pulled out a metal cosh. It crashed with a dull thud on the head of one of the engineers. He grunted and fell to the floor, his skull fractured. The sound of his fall made the three other engineers look around in shock. Nobody registered immediately what was happening, only that Gunther was lying spreadeagled on the ground and a man in black was standing over him. Then, suddenly, they understood all too clearly.

Only one of the remaining three engineers managed to shout a warning as the seven men attacked them in a mob, cracking skulls, windpipes or spines with their metal weapons. It was quieter this way, and besides they had been instructed to make it appear as though the workers had died in the explosion that was to follow. Satisfied that all the engineers were dead, the team leader posted one man at the door and instructed the others to get on with their assigned tasks. He checked that one of the boilers was still cold then went back into the antechamber and returned with a large suitcase. Getting into the Museum had been a piece of cake. The security guard on the delivery dock had checked the requisition for engineering supplies for the boiler room and allowed the team through. No questions had been asked. It had all been too easy.

Now the team leader unzipped the suitcase and took out an electronic timer connected to thirty kilos of

Semtex. He set the timer to explode in ten minutes and checked the radio frequency attached to the explosive. The second the timer ticked down to zero it would emit a high-pitched frequency which would activate the radio transmitter. The thirty kilos of Semtex would bring down most of this part of the building and blow out the windows in almost all the surrounding streets. It would cause massive panic all around the area; emergency vehicles would be hard-pressed to get to the building. The fire would spread and all traces of their labour in the basement would be burnt beyond forensic recognition. Piece of cake!

He doublechecked everything then picked up the suitcase, now as light as a feather. His team collected their things and changed quickly back into the clothes they had worn when they entered the building. They locked the outer door to prevent anybody accidentally entering the boiler room then left through the service area and delivery dock. A van was waiting there to carry them to their escape truck four streets away. As the van drew to a halt each man looked at his watch.

Heidi Schmidl had been a teacher for only four years when she was given responsibility for taking the thirty boys and girls in Year Six on their excursion to the Museum. She had organised two other teachers to help out with supervision, and the thirty-three of them were heading up to the Egyptology wing when a dull roar filled the air and the entire building began to shake and shudder.

At first Heidi didn't know what was happening. The children realised more quickly and began to scream. Heidi went to shout to the children to fall to the floor but the words never left her mouth. The floor erupted beneath them and the ceiling came crashing down from above, crushing the life out of everything in its path. In an instant the entire Year Six class was killed. Some of the children were holding their friends' hands as they died.

Like a giant house of cards the second and third floors of the Museum collapsed and the ground floor itself blew outwards into the street. Exhibits, glass, marble, columns, masonry and human bodies were carried upwards and outwards on the crests of massive waves of broiling flames, crashing on the hundreds of people milling about outside.

The force of the explosion had projected the three boilers in the basement up through the ground floor, killing the forty-two people who were queuing in the entrance foyer to see the latest exhibition of American Red Indian artefacts. Passers-by were lacerated by the razor-sharp shards of glass that flew from the windows into the street. Traffic swerved in all directions at the shock of the explosion. One car was even thrown onto its roof as the pavement beneath it erupted on a geyser of exploding gas from a burst main. The Museum itself was a tower of flames.

As the noise of the explosion slowly began to recede and the dust, rubble and debris slipped slowly groundwards again, a hideous and unearthly silence fell upon the area. Everything that had been alive minutes before was now annihilated. The only visible evidence of the life which had filled the Museum were the bleeding limbs protruding from the rubble. Priceless exhibits, the eternal record of humankind, was spilled like garbage all over the area.

Then the screaming began. As people realised they were alive so the horror became real. Horrified drivers screeched to a halt before the apocalyptic scene. Suddenly the air was rent with sirens. Sirens everywhere, sirens and bells. And beneath them a constant wail of grief, terror and pain. Police, ambulances, and fire brigades rushed to the scene but all were too late.

An old Berliner, a man in his early eighties, left his coffee and the café to view the destruction from the explosion. He shook his head in horror. 'Again,' he mumbled. The waiter next to him understood immediately what he meant. This was the Berlin of Hitler's last days. The Berlin people thought would never happen again.

CHAPTER 13

Amra was dazed with amazement and awe, her mind a turmoil of incomprehension. She had never seen so much water before. She had thought that the river which ran beside her village was vast, especially when the winter snows melted and swelled its waters, but when she had first espied the Great River, the river that the five rivers of the five valleys ran into, she had thought she was dreaming. In places it was so wide that it was impossible for her to throw a stone from one side to the other. But this! There was no end to this water. The Eternal Sea continued forever; from where she was standing on its shore she could look in the direction of the Sun God's birth and see no land; then in the direction of the Sun God's death and see no land either; and when she looked straight ahead the sea had no limit, it simply fell off the end of the earth.

Of even greater amazement was the way the water didn't run as it ran in other rivers she had seen. This water continuously swept up towards her feet, then back again. Up and back. Up and back. As though the God of the Seas was trying to claw his way out onto the shale and sand of the beach but was constantly pulled back.

'They're waves,' said the fisherman standing beside Amra. He marvelled at her awe.

'Waves?'

'You really have never seen the sea before, have you, child?' asked the old man.

Amra shook her head. He smelt different from the men of her village. He didn't smell of the fields or trees but of salt, of fish. A different sort of salt from that used to enrich the taste of food or to preserve meat and fish over the winter months. The salt of this man's smell, the salt from the sea, had a sweetness to it, a freshness and life.

'And you've never swum in the sea?' he asked.

Amra shook her head. 'Are there fish in the sea?' she asked.

'Many. We throw out nets,' he said, pointing to a bundle of black spider webs piled in the bottom of his boat, 'and we haul the fish caught in them into the boat.'

Amra was too amazed to say anything. She had heard tales from the travellers around the campfire in her village about the Great Eternal Sea, but she never in her life thought she would be privileged to see it. Yet here it was, stretching so far in all directions that it disappeared into the end of the world.

'What happens when you go past there?' she said, pointing to the horizon.

'It continues,' said the man.

'But how can it? It finishes there.' She pointed again to the distant horizon. 'Does the sea pour off when it gets to the end?'

Amra could not understand what happened at the end of the earth. One day she and her friends had run as far as they could across a large flat plain until they disappeared out of sight of those they'd left behind. But the world didn't end. Instead it continued, seemingly forever. Yet their friends said that they had become smaller until they disappeared; and when they looked back, those friends they'd left behind grew smaller and smaller until they disappeared. Where had they gone to? Where was the end of the world? And why didn't the sea pour over its edge?

'Where are you heading, child? And why do you have such a large and valuable horse? Did you steal it?'

Amra looked at the man in surprise. 'I am Amra the hunter. I come from a village many days' journey from here.' She pointed towards the northern horizon. 'I am going to the land of the Hittites.'

'They live beyond the sea,' said the fisherman. 'Over there.'

Amra stared at him in disbelief. Her map was unclear from here. The Headman had accurately traced the path of the river but beyond the range of great mountains his lines had become unsure and indistinct. The markings he had told her were the Eternal Sea looked nothing like what confronted her. 'But how can I cross? I can't swim that far.'

The fisherman laughed. He liked this girl. She would make a good wife for him if only his old wife would die, may the Gods curse her evil temper.

'Travel this way,' he said, pointing along the shoreline of the Eternal Sea in the direction of the Sun God's death, 'and you will come to the junction between the Crossing of the Dardan peoples and the Great Sea of Islands.'

'The Crossing of the Dardan peoples? Who are the Dardans?' Amra asked.

'An old race. This whole area now is part of the land of the Mycenaeans who came across the Sea of Islands in the time when the Gods walked the earth. They say that their God Zeus and Electra his wife had a son called Dardanus who was the forefather of the people who live here in the Troad, and he is the father of the Royal House of Troy. The Crossing of the Dardan peoples is the means of crossing from one land to the other. Otherwise you will have to return and journey all the way around the two great seas, which will take you a whole season, and then you will have to traverse the Land of the Giants. People get eaten alive.'

Amra recoiled in horror. Giants? Royal House of Troy? There was so much she didn't understand.

The old fisherman continued, 'You have to pay to cross the neck of the seaway. It's not a large distance but the water is very rough with fierce currents. A boatman will take you across.'

'How can I pay?' she asked.

'What do you have of value?'

Amra wasn't going to tell him. She didn't want to have to kill him if he tried to take her amulet from her. Anyway she had taken many things from the men who had violated her; she would use these to buy her passage across the sea. 'I have things to trade.'

'Then you should have no trouble.'

'How far is it to the land of the Dardan people?'

'On your horse,' said the fisherman pointing at Wind, 'two days, maybe three. It is an easy journey. Follow the shore of the Eternal Sea until you come to another sea, the Sea of Islands. There you will find the ferryman. Cross over to the opposite bank of this Sea and you will be closer to the land of the Hittites.'

Amra thanked him and walked back to Wind. The fisherman followed her. Amra instinctively reached for her knife.

'Why are you going to the land of the Hittites?' he asked.

'Because I need to find out how to make iron.'

'Where will you go when you get there?'

Amra didn't know.

'The capital is Hattusas. It is a great city but the people who are really skilled live much closer than that. Hattusas is still a long journey. I've never been there but I have been to Troy. Troy is where you should go. There are great palaces of stone in Troy. The people who live there know everything.'

'Troy?' said Amra.

The fisherman nodded. 'It is only a morning's ride from the bank where the ferryman will take you. You will learn what you need to know there.'

Amra thanked him again and jumped quickly on Wind to ride away before he could ask any more questions. It would be easy for her to be friendly to the fisherman but since her experience at the foot of the mountain she had become wary of people in general, men in particular. In the past seven days she had passed many villages, sometimes entering them and telling stories in return for food and shelter, sometimes avoiding them instinctively, knowing that there was something wrong, a reason for her not to be there. Even now, seven days after the evil men had violated her, she had only just stopped bleeding and her strength was returning. A woman's first bleeding should be a time of joy. It was when she was given her own room, when she joined the circle of women. Yet Amra's first bleeding was a time of horror for her. It was the wrong kind of bleeding. It was the bleeding of hate.

On her journey from the foot of the great mountains Amra had seen more and more groups of people tilling the soil, planting crops, burning trees and stubble to prepare the soil for the next planting season, or plucking weeds from the ground. Riding through forests she had seen many parties of hunters, and on the banks of the river, many fishermen. The world seemed to swell with people the closer she journeyed towards the Eternal Sea. And now this old fisherman had told her of another sea, the Sea of Islands. She knew from the traders' stories what an island was – a land in the sea. There were no islands in the Eternal Sea, or none that she could see as she scanned the horizon. Amra was quickly coming to the conclusion that there was much that she didn't know, much that she didn't understand.

The fisherman had told her the journey from the northern shore of the Eternal Sea to the Crossing of the Dardan peoples was an easy ride. Yet there were obstacles all the way. Long before she reached the narrow channel of water which separated the Sea of Islands from the Eternal Sea, Amra had to travel deep inland around two great arms of the sea. From the height of one of the arms, the land stretched out below appeared as the gigantic horn of a bull or a goat. The sun fell from the Heavens towards the sea and the land became first pink then golden, the tops of the distant hills ringed with fire.

Amra made camp on the heights and ate the provisions she had traded in a village for one of the copper pins her father had given her. The food tasted different from her food at home; the spices were sharper, the dried fish was salty, yet sweet, and even the water from one of the rivers, which she had collected in her goatskin during the morning, was softer, more delicious. This truly was a land of plenty.

Two of the traps she'd set further down the mountain before making camp had been sprung by rabbits, giving her enough food for the next three days. Even Wind seemed to be enjoying himself, frolicking in the grass, galloping to and away from where Amra was sitting, and forcing his nose into her panniers to see whether there were any carrots or turnips for him to eat. It was a game he had come to enjoy. Amra would hide his food the moment she made camp then Wind would search for it. Amra would surprise him by taking the carrots from under her dress and feeding them to him one at a time. It was a pleasant part of the day, a time when they were both tired yet excited by what they had seen, and not yet ready to settle down by the fire, eat and fall asleep.

It took Amra another two days to reach the northern shore of the Crossing of the Dardan peoples. The people here were very different to those she had met far back along the shores of the Eternal Sea. Those people had accepted her quite comfortably, but the men here, and to a greater extent the women looked at her as though she was from a different race. When she rode into the village nestled at the foot of the wide hills above the beach many people stopped what they were doing and stared at her. Wind sensed that things were not well. He reacted uncharacteristically by shying and frightening the children running alongside him.

Amra climbed down from her great horse and walked with him into the centre of the main street. It was lined with houses not dissimilar from those of her own village, though these were painted white and glared in the brilliant sun. A woman, then a man came out of the houses to look at her. Amra smiled at them but they didn't smile back. They looked astonished by her. Amra felt herself frowning. She walked further and more people came out from their houses. They began to follow her and Wind. She wanted to stop and ask them why but she sensed a menace about them. Her throat constricted in fear and she instinctively reached up to touch her amulet, then her knife.

When she arrived in what she judged to be the middle of the village a large silent throng greeted her. Had a messenger gone secretly from dwelling to dwelling to tell the inhabitants of her arrival? Amra's fear intensified. But when she looked more closely at the people she realised that what she had taken to be menace was simple curiosity. Suddenly she realised these people looked very different from the people of her own village and all the other villages in the valleys where she lived.

Amra stood holding Wind, staring at the people who silently returned her gaze. A little girl, aged about seven or eight, was the first to step forward and identify the difference. She walked over to stand directly in front of Amra, a look of intense curiosity on her face, as though a God had descended from the Heavens and was standing there before her. Slowly, cautiously, she raised her hand and traced with a finger the blue and ochre tattoos which described delicate whorls and lines across Amra's face, neck and arms. She licked the tattoos to see if they tasted of anything recognisable then plucked at Amra's tunic to uncover more of the patterns which extended from her arm to her breast.

Amra smiled her encouragement. The girl turned to her parents and burst out laughing and the other adults laughed too. The tense atmosphere was broken, the gap narrowed. None of these villagers had a tattoo. Their faces were as clear as those of newly born babies. How did their totems know who they were? wondered Amra. How could the Gods recognise them from up high in the Heavens? These were a strange people.

A tall man stepped forward. He spoke in a language Amra didn't recognise, pretending to shovel food into his mouth. Amra nodded and grinned then pointed to Wind. A woman, the man's wife, walked over and stroked Wind's nose then led him away for food and water.

Amra followed the man into a large house by the waterfront. It appeared to Amra that the house itself was somehow in the water until, once inside, she saw that it was suspended above the beach on thick treetrunks. Boats bumped and banged into the trunks as the water rose and fell. Inside the large house were many men, seated at long tables. They were drinking and laughing but they stopped when Amra and the tall man entered. One man was pouring ale into the pots the men were drinking from; he too stopped as soon as he saw Amra. He asked her something but she didn't understand. He repeated his question, this time in an approximation of her own tongue. He sounded strange but Amra understood him.

'Where are you going, woman-child?'

'To Troy,' she answered simply.

'And the men say you have a great horse. Your horse goes to Troy also?'

Amra nodded. The man explained to the others what she had said. The men nodded and made noises of understanding.

'Speak to me, woman-child. How will you barter with someone to take you and the great horse across the Crossing of the Dardan peoples into Troy?'

Amra remained quiet for a moment. If she told these people what was in her panniers they might kill her and steal her gifts. They were valuable and these men would know that. Yet how else could she continue the journey? She had made the mistake of leaving Wind and all her goods with the people outside because they looked kind and gentle. It was a silly thing to do and she regretted it now. She felt uneasy but she had to say something.

'I have some goods to trade for the journey.'

'Goods?'

'My father makes copper and bronze. I have hair pins, clips, buttons, jewellery, many things.'

Again the man translated what Amra was saying. A short squat man stood and walked over to her. He too marvelled at her tattoos. Like the child outside he put his finger to her face and traced the swirls which had been etched into her skin by her mother when she was a child. As his rude hands touched her skin Amra remembered clearly the pain she had felt as the needle her mother held bit into her, dragging agonisingly across her forehead, her cheeks and her chin. By the time her mother's needle had reached her arms she was beyond caring, having fainted. When she awoke her skin was mottled and raw and the wash of the dyes made her look as if she'd just fallen into a clump of berries.

'Show me these bronze jewels. I am a boatman. I'll take you across the Crossing of the Dardan peoples.'

'How do you speak my language?'

'I have ferried many different people across this stretch of water and have learnt many languages. Yours I have heard many times before. Some of the men I've taken across have had these markings on their skin, but I've never seen them on one so young. Why do you do these things?'

'They are to show our totems that we are faithful, to let them know where we are when they come looking for us.'

'And your totem?'

'The bee. That's why when I was very young this was put into my skin.' Amra pointed to the blue whorl on her forehead. 'It is the circle dance of the bee when he returns to his hive.'

The man nodded and translated again for the others. This time they nodded in understanding and appreciation.

'So will you take me across if I trade some of my jewellery?'

'That depends on what it is. But if it is sufficient, then yes, I will take you to the other side. But I warn you that the currents are fierce at this time of the year and there is always danger present. Many have drowned and never been seen again. Are you willing to take the risk?' he asked.

Amra nodded. 'And my horse?' she asked.

The man laughed and explained to the others what Amra wanted. They too burst out laughing. Amra was stung by the insult. She was inclined to reach for her knife but there were too many of them. She was Amra the hunter and because she was so skilled she knew never to take on an enemy more powerful than she unless she had the advantage of surprise. So she laughed with them. This goaded the men to greater heights of laughter yet she could feel fellowship developing.

The man behind the table poured her a glass of ale. It was more bitter than the ale her father drank but it was welcome in the heat of the inn. The men lifted their glasses and shouted something at her. They drank deeply, wiped their mouths, then demanded more ale from the man pouring. These were indeed a strange people.

It was already long past the middle of the day and Amra was anxious to get onto the boat and cross the water. From time to time the men looked outwards from the inn at the sea. There seemed to be more of the sea now than there had been when she first arrived. It was very strange. Boats which had lain on the sand were suddenly floating on the surface. Yet nobody had put more water into the sea. Where had it come from?

The ferryman explained that it was a tide. They could only sail on a high tide which arrived at roughly the same time twice each day, once early in the morning and once as the Sun God was falling towards the Eternal Sea. The morning tide was the water which erupted from the Earth Mother when she gave birth to her child, the Sun. The evening tide was caused by the Sun God falling into the sea, just like when a stone is dropped into a cup full of water and it overflows. Amra thought that these men were very wise.

'Do you really want me to take the horse? Has he ever been on the sea before?' asked the ferryman. Amra shook her head. 'Well, you must keep him calm. I have taken horses and cattle over before. Sometimes it's all right but sometimes it is as if the God of Tricks has got into them and they go crazy. They kick and neigh and jump all over the place. It is bad for them and bad for me. Any damage you'll have to pay for. Understand?' Again Amra nodded.

Suddenly there were shouts of excitement. Several of the men left the inn and headed off down a wooden ramp built out into the sea. Boats were tied to the ramp with coarse rope. The ferryman turned to Amra and said, 'Fetch your horse. And let me see what you have to trade in return for the journey.'

Excited that the final leg of her journey might be coming to an end after all the dangers and difficulties she had faced, Amra ran from the inn. She felt unsteady on her legs, the effect of the ale. She found Wind being fussed over by a large number of children in the main street of the village. The panniers were still there and seemed to be untouched. Amra was impressed by the honesty of the people in this village. But she also realised how stupid she'd been to have let the panniers out of her sight. The woman who had taken Wind had asked for no payment and she wasn't around for Amra to thank. She would make a point of stopping and thanking the woman properly when she returned to her people with the secret of making iron.

Amra pulled Wind away from the children and around the side of the inn. There they met the ferryman. He was fixing up the ropes on his boat. Amra saw that a number of boats were already on the water, sailing out to sea. Sitting in them were the men she had been drinking with; other men, also from the inn, were passengers. The ferryman looked at the great horse and shook his head vehemently.

'That beast will sink my boat. It's far too big and it will be frightened. You can see its spirit just by looking. No! Sorry, child. You will have to find another way.'

Amra's heart sank. 'How?' she asked.

'The long way. By land, all around the sea,' he said, pointing back in the direction she'd come from.

'How long will it take?'

'Twice the life and death of the moon. It's a fearfully long way. I don't know anybody who's done it.'

'But that is madness! Surely many horses cross these waters. What is so different about Wind?'

'Indeed they do, child. But your horse is like one of the royal horses that travel across on barges, boats much bigger than mine, often rowed by twelve strong men.'

'How much?' asked Amra simply.

'It's not a question of how much. It's a matter of size and strength.'

But Amra wasn't listening. She turned to Wind and took from her pannier the knife her father had made specially for her. It had a bronze blade and copper handle inlaid with filigrees of gold. The boatman looked at it lustfully as though it were at a naked young woman about to give herself to him.

'It's your risk,' he said, snatching the knife from her.

'That's for the return journey also,' Amra insisted.

The ferryman nodded. He knew just by looking at the knife that he wouldn't earn this much in ten full passes of the moon. This was a tool of incredible beauty and value. More valuable than anything he'd earned in his life.

Amra led Wind onto the ramp. The moment the horse left solid ground and heard his hooves resonating on the pier, he began to fret and shy. Amra put her arms around his neck and whispered comforting words into his ear. He calmed somewhat and allowed Amra to lead him to where the ferryman's boat rode up and down on the waves. The boat was bigger than it had appeared from the inn yet when Wind stepped down into it he appeared to fill all the boat's space. Knowing that he would be nervous until they reached the other side, Amra kept her arms around Wind's neck, whispering and crooning to him all the while.

The ferryman jumped down into the back of the boat. Wind shied in panic and the boat swayed perilously.

'Keep that horse still!' the ferryman yelled at Amra. 'Tie his forelegs together.' He threw her some rope but Amra ignored it disdainfully. She knew Wind, she could calm him, reason with him. But if she tried to restrict him, to tether him, he would hate her and try to bolt. Then he would bring them all undone.

The ferryman cast off the rope holding the boat to the pier and told Amra to untie the rope close to her at the front. The tide began to pull the boat to the middle of the lake and the man raised the sheet sail, tethering it to the edge of the boat. Immediately the sail filled with wind. Amra could feel the boat surge out from the land. She was thrilled. It was all so easy. The God of Wind blew into the sail and the boat flew across the water. But Wind wasn't reacting well. His nostrils flared and his back strained as he clopped about on the heaving deck. Amra sang him a song her mother had sung to her when she was a baby and refused to go to sleep, but for the first time in all their days together Wind would not be calmed. Even when the mountain lion had threatened them, Amra had managed to bring Wind back from the edge of frenzy, but now he was more disturbed than she had ever known him.

She held his head and hid the sight of the sea from him by putting her hands over his eyes. At first he tried to shake her hands away, but she kept them there against his will and slowly he began to calm as he could no longer see the horizon surging up and down. Amra thanked the Gods that she had found a way to stop him from moving about so fretfully. One good kick from his hind legs and he would hammer a hole in the side of the boat.

For the first time since they had set out Amra felt confident enough to look around her. She had never been in a boat before, let alone one which had sails and flew across the surface of the sea. It was wonderful. Her sense of adventure was fulfilled even if her movements were restricted by having to blindfold Wind to prevent his panic. She was stunned that the shore was already so far away. The God of the Wind must be happy for them to cross. The sail was full of his breath, and even as she watched the inn was disappearing, growing smaller and smaller all the time. Why did things grow smaller? she wondered. Where did they go to? What had happened to the large inn that she'd sat in? The one she could see now was too small even for her alone to fit into. She knew it was the God of Tricks playing a joke on her eyes, but where did he put the trees and the houses and the mountains when she walked away from them?

'Clever girl. Keep your hands on his eyes,' the boatman called over the freshening wind. And Amra would have done had the boat not entered a particularly rough passage of water halfway across the strait. Waves which had been gentle near the shore were now capped with angry white foam which washed over the side of the boat. The wind in the sail dropped and then roared again and the sheet whipped and cracked. Amra was tossed this way and that and even though she desperately tried to keep Wind's eyes covered, he shook his mighty head and dislodged her hands. When the horse realised he was in the centre of an angry inferno he was terrified. He let out a terrifying bellow and kicked frantically with his hind legs. Then he reared up, his forelegs clawing the air.

'Keep that damned horse tethered, girl! He's upsetting the balance!' screamed the ferryman. 'I can't sail if he's kicking.'

Amra wanted to shout back that she was doing her best but at that moment Wind pitched forward, his forelegs flailing the air, and sprang off the deck, landing across the edge of the boat, his hindlegs slipping and sliding to find a grip. Amra screamed for the boatman to help her. She was terrified that the boat would overbalance and toss Wind into the sea, but the ferryman was tugging at the rudder in a desperate attempt to gain some sort of stability. It was no use. The boat listed badly as the full weight of Wind's huge body bore down on one side. Water gushed into the bottom of the boat and the whitecaps jumped over the edge.

The boatman cursed. He should never have been greedy. Damn that dagger! Now he would not live to trade it. He manoeuvred unsteadily towards the terrified horse. 'Only one thing to do,' he shouted to Amra, 'the horse must go over. If not, we'll all drown.'

'No!' Amra screamed, but the wind whipped away her protest.

The ferryman heaved at Wind's hocks, straining to lift the huge beast. Finally he managed to push him overboard. The boat rocked from side to side, sending Amra sprawling onto the deck. But she could still see Wind, his head high in the water, desperately struggling to swim in the choppy sea. Amra screamed his name.

'Forgive me, child,' the ferryman muttered. 'A horse's life against mine.' He shrugged.

Amra was furious. She screamed abuse at the ferryman, calling him a murderer, then plunged into the sea to swim after Wind. The last thing she heard as her head disappeared underneath the waves was the ferryman shouting at her not to be such a fool.

The water was cold and it shocked her. It was different from any other water she had ever swum in; it moved in undulations, like a breathing person. Was this a God she was swimming in? But her mind was too distressed to follow such thoughts. Saving Wind from drowning was her immediate focus. As she struggled to the surface to breathe, she realised that the water was somehow forcing her upwards as though the God didn't want her to drown. But when she broke through the surface, a wave submerged her again and she choked on the salty foam.

Her fear of this environment overwhelmed her. She was a strong swimmer but was used to the smooth surface of the river. In this water the surface kept changing; one moment it was low and calm, the next it was high and her head was being forced under. Panic threatened her. She flailed the water with her hands, struggling to keep her head above the waves. She kicked hard with her legs but found that while at one moment much of her upper body was out of the water, the next she was totally submerged and heaving for air. The effort made breathing near to impossible. She didn't know when to gasp for breath; every time she opened her mouth it filled with salty water from the crest of a wave. Then the wave would dump her down again under the surface. She tried to keep her eyes open to see what was happening but the salt stung. She had to blink repeatedly to try to clear the pain.

Amra cried out for help but again water entered her mouth. She realised she was alone, that the boatman was not going to save her, that she had to do it herself. And so she drew on all the strength in her legs and kicked more furiously than she had before. This gave her time to gulp enough air to fill her lungs. Then it dawned on her that if she stopped struggling and allowed her air-filled body to rise and fall with the waves she wouldn't have to work so hard. She had found a technique. She quickly thanked the God of the Sea for helping her by pushing her upwards, enabling her to swim towards Wind without becoming too tired.

She could see that Wind was already a long way away from her. How had he managed to swim so far, so fast? And then she realised that the God of the Sea was pushing her towards the horse. Kicking and swimming more easily now, Amra was able to bridge the gap between them far more quickly than she would have been able to in the river at home.

She eventually swam so close to Wind that she could reach out and grab him around the neck. At first the horse was terrified, but eventually he too adjusted to the movement of the water. Soon both of them were swimming further and with greater ease than either had experienced before.

Amra used Wind as support and looked around to try to see the boat. As the swell carried her upwards, she saw it in the distance, becoming smaller and smaller. That meant the boatman was not even making an attempt to follow and rescue them. For that he would pay. Once Amra had fulfilled her mission she would look for him and demand back her knife. Why should he keep it when he had abandoned them to drown in the sea?

It took Amra and Wind far longer than she had anticipated to reach the opposite shore, even with the God of the Sea helping them. The trees and cliffs slowly became larger and larger, but whenever Amra put her feet down to try to stand on the bottom she found nothing solid. And every time they felt as if they were being swept towards the shore, another wave would sweep them back out again. Amra realised that to overcome this last hurdle she would have to lead Wind and force him to swim more strongly than ever. Her arms around his massive neck, she whispered into his ear, 'Wind, now you and I must work together as never before. This is very important if we're to get out of this sea. Here, friend, let me guide you.'

She turned on her back, the horse's head nuzzling her stomach, and kicked hard on either side of his forelegs. Sensing the forward movement, Wind joined Amra in kicking towards the shore. For what seemed like a long time they struggled against the tide trying to pull them back, but eventually Wind's hooves struck the seabed and his legs gained some purchase. Though he stumbled twice as the tide forced his body backwards, he managed to clamber up the shore, dragging Amra with him.

Amra fell back on the sand, exhausted. Wind too was tired; she could tell by his shaking legs, his beating heart. But they were safe. They were on dry land. They were wet, tired, spent, but safe. People gathered around them and Amra realised that once again they were staring at her. But she was too tired to worry. She closed her eyes.

Relief at her escape from death made her start to cry. A fat woman, old enough to be her mother, stepped through the crowd and knelt down. She nestled Amra's head in her lap, just as Amra had nestled Wind when he was in peril, and smiled down at the girl.

The fire roared and sparks flew up into the air. Amra was warm, well fed and felt truly secure for the first time since she had left her home so far away. The people of the fishing village had taken her from the beach, washed her face and hands with clean water and dried her. The old woman, who could speak much of Amra's language, explained that the salt in the seawater would make her skin feel pinched and stiff unless she washed it off with fresh water. Amra was amazed by the woman's knowledge. The meal was one of freshly caught fish, as well as a haunch of cow which had been slaughtered the previous day. Along with the flesh they served green leaves, beans, peas and a red root which tasted sharp but not unpleasant. They filled the rest of the cooking pot with cabbage. Everything was boiled in water then turned out onto a large cloth. The people picked at the vegetables in between eating their meat and fish. Amra didn't eat any of the fish even though the woman encouraged her, telling her it was delicious. She had eaten much fish on her journey and, although she had caught the occasional rabbit and hare, she was desperate for the taste of meat. She hadn't eaten cow flesh for longer than she could remember. In her village cows were used to give milk and their hide was used for clothing and shoes. The meat was eaten only by the adults at special feasts. Only when the feast was almost at an end, and when the guest had eaten his fill and was about to tell a story, were the children allowed close to the fire. Then Amra would sit in her mother's lap, eat scraps from her plate and listen in awe to the guest's tales of wonderful places and marvellous adventures.

Food wasn't the only way these people were different from her own. There was more laughter here, more friendship, more openness. The people had seen her emerge from the sea and had thought that she and Wind had swum over from the other side. When Amra told them that Wind had been thrown overboard by the ferryman, the people were furious and helped her more than they would a normal traveller.

Before settling down to eat around the fire, Amra had inspected the panniers. Everything was sodden. She was forced to throw out all of the food she had stored for the future. The kind old woman told her not to worry, that the villagers would give her enough food to last her until she arrived at her next destination. Amra washed all her other possessions in river water on the advice of her new friend, to remove the salt from them. It was then that she realised her ordeal had made her hungry. Now, after eating, she was ready to repay the villagers' kindness with the tale of her journey so far. The children, as well as the adults, gathered around to listen.

Amra told them of the mountain lion and how Wind had helped her kick it over the precipice, how the three men had violated her and how she had wreaked vengeance by killing them and cutting off their testicles. Many of the women nodded sagely and marvelled at the girl's courage. And when Amra told them of how the boatman had pitched Wind over the side of the boat and sailed off to leave her and the horse to their fate, they spat into the fire in anger and humiliation that one of their own could have committed such a vile crime. But what really made them breathless with surprise was Amra's description of the iron men from over the mountains, and how her village would be destroyed unless she brought back the secret of making iron.

'And where will you find the secret?' asked the old woman.

'Troy,' Amra said simply. The woman translated. The people shook their heads in sorrow and made concerned noises.

'How will you get into Troy?' asked the woman.

'I don't know,' Amra said. 'I'll just travel there and ask to speak to the one who makes iron.'

The woman shook her head. 'There are great secrets which are known only to the King and the priests. These secrets will not be told to one such as you.'

This had never occurred to Amra. Why should she not be told the secret?

'These are the secrets of the Gods,' the woman continued. 'They are known only to those to whom the Gods speak – the royal family of Troy and the priests who serve them.'

Amra was downcast. Had she travelled so far and endured so much to come to the end of her journey without finding out the secret which would save her people, and her sister Peta?

An old man with his bones showing through his grey skin walked over to the old woman and spoke rapidly to her. She smiled and nodded. She turned to Amra. 'You have skill with horses. Do you also have skill with other animals?'

Amra told her she did, although she felt uneasy at the question.

'Good,' said the woman. 'Have you heard of the Trojan bull?'

'No,' said Amra. 'But we have bulls in my village. They're very fierce.'

'They're nothing compared to this one. It has killed twenty men. They say that it is unkillable, that it is a God come to earth to take revenge on man for finding the secret of fire and lighting the darkness of the night.'

'What has this to do with me?' Amra asked, her voice suddenly timorous.

'Inside the bull's enclosure is a golden arrow. It is fixed high above the ground, stuck in a tree. Nobody knows how it got there but whoever removes it is granted whatever he wishes. No-one is allowed into the enclosure with a weapon.'

Amra understood all too clearly why the woman was telling her the story.

CHAPTER 14

'Those poor bastards.' David put down the paper.

Sarah was ashen. An entire wing of the Berlin Museum destroyed. Untold, irreplaceable treasures. And the cost in human lives – twenty people confirmed dead, dozens more injured, many critically.

David continued to read out loud as he scanned the newspaper. 'The neo-Nazis have already claimed responsibility. They say their mission is to force the German people to rise up and kick out the foreigners and Jews who are infesting the nation. They say that the wing of the Museum they blew up was full of degenerate examples of subhuman cultures, that the only culture which should be celebrated by the German people is the culture of Aryan people from Germany and Austria.' He put down the paper. 'Sound familiar to you?'

Sarah was too shocked to acknowledge the question. She was thinking about the picture in the paper of the Museum after the bombing; it looked like a crushed walnut shell. Dozens of men were frantically digging at the rubble of the building with their bare hands, trying to reach the mangled bodies inside. According to the report, the entire pre-history department had been attending a regular faculty meeting on the second floor when the bomb had been detonated. Most had been killed instantly as the pillars supporting the middle of the building blew out and the third floor collapsed onto the floors below. A school party visiting the Museum accounted for most of the other deaths and injuries. She shook her head, unable to comprehend the enormity of the disaster. 'Why? It's all so senseless. Why kill archaeologists, for God's sake? Politicians, judges, police

– I can understand the perverted logic behind that. But archaeologists?'

'They weren't targeting the archaeologists, darling. They were destroying the building and its contents. They want a culture which closes its eyes to all influences except those it creates itself. German art, German science, German logic. It's obscene, but it was the same rationale that drove Hitler and Stalin. Madmen like these neo-Nazis will go all out, regardless of who they destroy, in pursuit of their goals.'

'But priceless relics, David. Irreplaceable treasures. They don't just belong to Germany, they belong to the human race. And the people they killed!' Sarah shook her head.

David read on. When he discovered that the Museum had once been the repository of Schliemann's Trojan treasure – the very thing Sarah was trying to wrest away from the Russian government – he decided to keep his comment to himself. He sipped his coffee, despite the fact that it was now cold.

❉

Ever since the explosion and the resulting deaths, Feyodor Mikailovich Meconski had been torn between the desperate need to sleep and his fear of doing so. His dreams were filled with writhing bodies, children screaming, hands grabbing at him out of the rubble. Each time he awoke in a sweat, choking with terror and tears. Lomonosov kept calling, wanting to check on him, but Feyodor instructed his secretary not to allow any calls through.

He could not escape the horror, it was in every newspaper, on every news bulletin. Today's paper had a headline which particularly attracted Feyodor's attention: 'Neo-Nazis thought responsible for Berlin Museum horror'.

Could it be true, he wondered? Was it possible that the Mafia wasn't to blame, that Lomonosov had been calling

257

him to protest his innocence, that the whole thing was a hideous coincidence? The police didn't usually make mistakes of this kind, they obviously had reason to believe the neo-Nazis had planted the bomb.

As he was musing, the phone rang. It was Minister Vardian's secretary, a grey-haired bitch, uncompromising and unlovely. 'The Minister wishes to see you immediately,' she said. 'Please present yourself here within the hour. Good day.'

Who the hell did she think she was talking to? thought Feyodor. She was a mere office assistant; he was one of Russia's leading archaeologists and museum administrators. He wouldn't be spoken to like that. Not by her, at any rate. He took a mirror out of his bottom drawer of his desk. He was shocked by his appearance; dark patches of beard clung to his grey cheeks and his eyebrows were bushy above the red slits which masqueraded as his eyes. He stuck out his tongue; it was hard to differentiate it from the rest of his face, it was so grey and lifeless. God Almighty, he had to pull himself into shape. If it *was* the neo-Nazis it didn't diminish the depth of the tragedy but it did make him feel better about his own involvement. And it was probably the neo-Nazis. They were a hideous bunch of evil men. It was just the sort of thing they would do.

He took an electric razor from his drawer and removed the patches of hair he'd missed that morning. Then he went to the bathroom and washed his face, rubbing it hard with his hands and the towel to try to bring some colour back. He straightened his shirt and tie, combed his hair, put on his glasses to hide his red eyes, and instructed his secretary that he would be at the Kremlin for the next couple of hours.

By the time he got to the Kremlin he was feeling much better. He had decided that it definitely had been the neo-Nazis; not even Lomonosov could be so callous with human life.

The Minister's secretary glanced up from her desk and nodded for Feyodor to take a seat in the armchair outside the Minister's door.

'Are you aware of who I am?' he said haughtily.

She looked up, frowning. 'Of course.'

'I am the deputy director of the Pushkin Museum. I'm not accustomed to this sort of treatment. If it continues I shall report your behaviour directly to the Minister. Now have the courtesy to make me a cup of coffee.'

She gulped and stood, disappearing into an anteroom. A moment later she returned with a cup of coffee. He noted with some satisfaction that there was also a biscuit in the saucer.

'Thank you,' he said politely.

'It's my pleasure,' she said and returned to her desk.

The green light above the Minister's door was suddenly illuminated. The secretary asked if he would care to enter.

Without preamble, Minister Vardian launched into his attack. 'I thought we could breathe easily since the neo-Nazis bastards eliminated the Berlin Museum people,' he said, waving a fax in the air. 'I thought it might do us a bit of good, plunge the archaeological world into chaos, give us some time. But it hasn't. This arrived overnight.' He threw the fax contemptuously at Meconski but before he could read it, continued.

'It's from the Ministry of Antiquities in Turkey. They've said that they want their treasure back within a month without qualification or argument or they will seek leave to go to the International Court in the Hague. They say that they haven't heard from us since their first letter so now they are taking the matter further. Obviously they want to put on an exhibition and make a fortune from tourists. Just like we do.'

The deputy director nodded.

'The problem is,' continued the Minister, 'that neither you nor our legal people have managed to come up with any real grounds for us to retain it. The only suggestion is that we maintain our claim that the treasure is reparation for the loss inflicted on us by the Germans in the Great Patriotic War. But the fucking Turks weren't even in the Second World War so we have absolutely no grounds for refusing their request. They're basing their argument on the claim that Schliemann lied when he signed the contract with the Ottoman government, making that contract null and void. Add to that the fact that the Turks hate the Arabs and are doing our dirty work on the southern border fighting the Kurds and there's every reason we should bundle up the treasure and send it back with love and kisses. But it's worth billions and there's no way we can afford to lose an asset like that. My people estimate that it'll be worth hundreds of millions in income from travelling exhibitions around the world over the next couple of years.'

Feyodor shook his head. He didn't understand the problem. In their previous meeting the Minister had told him that the Turks would be making a claim for the treasure – why more fuss and bother now? The real problem had been with the Germans. Now that the German team was destroyed any other claims would just require delaying tactics. The Minister had been confident of sidetracking the Germans; there was so much hatred between Russia and Germany that there would have been another revolution if the treasure was given back. Only this morning he had even allowed himself a little relief knowing that the death of the archaeological team had put an end to his nightmare.

But now he had to think of Turkey. After that first meeting with the Minister, he had asked Lomonosov to use his contacts in Istanbul to determine who was really behind the push to recover the Trojan treasure there and what could be done about it. Certainly not another explosion – that would defy credibility! The contacts had reported back that the driving force behind Turkey's demands was the female Minister for Arts and Antiquities. She had brought in a young American woman lawyer as a consultant since she was an expert on reclaiming property stolen in time of war. But the Minister had already alienated everybody she worked with and even the government – which was in the process of being torn to shreds by militant Islamic fundamentalist opposition on one side and the secular army generals on the other – was losing interest in supporting her. Indeed the director of the department, an orthodox follower of Islam called Dr Yussef Barrak, was offended by the strident posturing of both the Minister and her lawyer. The contact confirmed that Barrak and his whole department was seriously estranged from the Minister and gave only the most grudging assistance to the American.

'What precisely does your Excellency want me to do?' asked Feyodor.

'Something! Anything! If I knew I'd have done it myself, idiot. That's why I've brought you here. When will your director be back from sick leave?'

'The director is still confined to her bed,' Feyodor replied.

'Pity! She would have had some sensible solution instead of asking *me* what to do. This is a terrible situation. A full-scale worldwide exhibition of the treasure could put bread on millions of Russian tables. The Egyptians made a killing out of Tutankhamen's treasure – that's how fucking crucial this whole thing is! Use whatever means are at your disposal to draft a reply to this Turkish letter. Find an archaeological excuse – say the exhibits are too fragile to move, or there's a Russian connection somehow, that the Hittites came from Moscow so the treasure was originally ours. Say it's propping up one of the columns of the Museum, if needs be, but for fuck's sake, say something! I'm getting serious pressure from the President on this one. It's become a government to government matter. I'm going to lose control of the situation soon and I've got plenty of enemies who will relish this matter being taken away from me. The department's lawyers are working on the legal aspects but I've got to have an archaeological answer as well. I want your response within forty-eight hours.'

The deputy director was dismissed.

CHAPTER 15

It was the owls that kept Amra pushing onwards. She needed to sleep to restore her strength but the screeching of the owls from their roosts in the cliff-faces prevented her from sleeping more than a short while each night.

The journey from the southern shore of the Eternal Sea to this plain upon which Troy was situated had taken two days of gentle riding. Wind was a different horse to the powerful and independent beast that had thrown her off his back at the very start of her journey. Now he behaved as if he were completely dependent on her. He seemed nervous and had lost that playfulness at the end of a day's riding when he would gallop around her in a huge circle so she could jump in feigned surprise when he suddenly galloped up to her behind her back.

It was his near death in the Eternal Sea which had caused the change. Amra had seen this loss of confidence when a horse's spirit was broken by a cruel owner. One final slap or one final crack with a stick and the horse would simply give in. Was this what the sea water had done to Wind? Amra prayed to her totem, the bee, that this wasn't the case. She would still be able to ride Wind, to get him to carry her from place to place, but he would no longer be the Wind she loved, her friend.

Whenever they came to a stream Wind would rear and flare his nostrils, and Amra would have to dismount and lead him across, singing soothing songs into his ear. She was worried about him. She was surprised too. The mountain lion had been far more frightening than being in the sea; maybe not for Wind though. Maybe she didn't understand him as well as she thought she did. But she did understand that she had to be gentle with her friend, kind and understanding. If his nerve was to return, if his courage was to come back to him, much depended upon her understanding of his needs. It was like when a hunter was attacked by an animal and lost his nerve – he might stop hunting for a time, stay in his hut whittling wood or pretending to do work – but eventually something would happen to drive him back into the fields with his bow and arrow, his spear and his knife. Amra was confident that something like that would happen with Wind, given time.

Their route took them through an orchard of trees, all bearing the same fruit. Amra had never seen such a place; she assumed it had somehow been created by the people who lived in this land. They passed increasing numbers of people hard at work in ordered fields, each with different coloured crops. How did the people control what the Gods gave to them? It took many prayers and sacrifices every year for the Gods to smile on the people of Amra's village and provide them with sufficient sources of food. Yet here the Gods had given strength to what looked like the entire country.

Amra noticed as she rode deeper and deeper into the plain that the houses grew in number. The houses of the fisherpeople who had helped her after she emerged from the Eternal Sea had been rough and crude, insubstantial structures that required rebuilding every year. But these houses – well, they weren't really houses at all. They looked more like huge rocks, with gaps in their walls where the people could look out and long fissures for doors. But, unlike rocks or caves in the walls of mountains, these rocks all looked the same. They were square and white. Amra knew they were made of stones with straightened sides, huge stones hewn from a mountain nearby, placed one on top of the other. They were not unlike the altar in the middle of her village. But her village's altar was small; these structures were enormous.

How did they manage to build so large? What tools did they use to make the sides of the stones straight so that one could sit on top of another with no gaps showing? Amra slowed Wind to a gentle trot for a better look. The people working in the fields stopped their toil and stared at her. Amra was used to it by now; she realised that her strangeness lay in riding a huge horse and in the markings on her face and her body. She ignored the stares. She was tempted to smile but there was nothing about these people to show they were friendly. Nobody smiled, nobody waved. They just stared after her, as though she were a God who had come down from the Heavens.

Amra put them out of her mind and thought instead about the bull she would soon have to meet if she was to claim the golden arrow, meet the king and be given the secret of how to make iron. She had come so far, yet it was only now that she truly understood how difficult her task would be. Back at home in her village it had all seemed so easy: go to the land of the Hittites and ask for the way to make iron. Then her father could turn the red earth into iron and make weapons for all of their people to defeat the invading army of the men of iron from the other side of the mountain. But the reality of being in a land where the Gods worked directly with the people was quickly dawning on her. These people were not like her own; they were strange and powerful. And she was travelling through their midst, alone and afraid. How could she meet and overcome a God so strong that he could make the crops in the field stand like soldiers? Her heart beat faster as she thought about her fears.

At the furthest edge of one of the fields a man called a young boy over to him. Amra saw him say something to the boy, who turned to stare at her, then ran off at high speed in the same direction as Amra was riding. He disappeared from view behind some houses, then emerged only to disappear once more, this time into a copse of woods. Amra knew that he was running to warn somebody of her approach.

Amra was frightened. Except for her ordeal by the riverbank the people she had met on her journey had been friendly and welcoming. But now, as she travelled closer to Troy, her fear of being attacked returned. Her throat tightened and she could feel the muscles of her back stiffening. She wanted to ride out of this place as quickly as possible. The people, even the Gods, seemed to be against her. She kicked Wind in the flanks and the horse responded immediately, carrying her swiftly through their fields. The people watched her silently; they were like the idols in the Medicine Man's prayer house, unmoving. What was in their minds? Did they mean her harm?

Quickly Wind carried her out of sight of the people, but Amra still felt their menace. This was a strange place. There were fewer trees here and the sun was hotter. The rivers and streams were fewer and the land was flatter. Unlike the villages in the valleys of the five rivers, which were joined by muddy tracks, it was easy to travel across the plain; the earth had been deliberately flattened to make a roadway.

Amra had been riding towards a large mountain for some hours before she fully grasped what it was made of. As she got closer she could see that what she had thought were huge boulders were actually houses, layer upon layer of houses which went upwards, ever upwards. She cried out in consternation and awe. This must be what the people in the fishing village had called a city. The buildings were bigger than any she'd ever seen, and they were all surrounded by a huge wall which was taller than the tallest tree Amra had seen in the forest. The wall was long too; it seemed to go on for ever, stretching as far as Amra's eye could see. Soldiers with spears stood atop the wall, patrolling backwards and forwards.

Amra pulled Wind to a halt and simply stared. The sun was burning down on her head and shoulders but she didn't care. She needed to absorb everything before going on. She could hear voices coming from the settlement, they were carried to her on the wind which blew in from the sea beyond the city wall. And again the screeching of owls, even though there were many hours yet before the God of the Sun went to his rest. Amra turned her head from the baffling sights which threatened to overwhelm her and rested her gaze on the sea which seemed to lap at the feet of the city mountain. This sea was blue, not green like the Eternal Sea which had tried to swallow Wind. And it was bigger by far than the Eternal Sea. Far out Amra could see tiny humps of land. She had reached the Sea of Islands. She had reached the city of Troy!

Amra dismounted from Wind. She owed thanks to her totem for allowing her to live and see this city. She removed her amulet from around her neck and placed it on the ground so that the bee was facing towards the city. She knelt and prayed softly. 'Great totem bee, thank you for protecting me. Thank you for helping me to reach Troy. Please make the people give me the secret of making iron so that I can return to my home and save my people and my sister.' Amra kissed her bee totem and put it back around her neck.

As she stood she saw a cloud of dust moving rapidly towards her. She looked around in amazement; there was only a slight breeze blowing, not enough to stir up that amount of disturbance. She reached inside her pannier for her knife and strapped it to her belt, then brought out her bow and arrow. A wheeled cart pulled by five horses emerged from the haze. Amra had heard that the Hittites used chariots in their battles; now there was one bearing down upon her. She was terrified, but she held her ground.

The chariot skidded to a halt and Wind reared up in alarm. Amra grabbed him by the neck and whispered gently into his ear, her voice calm despite her own nervousness.

The man driving the chariot spoke gruffly. Amra didn't understand what he was saying. The other man asked her something more gently in what she guessed was a different language. Again she didn't understand. He tried another tongue before finally speaking to her in a version of her own language.

'Who are you? What do you want? What rights do you have here?'

'I am Amra,' she responded, her voice firm. 'I come from the valleys of the five rivers beyond the Eternal Sea. I have come over the crossing of the peoples of the Dardan to reach Troy. I want to know how to make iron.'

The man stared at her. His face creased into a smile. 'You want us to teach you how to make iron?' he repeated.

Amra was worried. Had she said something wrong? The man was smiling but it was not a friendly smile, more one of contempt. He explained to the driver what Amra had said. The driver burst out laughing and responded sharply. The second man nodded.

'My friend says that I should kill you for saying these things,' he told Amra. 'He says you are a girl and that your face is marked like a statue. You are from a distant people, not a mighty city like Troy. We should kill you and return to the city.'

Amra realised that the merest show of fear would be very bad for her. 'Is this how you deal with people who come to you in peace?' she asked.

'It is how we deal with girls from distant places who live in straw huts.'

'My home isn't made of straw,' she said angrily. 'My home is made of stone, like yours.'

Again the man laughed. He pointed to the largest building in the city. 'This is the greatest city in the world ruled by the greatest King. All other kings bow down to our King.'

'Then why won't your King teach me how to make iron?'

'Such secrets cannot be told to girls.' But he softened enough to ask, 'Do you have things to trade from your village of five rivers?' Amra nodded.

'Show me,' he demanded.

Amra reached into her pannier and took out some of the bronze and gold objects her father had given her. The translator looked at them, his nose wrinkling in contempt.

'These are poor quality, as if made by a child. Take them back. They will bring you nothing from the mighty city of Troy. The people will laugh at you. Go back, child, to your village and your rough ways. Do not bother the King and Queen of mighty Troy.'

The driver flicked the reins of the chariot and the horses responded instantly. Wind shied again, the sight of animals in harness making him uneasy. But before the driver could turn the chariot back to the city Amra shouted, 'Stop!'

The driver looked at her in astonishment.

'How can I get into Troy?'

'You can't,' said the translator. 'It is forbidden to you.'

'Others get in,' she said desperately.

'Others are traders. They have things we wish to buy.'

'I have such things.'

'Show me,' said the translator again.

'I have things more powerful than bronze and gold jewellery. I have power.'

The translator laughed. 'You are a child. What power could you have?' He pointed to Troy again. 'Within those walls is a King who owns more chariots than wheat in the fields and has an army so large that no other king dares to speak his name. That, child, is power.'

'My power comes directly from the Gods. My power is the power over animals.'

The translator hesitated for just a moment, long enough for Amra to know that this was her way in.

'I have power over bulls. I am Amra the bull tamer. I have come to take the golden arrow.'

It was as if she had said a silent prayer and a God had suddenly appeared. The translator looked stern instead of contemptuous now. 'What did you say?' he demanded.

Amra repeated her claim and the translator informed the driver. The driver shook his head.

'Only warriors may try to take the golden arrow,' said the translator. 'The bull is a God, come to earth. We insult him by putting you into his arena.'

Amra remembered the words she had been told by the fishing people. 'I demand the right to take the golden arrow.'

The translator licked his lips then nodded curtly to the driver.

'Follow,' he said simply. The driver wheeled the chariot around and drove towards the gates of the city. Amra rode Wind behind the chariot. Wind wanted to overtake but she held him back.

The guards at the gate stood stiffly to attention. The driver halted the chariot and the other man turned and said to Amra, 'Wait here. Don't move. Don't attempt to enter the city or you will be killed.'

Amra waited. There was nothing to shade her from the merciless sun. Nor did she think to climb down from Wind's back. She had no idea how long she waited but it seemed forever. She felt the sun burning her head and shoulders. Wind shuddered occasionally. Amra could tell he was desperate for a drink but she could not help him. She asked him to wait quietly with her.

Eventually another chariot came out of the city gates. It carried a tall, grey-haired man who was wearing a cloak of deep blue. It was obvious he was powerful and rich. The chariot stopped in front of Amra.

'Are you the girl who has challenged the bull in the royal enclosure to a battle to the death?' barked the man.

Amra nodded.

'I am Mithrassa-Urbek, the King's secretary. Are you sure you know what you're doing, child?'

Again Amra nodded. Her voice had deserted her.

'Are you aware, Amra, that the bull has killed more than twenty strong men and is the most feared animal in captivity?'

It was obvious that Amra understood very little of what she was hearing. Mithrassa-Urbek shrugged. He had no more time to waste with this girl. He had explained the risks; now it was her choice. She would clearly pay with her life, but that wasn't his problem.

'You will enter the bull's enclosure when the sun is at its highest tomorrow. Enter the city by the main gate; the guards there have instructions to admit you. Is there anybody who should be told of your death?'

Again Amra shook her head. By the Gods, he wondered, where had this strange painted idiot come from?

'Amra, you are permitted no weapons to help you fight the bull.'

This Amra understood. 'I will take no weapons. I need no sword.'

'But you are a girl. How will you fight the animal? With your bare hands?'

'With my song,' she said quietly.

There was something in the child's eyes which told Mithrassa-Urbek to take the time off from his myriad duties to watch the battle the next day. For three years he had warned many foolhardy braggarts about the danger of what they thought would be easy. Yet each had been carried on a stretcher away from the field, bones broken, head or chest gored and trampled, face unrecognisable. It was a horrible death, especially as the crowd cheered their champion bull when it drew first blood. Well, soon it would have another victim. But a girl this time. A girl had never been so bold as to challenge the bull. It would definitely be an unusual battle.

Amra followed Mithrassa-Urbek's chariot to the city walls. She was committed now, there was no turning back even if she wanted to. She was afraid that were she to ride away the guards would chase her and kill her. She had offended them by asking for the secret of making iron. She was on the path to the future now. If she was brave, and if she could stop the bull from killing her, then she would be given the secret of making iron. She could take the secret back to her people and her father could make the weapons to kill their enemies. Then her family, her friends and everybody in the village would be safe. This is why she had come to Troy, why she had taken the risks, why she had suffered the loneliness and the fear.

The city wall towered above her head. The gate itself was three times higher than Wind. It swung open to admit the chariot, like a God opening his huge mouth to swallow an offering. Amra was terrified. She wanted to turn and ride away. But she couldn't. Too many people would die, and besides she was Amra the hunter, Amra the lion killer. No! She would not turn back. She waited for nightfall in the shadow of the city wall.

The middle of the next day was a long time in coming. For Amra the wait was excruciating. Finally the sun reached its spot directly above her; midday. She must go to the royal enclosure to deal with the bull.

As she approached the gate, the guards stood aside. A man in uniform emerged from a small hut next to the doorway and took out a long golden tube, held it to his lips and blew. Wind shied and Amra fell down across his neck.

As the trumpet sounded the two gates creaked slowly open. Amra saw inside the walls of Troy for the first time.

Amra gasped in sheer wonderment. This was how she imagined heaven. The city was crowded, vast numbers of people had poured into the streets to see this girl who had challenged the bull. The women wore beautiful multicoloured dresses, fixed together with metal clasps. The men wore shorter tunics, most of them made of white linen. But it was the way the houses were arranged which amazed Amra most. They were set in parallel rows which seemed to go on forever, all leading upwards to one massive building, the King's Palace.

Amra kicked Wind gently to urge him through the gates. She could tell from the way his body shuddered that he was nervous. Neither he nor Amra had ever been in a place like this. So many people with so little space between them, and so much to see, so much to understand.

There was a water trough at the side of the road. Wind nervously approached and drank greedily. The people stared at Amra, exclaiming at her coloured skin, her threadbare clothes. She didn't care. All she could think of was the ordeal awaiting her – its outcome would ensure her village's life or death.

The crowd ahead suddenly cleared for the King's secretary. Mithrassa-Urbek spoke to Amra quietly so the people could not hear.

'Amra, you are young. I want you to think very carefully about what you are about to do. There is no reason to give up your life like this.'

'I must learn the secret of making iron,' she said.

Mithrassa-Urbek shook his head. 'This secret will not be given to you.'

'If I take the golden arrow can I not ask for anything that the King can give me?'

'No! That is not right,' said Mithrassa-Urbek. 'It is commonly said by the peasants that this is the case, but it is not so. If it were the case then he who takes the arrow could ask for the wealth of the entire kingdom.'

'Then what do I gain by risking my life?'

'You will sit tonight at the table of the King. That is all.'

'And if the King says no to my request? Will my whole journey have been in vain?' Amra felt tears ready to choke her.

Mithrassa-Urbek shrugged his shoulders.

Amra thought hard for some moments. What choice did she have? If she won the arrow she could explain to the King how important it was for her to save her people. But if she left the city now her life – or worse, Peta's – would be sacrificed. At least this way there was a chance.

'Where is the bull?' she asked simply.

Mithrassa-Urbek's face dropped in sadness. He liked this girl's open way. It was a pity that she chose to die.

He escorted Amra to the Temple to the God Mithras which housed the bull's enclosure. As they walked he explained that Mithras was the God of Contracts and Obligations, as well as the God of the Sun, War and Justice. Amra knew that this Mithras must be a very powerful God.

'Why do you keep a bull in your God's temple?' she asked.

'Because we believe that Mithras will love us if we sacrifice a white bull in his name,' said Mithrassa-Urbek.

'The dead bull then goes up to the sky and becomes the moon.'

Wind was taken off to a stable, and Mithrassa-Urbek left Amra with the priestesses of Mithras. They dressed her in a white robe. Amra thought she looked very splendid and marvelled at the softness and thinness of the material, so fine she could see her skin through its pallor. She wished Peta and her father could see her. She wished she could see them too, be at home in her village once more, be anywhere but here. More and more people gathered on the platforms above the enclosure. The hot sun shone directly overhead but most of the crowd had covered their heads with white material and sipped water from stone bottles which they had brought with them. The noise grew; people shouted and whistled in anticipation of another kill.

The bull emerged from the tunnel which led into the enclosure. Amra's knees went weak. It was the largest animal she had ever seen. It stood almost as tall as a man and in length rivalled her house back in her village. Amra let out a cry of despair. In her village she was known for her way with animals. She could calm them when no-one else could even go near. Her people said that the Gods had given her special powers to communicate with the animals. She had ridden Wind and made him her friend. But this bull terrified her. It was like the men of iron beyond the mountains with their weapons, and she was Amra, defenceless and alone.

'It's not too late to walk away, child. Nobody will say anything. You have my word,' said Mithrassa-Urbek.

Amra saw his lips move but did not hear his words. The pounding of her heart and the rush of blood in her ears drowned out all other sounds. She stared at the bull, wondering how she would ever be able to get past him to the golden arrow, how she would become Amra the bull killer. She had said she didn't need a sword. But look at the bull. He was so angry. How could she possibly speak to him?

The crowd had filled every space on the viewing platforms. The noise was frightening the bull; it snorted and scraped the ground with its feet. A priestess came forward, kissed Amra on her forehead and intoned a prayer over her. Mithrassa-Urbek ordered the door to the enclosure to be opened and Amra was led gently forward. Before she stepped inside, Mithrassa-Urbek raised his Rod of Office for silence. At his signal the crowd fell into a hush. The silence would last until the bull had scored its first blood. Then they would whistle and shout and drive the bull into a frenzy while it tossed the girl around the enclosure like a child's doll.

Amra heard the gate click shut behind her. She kept her eyes on the bull. The beast raised its massive head and looked around at the crowd. The sudden silence unnerved him; he aggressively scraped at the grass beneath his lethal hooves. In the middle of the enclosure Amra saw a tall tree; high up in its branches was the golden arrow. But she knew that if she moved suddenly and ran for the tree, the bull would surely impale her upon its gold-covered horns. The arrow would have to wait.

The bull suddenly noticed her. She watched it shift its head from side to side, as if to get a better look at her. It snorted and pawed the ground then lowered its head, its horns pointing directly towards her. The crowd tensed. The bull was ready to charge.

Amra opened her mouth to sing to the bull but no sound emerged. She tried again. A squeak came out. Somebody in the crowd laughed, but was instantly silenced when Mithrassa-Urbek raised his Rod of Office again, this time with the threat of punishment.

Amra walked slowly towards the bull. Her voice returned and a calming song came to her. It was a gentle lilting tune, rising and falling like a breeze on a summer's day. As the tune drifted across to the ears of the bull Amra smiled. Something told her that the bull was listening. His shoulders became less rigid, his stance less threatening. Yet he continued to snort, unsure of the small figure singing to him.

Amra cautiously crept closer, her voice rising in volume until her melody filled the whole of the enclosure and drifted up to the astonished crowd. Still the bull didn't move. He stood, transfixed, watching the apparition in white move slowly towards him, lulling him gently with her song.

There was no further need for Mithrassa-Urbek's Rod of Office. Nobody in the crowd uttered a sound. As one they held their breath. Mithrassa-Urbek sent up a silent prayer to Mithras to save the child's life.

Amra's confidence grew steadily, but she knew enough about animals to realise that the slightest wrong movement on her part – too quick, too slow, too loud, too soft – would turn the bull from a curious animal into a dangerous one. She moved closer until she reached the shade of the tree. Instinctively she decided to stop there. The bull was used to being the lord of the enclosure and was unsure of this creature intruding in his domain. He was also curious. He tentatively approached Amra, moving in a roundabout way towards the tree in the middle of the field and the arrow which represented Amra's salvation.

Suddenly a gasp went up from the crowd. Amra had turned her back on the bull. She sat down in the shade of the tree, telling him that she wasn't concerned about his size, his strength, his power. The animal lumbered curiously towards the tiny cross-legged figure, the ground vibrating gently under his weight.

Amra glanced up at the crowd for the first time since she had entered the enclosure. There wasn't a man, woman or child whose eyes were not fixed on her. But where earlier she had felt that the crowd had been willing her to fail and become yet another victim, now she sensed their amazement and support. She returned her concentration to the moment and heard the bull's breath coming even closer. She turned slowly, still humming her song which moved between gentle ululations and lilting tones like a stream dancing over rocks. The bull's red eyes were fixed upon her. Still she waited motionless. She dropped her voice slightly so as not to alarm the beast. Finally he came to rest within an arm's length of her.

Amra had no idea what to do now. If she were to move suddenly and the bull took fright his horns would disembowel her as surely as a guard's lance would mutilate an attacker. Yet she had to move to maintain her tenuous hold over the beast. And so she reached out her hand, slowly and cautiously, until she touched the animal's leg. She rubbed his foreleg, her nails gently scratching the skin beneath the hair, just as she scratched her dog back in her village.

The bull snorted gently, as though enjoying the novel sensation of touch. Amra felt bold enough to move once more, this time climbing to her knees, singing gently all the while. She rubbed her fingers underneath the hair of the bull's shoulder, then stood up slowly and scratched his neck in the same place that Wind enjoyed being scratched. And all the while she continued her calming song. She felt a shudder in the bull's body and moved closer still so that her warm body was against his. Then she put her arms around the bull's neck, pretending that she was cuddling Wind, and sang into his ear.

The huge audience was transfixed. Amra whispered to the bull, 'Come, friend. I will take you back to where you came from.' And she gently encouraged the beast to follow her back across the field towards the tunnel out of the enclosure. Amra gently closed the gate behind him and drew the wooden bar across to secure it. Then, still in silence, she returned to the tree, jumped as high as she could and grasped the golden arrow in her hand. The crowd erupted in the loudest cheer the city of Troy had ever known. The people clapped and whistled and threw flowers down at her feet.

Clutching the golden arrow Amra walked towards the gate where Mithrassa-Urbek was waiting. To her surprise Mithrassa-Urbek threw his arms around her. His words tumbled over one another in his excitement but Amra didn't hear. She slid to his feet in a dead faint.

CHAPTER 16

Nothing was going according to plan. Every time Feyodor managed to escape one treacherous situation another bit him on the ankles. First it was the Germans. Now it was this damned Turkish Minister and her American adviser. Why the hell couldn't they just leave things alone? It was time to get back in touch with his Mafia contacts.

Feyodor had told his wife he was going to a Museum meeting. Once upon a time she had taken the trouble to question these meetings; now she just wasn't even interested. He nodded to the woman outside the nightclub. She admitted him immediately. He was known now; he was one of the group. Within seconds he was in Lomonosov's office, explaining the situation in Turkey. He knew he should ask whether the neo-Nazis had really been responsible for the massacre in Berlin but the truth was he just didn't want to know. Instead he fixed his mind on the Turkish Minister and the American lawyer.

'We could kill her,' Lomonosov mused.

Feyodor shook his head. 'Not so soon after the Museum deaths.'

'Who's the target?' asked Lomonosov. 'The Minister or this lawyer?'

Feyodor breathed deeply. 'I think it's the lawyer. If we get rid of the Minister then they'll just appoint another Minister. But she's called in an American expert because no-one in Turkey has the expertise to work out what to do. If we get rid of the American then my guess is that the enquiry will come to an end – or at least be delayed long enough to save our asses.'

Lomonosov shook his head. 'They'll just call in another consultant. America is full of consultants.'

'Not in this area, according to your people. This woman is an expert in reclaiming property stolen in times of war. She acted for some big time Hollywood film director to get his property back and then became adviser to the Czech government. Sure, there are other people in America who could do the job but think about it. They all lead busy lives. It would take months, maybe even years, for them to clear up their workload and fly to Turkey for the time period required. No, I think getting at this American woman is the way to go.'

Lomonosov nodded. 'We could scare the shit out of her. Threaten to murder her if she doesn't leave Turkey immediately.'

Again Feyodor shook his head. 'She'd simply get police protection. That sort of person always responds adversely to an external threat.'

From the dancefloor beyond Lomonosov's office came the dull percussive thump of techno music. Hundreds of sweaty young things gyrated on the dancefloor, their gaunt faces eerily lit by alternating blue, red and gold strobe lights. The airconditioning of the office was a profound relief compared to the inferno outside.

The Mafia boss decided to give the little archaeologist an insight as to why he was so involved in the matter at hand. 'You know, I have just as much interest in terminating this demand from the Turks as do you, my friend. If our profitable activities are exposed you will not be the only one to suffer. Once they have dealt with you this new anti-corruption watchdog will come sniffing after me. Our business venture is only a tiny part of my financial enterprise. This thing between us, small as it is, could blow up into an international incident, and the last thing I need is a spotlight turned on me. Regardless of the consequences we have to get rid of the problem.'

'But you can't terminate the American woman,' Feyodor protested. 'Not now. Not after the deaths of so many archaeologists in Berlin. It would cause an uproar, and raise too much suspicion.'

'What about her husband then?'

'She's not married.'

'Mother, father, sister, brother, lover? I don't care! Anybody whose death will hinder her willingness to continue.'

'But will that cure the problem? What I said before was true: it could be a long time before she's replaced, but eventually she will be. There will never be an end to this nightmare! There will always be others who will fill the gap. Others who will come after us. Maybe not immediately, but eventually.'

Lomonosov smiled. 'Not necessarily. If we're really smart, we could get rid of the American, the Minister and the problem all with one carefully constructed incident. Undermine the American, have the Ministry officials denounce the Minister as anti-Islam, get the mullahs involved and start a public outcry. That should keep the new Minister too busy to make demands on us. Simple.'

Feyodor smiled, more in deference than belief in the idea. He still had his own problems about what he could report back to his own Minister in two days' time.

❊

The Director of the Ministry of Antiquities for the Republic of Turkey, Dr Yussef Barrak, puffed hard on his pipe, biting the stem in agitation. The past three weeks had been the worst in his entire life. Since the arrival of that execrable American woman lawyer Barrak felt as though his very existence had been turned upside down. And his Minister, at the best of times an acerbic and vitriolic woman, had been particularly cutting, deliberately going out of her way to embarrass and diminish him during departmental policy meetings or in discussions with her cabinet colleagues.

After a little more consideration he had to admit to himself that his life had really begun to go to pieces after the election of this damnable secular government in Ankara, a collection of ungodly men and women dedicated to carrying out the anti-Islamic dictates of Mustafa Kemel Atatürk. For all of the wondrous things which the founder of modern Turkey had accomplished, the one thing for which he would be eternally damned in the fires of hell was his contempt for Islam. Without Islam there was nothing. Turkey without Islam was nothing, a puppet of the United States. And that was precisely the direction this government was taking. Genuflecting towards the almighty United States with its military prowess and its woman-loving president. The only consolation Barrak could feel was the knowledge that the government infidels would suffer the same fate as the evil angels Harut and Marut, condemned by Allah to hang by their feet in a well in Babylonia until the Day of Judgement.

It was the mullahs, the religious elders of Islam, who were the particular target of the more outspoken and secular ministers in this hideous government. Any time one of God's chosen made a speech critical of the government an orchestrated campaign against him would follow. And the Prime Minister, vacillating and ineffectual, allowed it all to go on. But it wasn't just the government that discriminated against Islam. The military had demanded the closure of Islamic schools, forcing the government's hand by claiming that they were acting in the secular spirit of the legacy of Atatürk. And even now the military was petitioning the courts to declare the Islamic People's Party — Barrak's own party — constitutionally illegal.

But Dr Barrak was increasingly certain that the people would not tolerate much more of the government's anti-religious attitude. Every day the religious faithful were out on the streets, demonstrating against the oppression of Islam by the government. There were massive public protests in Istanbul, Ankara and the cities of the Black Sea, the Mediterranean and the Aegean. Curfews had been imposed; the situation was looking critical. Every day, five times a day, the genius of Islam was proclaimed to the people of Turkey by the mullahs, high in their minarets. Every day Barrak and every other devout Muslim listened to the call, their azan: 'God is great! There is no god but God, and Mohammed is His Messenger.' Everyone in Turkey, from the Black Sea to the Mediterranean, from the Aegean to Mount Ararat, each and every one of its seventy million inhabitants joined with their seven hundred million brothers and sisters throughout the Islamic world in acknowledging that God is great. Islam was the religion of submission to the will of God. The people of Saudi Arabia, Libya, Iran, Indonesia – everywhere that the followers of Mohammed had prevailed – accepted the inevitable: that they must submit their lives to God and Islam. Yet this government, these western-looking, Godless infidels, sought to defy the will of the people and the demands of the mullahs. And those who knew the reality of the political situation, those such as Dr Yussuf Barrak, knew that the demonstrations would change nothing. As long as the military supported the government's secular policy against the power of Islam, and as long as the people feared the aggression of Turkey's insane neighbours, Greece, Syria, Iraq and Iran, the people would always support the military over the clergy.

Barrak silently intoned the words of the azan to himself as he waited for his visitor. They provided stability in an unstable world. How often throughout his childhood and his adult life had he repeated the simple yet eternal words to himself: God is great. There is no god but God, and Mohammed is His Messenger. Simple and straightforward for even the most childlike of minds; yet unlike Christianity and Judaism, which were struggling against an increasingly secular world, the followers of Islam heard the affirmation of their faith so regularly that it was like a heartbeat.

He sucked again on his pipe, realising with annoyance that it had gone out. He looked at his watch. His visitor should be here any moment. The telephone on his desk rang loudly and Barrak's secretary told him that his visitor was waiting in the lobby of the Ministry building. The man was precisely on time.

'Tell him I am in consultation,' he instructed, 'and will not be free for fifteen minutes. Give him a glass of apple tea. I'll ring when I'm ready to see him.'

In the world of Turkish officialdom, fifteen minutes was the minimum period one would allow to elapse in order to make a visitor realise his subservience. Barrak took out a newspaper and perused the articles he had not had time to read over breakfast that morning.

When the visitor was finally shown into his office, Dr Barrak professed his apologies for the inexcusable delay. He didn't recognise the man who had sought an urgent meeting and insisted on seeing the director himself, despite all attempts at deflection by his staff. His card showed that his name was Ozman Urzak. His profession was described as 'entrepreneur' with special expertise in 'import/export, consultative services, diplomatic missions'. Dr Barrak had no idea why an entrepreneur should want to see him.

For the first ten minutes Urzak covered numerous topics from the economy to the interference of the military in religious freedoms to the air pollution in Istanbul and other major cities. Dr Barrak knew the technique; the man was here to ask a favour and was trying to find a point of mutual interest. Why not just come straight to the point? he wondered, then realised that he began difficult interviews in precisely the same way.

'Mr Urzak, your conversation is interesting but I am an extremely busy man. I wonder if you could tell me why you have sought this interview.'

Urzak nodded. 'Mr Director, I represent a group of very wealthy businessmen who are being seriously disadvantaged by the actions of your Minister. Their businesses, their incomes have suffered enormously since the Minister introduced restrictive legislation concerning access to archaeological sites. Limiting the number of people who can visit those sites per day will send many of these businessmen – the tour operators, bus operators and so on – into bankruptcy.'

'But this legislation has been in force for nearly a year. Why are you protesting now?' Barrak prompted the man to get to the precise purpose of the meeting.

'We protested at the time of its introduction . . .'

'And my Minister explained in a lengthy statement to the National Assembly that the dangers of large crowds, not only to the priceless archaeological ruins but to the safety of tourists, necessitated . . .'

Urzak interrupted, something Dr Barrak was unused to. 'Sir, I know that the Minister had good reasons, but the loss of revenue for the government . . .'

'I presume you mean for your colleagues?' Barrak corrected.

Urzak sipped his apple tea and smiled.

Barrak continued. 'Why are you here? I assume that you're astute enough to realise that this conversation is a year too late.'

'It has come to our attention that you are unhappy with your Minister.'

Barrak was stunned. This sort of direct comment was unheard of. It was naive, seditious and politically dangerous. If it were overheard even Barrak's strenuous denial wouldn't be enough to remove the suspicion of his disloyalty. 'Explain yourself,' he said quietly.

'Surely a man such as you needs no explanation.'

'A man such as I has the power to have you thrown into prison unless you explain your remark.'

Urzak remained quiet for a moment, weighing up how best to say what should not have to be said. 'Let's just say that on occasion, and because of extreme provocation, you have been less than discreet.'

'Explain!'

'There are many, like myself, who admire you. Your Minister has been less than gracious. Your frustration has become evident. I think that sums it up.'

Barrak felt his whole body flush with fear. What could he have said that might have been overheard? He had to know so that he could limit the damage.

'You will tell me or I will call the guards,' he said quietly, hoping that the tension in his voice would be interpreted as menace.

Urzak shrugged. 'At a private dinner party with two other heads of ministries at the Yeni Hamsikoy restaurant you complained that your Minister was ruining ten years of your work, that she had the brain of a insect and the manners of a pig . . .'

'Silence,' hissed Barrak. 'Get out of my office or I'll have you thrown out. How dare you make up these slanderous . . .'

'Relax, Yussef. I'm not here to make trouble for you. I'm here because it's in both of our interests if your Minister quits politics; indeed, if we can bring down this government and replace it with a religious government dedicated to the ideals of Islam.'

'I'm warning you, I'll have you arrested if you don't remove yourself from my office immediately. I've never in all my life heard such treasonous nonsense. You could be thrown into jail . . .'

'Yussef . . .'

'Stop calling me Yussef!' Barrak shouted.

'Quiet, fool, you'll attract attention.'

Barrak's mouth dropped open. Had he heard properly?

'Stop shouting and listen to me. This is important. Your position is in peril. Your Minister is on the verge of firing you, all at the instigation of this American Jew lawyer. If you are dismissed, your bitch Minister will no doubt appoint a secularist, some un-Godly and unworthy man, in your place. Or perhaps even a woman! The cause of Islam will suffer another serious setback. I know these things because I have ears in places where you could not even put your head. My connections are at the very highest levels of the government . . .'

Barrak couldn't believe his ears. Was this really happening? How could this stranger, a man he had never heard of, know more about his career than he did? This man could be the world's greatest liar; or he could be one of those who truly did govern the decisions and direction of his masters. This could be either a test of loyalty, or some Machiavellian plot to undermine him. Certainly it was the most dangerous conversation ever to take place in his office. 'Who are you?' he asked quietly.

'All you need to know is printed on my business card. Beyond that you need know nothing – except that I can make one telephone call and one hour later be sitting in the Prime Minister's office.' Urzak smiled. 'And if I make other telephone calls I can be sitting in the offices of the Imams of Baghdad, Tehran, Cairo and Mecca. I am the man whom the Prime Minister relies on to stop the mullahs from whipping up the people into an uncontrollable frenzy of anti-government feeling. Of course he has no idea which way my personal preferences lie, but that ultimately is his problem. He thinks I am an honest broker between his government and God. Frankly he's terrified of an uprising . . .'

'Then why does he keep making anti-Islam statements?' Barrak interrupted, mystified.

'Mere posturing to keep the military on side. He is terrified of the mullahs, but he is even more frightened of a coup. Of course he's clever enough to know that the military are slow to move and that such a coup would be hugely unpopular with the people. But his real fear is of a serious uprising caused by the clerics inciting the faithful from their mosques – he knows that such a concentrated attack would inflame passions, pit the people against the military, and ultimately oust him from government. That is why he needs me. I'm a go-between to keep the lid on things.'

Barrak was stunned. He'd had no idea that all this was going on in the upper echelons of government – if indeed, what this stranger said was true. But it seemed rational, and it would explain much of what he had found puzzling about the government's actions.

'Now, Yussef – to matters at hand. Although this government believes I am working for peace, the opposite is true. The leaders of our faith know this, though they will always deny it. Now you know it too. I am approaching you because, in your present precarious position, you are the most likely departmental head to cooperate with us. Further, your Minister is the most outspoken and western. That means she will be an ideal target for the mob to identify when they rise up.

'We believe that it is in the interests of Islam to get rid of this government as quickly as possible. However, for reasons with which I am sure you will be in sympathy, the mullahs cannot be seen to be actively involved. The military would step in and there would be a bloodbath. For some time my associates and I have been seeking ways of engineering a major crisis for the government, a scandal which would alienate the populace, give the clerics cause to raise the ire of the people, and ensure the military refrains from intervening. I believe that with the employment of this Jew we have found the cause.'

Barrak wished his mysterious visitor would lower his voice. Softly he said, 'But the Turkish government has good relations with the Jewish community, and it will not do anything to alienate Israel. We are military allies with the Israelis against Iran, Syria and Iraq. We're selling them water; they're selling us military hardware and training our army.'

'Don't confuse a convenient alliance with the people's hatred of Jews.'

Barrak nodded. Again it sounded logical. The alliance with Israel was driven by the military, and there was an incipient anti-Semitism in Turkey, despite the swarms of Israelis flooding Antalya and other cities on the Mediterranean coast. In the days of the Spanish expulsion of the Jews Turkey had offered the refugees a home, but that was five hundred years ago, long before the growth of militant Islam in Turkey and the Moslem world's subsequent altercations with the Zionists.

'You want to get rid of your Minister. I and my associates want her to go in a blaze of scandal which will rock the very foundations of Ankara. This government has a knife-edge majority. If it were not for the military they would have been thrown out six months ago. Your Minister's intention to overthrow centuries-old Ottoman law to reclaim the Schliemann treasure is a disgrace.'

Barrak looked at him in astonishment. 'Why on earth would you oppose us getting back a treasure which rightfully belongs to the Turkish people?'

'Because it isn't as simple as that, my friend. Certainly this treasure should come back, but to declare that Ottoman law should be overthrown will undermine all of our legal traditions. Such decisions could undo the very fabric of our society.'

Barrak laughed. 'Your argument is very thin, I'm afraid. I was the one who advised the Minister on getting the treasure back. What I didn't count upon was her calling in this American lawyer.'

'This Jewish lawyer.'

Barrak frowned. 'I find your constant use of her religion in a pejorative sense insulting . . .'

'Your concern is of no interest to me. I have bigger fish to fry – the creation of a scandal. Join me and you will sail high on the crest of a wave. Fight me and you will sink with the rest of them. I have a large fund earmarked for the creation of this scandal. Naturally, with your impeccable credentials, the money will be under your control and we won't embarrass you by asking for an audit. So, are you with me? Will you join me in watching the shit fly, or would you rather be eating shit for the rest of your life?'

Barrak's silence was tacit agreement.

'Good!' said Urzak. 'Now tell me, this American lawyer – how good is she?'

Barrak thought. 'Very good,' he said after a moment. 'Acidic, arrogant, self-righteous, but according to my staff she has a wonderful mind and an excellent knowledge of international law and property rights. She is an expert in reclaiming property stolen in times of war. She is certainly no fool and must not be underestimated.'

Urzak nodded. 'That is what we've heard. So, your job is to create a scandal. It has to be aimed directly at her because your Minister has the reputation of being a pure spirit. Happily married, no affairs, no expensive property here or abroad, little money, works fifteen hours a day and was loved by her students when she was a professor. Which means that the Jewess has to be her Achilles heel, if you will forgive me using a metaphor from the Greeks. We must attack the Minister through her choice of this lawyer. And it seems as if the only way to do so is through the girl's personal life.'

The man's presumption frightened Yussef. It was too late, but he asked the question anyway. 'Why do you think I will help you in this mad scheme of yours? I am still thinking of having you arrested.'

Urzak smiled. It was a frightening sight. 'You won't, Yussef. As I said, this goes ahead with or without you. And it is in your very best interest to work with me. And in the best interest of Islam. As well you know.'

Urzak was so self-confident, so self-assured, thought Barrak, he had all the answers. And he had accurately targeted Yussef's own Achilles heel. Indeed he could have been sitting at the dinner table when Yussef had discussed these very matters with his two colleagues. Suddenly Yussef realised where the information had come from – one of his colleagues was an informer. It hit him like a thunderbolt. But which of his colleagues? And did it really matter after all? He had been wondering for some time how he might scuttle the Minister's career – embarrass her in public, expose her in a compromising situation, let the public have her head on a platter. Yussef found himself nodding. Too late he realised that he was supping with the devil.

❂

Sarah Kaplan lay in bed, waiting for David to finish in the shower. The joys and security of their live-in relationship in New York had flooded back to her. Since David had landed in Istanbul, she had continually been asking herself, 'How could I have left this wonderful man, just to pursue my career?' They had lived together for three years until a year ago, when she'd made the decision to stay in Prague for the war crimes trial. Sarah's mother and father, her employers and her friends had disapproved of her decision and begged her to come home, but Sarah had felt a need stronger than the trial to stay. Before going to Europe she had firmly believed that America was the future for Judaism, that Europe had nothing to offer but horrific memories. She had even made a public stand against Jews returning to 'the old country', writing editorials in major newspapers pointing out that Russia, Poland, Hungary, Germany and many other nations were the sources of millennia-long anti-Semitism. Even after the insanity of Hitler, these countries still festered with deep-seated hatred for the Jews. Yet grandparents in America still talked lovingly to their grandchildren of life in the *stetl*, of what it was like in the old village, the old town, the old city, the old country. Sarah and a group of young like-minded intellectuals had begun to think along very different lines to their parents' and grandparents' generations. Their perspective was that if Europe hated the Jews, then American Jews should have nothing to do with Europe. They shouldn't return, they shouldn't yearn for it, they shouldn't look back on it as the golden land where their forefathers and their religion had flourished. Rather they should accept America – and Australia and Canada and other western democracies which had accepted the Jews – wholeheartedly and without reservation. But when Sarah had been forced to go to the Czech Republic to fight for the return of her client's property, she had become swept up in the mystery of Europe and the history of her people there. It had appropriated her and to leave before she had explored and resolved those feelings would have been so very wrong. That was why Sarah had stayed.

But while her family's disapproval had been loud and clear, David's voice had been conciliatory, understanding . . . and then accepting. In the long phone conversations between Prague and New York, his had been the voice of reason. He had admitted that he would miss Sarah terribly, that he wanted to marry her but he would wait for her until she had worked out the conflicts in her own mind.

Sarah had been furious. David should have demanded her return to New York, should have begged and cajoled her. She had the answers ready to hurl at him when he did so. But David had proved to be precisely what he always was – gentle, understanding, loving, perceptive, generous and kind. Nevertheless, Sarah had felt intensely guilty for months after making the decision to stay on in Prague. It had turned out to be an exhilarating experience. For an entire year she had met with some of Europe's most senior advocates, had flown halfway around the world gathering evidence, promising the victims their revenge, and meeting regularly with representatives of other governments to explain what the Czech government was doing. But in the evenings, when she crawled back to her empty apartment in the Old City of Prague with take-away food and a copy of an English language newspaper, then Sarah had missed David terribly. Even though his career as a concert cellist had kept him busy, he had somehow always been there for her.

The last week with David, spending time with him, visting some of the greatest archaeological treasures in the world, had made her realise how lonely she had been in Prague. It was amazing that a life spent on the run, dealing every day with dozens of people and enquiries and situations, a life where she never had more than a couple of moments to herself, could be lonely. Yet walking hand in hand with David through the wondrous ruins of Ephesus and Aphrodisias and Bodrum had made Sarah feel incredibly homesick. She felt a yearning in the very pit of her stomach to return to the apartment she once shared with David, to wake up on a Sunday morning and go to their regular coffee shop for a breakfast of blueberry muffins or oatmeal pancakes, washed down with a strong caffè latte, to read those wonderful overflowing New York newspapers, even to visit their respective parents' homes on alternating Sunday fortnights and tread the minefields of parental disapproval. This week with David had helped her to make up her mind. Whether David would agree was another matter, but his warmth and the fact that he'd flown in specially to see her told her that his answer would be yes. Anyway, he'd been virtually begging her for years.

David emerged from the bathroom and Sarah looked at his lovely body in admiration. He was delicately built yet still masculine, lithe and lean. He took care of himself without being obsessive about it.

'I've made a decision,' she said as he towelled his hair. 'I'm returning to New York as soon as I've finished here and cleared up the odds and ends in Prague. They don't need me anymore. I could be back in a month.'

David turned to face her, waiting for more.

'When I come home I'd like to move back in with you, if you'll have me. And I'm going to ask your mom and dad for your hand in marriage. Then I'm going to have a baby and find us a house with a picket fence. With your permission, of course.'

David sat down on the vanity stool and stared at Sarah. He smiled broadly. It was what he'd been hoping to hear since they'd first moved in together. He loved Sarah desperately but there had always been something which prevented her from committing herself to him exclusively. Now she had overcome that obstacle. He began to speak, but Sarah interrupted him.

'Before you say yes – as I'm sure you will because I'm such a great catch – there's something I've got to tell you. Something that happened to me ... what I did in Prague. Something that will come between us unless I get it out now. So don't say yes until you've heard me out. Then you can decide whether you'll have me or not.'

'Sarah, I really don't want to know about what you and Josh, or you and Laco, or you and anybody else did while you were away from me. You see ...'

'I want you to know. I couldn't be married to you if there was something hidden.'

'Many married men – and women – have affairs. They don't come home and blurt it out to their partners. It's no big deal.'

But Sarah was intent on honesty, the catharsis of a full disclosure. 'Maybe, but I don't want dark spectres hanging over us.'

'Before you tell me your news, darling, why don't you let me tell you about Louise. And Monique. And Jessica. And Joanna. And Brunhilda . . .'

That was as far as he got. The rest of his admission was muffled by a pillow hitting him square in the face.

❃

Ozman Urzak sat astern of the ferry, watching Istanbul's Kabatas docks receding into the background haze. The further the ferry travelled from land, the more clearly he could see the amazing outline of Sultanahmet and the Old City. The minarets of the dozens of mosques which crowned every hill stretched skywards like candles on gigantic cakes. Is that how his Moscow colleagues would describe the scene? No, they would say that the minarets looked like rockets about to be launched from Baikonur. Whatever! To Urzak they were a marvel of artistic and architectural genius. Or hubris? Only time would tell. Some of them, like the Blue Mosque, dominated their surroundings; others were more modest, as though a lesser God was worshipped there.

The boat was full of tourists and locals travelling to the Red Islands. Once the exclusive resorts of the wealthiest inhabitants of Istanbul, now the Jews, Greeks and Armenians had built summer mansions there to take advantage of the cool breezes denied to the inhabitants of the city's closely packed precincts. From the moment Urzak had taken his seat, even before the boat left, hawkers had tried to sell him Pierre Cardin ties, Rolex watches, Parker pens, Gucci this, Hermes that – the plethora of falsification was overwhelming. His own solid gold Rolex had cost him thousands in New York; he could have saved his money. Nobody could tell the difference.

Urzak was so intent on the hawkers that he didn't notice the man who sat down next to him. But he recognised the gruff guttural voice which said, 'I've brought you a coffee. Yours is black, no sugar as I remember.'

Urzak smiled and accepted the coffee. 'For my performance I deserve Bollinger.'

The other man smiled and nodded to the two hawkers, bracing themselves against the roll of the boat, pushing their cheap copies to other tourists. 'I'm sure one of these bastards could sell us a bottle of the real thing. So, it went well?'

Urzak looked at his friend. They met on a weekly basis but he still only knew him as Piotr, an administration clerk at the Russian consulate in Istanbul. They had done business together for the past ten years, both making a fortune. Urzak bought drugs from those opium farmers in Turkey's distant eastern provinces who managed to avoid the eagle eye of the American DEA then sold them on to Piotr's Mafia colleagues in Moscow, in exchange for a very nice line in military hardware which found a ready market in Armenia, Iraq and Iran. It was a comfortable trade, only occasionally interrupted when consignments were caught in transit by a border official who hadn't yet had his pockets lined.

Urzak's current assignment, pretending to be a high-ranking undercover agent of the Islamic world in order to manipulate some petty Ankara official, was a very definite change of pace for him, though the fee he was charging would make a nice addition to his already considerable Swiss bank account.

Piotr nodded in approbation as Ozman described the interview.

'And he bought it? Completely?' he asked.

'Totally. One hundred per cent. His hatred of the Minister was the key. He was prepared to believe anything of her.'

'So what's the next step?' asked Piotr.

'I told him to come up with a scheme to embarrass the Minister through this woman lawyer. As you requested. Though God knows why. I mean, if you wanted to get rid of the Minister there are other ways.' He made his two fingers into a gun and winked. 'Assassination is a tried and true staple of Middle Eastern politics.'

Piotr nodded. 'I have no idea why my colleagues in Moscow want the lawyer embarrassed. They said it was something to do with some archaeological treasure dug up by some German a hundred years ago. More than that, I don't know. However, I imagine the Russian government would be severely embarrassed if it had to give back the treasure. Apparently it's worth a fortune. Billions of dollars. We can't afford it.'

'But how does that affect our Mafia comrades?' asked Urzak.

Piotr shrugged his shoulders. 'Mine is not to question. If they want this Jewish lawyer to be run out of town, then that's what I'll do. I don't ask any other questions.'

'But why not just terminate her?'

Piotr shook his head. 'That's not an option in these early stages. But certainly, if the first plan fails, it will be considered.'

CHAPTER 17

Sarah and David decided to drive back from Pamukkale to where they had first started their journey. Cappadocia had had such a huge impact on them that they both felt the need to go back there before returning to the chaos of the city. They informed the Ministry of their change of plan then spent the day wandering amongst the fairy chimneys in blistering temperatures.

When they got back to their hotel in Goreme, a message was waiting for Sarah. She read it twice and shook her head, trying to work out its ramifications. David took the message from her fingers and read it aloud: 'The Director of the Ministry for Antiquities, His Excellency Doctor Yussef Barrak, presents his compliments to Miss Sarah Kaplan and respectfully requests her to grace him with a telephone call this afternoon at six o'clock.'

'Where's the problem with that?' he asked.

'It's simple,' Sarah explained. 'He's resented me from the moment I got here. He's a misogynist, a typical Mohammedan. He distrusts women and likes to lord it over everybody who works for him. He's arrogant, vain, pompous and deceitful. He should have been operating at the height of the Ottoman Empire; that world would have suited him perfectly.'

'Maybe he's changed. Maybe this woman you're working for, the Minister, has forced him into subservience.'

Sarah laughed. 'He'd rather die than have to work with me as an equal. He's a real snake in the grass. I don't trust him.'

'Do you have to?' asked David. 'You're working directly with the Minister. You're in control of a special group that's outside his authority. He can't hurt you. Give him a ring and find out what he wants.'

Sarah looked at her watch. She was tired and hot. She wanted a cold shower, a sleep and then some dinner. Then she wanted to make love to David and finally sleep long into the morning, waking refreshed and ready to start again. If she followed Barrak's instructions, she had to wait an hour to ring him. 'Okay, but I'll ring him now,' she said to David, 'not when he "respectfully requests" me to.'

She picked up the phone and stabbed out the number Barrak had given as his direct line. A mellifluous Turkish voice answered.

'Dr Barrak, this is Sarah Kaplan. You wanted me.' She sounded both officious and efficient.

'Miss Kaplan.' Barrak didn't seem in the least surprised. 'I was expecting you to ring in an hour but I'm delighted you've chosen to ring me earlier. I was wondering if perhaps on your return to Istanbul you would join me for dinner. I'm arranging a small dinner party at one of the better restaurants in Istanbul. Just a group of archaeologists and academics but I'm sure you would enjoy their company. And your companion would be very welcome to join us, of course.'

Sarah hadn't expected this. 'May I ask the purpose of the invitation, Dr Barrak? Your relationship with me isn't that of a dining partner. You made that quite clear when I first arrived.'

'Miss Kaplan, when you first arrived I was unsure of your role and motives and therefore somewhat peremptory. For this, I ask you to accept my apologies. I have closely followed the work you've done and spoken to the staff working with you. They admire you greatly and it is obvious that I have made a significant mistake. I wish to repair this error by offering the hand of friendship, if you will accept it.'

His tone was gracious. Sarah had no reason to refuse the invitation and indeed his cooperation would make life easier for the people who worked for her, especially after she had gone.

'Dr Barrak, that's very kind of you. Yes, we did get off on the wrong foot and I'd prefer that we mended the fences. I'd love to join you. My companion's name is David Rose. Oh, and he's my fiancé.'

'Wonderful,' Barrak said. 'I look forward to dining with you upon your return. Tell me, how are you enjoying the wonders of our country?'

She spent several minutes telling him of the sights they'd seen. He told her of some special places they simply mustn't miss. They arranged a time to get together when they returned to Istanbul and Sarah hung up the phone. She shrugged her shoulders. 'We have a date with an Ottoman,' she said.

For a moment Yussef Barrak felt a twinge of regret. She was an attractive young woman, open, honest and uncomplicated. It was a shame that he had to devise a plan to destroy her, but she had meddled in things which were not her business – as had that woman who commissioned her to act so imperiously, as though she were a Moslem, a man!

He smiled. Ever since his conversation with his visitor earlier that day, he had been musing over ways to bring down Sarah Kaplan and subsequently his execrable Minister. Just as taking a brick from the lower concourse of a wall would ultimately bring the wall crashing down, so the scandal surrounding the Minister would collapse this government into a festering heap to be washed away by the clear cold tide of Islam. Barrak licked his thin lips and pondered again on the course of action he was planning to follow. Could he get the guardian to agree?

He smiled when he thought of the mosque of Mehmet Pasha. Praying there was always special. It had been built by the genius Sinan at the end of the sixteenth century, a marvellous godly man who, although born a Christian, spent his entire life devoted to the glorification of the Ottoman sultans, building mosques, palaces, tombs, schools, hospitals, fountains, aqueducts, caravansarai and almost everything else. In his ninety-nine years of life the great Sinan had constructed many of the edifices which today symbolised the Turkish nation. But that wasn't the only reason that Yussef Barrak found it easiest to give his mind and body over to God in the mosque of Mehmet Pasha. No, it was the four fragments from the sacred black stone meteorite in the Kaaba in Mecca which was the chief magnet that drew him there. Many centuries earlier, when the Ottomans controlled Mecca, they had taken small pieces from the sacred stone to use as focal points of worship in their own mosques in Istanbul. This was as close as Barrak could come on a regular basis to his spiritual home, a place where his heart and mind could focus on Mecca.

And now his audacious plan involved interfering with the most sacred object in the world. But the results would surely be worth it. There would be a massive outcry by the Islamic community against the American Jewess for daring to interfere with a fragment of the Kaaba. It would spread like wildfire throughout religious and ultimately secular Turkey and would bring down the Kaplan woman, the Minister and the entire rotten edifice that Barrak was forced to bow down to every day.

He smiled again and closed the files on his desk. It was the end of the day but he didn't feel like going home. He felt a strong, indeed overwhelming, urge to go to his mosque and pray.

He left his office without acknowledging any of the staff or their farewells. Tomorrow he would call his office and inform them that he had decided to travel to Istanbul. He sighed. The thought of being there didn't please him; it was too noisy, too fast. What he really wanted was to enclose himself within the eternity of Islam. He walked out of the Ministry grounds onto the main street.

To his left was the Sultan Mehmet mosque. He had watched the American woman begin to enter the building, but then turn and walk away. He didn't admire the way she walked; it was provocative, ungodly. But still he was fascinated by her western mannerisms, the complete opposite of the modesty of Turkish and Arabic women.

Yussef Barrak stopped at the gates and looked up at the huge dome and the four minarets. It was a comforting sight, the sight of eternity, of everlasting truth. It was the very opposite of the Ministry building he had just left, a building devoted to the snakes and spiders of political life. So odd that the two buildings were side by side: God and Mammon rubbing shoulders. Wasn't that exactly what Mohammed had fought? Mammon was the antithesis of pure Islam; he represented greed, commercialism, sensuality – everything which Yussef Barrak, as a devout Moslem, most hated, but was forced to deal with every day in his position as head of the Ministry of Antiquities. There was no reconciliation of the two sides of his life.

He walked down the path towards the mosque. He yearned to be inside, to be enveloped in its cool calm interior, to watch the beauty of the blue light filtering in through the high windows, the lovely arabesques in the tiles, the grandeur of the building as it soared upwards into a dome which looked like the palm of God. Next door he was an important man, but in the mosque he was one among equals. No worshipper of Islam was any more important than any other. Barrak could lose himself in divine anonymity. He could talk with his heart open to God Almighty.

This was Islam. This was the way. And in order to defend Islam, in order to rid Turkey of its secular government, Yussef Barrak knew that he would do anything, including sacrificing the American woman. For by doing so he was doing the work of Allah, and in doing the work of Allah he would make Turkey into a great and godly nation.

He entered the mosque and breathed in the dark cool air. He took his shoes off at the portico and felt the warmth of the carpet beneath his feet. He was home.

✳

This time they met in a Bulgarian restaurant on a small road between Kutuzov Avenue and Kiev Station in south-west Moscow. Lomonosov had chosen it because it was on his way back from a meeting at Mosfilm Studios in the Lenin Hills, before he took his children to the planetarium in the afternoon. A lunch with his friend, the deputy director of the Pushkin Museum, was not only in line but in order.

Feyodor didn't like to meet with Lomonosov so publicly but the phone call had been jovial, and he was keen to know what was happening in Turkey. Nothing was happening in Berlin. The last letter of demand from the Berlin Museum of Archaeology had come two weeks before the tragic bomb explosion. Now there were no records of the correspondence. It would take the Germans years to sort out the paperwork again.

Lomonosov was in the restaurant when Feyodor arrived. A huge man with a large appetite he was already eating as Feyodor was shown to the table. The restaurant was fairly busy and Feyodor was surprised by so much activity so far from the city centre. The business district of Moscow was usually crowded with lunchtime diners but he couldn't remember the last time he had eaten outside of the garden ring which surrounded the Kremlin, the Museums and Pushkin Square.

'Sit,' said Lomonosov expansively. 'The food here is wonderful. Whenever I visit my interests in Mosfilm I usually stop off here for a quick bite to eat. You must have the *khoresht beh*. They do it splendidly here. Try it either with lamb or beef. Trust me, it's delicious. It's eaten with rice, a subtle blend of sweet and sour flavours. It's wonderful. It's their speciality, even though it's not Bulgarian but Persian. Who can tell the difference?'

Feyodor ordered as he was advised and the waiter nodded and retreated.

'Well?' Feyodor asked.

'Things are going to plan.'

'What do you mean?'

'What I say,' said Lomonosov. 'Things are going very nicely. We're springing the trap for one Doctor Barrak, of the Ministry of Antiquities, so we can use him as a lever to bring down this American lawyer. The scandal should bring down the government too. It's very neat and rather clever. I thought it up myself.'

Feyodor was amazed. 'Where did you get the information? I don't understand.'

'The Mafia is like a family, my friend. When Gorbachev liberalised things here we needed help in setting up our branch. So we brought in the Sicilians. They were marvellous. Their contacts are nothing short of breathtaking. Suddenly Russia was connected with the rest of the world. It would have taken us years to do it ourselves but with their help we just plugged into an existing network.

'Sure, it was difficult getting rid of them, but eventually we succeeded. Now our own connections are worldwide.

You know, people are very blinkered when it comes to dealing with the Mafia. We're a global business. We have branches everywhere and friends everywhere. If you want somebody assassinated in New Zealand it will take me twenty-four hours to set up. If you want a banker in New York to give you an unsecured multi-million-dollar loan – forty-eight hours. So bringing down some American lawyer in Turkey isn't exactly difficult.'

The waiter set two glasses of vodka and a jug of iced water between the two men. He poured the vodka into the glasses which immediately frosted in the warm atmosphere of the restaurant. In admiration, Feyodor Mikailovich Meconski lifted his glass and toasted his business partner. Then he got to his main concern.

'A question. If I wanted to be made director of the Pushkin, would you find that difficult? I would be in your debt forever, naturally.'

Lomonosov smiled and leant back in his chair, wiping a paprika stain from his upper lip. 'Not a problem,' he said. 'Not a problem at all.'

Both men threw the vodka down their throats.

CHAPTER 18

Slowly they climbed the palace steps. Because he was such a busy man Mithrassa-Urbek usually bounded up them. But today his normal progress was hampered by the child next to him who was dragging her feet.

'What is it, Amra? What's the matter?'

'I was afraid of the bull, but I faced it because I understand animals. But this . . .' she nodded towards the palace, 'this is . . . I don't know the word.'

'Overwhelming?'

Amra shrugged. 'I don't know what that means, but it's frightening. I've never been in a place like this before. I feel as though I am in my dreams but I can touch the walls. They don't disappear like they do when I open my eyes in a dream.'

Mithrassa-Urbek smiled. Despite himself he was beginning to like this woman-child, this savage. She was refreshingly honest. In court – especially the court of King Praxis whose sons were constantly warring for power and whose jealous wives would do anything to advance the standing of their offspring – politics was everything. Honesty was dangerous in the court of any great king; if people knew what you were thinking that gave them an advantage. This girl Amra with her blue skin, crude clothes and simple peasant ways would not fit in at all. Despite her extraordinary skill with the bull she would be nothing more than momentary amusement for the royal family and their courtiers. It was a shame, thought Mithrassa-Urbek, because in the short time he had known her, he had grown to admire as well as like her; two emotions which he thought had been driven from his nature by the antics of those whom he was forced to deal with as the King's secretary.

By now Amra was used to unusual sights. She closed her mind, and sometimes her eyes, when things became too strange, but when she saw the palace doors at the top of the steps, high above her, she stopped dead, breathless with wonder. The doors were made of a shining metal like gold and were almost as large as the doors which had barred her entry to the city.

Mithrassa-Urbek climbed eight more steps before he realised that Amra was no longer by his side. He turned to hurry her along and saw her face. It was a mask of wonder, fear and incomprehension. He'd seen such expressions before on the faces of other primitives who had been granted an audience with the great King. It was good for him to be reminded that what he took for granted were works of sheer wonder to others.

Mithrassa-Urbek's mind flashed back to the first time he had mounted these steps, when he was a young boy. Fear had also been in his heart then. But, unlike him, this child of the wild northern lands had no way of understanding this or indeed any other building in the city. He had travelled to her lands many years ago and he had no reason to believe that the peoples of those lands or their way of living had changed much. This girl probably lived in a mud and stick house with her many brothers and sisters, and probably farm animals also, like pigs and sheep and goats. How could somebody who lived so rudely understand the magnificence of a palace whose rooms were three times taller than the height of a man, whose walls and floors were made of the finest marble brought from quarries twenty days' journey inland which was hauled in on specially constructed wooden rollers by teams of thousands of slaves, whose ceilings were painted the colour of the sky and traced with rivers of pure gold leaf, whose waters ran hot from underground streams buried deep within the earth or came freezing cold from mountain streams, and whose beds were covered with the finest silk cloth imported from exotic lands far to the east made by flightless moths and spun by a people whose language and customs were those of legend?

Nevertheless, it was difficult for Mithrassa-Urbek to believe that this child standing timorously at the foot of the steps leading up to the King's palace was the same child as Amra the bull tamer, whose fame was spreading throughout the city and whose heroic deed would soon become the toast of the lands of the Hittite kings, the girl who had done what not even the very bravest warrior had succeeded in doing. He ran back down the steps and stood by her side. 'Tell me, Amra, why are you afraid?'

The child remained silent for a few moments, staring up at the massive doors and at the huge Nubian guards in their gleaming armour. Even their black faces, impassive and unmoving, seemed to burn with a dull power in the light of the sun.

'Amra?'

She looked at Mithrassa-Urbek. 'It's so big. It's bigger than any of the trees in the forest where I live. I've never . . . there's no . . . and those guards. Their skin . . . I've never seen . . .' Her voice failed her.

'They are Nubians from Abyssinia. The king of Abyssinia is a great king and there is much trade between our countries. He sends us spices and precious stones, tin for our bronzesmiths from the darkest parts of Africa. And he also sends us warriors. Our finest men spend two years in Abyssinia as guards in the King's palace in the high hills of Gondar, and his men spend two years here. Our women love to have their children. They grow strong and virile and very handsome with a delicate dark brown skin.'

Amra nodded. She had never seen men with black skin before. This truly was a wondrous place.

Mithrassa-Urbek put his hand on her shoulder. He was not normally a man moved to gestures of understanding, and almost never to feelings of compassion for any but his own family. As the King's secretary his responsibility was to deal with ambassadors of foreign governments, to keep the huge staff of the palace as well as the King's unruly children disciplined and under control, and to act as diplomat, travelling to the outposts of the empire to support the King's princes in their dependencies when difficult negotiations with obdurate neighbours were required. He was secretary to one of the mightiest kings in the world. He had neither the time nor the patience for frightened children, except for his own, some of whom he loved dearly. But somehow Amra was special. Mithrassa-Urbek knew that she could learn much from Troy, but an instinct told him that Troy could also learn something from this strange and complex child of the natural world.

'Amra, this is a huge building and it's very beautiful, full of marvellous things. But it is nothing more than a building, just as the house where you lay your head at night is nothing more than a house. Your home is special to you because of the people who live there, not because of the materials it is made from or its size. It is important for you to realise that while there are many important people who inhabit this great and mighty building, they all must eat and drink and rid themselves of body water just like you. The King is one of the most powerful men in all the world. Other kings come to bow their heads to him. But he has sons and daughters whom he loves very much, just as your father and mother love you. The princes and princesses who live in the court have many fine things given to them by their father, just as you, I'm sure, have wonderful things made for you by your father.'

Amra looked at Mithrassa-Urbek and smiled. Suddenly the building didn't seem so overwhelming. She began to slowly walk up the stairs, trying to take in his words, but her knees still felt like water as she climbed higher and higher. She had never been so far off the ground. This was different to climbing a hill or a mountain; that was still ground. But here she looked around and could see that she was level with the tops of trees and houses. Grasping her courage she stopped, and looked around properly. She could see into the courtyards of the houses; most of them had trellises with green bunches of fruit hanging among fleshy green leaves. She could see the tops of the people's heads in the road below. Some of the men were bald. Amra smiled, her nervousness fading. It was good to be so tall. Much taller even than when she rode on Wind.

Her thoughts were interrupted by Mithrassa-Urbek. His voice had lost its momentary friendliness; it was now the voice of a Headman telling a villager what to do. 'You are about to enter the King's palace. It contains many rooms. You must stay on the path between the doors and not stray into the rooms themselves. Under no circumstances are you to touch any vases or ornaments belonging to the King. This is punishable by death. When you come to the King's meeting chamber you will see King Praxis. You must fall immediately to the floor and not raise your eyes until he tells you to approach. If the Lord King allows you to stand and walk towards him avert your eyes. Never look directly at him. Do not speak to him unless he speaks to you. If a prince or princess addresses you you may speak to him or her, looking them in the eyes, but you must not speak first.

'Do not be presumptuous, child. Do not be forward. Remember that you are treating with some of the most important and powerful people in the world, people who demand the respect of the lowly born. Do you understand, Amra?'

Amra nodded, though in truth she hadn't understood very much. All she wanted was to ask the King for the secret of iron so that she could save her people. Then she could leave this strange place. Her nervousness increased as the Nubian guards threw open the massive doors, banged their lances on the ground and shouted out incomprehensible words of power.

Immediately Amra noticed how much colder it was inside the palace than outside. Somehow the burning sun lost its heat as they walked through the great doors. Where had the heat gone? Amra felt the air to see if it was wet, but it was dry no matter where she felt. Mithrassa-Urbek looked at her strangely, wondering at her strange swimming movements. Then Amra saw the painted walls and her jaw dropped in amazement. Men and women were chasing each other all over the walls. She knew they were figures traced and coloured on the wall but they were so real. She herself had decorated vases that the potter made, but her paintings were white lines and red ochre circles. These paintings were huge. And so lifelike that she expected the people to turn and greet her.

Each room was a new experience and Amra's wonder grew and grew. She had often imagined the home of the Gods, but in all her dreams had never imagined such glory as this. Some rooms were a deep blue like the sky, others a bright red like the sunset, others yellow like the gold her father fashioned into jewellery. As they walked further into the palace Amra became increasingly disoriented. They turned corners, walked along corridors, through rooms, up stairs, past courtyards bathed in the brilliance of the sun. They walked so far that Amra felt they could have crossed from one side of her village to the other, yet they were still within the one building. This surely was the greatest building in the world. Was this where the Gods lived? Was her mother here?

And it wasn't just the size of the building which caused her heart to beat faster. The rooms they passed through contained the most fabulous treasures she had ever seen. Her own family had more possessions than most because of her father's wealth and position as the metalmaker and armourer to the village. They had vases and a rug which her father had bought from a trader, and statues of Gods which stood on niches built into the walls. They had lamps in every room, some of which they burnt all night. But Amra realised that compared to this palace her home had next to nothing. There were vases here, painted in the most exciting of colours, the colours of the morning, the colours of rivers, the colours of rocks glistening in the sunshine, with figures dancing around their rims. There were rugs on the walls and floors, rugs of the deepest blues, reds and golds. She wanted to reach out and touch them, to smell them, taste them, feel their wealth. But touching them was death. That she had clearly understood from Mithrassa-Urbek's warning.

Suddenly Mithrassa-Urbek restrained her from walking any further forward. She wondered what she had done wrong but then saw that they had reached a doorway guarded by a quartet of the black-faced men. Mithrassa-Urbek's face and voice suddenly became even more serious than before.

'Amra,' he said softly, 'it is time to enter the preserve of the King. This is the throne room. Every important person in the palace gathers here to wait upon the desires of the King. This is where ambassadors and kings paying tribute are brought to bend their knees to the majesty of King Praxis of Troy.'

Amra's heart was pounding. Her throat was dry. The rooms they had walked through were large, cool and magnificent but the throne room, which she could see beyond the arches guarded by the four Nubian guards, surpassed them all. In the centre was a throne made of gleaming marble and inlaid with pure gold. It looked like the creamy water of an angry stream, the whitest and most brilliant stone she had ever seen, and it seemed to glow in the light which shone in through the windows. Surrounding the throne was water – running water inside a palace? Amra blinked her eyes, thinking that the God of Tricks was making fun of her, but indeed there was a stream of water surrounding the King's throne. It seemed to be coming from underneath the floor, near one of the windows, and flowing out again on the other side of the room. A small bridge, made of gold, spanned the stream, enabling the King to reach his throne. Standing on either side of it were two Nubian guards.

The room was full of people dressed in beautiful clothes in the colours of the sky and the sun and the grasses and the trees. They were talking quietly, but Amra could hear one particular voice above all the others. Some of the people noticed her and stopped talking. Others turned to see what had caused the lull, and soon all conversation ceased. Even the King turned to stare at her – the strange blue-faced child everybody had been talking about. Amra stared curiously at the King. He was taller and older than most of the people in the room. Judging by his height, and what she could see of his body beneath his wonderful clothes, Amra thought that he must once have been very strong. He was still probably one of the strongest men there.

Mithrassa-Urbek touched her arm and whispered 'Follow me and do exactly what I do.' He walked forward then, suddenly and alarmingly, fell to the floor and touched the ground with his forehead. Amra stood where she was, too surprised to move. Then, thinking he'd fallen, she stooped down to pick him up. He swiftly pulled her down beside him and pushed her head down until it too touched the floor.

Amra could hear people moving around but she couldn't determine what was happening because her head was being held to the ground by Mithrassa-Urbek. And she realised that she mustn't try to lift it or Mithrassa-Urbek would be very angry with her. She recognised the King's voice and could distinguish what he was saying. In the short time she had spent in Troy Amra had realised that their language was not so different from her own. They just had a different way of pronouncing words.

'This blue woman? This is the bull tamer?' said the King.

Mithrassa-Urbek's reply sounded muffled. 'Yes Lord and Master of the World, this is Amra the bull tamer.'

'Many people speak of you. Word of your conquest has come to my ears.'

The King now stood close to where Amra's head touched the floor. She could see the tips of his sandals. Mithrassa-Urbek took away his hand.

'What trick did you use to charm the bull?' the monarch asked.

'Trick?'

Mithrassa-Urbek nudged her sharply. 'What?' she whispered.

'Say, "Yes, Lord and Master of the World".'

Dutifully Amra repeated his words.

'What trick did you use? This bull is the incarnation of a messenger of the God Mithras on earth. I am his high priest. I know that he is a messenger of the God because he has killed many brave men. The bull is protected by the great God Mithras with love and affection. That is why he cannot be killed. Yet if what I am told is true you sang to the bull and tamed it.'

Amra raised her head. There was a gasp from the courtiers. Mithrassa-Urbek couldn't see what was happening or he would have forced her head back to the floor.

'I used no tricks,' she told the King. 'I sang to your bull as I sing to all the animals at home. If you shout at a bull or threaten him with a sword, he will charge at you. But if you show him you are his friend, he will be friendly.' Suddenly Amra remembered where she was and whom she was speaking to. She bowed her head immediately, wondering if her sudden outburst would be punished. She knew she should be afraid of this King. Everybody else was. She quickly added, 'Lord and Master of the World.'

The atmosphere in the throne room had changed dramatically from curiosity to hostility. People muttered under their breath, outraged that this primitive had dared to look directly at the King. But King Praxis was amused. The child was a savage; he had nothing to fear from her disrespect. Were she an ambassador from a rival monarch her breach would have meant her life. He would have cut off her head and returned it to the offending king so he would immediately know how powerful was Praxis, King of Troy. But this woman-child was from the wild lands in the north, far beyond the empire of the Hittites. Her face and body showed that she was a primitive. He would treat her like one of the exotic animals given to him as tribute by the kings of Egypt.

'Stand,' he ordered.

Mithrassa-Urbek leapt to his feet and pulled Amra up beside him. He saw that she was looking at the King and smiling so he pushed her head downwards to look at the King's feet.

The King walked back to the centre of the room, crossed the golden bridge and ascended his throne. Amra began to follow but Mithrassa-Urbek restrained her.

When he was seated the King beckoned her forward. With Mithrassa-Urbek to escort her Amra walked as far as the stream surrounding the throne. The Nubian guards stood on either side of them.

'Why have you come to Troy, child? Was it just to tame the bull of Mithras, or for some other reason?'

'I came . . .' Amra began but Mithrassa-Urbek again forced her head towards the floor. She was beginning to get a bit tired of this. 'I came because I want to know the secret of making iron.'

Suddenly the King's eldest son, Prince Cormis, shouted out in rage. 'Father, this is too much!'

Amra turned to see who had called out. He was tall and young and dressed in a beautiful long blue gown. He wore gold bracelets on his wrists and a gold circlet on his head. He looked wonderful but his face was mean and bitter. Why was he so angry? The King had asked her a question which she had answered. Amra was about to ask him what she had said to cause him so much distress when the King spoke angrily. 'I will decide what is too much. I am talking to this child. You and everybody else will be silent.'

The King turned back to her. 'So, you want to learn from us the secret of the Gods, the way in which we make iron. Why?'

Amra explained to the King about the men who lived beyond the mountains, men who had so many iron swords that their army numbered more than the stars in the sky. There was laughter at her description, but it stopped immediately as the King glared around the room. Amra stared in dismay. Why were they all laughing at her? Why was it funny that her family and her friends were threatened with death? Or that she or her sister Peta would be sacrificed to prevent the iron men from coming over the mountains?

'Iron is the most precious of all the gifts of the Gods,' the King explained. 'More precious, even, than gold. More difficult to make than bronze. From the time of my father the King, and my father's father the King, our metalworkers have been trying to make iron. It is like the Gods of the sea – known but invisible. When they make bronze daggers they find the iron on the sides of the kilns. It is a gift from Mithras in return for our devotion and sacrifice. He gives it so we may enjoy our future prosperity. Sometimes iron falls from the sky. It is used for the most precious and expensive of our jewellery. And this mystery is the gift you seek from me? The gift of iron is not something which can be given to one such as you.'

Amra's heart sank. With these words all her hopes were dashed. Everything she had dreamed of had come to nothing and the horrors she had survived were of no value. She had succeeded in reaching the people of the Hittites, but now the King was telling her that not even the mighty people of Troy have the secret of making iron. The anxieties, the nightmares of the past weeks flooded into her mind, clouding her judgement.

'But I was told by the traders who pass through our village that you have the secret of making iron. They told us that you have iron swords and shields. Do they lie?' Her voice was louder than she intended.

Her vehemence took the King aback. 'Do not dare to raise your voice to me,' he shouted. 'I have struck men dead for less than that. Kneel!'

Mithrassa-Urbek pushed Amra to the floor and forced her to prostrate her body.

'You are a child. It was only because of your bravery in facing the bull of Mithras that I permitted you to enter my presence. You need to learn much before you will be allowed to stand here again. You will go to the palace of the women. There you will learn how to conduct yourself in my court.'

The moment the King finished speaking Mithrassa-Urbek's hand forced Amra to stand again. She was guided backwards out of the room, eyes lowered the whole time. It wasn't until they were out of the room, and the doors firmly closed behind them by the black Nubian guards, that Mithrassa-Urbek allowed her to stand straight.

Amra looked at him in shock. 'What did I do? What did I say? Why was old man King so angry?'

Mithrassa-Urbek's fury abated when he realised that the child genuinely had no idea of her impertinence. One more unfortunate remark and the King would have ordered her execution. Instead of dragging her by the scruff of her neck to the women of the court who would teach her some manners, Mithrassa-Urbek could have been strapping her delicate body between two chariots and watching her limbs pulled apart to the roars of the same crowd which had cheered her success with the bull.

'I warned you,' he said, some of his fury returning. Her impertinence could harm him. After all, it was he who had introduced her to the King, something his enemies would not forget or forgive. 'I told you what to do and what not to do. Yet you looked directly at the King, you answered him in a disrespectful way – you even dared to ask him a question.'

'Of course,' Amra said, beginning to get angry herself. 'How else was I to speak to him? How else could he have told me the secret of making iron?'

'That is not the way of Troy, Amra.'

'Well, that's the way things are done in the villages of the five valleys. If we want to know something we ask. I don't understand your ways.' Amra flung out her hand, her gesture sweeping the palace. 'This is a horrible place.

I don't like it. I want to go back to my home. Why can't I ask the King how to make iron?'

'It is not an appropriate question. I warned you yesterday but you didn't take my advice. It could have cost you your life. Now I must take you to the court of the women, who will dress you properly, teach you how to speak to the King and the princes and princesses, and how to behave in court.'

Amra realised she had upset Mithrassa–Urbek. She could tell by the look on his face. She wished she hadn't because she liked him, and she knew that he liked her. So she nodded in agreement. Mithrassa–Urbek relaxed for the first time that day.

The air in the room was full of the smells of flowers, grasses, and other scents Amra could not identify. The windows were covered in a thin cloth through which the sun shone; Amra could see through it into the distance. The cloth seemed to be part of the wind, to sway in the breeze, just as her white robe had gently fluttered when she climbed the palace steps just a short time before. In the middle of the room was a large basin of water. More water came out of the top of what appeared to be the stem of a huge flower; it cascaded down into the basin over and over again.

There was movement on the ceiling too. Amra looked up in surprise. A collection of feathers hung down from a gigantic bird, they wafted backwards and forwards, backwards and forwards. She stared, stunned into silence, and saw that there was a rope attached to the tail of the bird. She followed the length of the rope through various fastenings on the ceiling until she saw the other end. It was being pulled by a young girl sitting in the corner. How boring her life must be, thought Amra, just sitting on the floor every day pulling a rope, even a magical rope that made a bird's tail move. The tail of the large bird produced a continuous cooling breeze; it was like being in a field on a hot summer's day when a cool wind blew down from the distant snowy mountains.

The room was empty except for the girl in the corner and two older women who stared at Amra with suspicion and bemusement. The women's dresses were so fine that Amra could clearly see their breasts, and the sun shining through the cloth over the windows also shone through their clothes, showing the outlines of their legs. What were these clothes for, she wondered? They could provide no warmth in winter; and in summer why wear anything other than the cloths which the women in her village wore around their stomachs?

'So!' said one of the women, 'you are the girl Amra who insulted our great King.' Amra wasn't sure whether she was being scolded or whether she should reply.

'Does the paint wash off?' the second woman asked.

'Paint?'

'On your face, child. The blue paint. Does it come off when you wash?'

Amra shook her head.

'You mean you look like this all the time?' The woman sounded horrified.

Amra nodded. The two women whispered together and even though Amra's hearing was particularly good – she could hear a bird settle in a tall tree – she heard nothing of what they said. These women were obviously skilled at talking without anybody overhearing them.

Finally the older and taller of the two women walked over to her. Her face was gentle, if lined, and her hair was grey. 'I am Mattusa. I am one of the former wives of King Praxis. My job is to teach new wives the ways of the court. I have been ordered to smooth off the uncivilised roughness from you.'

Amra stared at her wide-eyed. 'I am to become a new wife?' she gasped.

Mattusa burst out laughing, as did the other woman. 'Of course not. The King wouldn't marry one such as you. His wives come from other royal houses. Our job is to make you into a woman of Troy.'

'Why?'

'Why?' repeated Mattusa. 'Because ... well, because you can't enter the presence of the King looking and speaking the way you do.'

'But I already have,' Amra said.

'Yes, and look what happened.'

Amra silently agreed that her first meeting with the great and powerful King hadn't proceeded as she had hoped. It had surprised her. She had dared to imagine that she would be welcomed like a hero into the court of the King as the woman who had taken the golden arrow from the tree. Around the fire in her village, her parents and the other elders praised the deeds of the heroes of their land. Amra had imagined that when she walked into the palace of the King she would be treated in the same way as her people treated heroes, and that she would be asked to tell the story of how she fought the great bull of Mithras and how she had killed the mountain lion. But nothing had gone as she had thought it would. Instead she had been laughed at, made to feel stupid and sent away to become more like them.

Thinking about her reception by the court Amra became angry. Angry at the way these people treated her, angry because she had risked death for the golden arrow but had been refused the secret of making iron, angry because these women said she wasn't good enough to talk to the King even though she had done what twenty men before her had not been able to do.

'Take off your clothes and we'll burn them,' said Mattusa. 'We'll find something for you to wear which will cover those blue markings on your skin then we'll teach you how to . . .'

'No!' shouted Amra loudly. Her vehemence stunned the women and the girl sitting on the floor stopped pulling the rope, her jaw agape.

'No!' she repeated. 'You will *not* burn my dress. You will *not* wash me. I am Amra the hunter. I have killed a mountain lion. I was attacked and entered by three men. I killed them and cut off their penises and wore their manhood around my neck. I am Amra the hunter. I am Amra the bull tamer.'

She stood defiantly in the middle of the room, breathing deeply, her face red, her heart pounding. The bird's tail no longer stirred the air. The two women stared at Amra, trying to comprehend her extraordinary outburst.

'Oh dear,' said Mattusa.

CHAPTER 19

There was something about the wording of the invitation that concerned David, it felt as though Barrak was trying to manipulate them. He expressed his doubts to Sarah before she kissed him goodbye at the Hotel Turkoman, but she laughed, told him not to be paranoid, and said she would see him for dinner later that night. But *was* he being paranoid? Why had Barrak insisted that David enjoy a private tour around the harem of the Topkapi Palace while he met Sarah alone at the mosque of Mehmet Pasha?

Sarah thought it was all perfectly reasonable. She had already seen the Topkapi harem before David arrived in Turkey; now it was his turn to be escorted there by Barrak's assistant, leaving Barrak himself free to explain more about the wonders of Islam by showing Sarah the essence of a mosque. 'The last thing I want to do is to go back to the harem,' Sarah had said. 'It's beautiful and wonderful and decadent and incredibly interesting, but there's so much to see in Istanbul and so little I've had a chance to see because of the pressure I've been working under. Anyway, Barrak couldn't have been more charming at dinner last night. He was a perfect host. I think it's his way of eating humble pie. He knows his head is on a platter because of his treatment of me so he sees improving his relationship with me as his way of getting back into the good books of his Minister.'

David watched her leave the hotel through their bedroom window. She crossed over the road into the Hippodrome then headed to the right of the Blue Mosque and down towards the small but apparently beautiful mosque of Mehmet Pasha. He looked at his watch. He would need to leave in a few minutes to catch the tram down to the Topkapi Palace if he were to be on time to meet Barrak's assistant at the harem entrance.

Sarah tried to escape the afternoon heat by walking in the shadows of buildings, but this necessitated staying on the pavement. If this was New York, she reflected, the pavements would have been condemned by the city fathers as dangerous to pedestrians. It was the same all over Istanbul: pavements suddenly disappeared into yawning holes that gave entry to building basements. There was no thought to safety, no concern for potentially twisted ankles or broken bones. If there was a cellar, there had to be an entrance to street level. Answer: dig a hole in the pavement. It was an expedient solution, but downright dangerous.

Everywhere was in disrepair. Flagstones were often missing completely or had crumbled and broken into rubble. Most people walked on the road, risking their life as they braved motorists who seemed utterly insane.

Despite the efforts of the city to hinder her, Sarah eventually reached the protection of the cool inner courtyard of the mosque of Mehmet Pasha. Although the outer perimeter of the mosque had been invaded over the centuries by urban sprawl, there were still plenty of trees to offer shade to weary pilgrims and penitents. As with every mosque there was a central pillar in the courtyard with running water for the faithful to wash their faces, hands and feet. Sarah chose not to wash as she wasn't entering the mosque to pray. According to Yussef Barrak, the mosque was the pearl in the crown of Istanbul. It was a similar design to the Blue Mosque, but smaller and far more intimate, he'd told her.

Sarah slipped off her shoes and opened the curtain which screened the entrance. As she walked inside the heavy curtain shut out the heat, light and the noise of Istanbul. She looked up in amazement. Barrak was right: the mosque was exquisite. It was quite small which meant she was capable of taking in its grandeur and its beauty at the same time, something which the enormity of the Blue Mosque or Hagia Sophia made difficult. The Iznik tiles which decorated the walls cooled the room and gave off a translucent blue light. Sarah felt almost as if she were underwater.

She walked gingerly across the carpet and looked up into the cupola. Its delicacy made her hold her breath in wonder and amazement; the intricate geometric patterns created such an impression of unity that Sarah could not believe the artist's brush had ever once lifted from its work. It was a miracle of design.

As Sarah waited for her guide, her thoughts wandered back to dinner the previous evening. Barrak had thoughtfully sent a car to meet her and David at Istanbul airport. The chauffeur had explained that he was to take his important passengers to their hotel and wait for them until they were ready to leave for the Mevsim restaurant for dinner with His Excellency. At that stage Sarah had been non-committal, David impressed. When they eventually arrived at the restaurant, elegant and ornate even by Istanbul standards, they were shown through the main dining area with its dozens of tables and taken up a set of stairs to a private dining room. Yussef Barrak and six other men stood as they entered the room. Dr Barrak kissed Sarah's hand and welcomed David as though he were a long-lost brother, telling the men – all heads of other departments within the Turkish public service – what a wonderful job Sarah was doing and how she had solved a problem not even the most proficient of Islamic lawyers had been able to come to terms with. He sat her at the head of the table, a move in itself unique in this traditional Turkish restaurant where men and women often dined at separate tables. Barrak even deferred to Sarah and David's religion by making a point of not ordering shellfish.

During the evening's conversation he had asked Sarah for her impression of Islam in Turkey. Sarah had demurred, telling him that she had not had the time to really consider any of the major differences between Islam and Judaism.

'Differences?' he'd said, seeming genuinely shocked. 'But my dear Sarah, we celebrate our similarities not our differences. We have one sovereign ruler in both Judaism and Islam. Our history was created when God created Adam and Eve. We believe, like you, in the temptation and the fall, the flood of Noah, the prophets Abraham, Isaac and Jacob. But unlike Judaism and Christianity, which concede nothing to other religions, Islam concedes that it is based in both. For we revere also the prophet Jesus as one of the creators of our religion. The difference, however, lies in the fact that your Judaism, my dear, claims Moses as its founder. But it is the similarities which cause me the greatest pleasure. Correct me if I'm wrong, but I believe that the focal point of Judaism is not the worship of its prophet Moses but its reverence for the Holy of Holies, the Ark of the Covenant. From the time of Solomon and the building of the Temple all your worship has been temple-centred.'

Sarah nodded, wondering where he was going with the discussion.

Barrak continued. 'In Islam we have another focal point of identification with God and that is the Kaaba. The house of Allah. Like Jews who face Jerusalem, Moslems face Mecca. And like Moses, Mohammed is only a prophet whereas Allah or God is the source of worship. It has always interested me that Jews and

Moslems revere a place of worship and what it contains – the Holy of Holies and the Torah in your case, or the Kaaba in ours. However, our Christian bretheren have an entirely different perspective. They believe that the worship of God involves the worship of his son, Jesus Christ. The Christians have no place to turn to, nor any source of God or Holy of Holies to identify themselves directly with God.'

Sarah had nodded again.

'What do you know about the Kaaba?' he asked.

'Very little,' she had admitted.

'Then tomorrow,' he said conspiratorially, 'I will show you the Kaaba.'

Sarah laughed.

'Not in Mecca of course. You would not be welcome there, for reasons of which I am sure you are aware. But we have a piece of the Kaaba in a most beautiful mosque here in Istanbul, the mosque I worship in. Why don't you let me show it to you?'

'That would be lovely,' Sarah had told him.

And now here she was, a few minutes past their appointed meeting time. According to everyone who worked for him, Barrak was always punctual – if you called keeping everybody waiting fifteen minutes punctuality. She wondered where he could be. She looked around for somewhere to sit but there were no seats in the mosque. Everybody prayed on their knees. She wandered over to the benches that had been placed against the outer walls. As she sat down she heard the wailing of sirens in the distance. They seemed to be coming closer and closer. It reminded her of New York, sirens everywhere, all the time. They were definitely nearer now. Sarah felt her shoulders stiffen. Suddenly they stopped and their piercing noise was replaced by the menacing screech of tyres and the pounding of running feet. It was so close it sounded as though it was in the courtyard. Suddenly half a dozen police officers burst in through the curtain over the doorway, shouting as they ran towards her.

Sarah screamed in shock as one policemen grabbed her arm roughly and pulled her into the light in the centre of the mosque.

'What the hell do you think you're doing?' she cried out. 'Let go of me.'

A young cleric burst through the curtain and immediately pointed at her, screaming in Turkish. The policeman in charge barked at her aggressively.

'What the hell is this?' she shouted. 'Who are you and what do you want? Tell these men to take their damned hands off me immediately. How dare you touch me! I'm an American citizen.'

'Silence,' said the policeman in heavily accented English.

'You be silent!' Sarah was beside herself with fury. 'Let me go immediately or I'll sue you for assault. How dare you touch me.' She tried to shake her arms free but the more she resisted the tighter they held her.

'Silence,' the policeman said again and this time he struck her across the face with the back of his hand. Sarah stared at him wide-eyed with shock. The danger of her position suddenly became horribly clear. She stopped struggling and tried to calm herself in case he decided to do her anymore physical harm. She was overwhelmed. Nobody had ever hit her before. Her face stung where the man's heavy gold ring had cut her chin. She wanted to scream in pain and shock, but forced herself to be silent, to comprehend the situation.

'What is your name?' the officer demanded.

She had to retain the upper hand. 'What's yours?' she responded as menacingly as she could. She knew it would irritate him but it was a power ploy. If she pleaded or showed any sign of weakness, she was lost. Yet Sarah was terrified. 'I don't know how good your English is but try to understand this. I will prosecute you in the highest court in Turkey for striking me.' She sounded calm but her courage was only an act.

'Your name?' he demanded again.

'Sarah Kaplan. I'm an American lawyer.'

'How long have you been here in this mosque?'

'About ten minutes. Why? What am I supposed to have done?'

The policeman didn't answer. He turned to the cleric who was still talking and gesticulating and beckoned him over. 'This man says you have stolen pieces of the Kaaba from the mosque. He saw you do it and called us immediately.'

'What?' Sarah exclaimed. 'Don't be ridiculous. I've only just got here. I've no idea where it is. How could I steal it?' She knew she was babbling. She had to control herself, moderate her voice.

The cleric grabbed Sarah's handbag from her shoulder. She shouted at him but was powerless to move. The policemen were holding her too firmly. The cleric's robes fell across the bag as he opened it and tipped its contents to the floor. He picked out a tiny sliver of stone, black and pockmarked, and thrust it angrily in Sarah's face.

'I have no idea what this is,' she said.

The cleric shook his fist in her face and shouted at her. His spittle hit her lips and nose, making her wince. He grabbed at her clothes and pulled at her aggressively. The three policemen began to frogmarch her towards the door but the cleric stood in the way and jabbed his finger towards the pulpit, shouting at Sarah in disgusted tones.

The lieutenant in charge explained. 'He says that he saw you take this stone of the Kaaba from the pillar here.

He says you have defiled Islam. That you must suffer the consequences of Islam.'

'I never touched it,' Sarah insisted. 'I only just got here. Ask Dr Barrak. Yussef Barrak. He's the Director of the Ministry of Antiquities. He's supposed to be here now. He'll vouch for me. I swear to you I never touched this stone. Never.'

The policeman questioned the cleric to ensure that his story was correct. Sarah, her arms pinioned by the three policemen, began to realise that she was in very real trouble. It wasn't just the fact that she was accused of theft – though in Turkey, with its repressive laws, that was frightening enough. She was accused of having violated Islam, of blasphemy. Terrifying consequences began to unfold in her mind, each more frightening than the last. She remembered that in Saudi Arabia they stoned people for transgressing Islamic law, and in Iran they beheaded them. What was the law in Turkey? And where was Barrak when she needed him?

'You took a knife from your bag and levered the stone out of the wall. This is what the holy man says.' The police officer was getting annoyed with her obstinacy.

'I have no knife. Look.' Sarah nodded towards her bag, its contents spilt on the floor. 'Will you tell these three goons to let me go? Can't you use your damn eyes. Look on the floor – there's no knife there. Where did I get a knife from? Ask him that. That'll prove that he's lying.'

But before the policeman could pose the question, the curtain was pushed aside, admitting light into the mosque. A tall thin figure was haloed in the doorway. Sarah felt her knees go weak with thanks and gratitude.

'Yussef,' she called out. 'Yussef, for God's sake come and help me. These people think I stole the Kaaba stone. I've been arrested. It's all a hideous mistake.'

Barrak quickly crossed the carpeted floor. Sarah continued to speak fast and low as he got closer. 'I don't know what game these people are playing, Yussef, but I'm beginning to get very angry. I'm being accused of being a common criminal. I think I've been set up by this man.' She nodded towards the cleric. 'Is this common behaviour in your country?' she asked coldly. 'And I've been struck in the face by this policeman. Tell him that's a criminal assault and that I'll be going after his blood.'

Barrak held up his hands in an effort to take control of the situation. 'What on earth has happened? Why are you being held like this? For God's sake, tell me what happened, Sarah.'

'This man, this priest, says that he saw me take the stone out of the wall with a knife. I have no knife. Yussef, he's lying. Please, help me. I'm being falsely accused –'

'My dear Sarah, please. Wait a moment. Let me find out the facts first.'

Barrak snapped at the policemen to release Sarah's arms before turning to speak to the cleric. She felt overwhelmingly grateful as the feeling flowed back into her limbs. The cleric nodded and gesticulated wildly towards the stairs ascending to the pulpit then pointed down at the contents of Sarah's bag on the floor. Sarah had no idea what they were saying but assumed that Barrak was covering the same ground as the policeman.

Barrak turned to Sarah. 'He says you used a knife.'

Before Sarah could respond the officer in charge intervened. 'Do not question or talk to the accused. Who are you? I am conducting this investigation. What business do you have here?'

Barrak answered him imperiously, 'I am Dr Yussef Barrak, Director of the Ministry for Antiquities. This woman, Miss Kaplan, is a consultant to the Ministry, an

American citizen, a friend of the Minister and a guest in our country. What right do you have to arrest her?'

The officer explained again what had happened and why he had acted.

'And where is the knife she is supposed to have used?'

The policeman shrugged his shoulders.

'You have no evidence against this woman. Let her go immediately or I'll have your job.'

The policeman smiled. The days when a bureaucrat could intimidate an officer of the law were long gone. 'We have a lot of evidence. The stone was found in this woman's handbag. There was no-one else in the mosque when we arrived. The cleric is an eyewitness who saw her stealing it. That's enough for me to arrest her.'

'But the knife?' demanded Barrak.

The policeman shrugged again. 'Maybe her back was turned to the cleric when he was looking so he couldn't see what she was doing properly. Maybe he thought she used a knife when she actually used her fingernails. I don't know. My job is to arrest this woman and let the prosecutors make a case.'

'You can't arrest her,' Barrak insisted. 'She is a highly placed lawyer from New York. It would cause a major international incident. Let her give back the stone and we'll forget about it.'

The policeman turned and said something to the priest who shook his head, gesticulating violently at the empty scar in the pulpit and then towards Sarah's bag.

Barrak turned to Sarah. 'I'm afraid the cleric is insistent. I know this man. I'm sure I can persuade him to change his mind. In the meantime, please go along with these policemen. I'm sure we'll have this tragic misunderstanding sorted out by nightfall.'

'I'm not going along with anybody, Yussef. Once I'm in jail I will have no power to fight this. This man is lying.'

'Sarah, I'm afraid you don't have that choice. I will look after your interests – of that you can be assured.'

The three policemen again gripped Sarah by the arms and started to push her towards the door.

Sarah turned her head and spoke urgently to Barrak. 'Tell David what's happened. Please. Get him to come and see me. Yussef, please. And phone the Minister.' Her tone grew shriller as she neared the door. 'Tell the Minister I've been wrongly accused. Tell her to phone the American ambassador. I need the ambassador to get this sorted out. Please, Yussef.'

The policemen pushed Sarah through the heavy curtain covering the door. Her last glimpse was of Barrak standing beside the cleric. She couldn't see his face properly in the half light of the mosque but she was certain that he was smiling.

CHAPTER 20

An elderly Imam looked out of his office window at the commotion below. He had heard the police arrive and run into the mosque. He had descended the stairs from his office to see what the fuss was about but one of his young clerics had met him at the bottom of the stairs and deferentially suggested that the holy man not bother himself with matters concerning the police, that he would attend to whatever it was that the police were there to investigate. The elderly Imam was above such worldly concerns. He had begged the Imam to wait in his office, saying he would return shortly and inform him of what was amiss.

The Imam watched the girl being pushed into the car. Clearly she was a tourist. She was dressed like an American. It was very strange. Even stranger was the fact that his young cleric didn't appear immediately to let him know what the police had wanted. Instead he was standing in the courtyard talking to one of the mosque's most glorious patrons and congregants, Dr Barrak of the Ministry of Antiquities.

Sarah was bundled roughly out of the car and into the enormous police station with its large airless rooms filled with clouds of grey cigarette smoke. Her guards impelled her forward until her body was forced up against the desk. A man whose epaulettes and badges showed him to be a sergeant stood behind it. The officer who had arrested her gave details which the sergeant wrote down furiously.

'I have a right to know what you're saying and what I am being accused of,' Sarah said.

'You are being accused of theft and of tampering with a religious article. That's all for the moment.'

'For the moment?'

'Yes, for the moment! It is possible that the priest may bring a further charge of blasphemy against you under Islamic law. In his eyes you are an infidel. To have touched this holy stone is an offence in his law.'

'I demand to see the American ambassador.'

'Of course,' said the lieutenant. 'That is your right as an alien.'

'This is ridiculous, you know. There is not a court in the world that would accept the lies that this cleric has told. You're just wasting my time, your time and causing a huge incident. You know this is going to get onto the front page of the *Washington Post*, don't you? Can you imagine what that will do for tourism in Turkey? Who is going to come here from America if they know they can be thrown into prison on the slightest whim? This could cost you hundreds of millions of dollars in lost revenue. You know what's happened in Egypt and Algeria because of their treatment of tourists. Well, the same –'

'My job is to act on information, which is all I'm doing. Other people worry about the effects of those actions.'

'Look, I understand your job. I'm a lawyer in America. I know that you're only acting on a complaint. But you have to appreciate that without the knife to prove that I did it, this piece of stone could have been planted in my bag by the priest. In fact, it's the *only* way it could have got there. It's going to be his word against mine in a court of law. Can you seriously see any fair-minded judge finding against me?'

The policeman shrugged. 'That is not my concern.'

'Well, you ought to make it your concern. I'm not sure about the law in this country but in America there's such a thing as vexatious prosecution. If you press ahead with this, you may find yourself on the wrong side of the dock.'

The officer shrugged again.

Sarah gave up. 'I assume I have the right to see a lawyer and that I have the right to be freed on bail?'

'Your rights will be fully protected. We are not a barbaric country. In the meantime you will be fingerprinted and formally charged. We will inform the American consul in Istanbul of your arrest. After that, the processes of law will take effect.'

As a musician David Rose was used to waiting. He waited for orchestras to play their set pieces before he was called from his dressing room to perform his solo; he waited for imperious conductors to invite him to join them on the platform; he waited for his agent to call with offers to perform at concerts by impressarios who didn't know Dvorak from Kojak. And now he waited for a Turkish police lieutenant to tell him why in God's name his fiancée had been arrested and thrown in jail.

Of all people, Sarah was the last human being on earth who would commit a crime. She used to infuriate him on drives up Long Island to see her parents by telling him he was driving above the speed limit when he was just keeping up with other cars; if she saw somebody in the street who even looked like he was going to commit a felony she would wait in case she could assist the police with their enquiries, or would search out the nearest police officer. This accusation of theft was ridiculous. No! It was more than ridiculous, it was a total set-up. David was certain of it. And he was also certain that it was Yussuf Barrak who had set her up. Why else separate him from Sarah so there would be no witnesses to her alleged crime except for some low-life Islamic priest who was obviously lying through his teeth?

The immediate question was what to do now? Foreign nationals in trouble called in the big guns from the embassy, which is precisely what David was about to do.

Once he had seen Sarah. But that was taking an extraordinarily long time. He had been given an array of excuses: she was being processed, she was being interviewed, she was being informed of her rights under Turkish law, she was resting. Anything to prevent him from seeing her, anything to make him feel subservient to the petty little bureaucrats behind their high desk.

He rose from the hard wooden bench and once more walked over to the duty sergeant whose job, it appeared, was to sit behind his desk sipping an inexhaustible supply of apple tea and writing laboriously in a massive official-looking tome.

'Can you tell me how long now?'

The desk sergeant looked bored. 'As I told you before, sir, you may see the accused woman when you may see her. Not before. Not after. Only when.'

'You have been delaying my seeing her for the better part of three hours now. The time has come for me to telephone the American Embassy in Ankara. Are you aware of the consequences of my doing so? Do you realise the trouble you'll be in for preventing me from seeing my fiancée?' David tried to sound menacing but the desk sergeant just shrugged his shoulders and bent his balding head to his work again. David hadn't felt this impotent since he was at school.

He returned to the bench and looked at his watch. It was just past ten in the evening. The chances of him seeing Sarah before morning were growing increasingly slim. Not even the arresting officer had come out to speak to him. He would sit here for another few minutes, make another empty threat to the desk sergeant then return to his hotel room to hit the phones and make as much noise as he possibly could. The US ambassador in Ankara, the American Consul in Istanbul, the White House – damn it, why *shouldn't* he phone somebody in the White House? After all, he had played cello for the President – the State Department, Sarah's old law firm in Wall Street, the *Washington Post*, the *New York Times*, *B'nai Brith*. He would phone anybody and everybody who would listen and would make the biggest noise anyone had ever made about wrongful imprisonment.

But as he sat there waiting, going over in his mind what he could do to help Sarah, he realised that this was a much bigger issue than simple theft. Sarah had been accused of defiling an Islamic religious artefact; the real issue now was Islam versus Judaism.

David's musings were interrupted by the hum of human voices in the distance. He listened more attentively as the chanting grew louder and louder; it sounded like a body of people coming towards the police station. Even the desk sergeant, previously impervious to all outside influences beyond his ledger book, looked up and frowned. The atmosphere in the police station changed suddenly from one of boredom to activity. Several policemen came running in from outside, speaking animatedly and waving their arms in obvious concern. The desk sergeant exchanged a few words with one of them, then grabbed the phone and barked instructions into it. Within a few minutes extra police appeared and began closing the shutters inside the barred windows, locking them into position.

David walked over to the desk sergeant. 'What's going on?' he demanded.

'Demonstrators are coming this way.'

'Demonstrators?'

'We believe they want your companion. They say she has defiled Islam and must be punished.'

'What?!'

'Please sit down,' said the desk sergeant. 'You are in the way.'

'To hell with that!' shouted David. 'If there's a mob outside wanting Sarah I want reinforcements here immediately. I want her moved to somewhere safer. Now! Jesus Christ!'

The desk sergeant resented the westerner's interference. 'Sit down! You think we haven't handled mobs before? There's always a demonstration somewhere in the city. There's a procedure to follow.'

'The hell with your procedures. Have you got enough men? Have you got riot gear? Have you got tear gas or whatever you use?'

'We have everything we need to quell a riot. Now sit down out of the way or I will have you placed in a cell.'

The shouting was more distinct now. It was both terrifying and menacing. For the first time since entering the station David actually agreed with the sergeant. This wasn't a place for him to be. 'I'll go then,' said David. 'I'll go back to the hotel. For God's sake, look after Sarah.'

The police sergeant looked at him as if he was a lunatic. 'You are a crazy man. You will stay here. A mob will tear a man like you to pieces. Don't be a fool. Sit down and remain quiet until we have handled the situation. We have much to do.'

The sergeant began to shout orders to the young police officers. David retreated to the bench in order to ride out the storm.

And the storm was long and nasty. The mob of several hundred young men was led by four clerics, one of them the man who had falsely accused Sarah. They stood in an eight-deep phalanx outside the police station, blocking the main road. They carried placards which one of the nervous young policemen, peering between the slats of the shuttered window, translated for David. 'Death to she who blasphemes against Allah' and similar messages.

One of the clerics addressed the crowd, screaming invective and jabbing his finger towards the door of the police station. The crowd screamed their chants in response. Despite the shuttered windows and the locked door the noise seemed to seep in through the very bricks and reverberate inside the walls of the station.

Deep within the prison, locked in an airless room two floors below street level, Sarah lay curled on a hard wooden bunk, her knees folded tightly below her chin, her arms hugging her legs in foetal position. The muffled roar of the demonstrators' fury permeated the cell. Sarah knew they had come for her. She recognised a lynch mob when she heard one. How long would she last if the mob broke into the prison and found her, she wondered? The other prisoners were not making her anxiety any easier. They banged their fists against the water pipes, and rattled tin plates and cups against the cell bars. The cacophany pounded into her very brain.

Sarah had stayed calm when she was being interrogated. She had been aggressive, legalistic, hard-edged. But she was alone now and she could smell the prison deep in her nose, the decades of grime, filth, the stench of human sweat. She tried to read the graffiti on the walls to distract herself from her abject fear of what was happening outside, but nothing could block out the dull roar of the clerics and the mob who screamed for her head. Sarah hugged herself closer and tears welled up in her eyes. She began to hum a nursery rhyme tune.

David begged the desk sergeant to let him speak to Sarah. The noise of the mob outside terrified him so he could imagine now it would be affecting Sarah. Locked in a cell, cut off from the world, with no-one she loved to help her and reassure her that she was safe, she must be at her wits' end. But the sergeant just motioned him back to the bench.

The policemen inside the building seemed to be doing nothing except standing by tensely, waiting for something to happen. Each was armed with riot gear: flak jackets, helmets with perspex shields, vicious-looking wooden batons, and plexiglass riot shields. Some had exchanged batons for sub-machine guns and others for cans of pepper spray. But they weren't going out to face the mob; instead they stayed inside while the room reverberated with the mob's violence. The desk sergeant, animated for the first time since David had entered the police station, was pacing the room, occasionally giving instructions to his men to overcome their nervousness. David hurried up to him again. 'For God's sake, tell me what you're going to do. Why are your men just standing there? Why don't they go outside and confront them, send them away?'

The sergeant unexpectedly felt a degree of compassion for the young man. He explained, 'Mobs like this shout themselves into exhaustion. They'll soon be out of energy and will simply wander off. But if any of my men were to appear in riot gear, it would incite the demonstrators to physical fury and the situation would become very serious. Right now they're just throwing a tantrum. Better we let them do that than show our strength. A mob after destruction doesn't shout. It does.'

David was desperate to look out the window to see how many there were in the mob and what they were doing. From the volume of voices he could easily envisage a crowd of thousands. Suddenly the cleric's voice broke through. 'Allahu al Akbah,' he shouted, Allah is great. The mob responded and suddenly the demonstration was over. The mob sang an Islamic song which grew softer as they retreated slowly in a body away from the police station to be enfolded by the darkness of the night. The relief inside the station was palpable. The sergeant smiled and nodded to his lieutenant and to others in the room. Someone told a joke which David didn't understand but everybody roared with laughter. It was a means of releasing the tension. David was shaking. He hadn't realised the extent of his terror for Sarah.

The sergeant turned to him and said, not unkindly. 'I suggest you return to your hotel. I will send you in a police car for your protection. Come tomorrow at nine. You can see your lady then. Tonight is not suitable.'

David argued that he needed to comfort Sarah, to reassure her, but the sergeant was adamant. Eventually David had to nod and agree. Besides he was desperate to get back to his hotel to start calling people who could help. Before the mob had arrived, his main concern had been for Sarah's liberty. Now he was desperately frightened for her life.

In the bowels of the prison, Sarah lay on the filthy bunk, her hands over her ears. She had tried to block out the noise of the protesters by clutching her amulet, and trying to decipher the graffiti around her, but eventually her terror became too much. She had resorted to what she did as a child in a thunderstorm – closed her eyes and covered her ears and pretended it wasn't happening.

David slammed down the phone, hoping that the noise would damage the ears of the arrogant, officious, self-righteous pompous piece of bureaucratic slime on the other end. For much of the previous night and for the first hour of the morning, David had received nothing but superficial concern and shallow and patently obvious advice from the US ambassador's office in Ankara down to the US consulate in Istanbul. Everybody offered their deepest sympathies for Sarah's plight and their guarantee that immediate action would be taken on her behalf. But when he pressed them for what action, when, where and how, the evasions began.

'As soon as the time is apposite, sir, which means calling the . . .'

'You will appreciate, of course, the delicate diplomatic balance we have to maintain, but be assured Mr Rose that . . .'

'American and Turkish interests, as both nations are members of NATO, preclude any precipitate action, however . . .'

'Turkey is an ally of the west, and it would be unwise for us simply to march in there like John Wayne and . . .'

Everybody was concerned about America and Turkey but nobody seemed to give a damn about Sarah Kaplan, stuck in a stinking Turkish prison on spurious charges.

The call to the State Department the previous night had been spectacularly unsuccessful and still rankled with David. He had been passed upwards from an administrative assistant, to a situation officer, to an area expert, and the higher he got the less notice seemed to be taken of Sarah's plight. Their main concern was not rocking the Turkish boat. Eventually he had been put through to the Undersecretary of State charged with special responsibility for Southeast European affairs. The memory of the conversation still infuriated him.

'So, David – I may call you David?'

'You can call me anything you want as long as you help me get my fiancée out of prison.'

'You say you know the President, you've played cello at the White House?'

'Yes,' David had told him, 'but I used that to get to somebody as high as you. I have no special connection with the President other than having shaken his hand.'

'What did you play? I'm a devotee of classical music myself.'

'Does it matter what I played? For God's sake, we're not talking about me and my career. We're talking about my fiancée stuck in a Turkish jail!'

'Sure. Now run it past me one more time. Why precisely did she steal this holy stone from the mosque?'

'She didn't steal the damned stone! Will you please listen to what I'm saying. It's a put-up job. She's being framed. She's run foul of a heavyweight in the Turkish Ministry of Antiquities and he's concocted this bullshit story in order to get her out of the way. I've just come from the prison. There was a damn riot there. People want to tear her limb from limb. Do you understand what I'm saying to you?'

'Sure, Dave. Sure. I think, though, that it's important that you keep calm, and that you allow us to handle the sensitive diplomatic negotiations to extricate your fiancée from what is a very difficult situation.'

David had slammed down the phone. Since then he had slammed it down four more times that night and then twice this morning. Now he sat slumped on the edge of the bed, his face in his hands. What next? He straightened up again. If official America wasn't going to place diplomacy above the safety of one of its citizens, then he had to approach other avenues: Sarah's former law firm and the media. This was definitely a big enough story for him to get straight through to the editors.

It took three phone calls before he was satisfied. The night news editor of the *New York Times* had taken the story first, setting up a conference call with his foreign news editor, his diplomatic correspondent and David. The night news editor remembered Sarah from her defence of Frank Darman, the Holocaust denier, in a trial two years earlier. While they were obviously much more interested in the political details than getting Sarah out of jail, all had assured him that if what David said was true their front-page headline would put overwhelming pressure on the American government as well as bringing out the militants who would put pressure on congressmen.

But it was Morrie Friedlander, Sarah's old boss, who went ballistic. He shouted to David that he would take this matter up with friends in Congress, in the White House, in places of importance all over America. It was Morrie's voice which still resounded in David's ears when he got up from the bed to shower and to go to see Sarah.

There were more policemen outside the police station this morning than there had been the previous night. There was a different desk sergeant too. David explained who he was and asked in as cordial and open a fashion as he could muster whether he was now permitted to see Sarah.

The desk sergeant shrugged. 'Of course. This is not a problem. Your fiancée is down this corridor. Speak to the man sitting at the desk.'

David's body sagged with relief. He followed the musty smoky corridor until he reached the end. There was a desk there in front of a ceiling-to-floor grille. A fat policeman with a single stripe on his shirt sleeves looked at David quizzically. His telephone rang before David was able to say anything but the guard nodded, smiled and opened the grille, admitting David to a further corridor lines with cells. The guard shut and locked the grille behind him and escorted David down two flights of stairs into the bowels of the building where prisoners were incarcerated.

It had been hours since Sarah had spoken to anybody. Not content with taking away her dignity, her self-confidence, her freedom, even her name, they had also taken away her watch, her belt, her shoelaces and her jewellery. She had no idea what time it was, but she clearly remembered the hideous, leering guard who had won an obscene lottery with the other guards to see who would search her. His body stench reminded her of the driver in Cappadocia and she was powerless to free herself from him.

First he put his hands on her shoulders. Then he felt her arms. She had slunk back against the wall trying to get away from him but he had shaken his head, explaining mimetically that this was his job. Four other men in the fingerprinting room smiled as they looked on. There was no escape.

Her body, rigid with fear, disgust and self-loathing, was about to be invaded by this hideous man's hands. He moved slowly, like some maniacal photographer, from one of her arms to the other, his fat gut almost touching her. He put his hands around her back and felt her waist and then the bottom of her skirt. He turned and nodded to the other guards; they were enjoying the performance. She tried to force her mind to go elsewhere, but the guard's wandering hands kept bringing her back to reality. She felt ill.

Slowly the guard brought his hands around from her back to her front, and placed them inside her skirt and felt the top of her stomach. Sarah was sure he had an erection. His hands roamed freely as he forced them around her thighs, her bottom, then down her legs. Then he brought them upwards slowly in a vulgar parody of foreplay, and began to trace the outline of her bra with his pudgy sweaty fingers. She was about to throw up all over his greasy, bald pate when he removed his hands, nodded professionally and indicated to his colleagues that she was carrying no concealed weapons. They burst out laughing.

When she had been taken back to her cell, she had wept. Once again she was alone with her nightmare, the only thing that kept her going was the thought of David, and the hope that he might rescue her. But the longer it took, the harder it became to steer her mind away from the debilitating feelings of loathing, anger and fear. The explosive mood of the demonstration on the street, which she knew was directed against her, had been terrifying. Where was David? She knew the difficulties in getting people out of jail, she had done it herself. It was hard enough in America, let alone Turkey. God, where was David?

And then she heard footsteps.

When the door to her cell was opened David reacted in shock; it was worse than he'd imagined. The walls were covered with scrawls – the frustrations and fears of previous prisoners and it stank of fetid body excretions. Wincing, he adjusted his eyes to the weak light given by the lonely electric bulb dangling from the ceiling. There was no window and little air. A figure had risen from the single bunk, and cried out with fear, and then gratitude. It was Sarah. She had obviously been crying, her hair was a mess and her clothes were creased and dirty. She looked like a wilted weed in a dark, tropical forest.

Sarah began to sob. 'David. Thank God you're here. I've been frantic. Oh David, thank God.'

He kissed her, stroked her hair and hugged her. She wouldn't let him go, but kept hugging him until David was forced to untangle himself and sit them both down on the bunk.

'What's going on, David?' she asked, still sobbing. 'What's happened? This is all a put–up job. I've been framed. You know who's responsible?'

David put his finger to her lips. 'I know all about it, Sarah. It's Barrak. He separated us so that he could entrap you.'

Interrupting was entirely the wrong thing to do. What Sarah desperately needed was to talk, to get her fears off her chest. Her distress turned to anger and she began to sob again, the fear, the nightmares, all welling up inside her. 'Do you know how frightened I've been? Why the hell didn't you come last night? Why did you leave me all alone? I was going frantic.'

'Sarah, I was here. I was sitting outside for half the night. They wouldn't let me see you. I left late and I've spoken to the State Department, the local consulate here, the ambassador, the *New York Times*, the *Washington Post*, Morrie Friedlander. Everybody, Sarah. We're going to have you out of here in no time flat. This is the biggest lot of bullshit since Adam was a boy. Nobody believes you stole that damn stone. Do you hear what I'm saying, Sarah?'

She looked up at him, tears coursing down her cheeks. 'How?' she said, her voice catching. 'How are you going to get me out?'

'We're going to force them to let you out, honey. We're going to apply for bail.' He moved his head closer to hers and whispered, 'And then, if necessary, we're going to skip the country. I'm not going to have you facing a court here with the Turkish system of justice.'

She nodded and managed a slight smile. 'But if we skip the country I'll never be able to come back for a holiday.' David looked at her in surprise and they both burst out laughing. The tension between them dissipated.

'David, let me tell you what happened last night.'

He put up his hand, wanting to spare her the pain but she insisted. 'I've got to tell you, David. I'm going out of my skull. When I first got here they were okay. I warned them what would happen if they tried to fuck around with me. But then they put me into an interrogation cell with some animal sergeant. He stank of BO and was smoking horrible cheap Turkish cigarettes. I nearly retched. He kept on blowing the smoke into my face. He tried to make me admit everything.' She managed to laugh at the thought that she would give in to such crude methods. 'I told him a thing or two about the law of theft and proof of complicity. But it was above his head; he was just an ape. They gave me some dinner which nearly made me throw up. It was over-cooked meat swimming in fat. The breakfast was terrible too so I haven't eaten at all. I haven't spoken to anyone except that pig either since I was put in here. That's why you have to listen to everything I'm going to tell you and act on it. Do you understand me?'

David looked at her in surprise. Her tone had suddenly become cold and analytical. He saw that she had pulled back from the edge of hysteria and her rational mind was taking over.

'You have to hire the best lawyer in town, somebody who is literally straight out the top drawer. He's got to find out why Barrak is doing this and get him to give evidence. Then he has to go to the Minister. She'll be behind me, that I can promise you. She and I work very closely together and she knows my sense of ethics. She knows I would never steal that stone. She'll speak for me and she's a heavyweight in the government. Barrak won't be able to stand against her once she moves into action. He'll fold.'

David started to ask a question but she put up her hand. He realised she needed this, to direct her future. For the last twelve hours she had been powerless. Through this she was regaining her sense of self.

'Then that fucking priest. We have to find out who he is and what his motivation is. Why he's lying at the behest of Barrak. Find the link between those two and you'll blow them both apart.'

David nodded.

The guard opened the door wide and beckoned to him.

'David,' Sarah called as he was escorted out of the cell by the guard. 'Don't let me down.'

'Sarah, how could you say that?'

'I know, but without you I'm in the most terrible trouble. You're my lifeline, honey. Don't go limp on me.'

'Sarah!'

The guard took his arm and began to pull him out of the cell. David shook free and walked quickly back over to Sarah and threw his arms around her. He whispered in her ear. 'I love you. I won't let you down. You can rely on me. I swear.'

He felt Sarah nodding against her shoulder.

'Thank you,' she said simply.

CHAPTER 21

The clothes felt like the wings of butterflies on her skin. How often had she stood in a field, marvelling at those glorious colours in flight? Now she was a butterfly herself. Or perhaps she was wearing a spider's web studded with drops of dew that shone like precious stones in the early morning sunlight. Amra held it over her spread fingers; she could hardly feel it. She lifted it to her eyes and saw the room clearly and distinctly through the material; the walls were suddenly swathed in the colours of Heaven. Blues, yellows, greens, golds, silvers. She let the cloth fall but, unlike her own dress, it didn't drop straight back towards the ground; instead it floated gently downwards, like a cloud enveloping a mountain top. Amra picked up the dress again and held it to her face. She breathed in and the cloth was sucked towards her. She puffed her breath out and it billowed away from her like the sail of the ship she and Wind had crossed the Eternal Sea in.

And the colours were like bubbles of water in a waterfall. Sometimes, when the sun was shining brightly into her face, Amra had seen the God of the River jumping out of the waterfall in a large colourful arc. Or they were like the vivid blues, purples and greens left behind by the God of Rain when he had finished his work of having sex with the earth.

This cloth was so beautiful, so delicate – she had never seen anything like it. Amra's mother had taught her to make her dresses from flax and cotton, but they were harsh compared with this wondrous fabric which the women had placed around her shoulders and across over her body.

Amra looked at the women and saw that they were smiling at her wonder. She allowed the dress to fall to earth again and looked around the room. There was a polished wall of glass facing her. In it she could see a dark-skinned young woman. As Amra walked towards the wall, the girl walked too, then when Amra stopped she stopped too. Amra moved away from the glass and the girl disappeared. But when she moved back the girl was there again.

At first Amra thought the young woman was looking at her from behind the wall. She walked closer and touched the glass. The young woman put out her hand at the same time. Suddenly Amra realised it was her own reflection, something she was only used to seeing in the water. Some people in the village claimed it was her spirit she saw, caught forever below the water, and it could only be freed by deeds of bravery. But Amra didn't believe that. She knew that the face in the water was her own. Just like the face and body in this polished wall were her own. A yellow–brown face and body, the colour of bronze but somehow with silver in it. She was surprised by the way she looked; her face was older than she thought. And she was tall. There was much she could learn about herself from this polished wall. Amra looked at herself again and saw the way the dress seemed to become part of her body, hugging her breasts, wrapping her slim waist, protruding where her belly protruded, outlining her legs.

She breathed in deeply and smelled again the fragrance of the bath. The women had poured warm water and white oil on her skin and rubbed a different oil into her hair. It had felt slippery and cool. Then they had scraped her head with an instrument which felt like fingernails, hurting her as it pulled her head backwards. They had washed her hair three times before the prongs went through it cleanly. She had felt odd when she got out of the bath, but as the warm water dried on her body and the women scrubbed her skin with dry cloths, a fragrance had emanated from her arms and shoulders, even from her hair. It was a fragrance which she had last smelt while riding in the forests of her home – the aroma of mountain flowers. The women in her village used flowers and grasses to make their homes smell nice, and many adults chewed herbs to freshen the inside of their mouth. But she had never known the aroma of actual flowers to come from a person's skin. Traders often carried tiny jars which smelt of flowers, but Amra had thought that the jars held the juice of the flower itself. Had the juice been made into something which still kept its scent when rubbed on her skin?

The smell of the mountain flowers suddenly made Amra feel lonely and homesick for her father and sister. How did a smell make you remember? she wondered. She remembered the times of excitement when traders had visited her village, those wonderful nights around the fire. The traders would reach into their bags and pull out one mystery after another. For Amra the most wonderful had been those small bottles with cork stoppers. She especially loved it when one of the men passed the opening of the bottle under Amra's nose and she could smell the flowers inside. The traders had laughed at her delight. The villagers had laughed, and Amra had laughed. But there was no laughter in Troy. The women who had put the liquid onto her skin hadn't laughed when Amra's nose twitched. They were very serious in their task.

Mattusa, who was charged with training new wives for the King's use, was amazed by Amra's naivety. Everything this savage girl touched was a surprise to her. It was as though she had never seen cleansing oils before.

'Can you feel the difference in your skin, in your hair?' asked Mattusa.

Amra touched herself. Her skin was somehow slippery, like a river stone, or the skin of a dog after the rain. Her hair was different too. She stroked the wet locks and her fingers seemed to catch in them. She pulled a lock of her hair around under her nose and sniffed it. It smelt of young rosebuds which had just opened to the warmth of the morning sun. At home Amra washed herself in the river to rid her skin and hair of dirt and insects. She wondered whether more insects would be attracted to her now that her hair smelt of flowers. Maybe wasps would come. Or bees. Maybe they would think she was a flower and would try to drink her seed to make honey. Would they sting her when they realised that she had no seed for them?

'You are a very sensible girl to let us do to you what had to be done. We thought you would continue to fight us. You will soon come to understand that this is the only way the King will allow you back into his presence,' said Mattusa.

'But this isn't suitable clothing for me,' Amra protested. 'Look,' she held up the delicate fabric of her dress, 'this is a robe for a woman living in a royal court. I am Amra the hunter. My work is to hunt animals for food, or to make clothes for my father, or to cook meals so that he and my sister won't go hungry. Now that my mother has gone to the land of the Gods, this is my work. How can I wear this?' She let her dress waft softly to the ground. 'If I were to go into the fields in this robe it would tear on every bramble. I would come back naked.'

'Many of the women of Troy also work in the fields, helping their husbands,' said Mattusa. 'They don't wear clothes like this. But some of us are born to be the wives of great kings. I was born in a large house. My father was the chief architect and builder of monuments for the king of another land. When I was twelve and very beautiful, the king of my country gave me as a gift to Praxis. I was to be one of his wives. I was a good gift because there has been no war between our countries since my marriage. And since I was younger than you are now I have lived happily in this palace.'

Amra shook her head in surprise. 'Have you ever been outside?'

Mattusa laughed. 'Of course. I am not a prisoner, nor am I a slave. I go into the market often and talk to the people. I walk down to the sea and along the shore. I see many things there. I look for ships which sail up and down the coast or over the water from the other end of the sea, from the land of the Archaens. My life is very full. When I became too old to please the eye of the King he put me here in the hall of the women where my job is to train young women to be wives of the great Praxis.'

'And you do nothing more?' asked Amra.

Mattusa frowned. 'There is nothing more.'

'But what about riding a horse like Wind? What about the thrill of hunting, or gathering herbs or food? What about making clothes? Don't you do this?'

Mattusa shook her head. 'These things are done for us, child. We have slaves from Egypt, India, Phrygia, Harran, Canaan. They are the ones who do the work. A woman who was once Queen of the Hittites is not required to work.'

Amra nodded. 'I see. Can I go and see the King now?'

Mattusa laughed. 'The King will call for you when he is ready.'

'When will that be?' asked Amra.

'You are not permitted to know that.'

'Why not?'

'Nobody knows the mind of King Praxis. When he wants to see you he will call for you. Until then you will wait here.'

'But how long might that be?' Mattusa shrugged.

'Tomorrow?' asked Amra. 'In many days?' Again, Mattusa shrugged.

'Longer?'

'Nobody knows, Amra. The great King has much to occupy his mind. When his mind turns to you he will command your presence. Until then you must wait.'

'But what if he forgets me? I can't just sit here. I have to return to my village. I have already been away for one full passage of the moon. Before another two passages have been completed I must return to my village or my sister Peta will be sacrificed.' Agitated, Amra raised her voice, much to the consternation of Mattusa and the other women attending her. 'Don't you understand that? I can't wait here for the King to choose to call me. I have to talk to him now.'

'Amra,' said Mattusa insistently, 'nobody demands anything of Praxis, great King of the universe.'

'I am Amra,' came the reply. 'Amra the hunter.' But her voice had lost its ring of confidence.

'You must understand,' said Mithrassa-Urbek, 'that I am a very busy man and that this is a great privilege.' Amra nodded in gratitude. 'I wouldn't normally waste my time with a girl such as you.' She nodded again. 'It is only because of your skill with the bull that I have agreed.'

'Thank you,' said Amra simply.

'Unfortunately I am unable to help you.'

Amra was sitting on the banks of the stream which flowed below the hill on which the city of Troy was built. Mithrassa-Urbek had agreed to meet her there as he did not wish to be seen with her in public. To talk to her without the King's knowledge or express instruction could start tongues wagging and endanger his career.

'I am also here because of Mattusa. Like you, she came to the palace as a young girl many years ago. I was much younger then too, of course, and my position was quite lowly. We became friends and I helped her to understand the complexities of the court. In time she also helped me to gain favour with the King. That is why I am his secretary now. If she hadn't intervened on your behalf, especially after your behaviour in the presence of the King yesterday, I would not have endangered myself by meeting you here.'

Amra couldn't understand why Mattusa wanted to help her. Amra knew that she had been rude when she had first arrived in the palace of the women, yet Mattusa had smiled at her annoyance, much as her mother had smiled when Amra had thrown tantrums as a little girl. And she had agreed to ask Mithrassa-Urbek to meet Amra, to see if he could help her to see the King.

But Mithrassa-Urbek was different now. He seemed sly and secretive, unhelpful and unfriendly, not at all as he had been when he had taken her into the King's presence just a few days ago. Amra knew she had upset Mithrassa-Urbek and even endangered him by being rude to the King, but she had no other friends to turn to in Troy. She bit her lip as she felt tears welling up in her eyes.

'If I go home now without the secret of how to make iron, my life will be sacrificed,' Amra said. Mithrassa-Urbek nodded. 'But if I wait for the King to see me I may be late in getting home and then my little sister Peta will be sacrificed in my place. I don't know what to do.'

Mithrassa-Urbek's mind went back to earlier that day when he had come to the court of the women to collect Amra. Before he took her away, Mattusa had whispered into his ear: 'She is only a child even though she appears like a woman. Her mind is the mind of a savage and she has nothing of what a woman needs to live in the palace. Yet there is much about her which is strange and exciting. She knows things I don't know. She tells me of things I find frightening. She has lived through things that only an adult lives through and yet she can still smile and be happy. Be kind to her, Mithrassa-Urbek. She is a special girl. Although she doesn't realise it I believe she may have been sent to us.'

Mithrassa-Urbek put his hand on Amra's shoulder to comfort her. 'It is not an easy situation, Amra. Our ways must be strange to you, as yours are to us. You are a very unusual girl. Your body is painted in a style favoured by the black-skinned Abyssinians who live in the far reaches of our empire yet your skin is fair. You have a bravery the like of which I have not seen in men twice your age and size, but you also have a roughness, a crudeness, which is not welcome in our court. The court is very much like a peacock. Do you know what a peacock is, Amra?' She shook her head. 'It is a bird which comes from the land around the river Indus, which has an extraordinary tail which fans out into a rainbow of colours and eyes. It also has a crown on its head which makes it look royal. A peacock looks beautiful from afar, but get too close and its beak will take off your fingers. In many ways, Amra, you and the court have much in common: both of you are colourful and exciting like a peacock, but like the bird your bite could be very dangerous. Your crudeness could get us all in trouble.'

'Who with?' Amra asked ingenuously.

'With the King,' Mithrassa-Urbek told her.

'Why is your King so powerful?' she said, shaking her head. 'Our Headman is powerful. But the law of the village says that he can do nothing without first talking to the Great Council, and their decisions must be approved by the Gods who speak to the Medicine Man.'

Mithrassa-Urbek stood and walked down to the river. He splashed his face to cool his head in the hot sun. He turned back to Amra. 'You come from a village of very few people. I visited your region many years ago when I was a young man with a quest for knowledge of the world and its peoples. This is how I know your tongue. And I know your people, Amra. They're a people without art, without music, without the skills we have here. Your people have no wealth, nobody pays tribute to them. Troy,' he said, gesturing to the mighty walls which overshadowed them, 'is one of the greatest cities on earth. You may have heard of others such as Hattusas, Midea, Tiryns, Mycenae and Thebes, but Troy is the city which the great God Mithras created to dominate and rule over all other cities.'

'But I spoke to Mithras,' Amra said, thinking he meant the bull. 'I know Mithras.'

Mithrassa-Urbek smiled and shook his head. 'The bull is merely a messenger sent by Mithras. Some people say that the bull is the God himself come to earth, but nobody of intelligence believes that. On one occasion the bull was wounded by a soldier who tried to take the golden arrow. Although the bull pierced the soldier with his horn and killed him instantly, it still bled from the wound. Gods don't bleed, Amra. This bull is a messenger from the Gods, not Mithras himself.'

'Tell me about Mithras,' she asked.

Mithrassa-Urbek smiled and shook his head. 'This is secret knowledge, child. Besides, women worship the great mother of all the Gods. Some call her Cybebe, others Cybele. She is also known by many other names. This is the goddess whom you should worship. Mithras is not your god. Anyway, our King is the Chief Priest of Mithras. It is he who understands the God's will.'

'But I've spoken to Mithras,' Amra insisted. 'I have been with him. I know you say the bull was only sent by Mithras, but he spoke to me. He told me he was the God.'

Mithrassa–Urbek looked at her silently. She was such a strange girl, and with so many unusual powers that he was loath to discount what she said. 'You have spoken to Mithras?' he asked quietly. Amra nodded. 'Why should I believe you? Only our priests and priestesses can speak to Mithras. Even Praxis is in despair because the God hasn't spoken to him for a long while. He is taking it as a bad omen.'

Amra shrugged her shoulders. 'At home I speak to the Gods. They come to me in dreams. I tell the Medicine Man what they say and he tells the people in the village. They speak to me all the time.' It was a lie she had used successfully before. Maybe it would work again.

If she were a girl of the city then Mithrassa–Urbek would have struck her down for blasphemy. Nobody spoke like this of the great Gods. But this girl, this Amra, there was something about her which was otherworldly. It made him hold back his condemnation. How *had* she managed to enter the enclosure of the white bull, to sit down beside him without him tossing her on his horns from one side of the enclosure to the other? How had she led him back to his stall as though he were nothing more than a sheep? There was much he didn't understand about Amra, but from the very first time he saw her he had known that one day he would learn something from her.

'What did the God say to you?'

'I cannot speak of that,' she said.

'You must tell me, child.'

'Then you must tell me about Mithras.'

'Don't dare to bargain with me,' he growled. 'Mithras is the God of Contracts and Bargains. Not Amra.'

Amra held his stare. She was playing a dangerous game but she knew only what her instincts told her. She had not practised or thought through this moment. She was using the same cunning which enabled her to trap rabbits, hare and deer. Could she trap a man as clever and knowledgeable as Mithrassa-Urbek?

His curiosity forced him to speak first. 'If I tell you something of the great God Mithras will you tell me what he said?'

Amra thought deeply for a few moments and then nodded, as if agreeing to a hard-won concession. When she saw him smile she wondered if perhaps she had for once gone too far. Amra the hunter was always taking risks, but she was so far from home here and in such a strange land, did she dare rely on her skills? And when Mithrassa-Urbek had told her about Mithras, what could she tell him in return? This game could cost her everything, including her life.

Mithrassa-Urbek began to speak. 'What I tell you is known to many people in Troy. King Praxis has much secret knowledge that he, as High Priest, shares only with the priestesses. But as I said, for a long time now Mithras has not spoken to King Praxis. The priestesses say that sometimes the God speaks to them, but the omens are not good. War is gathering on many of our borders. But Mithras has always been there to help us in the past, and we await his coming again. So, in telling you of Mithras I will talk to you as though you were about to be initiated into the worship of the God. Is that understood?'

Amra nodded.

'And is it further understood that you will repeat nothing of what I say to the King or tell him that your knowledge has come from me?'

Again she nodded.

Mithrassa-Urbek spoke to her then in a low and serious voice. 'Mithras is the God of all things. I have already told you that he is the God of Contracts and Bargains, but he is much more besides that. He is the God of Friendship and of War and of Soldiers. He is the God who created the whole of the world. Once, at the beginning of the world, at a time before time, the Sun God sent a messenger, a black raven bird, to Mithras commanding him to sacrifice a large bull. Mithras didn't want to because he loved all things, but he knew that he must obey his father the Sun God and so he led the bull into a field. He raised his knife to slit the throat of the great animal and killed the beautiful animal with great sadness. But as the blood flowed from the bull, an astonishing thing happened. The white bull was carried on unseen wings into the sky. There he rested and became the moon. Mithras watched in shock and delight and as he gazed into the sky, his cloak was suddenly snatched from his shoulders and taken up into the sky where it became the very stuff of the stars. The tail of the bull and the blood of the bull gave rise to the grain and grape which have given food and wine to men ever since. The bull's testicles gave their seed into a mixing bowl and every creature on earth that you see around you today came from that mixing bowl and was created from that very seed. In the Heavens the moon began its monthly cycle and every month it grows small and then large again, as the bull grows large when it becomes an adult only to grow small and frail when he is old and waning. Night followed day and the seasons of warmth alternated with the seasons of cold, the seasons of plenty with the seasons of little, and as the moon danced its rhythm so time itself was created.

'But all was not well in creation. Because when day came with its piercing light, the creatures from beneath the earth were awakened and the serpent drank the blood of the bull and the scorpion tried to suck the seed from the bull's testicles. Good and evil were begotten, the evil which men suffer from today. From the raven, from the serpent, from the mixing bowl and from the lion which came also to feast on the bull's seed were created the elements of air, earth, water and fire.

'Mithras went to the Sun God and together they ate a last supper of meat and bread and they drank wine. Mithras climbed into the chariot of the Sun God and drove with him across the ocean, through the air, to the end of the world.'

Amra had not understood all of Mithrassa-Urbek's story, but she had heard enough to realise how powerful Mithras was.

'There is more, Amra, but that I cannot tell you. Most Trojans know the way in which the God Mithras's twelve disciples behaved. They also know of Mithras's birth from a virgin and of the God's last supper on earth before being taken up into the sky by the Sun God. But there are other things, Amra, which are known only to the priests and priestesses of Troy. Matters which the great God Mithras has made known to them, and which are so deep, so secret, that you as a savage cannot be permitted to know them.'

Amra knew he would say no more but she had learnt enough. 'You have told me a lot, Mithrassa-Urbek. I am very grateful.'

'I have told you because I trust you. Because I believe you when you say that Mithras did talk to you in the enclosure. Now tell me what he said.'

Amra gulped. She had no idea what to say. When Mithrassa-Urbek had collected her from the court of the women he had been angry because of how she had spoken to the King. But while they had been talking, he had changed. Now he was kind and honest, open and helpful. He had told her many things about Mithras which she knew he should not have. She was not of Troy, she was an outsider. If it ever became known it could cost him his life. She felt a profound sense of guilt at the lie she was about to tell him.

In a faltering voice, she said softly, 'The God Mithras spoke to me. That was why I was so rude to the King.

Because I came to him with the words of the God in my mind but he didn't want to listen. I wanted to tell him the words but he wouldn't allow me to speak.'

Amra looked beyond Mithrassa-Urbek to the river which ran outside the walls of the city. She followed the water with her eyes until it descended to the sea. It was a huge sea and from where they were standing she could see islands far out into it. They looked like jewels buried in translucent ice. On top of the sea was a boat, its single sail full of wind. And as she focused on the boat thoughts came unbidden into her mind. Without thinking, she spoke them aloud. 'Men will come from beyond the sea. Men in ships. They will land on your shore and they will try to attack your city.'

Mithrassa-Urbek caught his breath as she spoke, though what she said surprised him. The attack was predicted to come from the desert border in the east, not from the sea. 'But we are well defended and our walls are thick,' he said. 'Who are these men? Where will they come from? Are they Arcaeons? When will they come?'

'They will come from the other side of the ocean, where the sea falls off the earth.'

'How many will there be?' he asked.

'How many grains of sand are there down there?' Amra nodded towards the beach.

'Did the God Mithras tell you when these men will come?'

'He said they will come when the people of Troy stop listening.'

Mithrassa-Urbek frowned. 'Stop listening? Listening to what?'

Amra shook her head. 'I don't know. All he told me was that when the people of your city stop listening, the men from over the sea will come.'

'But if they do come,' he demanded, 'what can they do? We have food and water to last us forever. We can withstand a siege for years.'

'They will be able to get into the city,' she said.

'How?'

'That is something I can only tell the King. It is from the mouth of the God Mithras for the ear of the King. That and nothing more. I'm sorry.'

Mithrassa-Urbek walked back up the bank and sat beside Amra. He watched the river flowing swiftly down into the eternal sea. For a long moment he considered her words, then said, 'Tomorrow you will see the King. I will make sure of it. But let me down, endanger me in any way, and it will be the last act you ever do.'

Despite his warning, Amra smiled in relief. It wasn't until later that she realised how dangerous her meeting with the King would be.

Amra felt as though she was floating as she walked slowly behind Mithrassa-Urbek towards the inner sanctum of the King. The chief priestesses of the God Mithras also formed part of her escort, one on each side of her. Mithrassa-Urbek had told her that, after King Praxis, these priestesses were the most important people in the city. Amra's mind was in turmoil. She was desperately trying to think of something which would compel the King to tell her the secret of making iron, but despite lying awake all night each lie she had come up with sounded more outrageous than the next.

Mithrassa-Urbek had informed the priestesses of Mithras about Amra's conversation with the God through the great white bull. Amra mystified the priestesses too: such a strange girl. Perhaps she *was* a conduit for the God's mind, although they could not help but be sceptical. But Mithrassa-Urbek had convinced them there was good reason to believe her and so they had decided to accompany her to her audience with the King.

Amra stood behind Mithrassa-Urbek at the threshold of the court. The throne room was before them. She could see the King sitting on his throne, surrounded by the moat of water. All around, sitting on low stools, standing or reclining against pillows the men and women of the court were gathered. Unlike her previous visit, when she had looked and smelt strange, Amra did not feel such an outsider. Her hair smelt of flowers, her body was perfumed, her skin was smooth and she was dressed in the same fashion as the women around her. Her robes were coloured like the evening sky. Only the markings on her skin made her stand out.

Mithrassa-Urbek shouted out the usual preliminary greeting: 'Great Lord of the world, Majesty Praxis, King of the universe, God on earth, friend and follower of Mithras, High Priest to all the Gods, Protector of Life on Earth, feared above all others. Your servant Mithrassa-Urbek begs you to receive Amra of the people of the north.'

Amra knew now how to behave in the presence of the King. She cast her eyes downwards, as did Mithrassa-Urbek and the priestesses, and followed her escort into the room. They all knelt at the stream around the King's throne, their heads touching the floor in obeisance.

'Stand.'

Amra stood while the two priestesses and Mithrassa-Urbek remained kneeling. She looked at the water, not daring to look directly at the King. She had been well taught by Mattusa.

'I am told that you received a message for me from the great bull.'

'I did, great King of the world,' Amra said, her voice cracking in fear.

'What is the message?'

Amra knew this was the moment to speak, but she had no words. Her mind was reeling but her voice was silent. All she could think was that any moment the King would stand in fury, draw a massive sword from his scabbard and strike her dead. Then all the people in her village would die along with her. Still nothing came into her head. These people were too clever to trick. What could she tell him? Nothing! And soon her life would be nothing.

'Well?' demanded the King, his voice bordering on anger. Amra looked down at the crouching back of Mithrassa-Urbek and realised that he too would die as a result of the King's displeasure.

'The God is the bull,' said Amra tentatively.

'How can that be?' said the King irritably. 'That is what fools believe. I am the High Priest, I know the truth. The bull has been wounded by men. He has bled. No God can bleed.'

'The bull has two beings, great King. One is the inner being which is the God and which cannot be hurt by swords or daggers. The other is the outer being which grows old and dies and which can bleed and be hurt.'

The King remained silent. Amra was merely repeating some of the secrets her father had told her about their own Gods, things which the Medicine Man had told him. But she had to tell the King something more, something new and astonishing.

'Is Mithras your god?' the King asked.

'No, Majesty,' said Amra. 'I had never heard of him before I came to the city of Troy.'

'Then how do you know these things?'

'He told me.'

The King's voice had lost some of its harshness. Amra wanted to raise her head and look him in the eyes. She could only ever really speak to people if she looked them in the eyes. But she didn't dare. She heard him rise from his throne and walk down towards her. 'Can I see the God within the bull?' he said. 'If I kill the body of the bull, will the God spirit come out? Did the bull tell you that?'

Amra shook her head. 'Kill the body and the spirit will go to another bull. It will search the world until it finds another bull and that bull then will become Mithras on earth when he comes down from the heavens.'

The King lifted his Rod of Office and touched one of the priestesses on her shoulder. She rose immediately to stand beside Amra. 'Could what this girl says be correct? Why did you not know these things?'

The priestess nodded. 'Great King,' she said, 'you more than anyone in Troy know the deepest secrets of Mithras. You are the High Priest, the confidante of the Gods. You fill the world with your knowledge and help your people understand that our cult worships and venerates the bull as the embodiment of Mithras. We in the priesthood know that Mithras sent the bull to us. The reason that you allow men to challenge for the right to kill the bull is to challenge the strength of the God Mithras, to prove to all nations that Mithras loves and protects us and our city of Troy.'

She stopped speaking for a moment, gathering her thoughts. 'But what this girl says has come to us from the very God himself. Why he has chosen this savage to be the vessel through whom he talks instead of your most venerated and powerful self, I do not know. But if the God is inside the bull, as we have often thought, then it is only logical that he might very well speak to you through your priestess or through this girl.'

'So what she says could be true?'

'We need to know what the God Mithras said.'

'Well?' said the King, touching Amra with his rod. 'The God Mithras spoke to you. What was it he said?'

'He said that ships will come across the sea. He said that they will come from the other end of the ocean from a land in the sea before the ocean falls off the earth.'

'The land of the Archaeans?' asked the King.

'I do not know. He told me only what I repeat to you now.'

'It is for you, great King, to interpret the words of Mithras. Only you can know the God's meaning,' said the priestess.

Ignoring her, the King told Amra to continue.

'The ships will attack your city. The men on the ships will raid your city.'

'How will they get into our city?' said the King. 'We have food for many years in our granaries and storerooms. We have water flowing into the city from underground streams which cannot be blocked or poisoned in a siege. We have walls thicker than two tall men on each other's shoulders. How can an army, no matter how great, get into our city?'

This was the question Amra had feared most. She knew she would have to answer but nothing had come to her. She looked up at the King, daring to stare into his eyes. Praxis was too absorbed by what she was telling him to worry for the moment about protocol. Amra thought about her village, and how, during ceremonies the Medicine Man and the Headman became the animals which the men and women of the village hunted. They put on the heads and skins of the animals and became them. And then she found the words came easily into her mouth. 'When the sailors leave their ships they will climb inside animals. And the animals will wander into your city because you will not recognise them as an army. And once they are inside your city they will kill everybody.'

A gasp erupted in the room. Even the King was surprised. 'Mithras told you this?' he asked, his voice quizzical. Amra nodded. 'Did he tell you more? How many animals will there be? How big will they be? How many soldiers can get inside an animal? What animals will they be? Horses, dogs, cats, bulls?'

'The God has told me nothing more. He said only that just as he was able to become invisible inside the bull, so the invading army will be invisible inside their animals.'

The King shook his head in wonderment. 'But how will an army get inside an animal? Even inside the biggest bull there is not room for more than three men.'

Amra also shook her head. 'I do not know. But I do know one other thing: Mithras told me that the army will come only if the people of Troy stop listening to him.'

'Yes,' shouted the priestess. In her excitement she jumped to her feet and grasped Amra by the arm. 'Yes,' she said again, 'the girl is right. The people of Troy are too careless with their worship. They enjoy life too much and do not make sufficient sacrifices to Mithras. Now we have been warned that when the people of Troy stop listening to their priestesses and to the great God Mithras a great army will come from over the seas and destroy their city. For some reason, great King, Mithras has decided to speak through this child with her painted skin. This child sang to the God when she went into the palace enclosure and the God listened. She has come to us because she has been chosen. Mithras has sent her.'

The King was still bemused. 'But how can a great army get into an animal? Even a dozen large animals like bulls – we could kill them all. We have an army of the strongest men from all the lands around Troy. And we can arm a thousand slaves to serve us. Why should we be scared of a few men hiding inside animals?'

Amra lowered her voice, just as the Medicine Man lowered his voice to the growl of a dog when a god spoke through him. Then she stood rigid and lifted her face to the ceiling, her eyes staring. She growled, 'Do not dare to question the words of the God Mithras. You are a great

King but Mithras is King of everything. The seed of Mithras is in the seed of every living thing. Flowers, trees, animals and men and women.'

The King stared at the child-woman in astonishment.

The priestess, transported to another plane by evidence of the presence of the God, spoke to the King as though he was merely her husband. 'Praxis,' she said, her voice, like Amra's, deepening with authority, 'Praxis, listen to this child. Pay heed to this crude vessel through which Mithras speaks.'

The King was even more astounded. No-one had ever addressed him with as much familiarity as this priestess and this savage were doing. Suddenly both women realised their peril and hastily looked down. But to their surprise Praxis spoke softly to them. 'If I send the child back into the enclosure will the God Mithras tell me more? Will he explain to me how an army can hide inside a bull?'

Amra shook her head. 'Mithras told me that he will say nothing more. His message is that evil things will happen when the people of Troy stop listening. You must obey him, King Praxis.'

The King turned and walked over the bridge back to his throne. He sat down heavily. Suddenly he looked older, like a man with great troubles on his shoulders. Finally he spoke: 'I will issue a decree that once a week every person in Troy must bring a sacrifice and token to the temple of Mithras. Once a week people will offer part of their food for the enjoyment of the God. A roll will be kept of every person who lives within the city walls. Anybody failing to make offering to Mithras once a week will be strung between two chariots, the horses will be spurred and their limbs will be torn from their bodies.'

The King looked at his kneeling secretary. 'Mithrassa-Urbek, stand.' The man rose immediately. 'Write the decree and I will sign it with the great seal of the city of

Troy. Mithrassa-Urbek, you have done well. The priestesses confirm my view that Amra is the voice of the God Mithras. Had I not listened to you I would not have listened to the God. And the God would have destroyed this city. You are offered a reward which you may take from the treasury.'

'You child,' the King said, looking at Amra, 'You are a strange child. A King does not treat with a child. Yet you have the bravery of a grown man. Though your ways are not the ways of Troy, you will stay in my court. I do not believe that you have yet fully realised the purpose of the God Mithras. You will stay here until the God decides to speak through you again.'

Amra shook her head vehemently. 'No. I must return to my people.'

Praxis banged his rod on the ground. 'Enough!' he said. The priestesses led Amra out of the King's presence.

Amra was shorter by a head than the two women. She looked at them surreptitiously as she walked between them. Their skin had the lines of age yet their eyes were clear. They were dressed simply in white linen robes; they were very different to the women of the court who looked like the colourful birds which Amra had seen flitting from tree to tree in the city.

'I am Isha-Mithra,' said one of the priestesses, 'and this is Ishta-Mithra. Jointly, we are the chief priestesses of the temple of Mithras.'

'Why am I coming with you?' Amra asked.

'The King has commanded that you stay with us. He thinks that the God Mithras will speak through you again and inform him of who these invading men will be and how they will climb inside animals.'

'And if I tell him will he let me go?'

'No-one can know the mind of the King.'

'But you are the priestesses. Surely you can tell the King what to do?'

Isha-Mithra laughed. 'Praxis is the King of the world. The kings of Egypt and of Canaan and all the other great lands bow before him.'

'But you are the priestesses! Is he higher than the Gods?'

'Nobody is higher than the Gods, especially the God Mithras. That is why Praxis wants to keep you. For many years we have been seeking word from Mithras about the sea people. They are a violent people and have destroyed towns in other lands. We have word from traders of their violence. We have to prepare ourselves for when they land on our shore and dare to attack the great city of Troy.'

The other priestess, Ishta-Mithra, interrupted. 'We have made sacrifices, fasted and prayed for the God Mithras to tell us what will happen when the sea people arrive. We are strong. We have great reserves of food and water and our walls are thicker than the height of two men, but these sea people have destroyed other strong cities. Even our King Praxis is worried. He has sent messages to other kings to form a great army to go to battle against these sea people. The problem is we never know where they are because they travel by sea and suddenly arrive at a city and destroy it. It is like trying to capture the spring dust from flowers: it is everywhere and nowhere.'

They came to a large door guarded by Nubian sentries. In the lamplight their shadows flickered black and menacing. Beyond the door was a room almost as large as the King's throne room. There was a pool in its centre; four naked women sat in its waters. Hanging on one of the walls was a large idol with candles burning at its base. On another wall was a huge painting of a rock and a cave and the face of the same idol appeared from inside the cave. It was painted in red, blue and yellow and looked quite frightening. Had Amra not seen the paintings on the walls in other parts of the palace she would have dropped to her knees before such a thing. There was nothing like this in her own village. This palace, this city, were beyond her understanding. All she could do was to look and try to understand and not feel overwhelmed by fear.

Ishta-Mithra held Amra's hand, recognising her sudden fear of the room's enormity, its beauty and its mystery. This was a simple painted girl from a primitive tribe. What could she possibly understand of the ways of Mithras, of the greatest palace in the greatest city in the world? And yet it was through her mouth that the God had spoken.

'Amra, you see before you the inner sanctum of the priestesses of the God Mithras. Each of us here has been chosen by Mithras to be his servant. Each of us here was taken in childhood from our home and brought up to worship the greatest of all the Gods.'

Amra looked around. In another part of the huge room women were sitting around tables, talking in hushed and urgent voices. 'This is where we conduct the business of Mithras,' said Ishta-Mithra. Amra wondered what that business could be.

As they moved further into the room Ishta-Mithra pointed to a group of priestesses in one corner, also wearing white robes. 'Those priestesses direct the buying and selling of grain for our God. We take a portion of all the grain grown in the fields as tribute and then store it until the time is right for us to sell it for a profit. Those women,' she said, pointing to another group, 'trade in slaves. Their work for the God Mithras is to take one quarter of all the slaves brought to Troy by traders as tribute to the God Mithras. Those slaves who are strongest and fittest we keep ourselves for the worship of our God. Others, as these priestesses decide, are sold in the markets. And this other group of women –'

'I don't understand,' Amra burst out. 'Aren't you priestesses?'

'Yes.'

'But your work is in . . . You . . .'

'In your village, Amra, priestesses may simply worship their gods, but our God, Mithras commands us to increase his wealth. This is our sacred duty, it is what we must do.'

Amra nodded. It sounded very strange, but then the whole day had been strange.

'Why have you brought me here?' she asked again.

'The King has commanded that you must learn our ways. The God Mithras may speak to you again.'

'Why doesn't the God Mithras speak through you?' Amra asked.

'He does. But the words he puts into our mouths are not the words he put into your mouth. For reasons which we can't yet understand the God Mithras has chosen to speak through you, a blue-painted savage. Maybe it is his joke. Or maybe you yourself are a god without realising it. Mithras and Cybele, the great mother of all Gods, work in ways which even we priestesses cannot understand.'

'Am I a prisoner?' Amra asked as she was led deeper into the room. Now she could see there were beds in the corners and against the walls, and other doors leading, she assumed, to rooms where the servants slept.

'No,' laughed Ishta-Mithra. 'Of course not. Nobody can confine the voice of Mithras. You are free to come and go from this place as you will.'

'Then I can leave the city?'

Ishta-Mithra shook her head. 'That you may not do. Within these walls I and my priestesses are in command; nobody, not even Praxis, can tell us what to do in here. But outside of these walls, Amra, you are the subject of the King.'

'But I have to get back to my people. The men with iron weapons are coming to attack our village. I must find out the secret of making iron and take it back to my people so that my father and the other metalworkers in the valleys of the five rivers can quickly make iron weapons to stop our homes from being destroyed.'

Ishta-Mithra looked at her in surprise. 'You have come here to find out the secret of making iron?' Amra nodded. 'Child, nobody knows how to make iron. Iron is the most valuable of all metals.'

She lifted her finger and showed Amra a ring. In the centre of the ring was a tiny round glistening dark grey stone. 'This is iron, Amra. This was given to me by the King's armourer. These tiny pieces of iron are sometimes found on the sides of the kilns when the men are making bronze. Or sometimes in the fields they find a rock which gives them iron when they heat it. Sometimes it is used for jewellery for the ladies of the court. But they cannot make weapons from it. There is not enough.'

Amra looked at the priestess in shock. 'But the iron comes from the rock which is found everywhere, the red rock. My father and the other metalworkers in the five valleys know this. But the iron they get when they crush the rock and heat it is light and breaks easily. It cannot be used for making weapons. No-one knows how the men from beyond the mountains make their swords and daggers with this iron, yet there are many of them with these weapons and they will soon travel over the mountains and attack us. The traders told our people that you know how to make iron. That your people make it all the time.'

Ishta-Mithra looked at her sadly. 'You have been misled, child. Nobody here knows how to turn the rocks of iron into metal for weapons. It is a secret of the Gods. Our wealth comes from gold and bronze. I see that you wear a gold amulet yourself.'

'But gold is useless,' said Amra. 'It is the secret of making iron weapons that my people would most value.'

'Our power comes from our army,' replied the priestess. 'We have a thousand chariots and horses. Nobody can challenge the power of Troy. We are the greatest city on earth, rulers of the world. But not through iron, child. Only through our chariots.'

Amra looked at her in horror. She had travelled so far. She had faced so much hardship. Her body had been so badly hurt and finally, now that she had arrived in Troy, she was told that her journey had been a waste. As she realised that she would never know the secret of making iron and her family and friends would all be killed, Amra sank into a despair of black and menacing shadows. Overwhelmed by its weight she fell to the floor in a faint.

CHAPTER 22

Sarah's only means of working out the time of day was through the noises around her. Night-time was heralded by a crescendo of coughing, spluttering and shouting, various scrabbling sounds as prisoners settled themselves on stinking mattresses, scratched their body sores, removed lice and shooed away the ubiquitous rats, followed by relative silence. Occasionally she would jerk awake to the clang of batons against metal grilles and voices raised in anger, but generally the night was distinguishable from the day by the general aura of quiet into which the prison sank.

She certainly couldn't use mealtimes to tell the time; each meal was fundamentally the same: bread, gelatinous soup, a concoction of fried meat and rice topped with rancid-tasting pastry. Which was breakfast, which lunch and which supper?

When her cell door was suddenly opened outside of the normal mealtime Sarah got a shock. She stood; her knees were cramped. She had tried to do exercises in the cell to keep herself fit but had gradually been overcome by lethargy and depression. The guard stood in the door, silhouetted in the light from the corridor. He beckoned her to follow him, and heart pounding, Sarah did. Her spirits leapt at the hope of release, but she firmly dampened them down, not wanting to count on anything that might lead to further disappointment and distress. Still, it felt good to be out of the cell and walking along the corridor, even though the smells were the same. She followed the guard up the stairs. When she had initially been dragged to the cell the two guards had left bruise marks on her arms. But now she was walking freely –

what the hell was going on? As they climbed flights of stairs, marched along more corridors, the lights became brighter. Gone were the bare lightbulbs, replaced by strips of neon, glaringly white like the light of a hospital.

The guard stopped and opened a door, motioning Sarah into a bare room with a table and chair. On the other side of a table sat a young man. He stood and beamed a smile in greeting. He didn't look Turkish.

'Miss Kaplan, it's a pleasure to meet you. My name is Ben Hills. I'm attached to the US consulate in Istanbul. We heard just a short time ago about your incarceration and I've been making enquiries ever since. Please, sit down.'

Sarah gulped and shook her head in disbelief. Was her nightmare over? She forced herself to remain calm.

Hills looked at the officer. 'Would you please close the door?' he said then repeated himself in Turkish. The guard turned his back and slammed the door shut.

'Please sit down, Miss Kaplan.' Hills took out a packet of cigarettes and offered her one.

'I don't smoke, thank you,' Sarah said softly.

'Neither do I, but sometimes when you're dealing with American kids who've been caught dealing in smack, offering them a cigarette is a good way of showing them that you're not hostile.'

Sarah nodded.

'Well,' he said, 'this is a bit of a mess, isn't it?'

'How quickly can you get me out of here, Mr Hills? I've been here for days. Apart from my fiancé, nobody's been near me.'

'Why don't you call me Ben? I'll call you Sarah. Let's drop the formality.'

'How quickly can you get me out of here, Ben?'

'Unfortunately, Sarah, these things are never as simple as they seem at first sight. Your fiancé, David, has been phoning just about everybody from the President of the

United States down. He's called the Secretary of State, various Under-Secretaries, journalists in America – God knows who else. It's not the sort of thing we recommend and we've advised him to tone it down. You see, calling in the Marines isn't the way to achieve a diplomatic solution. Now, I know that might sound contrary to what you want, but whichever way you cut it this *is* a diplomatic incident and we have to play it a certain way.'

'It's not a diplomatic incident, Ben,' Sarah said, maintaining her composure. 'I've been falsely accused of a crime I didn't commit. The evidence was planted on me. We're not dealing with drugs, firearms nor the theft of confidential government material. We're dealing with a religious object which is of no value or interest to me. Now, I'm a lawyer . . .'

'So am I, Sarah.'

'Then you would be the first to understand that the police can't hold me without presenting evidence to a court of law.'

'In an ideal world, yes. But this is Turkey and there are numerous demonstrations which are just bubbling up in the streets. Clerics are whipping the population up into a bit of a frenzy, I'm afraid. You're a woman, you're an infidel and you're Jewish. Three strikes unfortunately.'

'What's that got to do with the rules applying to evidence? What's that got to do with *habeas corpus*? I don't know Turkish law, but there have to be some standards of human rights for God's sake! This isn't Saudi Arabia or China.'

'It's not a question of law or rights, I'm afraid. Those went out the window when the demonstrations started. You're now being held in custody for your own protection.'

Sarah was stunned. The blood drained from her face. 'What?'

'The police are holding you here to save you from the mob. The people I've spoken to at the Ministry of Justice, as well as in the upper echelons of the police here, tell me that your life would be in grave danger were you to appear on the street. Accordingly they have decreed that until further notice and for your own protection you will be incarcerated.'

Sarah let the words settle into her mind for a few moments. Then she began to laugh. The reaction was pure nervousness. For so long she had been working out ways to organise a bail application, appeal or just plain escape, and now she was being told that she had to stay in that hideous cell for her own protection.

Ben reached over and held her hand. 'I'm sorry. Our hands are completely tied.'

'Can't I be released to the safe custody of the American Embassy? I'll happily go to Ankara.'

'We've asked. We have a guest wing there, and we've got marine protection, but the Turkish authorities won't countenance it. They say the way the mob is feeling towards you, we could end up with another Teheran stand-off. It's just too risky.'

'So what are you going to do?' she said. 'What can I do? What does it mean?'

'It means, Sarah, that you have to wait here for a little while longer until we can sort out something. Maybe passage out of the country to somewhere a lot safer and much more salubrious. I can't say more than that at the moment. I'm sorry.'

'Who's running this case, Ben? You or somebody higher? Does the Ambassador know?'

'Of course he knows. He's the one who gave me the briefing before I came here.'

'And State in Washington, do they know?'

'Absolutely. They're onto the Turkish Embassy. They

called in the Ambassador and spoke to him. And they've made behind-the-scenes representations.'

'Fuck behind the scenes!' Sarah was losing her composure now. 'Behind the scenes and I'll be stuck in here. I want this in front of the scenes. I want America to read about this. I've been falsely imprisoned. I'm a member of the American Bar Association, I've been a government adviser in the Czech Republic and in Turkey. I'm not some twenty-year-old kid who's got into trouble on her first trip abroad. To hell with behind the scenes, Ben. I want this to be front-page worldwide news.'

Sarah withdrew her hands from his and folded her arms across her chest. She realised her amulet wasn't hanging around her neck. The guards had taken it, along with her rings and her watch. She prayed it would be safe.

'Sarah . . .'

'No, Ben. I'm in serious trouble here. One wrong move and I could be dead. If this is handled covertly I stand a good chance of falling through the cracks. This has got to be out front, in the newspapers. It has to embarrass the government. People have got to run scared in case the spotlight falls on them.'

Ben Hills sat back in his chair and sighed. 'I was afraid you'd say that,' he told her.

David Rose lay on the bed; he was too tired to move. He needed to eat and there were plenty of restaurants close to the Hotel Turkoman, but that meant moving from the bed when all he wanted to do was sink deeply into its pillows and sleep. That much he deserved, even in the service of something as urgent as freeing Sarah from jail. When he was a young musician with no money he had walked from concert hall to concert hall to save cab fares, not daring to trust his cello to the subway. Lying on the bed brought back those days of penury and exhaustion. Even though he'd been travelling by cab throughout the length and breadth of Istanbul, his weariness was just as intense.

Lawyers, government and prison officials, people from the consulate who had suddenly been galvanised into action by frantic calls from the *Washington Post* and the *New York Times*, police lieutenants, Islamic jurists – David had spoken to everybody who could possibly have some influence on getting Sarah out of jail. Most had offered to do all they could. Most, but not all. The Islamic lawyer he'd gone to see to had turned out to be a cleric. The interview, conducted in broken English, had begun coolly and ended in open hostility. The lawyer explained to David that what Sarah had done was far worse than simple theft; she had defiled one of the most venerated Islamic symbols of faith and worship. Just the fact of her touching the stone was enough to bring the crowds of the faithful out to protest on the streets.

And protest they did. It was as if a charge of negative electricity had surged through Istanbul. On street corners throughout the city centre, rabble-rousers stood on makeshift podiums, haranguing the quickly gathering mob to action; in parks, lunchtime crowds were assailed by indignant clerics who came out of their mosques to decry what the Jewish infidel had done; on radio – so the taxi drivers explained to him – commentators uttered dire warnings about how the incident could undermine the cordial relationship between the United States and Turkey unless the US government repudiated Sarah Kaplan's actions; and ultra-right-wing opposition members of parliament sought every media opportunity to attack the Minister for Antiquities for having given over matters of national importance to a foreigner who was now in jail accused of blasphemy. Yet again, Sarah had become a cause célèbre, vilified by all who didn't know her, defended by none other than those who had proved virtually useless.

But right now David was incapable of any more talking. All he wanted to do was sleep then start again in the morning. Because start again he surely must. If this day had taught him anything it was that nobody else was going to get Sarah out of jail. The morons at the US consulate were only capable of making promissory noises and phatic assurances – anything to defuse David's anger and ensure that he left everything to their subtle and useless diplomacy. And the local lawyers he'd interviewed hadn't been much better. Once they found out who David was asking them to assist their interest failed. No-one was willing to fall foul of the growing mood of Islamic militancy against Sarah.

Even his visit to Sarah late that afternoon had been discouraging. After the initial hugs and thanks, Sarah the composed lawyer had taken over and rattled off a series of instructions, as though David were trying to organise everything in New York with all tools at his fingertips. He nodded enthusiastically to keep up her hopes, but how could he tell her that he hadn't even managed to find a lawyer yet who was willing to represent her, let alone anyone desperate to lever open the door to her cell?

David lay on the bed at his wit's end, staring at the ceiling fan as it gently pulsed the heavy air currents. At first this room had been a sanctuary, a haven of rest and recuperation, of love and rejoicing. Sarah had been wonderful, her old self. He had rediscovered the woman he had loved so much for her level-headed, no-nonsense approach to life in New York. And there was also the sexual Sarah, rampant and vital, as though she was making up for the year they hadn't made love. Things between them had been on the cusp of getting back to normal in a spectacular way. And then this hideous event had happened.

On the bedside table was a stack of messages which David knew he would have to respond to soon. Sarah's parents, his parents, Morrie Friedlander – all desperately wanting news. Messages from the US State Department, the US Embassy in Ankara, even from members of his quintet in New York who had read about Sarah's predicament in the *Times*. There was even a message from the White House – which had impressed the pants of the man in the Turkoman's small reception area – as well as the *Washington Post* and the *New York Times*, Sarah's friends, David's non-musical friends, his agent – everyone wanted to 'touch base' and get him to pass on their love and thoughts to Sarah. Eighteen international calls in all. At an average of ten minutes a call that came to three hours. That meant he'd be talking until eleven at least, without the prospect of dinner or even a cup of coffee. So he'd told the guy at reception that he wasn't prepared to accept any calls unless they were from Sarah.

'And if the American President rings from the White House?' the receptionist had queried in all seriousness. 'I am to say no to the President?'

'Especially the President,' David had told him. 'He talks too much and says nothing. And I'm fed up with lending him money.' His only regret was that he'd turned his back and was halfway into the lift before finishing, so was unable to see the expression on the receptionist's face.

He would return all the phone calls in the morning. He closed his eyes and began to sink into that halfworld of fears, hopes and anticipation. The regular squeak of the ceiling fan drew his mind upwards and outwards from the hotel room to another place where he could lay aside the tensions of the day and drift into a desperately needed sleep. Suddenly the phone shattered the relative calm. David grabbed it from the cradle; it was probably Sarah calling from jail.

'Sir,' said the receptionist, 'two men are here and they insist on seeing you. I tell them you are not to be disturbed but they say no matter.'

By the time the knock sounded at his door, David had had time to wash his face and comb his hair. He recognised one of the men, who smiled at him and warmly shook his hand. Both were dressed in smart, yet casual clothes, and David felt unkempt beside them in his crumpled sweaty shirt and badly creased trousers. But they didn't seem to notice, or if they did, they didn't care.

'Hello, David,' said the man he recognised. 'I am Mustafa Bengazi. We met briefly when you first landed in Istanbul and came to the Ministry. But you didn't meet my colleague, Ibrahim Satap. As you probably know, David, we worked with Sarah on behalf of the Minister of Antiquities in trying to reclaim the treasury of Heinrich Schliemann.'

'I'm afraid I can't offer you even a cup of coffee, Mustafa . . .'

Bengazi held up his hand. 'No matter. We are not here for social reasons. We are here because we must help you release poor Sarah from prison. She has been falsely accused and wrongly imprisoned. She is a victim of a man called Yussef Barrak . . .'

'I know all about Dr Barrak. Sarah's told me everything. How can you help me?'

The two men looked at each other and nodded. 'Sarah spoke much about you while we were working together,' said Bengazi. 'We know that you are a musician not a lawyer. But even a lawyer would have difficulties in this matter for there are many complications.'

David told the two men what he'd spent the day doing. They were not surprised at the run-around he'd been getting from the Istanbul legal circles.

'There seems to be an orchestrated campaign to stir up a lot of resentment towards Sarah,' said Bengazi. 'But this whole scenario is only peripherally to do with Sarah, I'm afraid. It's all obvious to us now we can see the way things are operating: Sarah has been arrested to embarrass the Minister of Antiquities. The Minister is a woman, an intellectual, an atheist, a secularist, a modernist and she stands against the power of the Islamic clerics. Consequently she is hated by men like Barrak who want a return to the certainties of Ottoman rule and the power of Islam. She is detested by the clerics for her stand against Islamic education, and because she is demanding a contraction of the armed forces so that the money Turkey spends on armaments is spent instead on hospitals, schools and public transport. She also wants to make peace with the Kurds. For all these reasons she is hated by the mob and hence is the weakest link in the government. The fact that she is beloved by the intelligentsia in Turkey is of no matter. Barrak recognises that she is a weak link, and if he can break that link he can break the government.'

David sat down on the bed, stunned. Something had told him from the very beginning that the nightmare of Sarah's arrest had more to it than met the eye; that it was more than an accusation of theft. Things had quickly got out of control, and now suddenly he understood why.

'David, we are not here just as the bearers of bad news,' continued Bengazi. 'Since we learnt of Sarah's arrest, we've spent time working out why she is being made a scapegoat. Satap and I wrote down all the possible scenarios, from her being a simple thief to some Machiavellian plot to bring down the government. By the end of the morning the plot to bring down the government no longer looked Machiavellian but Barrakian. Yussef Barrakian to be precise.'

'Do you have proof?' David already knew the answer.

'To get proof we must determine the nexus between this lying cleric from the mosque and Barrak.'

'Yes, that's what Sarah said right at the beginning. But why involve Sarah?'

For the first time Dr Satap spoke. 'Precisely because she's Jewish and American. This was the fuse Barrak realised would ignite the bomb. It would incite religious extremists to rise up and attempt to overthrow the government.'

'But why?' David moaned again. He wanted to shout but he was too tired. 'Why should he want to do that? He's a public servant. Does he hate Sarah that much?'

'Yes and no. Yes, because she usurped his position in the Ministry and embarrassed him before his staff when she first arrived. But mainly, no. His real enemy is his Minister. He knows she is waiting for a chance to replace him and bring in her own head of department. Her position is too precarious to do so at the moment, but given an opportunity she'll get rid of him in a flash. Barrak knows that and this is his way of defending himself. And if attacking the Minister means bringing down her very shaky government by creating a scandal, then so be it. He's a typical Ottoman. Of course, if the government *is* brought down by this scandal, there will be a new election. And the people will be so enraged at the actions of the current secularist government, in particular the Minister's appointment of the supposed Jewish woman thief, that they will elect an Islamic government.'

David couldn't believe what he was hearing. Suddenly the small hotel room felt very claustrophobic. 'Okay, so what do we do? I'm all at sea here, fellas. I can't get a damn lawyer to take the case, and America, with all its resources, isn't going to be any use in this country if what you're saying is correct. What the hell do I do now?'

Bengazi answered. 'We can always find a lawyer. You were speaking to lawyers with a special knowledge of Islamic law, which means they're already committed to the other side. We'll have no trouble finding somebody who'll act for you, but even with the best will in the world, all he'll be able to do is shake a few branches, loosen a couple of leaves. No! The real issue lies with the infamous Dr Barrak and what has gone on in his office. We need to enlist the support and help of somebody who works closely with him, somebody who knows his office.'

'And somebody who is willing to give us information about their boss!' David said sceptically.

Satap smiled. 'They will be queuing up to help. Barrak is not popular with his staff.'

'The next thing,' said Bengazi, 'is to interview the Minister. She has to be appraised of the situation.'

'Not so easy,' David told him. 'She was the first person Sarah told me to call. I've phoned her four times and she hasn't returned any of the calls.'

Bengazi nodded. 'Then she's gone to ground. She's distancing herself from Sarah. It was to be expected.'

'Why? I'd have thought she would be the first to come to our aid. For God's sake, if Sarah goes down, so does she. Surely she, above all, would be determined to prove Sarah's innocence?'

'In an ideal world, yes,' Bengazi said, 'but this is far from an ideal world. Right now she's being a politician and protecting herself and her government. There are demonstrations going on all over the country. However, I agree that we have to speak to her. It's vital that she's informed that Barrak is behind the current imbroglio. Once she sees the complete picture I have no doubt that she'll use every device and trick in the book to prove the link between the theft and Barrak, and then Sarah will be out of prison and back in your arms.'

David wasn't convinced. It was all too risky and left Sarah hanging by a thread. Suddenly her freedom and safety were dependent on getting people to cheat on their bosses and trying to convince a minister to take phone calls. And just because Sarah had a good relationship with Bengazi when things were going well for her was no reason for David to trust him, or his companion, now that they were going haywire.

'No. Sorry,' he said firmly. 'There has to be another way. What you're suggesting is too precarious. If necessary I'll go to the International Court, Amnesty International, the United Nations. Someone must be able to get her out of there.'

The two men's silence was testimony to Sarah's plight.

David realised that he had no option but to trust them, even though it went against his instincts. He was a stranger in a strange place and two local men were extending a helping hand. He had no choice but to grasp it. Slowly he nodded. 'So, how do we uncover the link between Barrak and this guy from the mosque?' he asked.

The following day brought no relief from the demonstrations; if anything they seemed more virulent than on the day of Sarah's arrest. It was Sarah's third day in jail. Every couple of hours she banged on the cell door, demanding to know whether the writ of *habeas corpus* had been delivered to the prison officials. Her mood veered between cold hard calculation and nervous insecurity. In reality she was lost in a mire of political and religious machinations, and the fact that she was being held in protective custody only made matters worse. Once removed from the jurisdiction of the courts, she was in danger of slipping through the cracks altogether.

David visited her that morning. Sarah was stunned by his dereliction of the duties she had set him the previous day.

'You mean, not one lawyer would agree to represent me?'

'Not one.'

'How many did you see?'

'Four or five. Five, I think. By the end of the day I was at screaming point.'

'My God,' Sarah hissed, her fear making her furious. 'I told you not to go limp on me, David. Don't you see what's happening. This is a conspiracy . . .'

David held up his hand. 'It's not a conspiracy, Sarah. I just went to see the wrong lawyers. It's obvious to me now – I should have gone to ordinary lawyers. I thought that an expert on Islamic law was the way to go but I made a mistake.'

'You made a mistake! You made a fucking mistake and I'm still in jail,' she snapped. 'I had some idiot from the American consulate visit me yesterday. I think it was yesterday – I've lost track of time in this hellhole. He said I'm being held for my own protection against the mob and there was nothing he could do. I've been relying on *you*.' She sighed and her body seemed to deflate. 'Oh, David, I'm so sorry. This is just driving me crazy.'

'Darling, I'm doing everything I can.'

'I know you are. But you have to see it from my point of view. I'm powerless in here. I've lost every means of defending myself. I'm entirely dependent on you. And now you come and tell me that you've been going to the wrong lawyers. For Christ's sake, David, can't you see why I'm angry?'

'Sarah, I don't like this any more than you do.'

'Why the hell not! You're not in some stinking jail.'

David looked crestfallen. Sarah hated herself for shouting at him but it was her fear causing her to hit out. She was in a state of panic, desperate to leave this jail, this country.

'The consul actually had the gall to tell me that matters concerning the Islamic religion were very sensitive and for the sake of the relationship between the two governments he has to tread a very narrow path. For God's sake, I'm an American citizen and he's sitting on his rich ass examining things this way and that. He told me I have to sit tight and not to worry, that he will move heaven and earth to get me out of here.' She laughed dismissively. 'Not to worry!' she repeated sarcastically. 'You hear that? There are demonstrations all over the fucking city – the police here take great pleasure in coming in and telling me where the next one is taking place, taunting me – and he wants me to sit tight as if nothing has happened. Jesus!'

Her mind flashed back to the previous night. She had asked for some English reading material to stop her mind from atrophying and an elderly policeman had brought her a magazine. He had unlocked the cell door and walked proprietorially into the room. He stood next to her bunk, towering over her, positioning himself so close that Sarah she couldn't get up without touching his body. He had leered at her and Sarah had suddenly lost her bravado and become horribly frightened. She was convinced he was going to rape her. She hadn't been able to even scream, she was so frightened, but her terror must have showed in her eyes for the policeman smiled in conquest, threw a cheap magazine at her and walked out of the cell. Sarah hadn't been able to move for half an hour. Finally her fear had dissipated enough for her to burst into tears.

And now she was venting her anger and fear on David. Suddenly she was ashamed of her behaviour. He had assured her that he was doing everything in his power to help her and that he would continue to move mountains for her, because of his love for her, his concern. He was trying to remain calm in the face of her strident aggression. How could she be so cruel. David was her only hope and she was bawling him out like he was some negligent paralegal. Sarah threw her arms around him and held him close.

David left the prison desperately regretting not being able to tell Sarah about his conversation the previous night with her two former colleagues, Bengazi and Satap. If only he could have told her what they were planning to do, but spies were still everywhere in Turkey. Sarah could inadvertently leak the information that David was investigating Barrak's involvement with the Islamic cleric and the danger was just too great. No, Sarah of all people must be kept in the dark. She was as touchy as a firework and telling her about the suspected conspiracy to bring down the government might be the spark which sent her into orbit. Of course she already knew of Barrak's lies and manipulation – she had been screaming about it to everybody who would listen – but the vital link with the cleric was something she hadn't thought through yet, and the larger conspiracy which followed simply had not occurred to her. And that was precisely the way it had to stay.

David had discovered from the police that Barrak had been interviewed. He had confirmed that he was due to meet Sarah at four o'clock on the day of her arrest, but had been unavoidably delayed by a visitor. The appointment was noted in his diary. The visitor was due to have departed at three-forty-five but stayed until four which meant that Barrak had not been able to get to the mosque until four-fifteen, just in time to see the police arresting Sarah. He was devastated, claiming that if only he had been there on time he might have prevented the terrible blasphemy. He had volunteered the information that the stone in the mosque from the Kaaba had been one of the major topics of conversation with Sarah at dinner on the night before her visit to the mosque. He had explained its value, its place in the Islamic life of Istanbul to Sarah and she had been fascinated. Perhaps too fascinated, but she was so open he had seen no reason to be circumspect. Now, of course, he regretted having been so free with his information. He had not taken her for a liar, a thief or a blasphemer. He had assured the police lieutenant that in future he would be more cautious about what he said to whom.

David pondered Barrak's duplicity as the taxi carried him to Dr Bengazi's office in the Topkapi Museum. Bengazi greeted him with a drawn and worried face.

'The forces of darkness have been active overnight,' he said, dispensing with the usual pleasantries. 'There have been demonstrations against Sarah in many different parts of Turkey, even in other countries such as Iran, Egypt and Algeria. The fundamentalists are whipping up a mighty storm. There was even a demonstration in Jerusalem in the Al Aksa mosque. Thousands of young men came out onto the streets and the Israeli police were forced to use riot control gas.'

'Jesus,' said David.

'It was on the news this morning,' Bengazi told him. 'The situation is getting very bad, David. Very bad. I am afraid for Sarah's safety.'

'I've been afraid for her all along. The only consolation is that she's in a police station.'

'But police stations have been stormed before.'

'Do you think Barrak knew it would go this far?' David asked.

Bengazi shrugged. 'He has unleashed a tiger. I don't think anybody can predict what a tiger will do when it is angry.'

'It's all getting beyond us,' David said. 'Last night it seemed so simple: we co-opt somebody on Barrak's staff, find the evidence and blow Barrak apart. But if this thing is turning international . . .'

'It's still the only way. No matter what happens, the man with the key to it all is Yussef Barrak himself. He was interviewed by the police yesterday. A friend working in his department told me. I have no idea what was said though.'

'You have a friend working in Barrak's department?'

'Of course. My work as an archaeologist means I have much to do with the Department of Antiquities.'

'Why can't your friend help us?'

'Why should he, David? Why should he risk his career, his life even, by going against a powerful and vindictive man who could ruin him, just to help Sarah?'

There were a thousand answers but none of them held any weight. All David could do was nod in agreement.

'Money?' he asked simply. Bengazi looked at him quizzically, a smile appearing on his face. 'We have considerable resources available to us in America. If it's a question of buying information, I have no problem with that.'

'Yes,' said Bengazi. 'It is something I was going to suggest, but not as soon as this. I was hoping other means might work. But with the rapidity with which things are happening, I fear we have no time for other contingencies. Money might be the answer; it's a tried and trusted way of doing business in Turkey. I think maybe we should offer a couple of thousand American dollars to one of my friends in the Ministry to assist us in unlocking the secrets of Barrak's appointments diary.'

'Who will you ask?' asked David.

Bengazi laughed. 'My friend, you're the last person I would tell that to. Your hands have to be as clean as possible in all of this. You will make a donation of a couple of thousand American dollars to the Museum. After that you must leave it to me. You will of course have an official receipt and my thanks for your generosity. Now, David, I suggest you leave here for the next hour or so and I will get on with some urgent work which doesn't involve you.'

David left Bengazi's office and wandered around the vast grounds of the Topkapi. He stopped for a coffee at the café overlooking the Golden Horn, the same café in which Sarah and he had enjoyed their first meal together when he arrived in Turkey. Ships glided into and out of the bottleneck of the Bosphorus, entering or leaving the Black Sea. It was a narrow and incredibly busy waterway and David could easily have spent a couple of hours just watching the huge tankers ply their way along the shore, cleaving a path between Asia and Europe. In David's short time in Turkey, the differences he had noticed were remarkable. He was a citizen of America but his Jewish culture looked back towards Europe. Turkey, also, clung to Europe, its landmass north of the Bosphorus claiming a toehold in western civilisation. Yet south of the Bosphorus was Asia with its alien customs, as unfathomable to the European mind as heavy metal music would be to Buddhist monks.

He was lost in his thoughts when there was a tap on his shoulder. He turned around in surprise, realising that he must have been staring at the sea for an hour or more. Bengazi grinned at him. 'I have good news. Come with me.'

David threw some coins on the table to pay his bill and followed Bengazi up the steps from the café, along the terraces behind the harem and into the private offices of the archaeologists who worked in the Museum. When they were behind a closed door, Bengazi unlocked a filing cabinet and withdrew a small sheaf of papers. 'Photocopies of Barrak's diary. They were faxed to me by a close friend in the Ministry in Ankara. And at a very good price. Only one thousand US dollars.'

'Keep the other thousand for the museum,' said David, reaching over for them.

'You're very generous. And God knows we can use it. But first, my dear friend, you have to put the money into the account,' said Bengazi with a smile.

David scanned the papers but, of course, Barrak's notes had been made in Turkish.

'Tell me,' he said, 'why do you think that a man as careful as Barrak would have left any clues in his diary? I would have thought it would be the last place he'd write anything which might have anything to do with a conspiracy against the government. He'd have to be crazy to have committed that sort of thing to paper.'

Bengazi nodded. 'True, but we're not looking for a document. Like you say, he's far too sophisticated for that. What we're looking for is anything which might indicate a change of routine, something slightly out of the normal. Men like Barrak are frighteningly predictable. They leave home at the same time each day, they delay precisely the same amount of time before admitting a visitor to a meeting, they eat lunch at exactly the same time. They're horribly boring, and that's their weakness. Because anything they do out of the ordinary sticks out like a sore thumb.'

'And are there any sore thumbs in these papers?' asked David.

'I've only read them very quickly. Over the last six days, he's had fifteen visitors and numerous meetings. My friend who photocopied the diary has already helped me to discount eleven of the names. They are either officials or visiting dignitaries, or people who are highly unlikely to have had any contact with Islamic clerics. That leaves only four names: my friend in Ankara is currently checking on them. But there's one that stands out – even in Barrak's mind because he's put a question mark beside it.' Bengazi pointed out a late afternoon appointment held five days earlier. The name was Ozman Urzak.

'Who is he?' asked David.

Bengazi shrugged his shoulders. 'I don't know. My friend is currently checking.'

'Is he a cleric? An Imam?'

'I don't know, David. I don't know. There's no point getting excited until we've traced him. And what you said is probably right – Barrak's too smart to have written down anything which might incriminate him. But it's the first place to start. If nothing turns up from this Urzak fellow then we'll have to try getting information from people who know Barrak well. And we'll have to go to the Islamic officials in the mosque. Maybe there's somebody there who doesn't like him, who might give us information.'

'When will we find out more about this Urzak guy?'

Bengazi shrugged. 'Maybe today, maybe tomorrow. It might take a few days longer. It's our first positive link though. If he's an Islamic fundamentalist, as I suspect, then we just have to tie him in with the cleric at the Mehmet Pasha mosque, the man who allegedly saw Sarah stealing the stone. Once we've done that, we have enough evidence to present to the police. Certainly enough to get Sarah released on bail.'

David laughed. 'Even if Urzak is what you say, Barrak can deny all knowledge. He can just say that the guy visited him to talk antiquities.' Bengazi looked disappointed by David's response.

'I'm sorry, Mustafa. You've done a hell of a job. It's the first ray of sunshine in all this darkness. Don't think I'm not immensely grateful for all you're doing. But I think it's going to take more than an appointment diary to clear Sarah.' David was suddenly exhausted. He put his hands to his eyes and shook his head. 'Mustafa, I can't begin to thank you enough for what you're doing.'

Bengazi raised his hand dismissively. 'You would do the same for me.'

'Of course,' said David, 'but that's not the point. The point is that you've gone out of your way to help somebody you hardly know. Sarah and I owe you our deepest gratitude.'

Bengazi nodded. 'Show me your gratitude by depositing one thousand dollars in my friend's bank account in Ankara and donating one thousand to my work in the Museum.'

David laughed. 'With the very greatest of pleasure.'

❀

Ozman Urzak browsed through the newspapers, sipping his cup of coffee and reading about the increasing tensions in Turkey and overseas. His home, a mansion in the hills overlooking the city of Edirne, was a stone's throw from the Bulgarian border yet only two or three hours by car from Istanbul. So close to Europe, so near to Asia. What a life! Straddling two great continents. Literally a middleman. Beloved by the border guards of both countries for his generosity and understanding of their desire to give their families a better life.

A face stared up at him from the newsprint — the middle-aged visage of the Minister of Antiquities. It was no longer the face of Turkey's earth mother, assuring her people that everything would be all right if they simply listened to her. No! This was the face of a woman under siege, a woman — what was that expression they used in the west? — hoist on her own petard. Well, she wasn't nearly as smug as she had been a couple of days ago at the opening of the newest extensions to the dig at Ephesus. There she had told the world's media that Turkey was the great unknown of the western world; that while everybody had looked towards Greece as the cradle of civilisation, now archaeology was proving that Anatolia was the birthplace of western mythologies and western culture. How was she feeling now, Urzak wondered, with the Islamic world looking to her for an explanation of how she could have allowed the Jewish infidel to abuse a holy relic?

Urzak smiled and continued to sip his coffee. The plan was working brilliantly. And it would continue to do so if only Yussef Barrak kept his head. It was all so simple. This scandal would unseat the already unstable government, necessitating an urgent election which would sweep the Islamic party to power. For the next couple of years, at least, the question of the ownership of Schliemann's treasure would cease to be a pressing issue, especially now that the German team had disappeared into a puff of smoke.

Yes, things were proceeding nicely. As was everything else in Urzak's life. He was making a fortune, he had substantial bank accounts in Liechtenstein, several false identities any of which he could assume in an instant, charming mistresses in apartments in Moscow, Paris and New York, and an impenetrable front of respectability. And things would continue to travel along their merry way for as long as he could foresee. After all, the world would always need heroin, and the Kurds would always need guns.

Provided Yussef Barrak kept his head. If not, he'd very quickly lose it anyway.

One thousand miles north of where Ozman Urzak was sipping his coffee, Feyodor Mikailovich Meconski was tucking into a freshly baked croissant. In the old days he had suffered his wife's idea of breakfast: two-day-old black bread, slices of greasy ham and stewed tea left over from the previous day. As far as he knew, she was still eating the slop that she used to force into him. Not that he gave a damn anymore what she ate. He had roubles bursting out of his wallet and could afford anything he wanted. He had a stock of American dollars in a safety deposit box which he could use any time to treat himself and his lover, Natalie, to a wonderful time.

But what he particularly enjoyed was to leave his apartment as soon he had shaved, showered and dressed and catch the bus to the restaurants close to his office. They stimulated his appetite with their welcoming smells of delicious warm pastries and cooked meats, but he passed them by. Instead he walked to the GUM department store and took the lift to the sixth floor café where a special window seat was waiting for him. There the waiter, who by now knew him well enough to reserve his seat for seven-thirty every morning, immediately brought over a bowl of freshly brewed steaming black coffee as well as hot buttered croissants, crisp breakfast rolls and preserves. Meconski could never have hoped to afford such luxuries on his meagre salary. How things had changed.

He opened the paper and turned to the foreign news section. He smiled when he read the story about the riots in Istanbul, Ankara and other towns in Turkey, demonstrations against the desecration of one of Turkey's holiest sites by an infidel woman.

The headlines and report were delicious, as tasty as the croissant, as appetising as the coffee. Meconski felt an overwhelming admiration for his business partner, the very clever and unbelievably resourceful Maxim Nikolaivich Lomonosov.

CHAPTER 23

The three days during which Amra rested in the inner sanctum of the priestesses of Mithras came as close to happiness as she had known since leaving her village. Although the knowledge that she had failed in her mission constantly preyed on her, Amra allowed herself to give way to the bodily pleasures that the other priestesses spent much of their day enjoying. After weeks of sleeping outdoors, after being raped and brutalised, forced to catch her own meals, being constantly tired and prey to both the whims of the Gods and the elements, Amra's time in the inner sanctum gave her a much-needed opportunity to renew both her mind and body.

On the first day of her resting, she felt a sense of guilt that she had let down her family and village. They were waiting for her return, worrying about her, wondering whether or not she had succeeded in saving them. Yet, instead of continuing her quest, here she was being feted by the priestesses as an honoured member of the cult of Mithras. But on the second day, after feasting on more delicious food and beer, Amra's guilt was swamped by the heady sensation of being completely sated. This, she imagined, must be how her parents felt after a feast. On the third day, when she swam in the priestesses' pool, when the Nubian slave scraped her skin clean with a sharp curved scythe, when hairdressers attended to her hair and washed her body with warm oils, when perfumiers giggled around her and experimented with different scents on her arms, legs and her most intimate parts, when fat men with childlike high voices sang to her, she gave herself over to the joy and luxury of the palace. She forgot her family and her friends. She became a Trojan priestess.

But when she awoke on the fourth day, her sense of responsibility took over and she said to Ishta-Mithra, 'I must see the King.'

The priestess opened her eyes wide and shouted aloud her pleasure. 'Mithras visited you during the night! We have been praying for this. You have a message for the King?'

Amra knew that if she admitted there was no message, she would be refused admission to Praxis's presence. And so she nodded coyly. Runners were sent, messages were passed and in a short while Amra was told that she would dine that night with the King.

Amra visited Wind later that afternoon. Walking through the gate of his enclosure, she smiled at his grace and strength, recalling the pleasure he had brought her in her loneliness. Wind whinnied in pleasure, cantering over to see her. Amra jumped onto his back for the sheer joy of feeling his body and rode him around the field. She whispered into his ear, 'What will I say to the King tonight? How will I explain that I haven't spoken to the God Mithras, nor he to me, that I know nothing, that all I want is the secret of making iron?'

She reached her arms as far as she could around the huge horse's neck, holding her hands together so that she was embracing the black beast as men embrace their wives. She felt the power of his huge warm muscular body. It gave her a confidence which she hadn't enjoyed since she had arrived in Troy. If only everything were this simple. If only she could stay on the back of this wonderful horse, ride out of the gates of Troy, back over the land she had come from, back into her village to say to her people: 'I have found the secret of making iron weapons. I know how it is done.' But she knew this was all a dream.

In the evening, the priestesses dressed Amra in a clean white dress and placed a garland of red roses upon her head. They escorted her along the corridor, singing and chanting, the two chief priestesses on either side and ten lower acolytes following behind.

On the threshold of the King's throne room all fell to their knees and lowered their heads to touch the cold marble. Mithrassa-Urbek came forward and told them to rise. He led Amra towards the King, the priestesses still flanking her. Amra was surprised to see that the room was filled with huge banqueting tables which groaned with food and goblets of liquid. Ornately carved golden chairs were placed around the tables and, on a raised plinth, level with the height of the King's throne, was a smaller table and six chairs. On this table was an exquisite carving of a peacock. The bird appeared to be lying on the table with its tail fanned out so that it spread like a cloth, falling and covering the marble floor below.

Raising his voice, the King commanded, 'Come. Mount the stand and sit beside me, Voice of the God Mithras. During our feast you will tell me what new things Mithras has confided to you.'

Amra walked confidently towards the King, though in her mind she was feeling anything but self-assured. All she wanted to do was get onto Wind and ride away from this place. No matter how beautiful, how brilliant the court might be, she belonged in her village with her own people. She just wanted to return home to her loving family.

Once the King had sat down, Amra took her seat and looked carefully around her. On the King's other side were his two youngest wives and his two eldest children. One of them, a prince named Cormis, stared at her. Amra had noticed him before; he had spoken out against her when she had first arrived at the court. He made her feel uneasy by the looks he gave her. He was a handsome young man with black hair and dark sad eyes. His skin was very smooth like a baby's, although he kept hair on the bottom of his chin and across his upper lip. He was dressed in similar colours to those of the peacock.

The servants entered carrying trays laden with jugs of wine. The Chief of Service walked before them. He approached the King, bowed low and poured wine into his goblet. The King's food taster stepped forward and sipped the wine, pronouncing it good; then Praxis picked up the goblet and turned to Amra, lifting it towards her.

'Well, child. What do you think of our court?'

'It is wonderful, Great King and Majesty of the World. I have never seen anything like it.' The King smiled. Amra was glad that she had finally learnt how to address him.

'In your home what do you do to feast?'

'We have a large fire which we light at night in the middle of the village. The women cook meats and wrap vegetables in leaves then bury them in the ground close to the fire so that they cook. When everything is cooked, the villagers gather around, the Headman and the Medicine Man say prayers, and then we eat.'

'And do you drink?' asked the King. 'Do you drink wine as fine as this?'

Amra sipped the liquid. It was her first drink of wine; it tasted of fruit. She shook her head. 'No, Majesty. We drink beer and water. Beer is the juice of the hops that grow in our region. Sometimes we drink the juice of the fruits which grow in our valleys.'

'We also drink beer, but beer is not the drink of banquets. For occasions such as this, when we celebrate an agreement with a mighty nation such as Egypt, we drink wine.' The King raised his goblet towards a dark-skinned man sitting at the head of one of the tables below. The man raised his own glass and proposed a toast which Amra didn't understand. But everybody seemed to be happy, which made her happy. Amra sipped from her goblet again. Even though she'd only taken a few small mouthfuls she could feel the wine beginning to make her head peculiar, as though she were in the room yet wasn't really there.

Once the King and his wives had filled their platters, Amra filled her own and began to eat. There were many different kinds of meats: one she recognised as cow, another as sheep. Apart from the meats, there were great bowls of lettuce, parsley and cabbage, and also yellow and red flowers. Then there were pots of honey, and small trays with colourful powders in them which Amra began to taste. The man next to her told her their names. Saffron, a vivid yellow powder coloured like the sun, which came from India; garlic, a white paste grown in Troy; sesame, onions and mustard seeds for sprinkling on the meat to add taste and zest. Amra sprinkled some saffron on the cow meat, and was amazed at the way it tasted different from how it had tasted the last time she had eaten it in her village. She tried other spices, enjoying the different sensations on her tongue. But her amusement came to an end when the King turned to her, and said: 'The Chief Priestess informs me that the God Mithras spoke to you in a dream last night. Is this true?'

Amra's good humour evaporated instantly. The spices turned to dust in her mouth and all she wanted to do was to ride far away from this court and its dangers. While everybody was smiling at her now, she knew she was in great danger. A distant voice called to her from far away. She took another sip of wine. If only she imagined she was riding Wind in the cool fresh breeze, her mind sharp and free from the effects of the wine, she would be all right.

'Well?' demanded the King, becoming impatient. Courtiers began to look in their direction as they heard the King raise his voice. 'Did Mithras speak to you or not?'

'Yes,' declared Amra. This time her voice was less deferential, slightly higher-pitched. 'Yes, he spoke to me.' She had forgotten to add 'Lord and Master of the World', but it didn't seem to matter much anymore.

The background noise fell away as the courtiers strained to hear what Amra was saying. Her tone intrigued them. No-one ever dared to addressed the great Praxis in such a way. No-one raised their voice to the King and lived. Without realising the danger she was placing herself in, Amra continued. 'Mithras spoke to me about you, Praxis.' She pushed her chair away and stood up, swaying a little from the wine, towering over the King. Praxis looked up at her in astonishment. The courtiers gasped and the Nubian guards began to move away from their place around the walls to protect their monarch. No-one was allowed to be higher than the King in his presence. No-one! It was instant death to place one's head higher than the King. What was the girl doing? Didn't she know the law?

Amra looked down at the King. 'You, Praxis, Mithras spoke to me about you.' She heard her words ringing in her ears; they sounded strange. Like the old men in the village after a feast. The King stared at her in shock. 'He said that you, more than anybody, do not listen. Mithras has sent me to tell you things but you do not listen to me.'

Praxis was amazed. Was this truly the earthly embodiment of the God Mithras talking to him, he wondered? Only a god would dare treat him so disrespectfully.

'They will come as horses, Praxis. Horses like Wind. That is how they will attack you. Big horses.' Amra's hands flew out to encompass the room. 'The biggest horses in the world. And they will come, Praxis, they will come over the sea and will kill you. You cannot fight the horses.'

Amra sat down heavily in her chair, her face flushed. She took another sip of wine. Praxis continued to stare at her in amazement; this child really was possessed by Mithras. He turned to Mithrassa-Urbek. 'Are the priestesses here?' he asked urgently.

The priestesses hurried over at Mithrassa-Urbek's summons and fell to their knees at the threshold of the King's table. The savage girl was flushed, a silly grin on her lips.

'You heard what this girl said,' thundered Praxis. 'She says that the men will come inside the bodies of horses. What does she mean?'

'She means,' said Ishta-Mithra, desperately trying to interpret the girl's words, 'that great horses will come from over the sea.'

'Great horses? Bigger than the horses which draw my own chariot?'

'Bigger, Majesty. As tall as the tallest building.'

'And will these giant horses travel across the sea by boats?' demanded the King.

'I do not know, Majesty, but when they land on our shores they will be bigger than the biggest horse in the land of Troy.'

'How do you know that?' asked the King.

'I interpret the child's words. This child speaks with the voice of Mithras. Mithras speaks in a way which can only be understood by those who follow his ways.'

'I follow his ways,' shouted the King in fury, 'and I don't understand what she's talking about. Has she had a vision or is she just a child drunk on wine?'

'She is not drunk, Majesty, although the wine . . . maybe . . . I don't know.'

The other priestess burst in. 'If she is affected by wine, Majesty, it is because the God Mithras has made her so. If she speaks with his voice, with his authority, then her words must be heeded.'

'Giant horses?' repeated the King.

'Father,' interrupted Cormis, 'let me take this girl away from here and talk to her. I am a warrior skilled in battle. Before each battle I speak directly with Mithras. He heeds my prayers and I have never yet lost a battle. Even the priestesses say that Mithras smiles upon me for my victories and my courage. Therefore he may be willing to disclose more to me than in this company.' The prince pointed to the astounded people seated at the banquet tables.

'Amra,' said the King. 'Is there anything more you have to say to us? Did the God Mithras say any more?'

Amra shook her head. 'Wind,' she said. 'A horse like Wind.'

The King turned to the priestesses. 'They will ride on the wind?' The women shrugged their shoulders.

'Very well,' he said to his son, 'take Amra to your quarters. See if the God will speak to you. Return the moment you know more.'

As Cormis helped Amra from the table the room remained in total silence. Never before had such a thing happened in the court of King Praxis, nor in the time of his father before him. This was the stuff of legends, a story that the courtiers would hand down to their children and their children's children.

Amra walked unsteadily beside the prince, held upright by his arm on hers. Her knees felt strangely weak and unreliable, like at the end of her first day's ride on Wind. She knew she must not fall for then she would be laughed at by everybody. The walls kept moving backwards and forwards. Why, she didn't understand, but she knew enough to realise that she must be careful not to fall against them. Cormis took her out of the throne room and into a corridor which was bright with torches and covered with wondrous paintings of naked men and women, and the Gods in their blue sky.

'These are the private chambers of his Majesty King Praxis, his wives and the princes and princesses,' Cormis told her. 'Nobody comes here except for the royal family and the servants who attend us. Not even the high priestesses. You are a privileged girl, Amra,' he said.

His voice was gentle yet strong, like a singer of legends and stories around a village fire. He was taller than her by a head and his skin shone with cleanliness and oils. He smelt sweet like a flower yet Amra could see clearly the outline of his muscles.

'Tell me about your home,' he asked. 'I have never been north of Troy. My life as the commander of the Trojan army takes me only south and east to where our enemies gather at the borders.'

'What do you do?' Amra asked, not understanding what a commander was. She was embarrassed to hear her voice slurring over the words.

'I lead the army. I force rulers who refuse to pay us the tribute they owe to bow down before the great Praxis. I ride with my army to extract taxes from the people. Where there is a murder of an official like a tax collector, it is I who takes an army to make the people obey and to punish those who would dare to raise their hands against Praxis.'

'You must be very strong,' she said. She wished her voice would steady.

'I am strong. So is my army. We have over one thousand chariots in Troy. Their upkeep is very expensive. It is my responsibility.'

'I have seen the chariots,' Amra said. 'They ride outside the village. I don't understand how they work.'

'Tomorrow I will show you,' he said, 'but in the meantime you must tell me what Mithras means when he says the men will come in horses.' He stopped beside a large door. 'These are my chambers, Amra. This is where I live.'

He opened the door and revealed a series of rooms that disappeared into the distance. A group of servants cleaning the chambers were taken by surprise at the sudden appearance of their master. They flung themselves full length onto the ground and lay still as he walked in. Amra followed. He barked a command at the servants and, almost as one, they stood and ran crouching out of the door, closing it quickly behind them.

'Now,' said Cormis, turning to Amra. His gentle voice suddenly vanished. 'You aren't the voice of Mithras, are you? I've been watching you closely since you first arrived at our court, Amra. You're just a savage girl from the wild north. You have no ability to hear the Gods. You don't hear the voice of Mithras, do you?'

When Amra did not respond, his tone changed again from anger to one of conspiracy. 'Come over here. Sit with me. Let's talk about you and Mithras. And about how you managed to stay alive with that bull. What tricks did you use? Tell me, girl. I could use those tricks myself.'

Amra didn't fully comprehend Cormis's words. She followed him to the sofa and sat down beside him. All she wanted to do was close her eyes and go to sleep. Her head was spinning. So were the walls and the curtain across the wall behind the sofa was flapping strangely. Cormis moved closer to her the moment she was seated.

'You fascinate me. You're so . . .' he searched for the words, 'rough and crude. So much like a peasant with your painted skin and your lack of refinement. But there's something about you which is different. You're a fascinating girl, captivating. You have a wild spirit which I admire. Anybody else who spoke to my father that way would have had their head parted from their shoulders. But you didn't think of that, did you? You just wanted to prove to him that you were the mouthpiece of Mithras. Nobody has ever dared talk to my father like that. But for all your bravery, you may have miscalculated. He may still cut off your head when he realises that you're not a priestess of Mithras at all.'

'I am,' Amra said uncertainly. 'Mithras speaks to me.' She began to realise that there was danger here. Cormis changed his mood so quickly; she didn't trust him. Her head was beginning to clear and the things he was saying to her were threatening. 'Mithras speaks through my voice. I don't understand what he says. I'm not his priestess and yet he has chosen to speak through me. Why are you saying these things?'

'I am saying them, Amra, because I don't believe you. I think you're here to get the secret of making iron. This is a secret which is known to only a few – my father and his armourer.' He looked at her closely, 'And me.'

Amra shook her head. 'No! You're wrong. I've spoken to the priestesses. They say that nobody knows how to make iron. Not even the King. They say that my journey here has been wasted.'

'They know nothing. They spend their days trading in sacred prostitutes and slaves, corn, wine and spices. Arms and metals are not their province.'

'But they said . . .'

'What they said is of no importance, Amra. I *know* how to make iron.'

'Will you show me?' she asked.

He shrugged. 'First tell me if you are truly the voice of Mithras.'

'Yes,' she said, realising that if she told the truth, she would immediately lose her life. She had to continue the deception at all costs. She was glad that her head was clearing and the walls were stopping their movement. 'Yes. I am the voice of Mithras.'

Cormis moved closer to her and put one arm around her shoulder and his other hand upon her breast. She tried to move away but he gripped her powerfully. He moved his hand from one breast to the other and then down between her legs.

'Stop it,' Amra said pushing him away. 'I am a priestess. Stop it now!'

Cormis laughed. 'You're not a priestess. No god would speak through a thing like you. Come here, thing! I am Prince Cormis, son of the great Praxis. The law of Troy says that I may have any woman I want. I want you. I want to feel your savage ways. I want to know your body. These women in the court, they are all perfumed and mannered. They give way to me without a fight just because I am Cormis, son of Praxis. You are different. I want you. You are strong-blooded and you will fight. That will make for good sex.'

Amra was terrified. She could see in Cormis's eyes that he meant to possess her. Suddenly she smelt again the three filthy men, the three hunters, their foul breath, the stink of their bodies. She felt their bodies on top of her yet again, the way their hands touched and groped at her, the searing pain that ripped through her body as they forced their huge penises inside her. She smelt the smell again. She felt the fear.

Amra backed away until she came to the end of the sofa. Cormis was smiling. He stood. 'Stay where you are. You will do as I tell you.'

Amra stood and backed away from him further, towards the door. Suddenly furious, he shouted: 'Do not move! You are commanded by me on pain of death to take off your robes. I want to see your body.'

But Amra continued to retreat, unable to look away from him, transfixed as a rabbit before a snake. Cormis rose from the sofa and moved towards her. His movement broke the spell and Amra turned and ran towards the door. But Cormis crossed the gap faster than she did and as she tugged on the door handle, his hand forced it closed. He drew his knife and thrust the point into her throat. Amra could feel it cold and sharp against her skin. Was this how Annka and Henk had felt when the Headman cut their throats and ripped out their hearts? Terrified and powerless?

'How dare you run away from me,' Cormis growled. 'I am a prince of this court. Nobody disobeys my orders. I could have you killed for this. Now, get into my bedroom or truly I will kill you right now.'

Amra's body felt weak and flaccid. In the four days she had been in the Trojan court she had lost her guile, her cunning. Her edge had been blunted by luxury, good food and drink and now she was in the greatest of danger. She felt tears welling up but forced them back, knowing they would only incite the prince further.

But slowly, from the deepest reaches of her body a mantle of courage settled on Amra's shoulders, and with it fury. Fury that, yet again, her body was being taken from her. Fury that for the second time in her short life she was to be victim to a man's lust. Fury that she had lost control of who she was and what she was willing to do. Well, not again. Not a second time. She would rather die than feel him inside her. This time she would fight to her death.

Amra drew herself up tall and looked at Cormis with icy determination. Her fear evaporated. She hissed, 'Touch me, Cormis, and I swear that you will die.'

A flicker of worry passed momentarily across his face but then he laughed in her face, his spittle spraying her lips. 'Die? You are nothing. You would dare raise your hand to a prince of Troy? Where are your weapons, savage?' His free hand felt her body for a dagger which might somehow be concealed there.

'You will die because I am a priestess.'

'Liar!' he said, laughing. 'Fool! I know you are not a priestess of Mithras. You said so yourself. All you are is just a savage from the north, smelling of earth and trees.'

'I am not a priestess of Mithras,' Amra said. 'I am a priestess of the Goddess of the Moon. I am her soul on earth, through my dreams she talks to our people. It was she who sent me here. It was she who told me to come to Troy so that Mithras could speak through me.'

'What has this to do with me?' Cormis mocked, his confidence returning as he traced the point of his knife in a circle over the delicate skin of her throat.

'Simply this, Cormis. I am a virgin. And I will die a virgin because any man who puts his penis into my body will die. As he is inside me, he will suddenly freeze, colder than ice. Like the cold moon on a frozen evening. And then the Goddess of the Moon will strike an arrow through his frozen heart.'

Cormis withdrew the knife from her throat. 'I don't believe you. You're lying, just as you have lied since you came to Troy.'

'Yes,' said Amra, her tone mocking him in return. 'You're right. I am lying. Make love to me, Cormis. Put your body inside mine. I welcome it. I welcome your lovemaking. I welcome seeing you turn to ice. Come on. Take me into your room, lie me on the bed. Put that thing of yours into me and I will have the pleasure of dragging your dead body along the corridor and throwing it at your father's feet. It will be my joy.'

Cormis recoiled slightly. Amra could see the fear in his eyes. Should she tell him more? Should she tell him that if he thrust his dagger into her throat, then he would die immediately? No, she had said enough. The threat was there. She was in his hands now.

Cormis remained silent. 'Come Cormis,' Amra taunted, her mouth overriding her mind. She was furious

417

that he had touched her breasts, that his fingers had groped into the private recesses of her body. 'Come. Take me inside. I want to feel your frozen body. I want to see the Goddess of the Moon pierce your heart with her arrow. I want to see the look of death on your face when she strikes you.'

Cormis did not move. Amra smiled, reached behind her and opened the door. She walked out of the room alone. The servants who were waiting outside stared at her in astonishment. She walked back along the corridor and into the throne room.

When she appeared at the threshold the loud hubbub of voices was suddenly stilled. King Praxis turned towards her. Still furious at Cormis's violation, Amra raised her hand and pointed her finger directly at the King. 'Your son Cormis tried to take my body. If ever he or anybody in this court touches me in that way again I will call down the wrath of my goddess, the Goddess of the Moon, and they will be struck dead.'

Praxis rose from his seat with dignity and demanded: 'Explain what you have just said.'

'I shall explain nothing further,' said Amra, mustering as much self-confidence as she was able. 'Your son Cormis is alone in his room. The great leader of your army is shaking with fear, like a day-old calf. He is terrified of my power. You, great King Praxis, will soon know the full might of my goddess, the Goddess of the Moon. She and your God Mithras speak together in the Heavens and this is why Mithras speaks through me. But now the God Mithras will tell you nothing more. You will tell me now how to make iron so that I can save my people. This is fair.'

The King nodded. 'Come, voice of the Gods. Sit and finish the feast.'

Amra walked slowly over to the seat she had occupied earlier. Everyone was staring at her, marvelling at her control over the greatest king in the world. She sat beside Praxis and picked up her glass of wine, then put it down, realising that its effects were too unpredictable. She knew she had gone as far as she could go with her demands before Praxis lost his patience and ordered her death. She knew she had been unbelievably lucky in the way the events of the evening had turned out. Or was it her totem, the bee, looking after her? She had seen many bees since she had been in Troy, fat bees with unusual markings on their bodies. Somewhere close by there must be lots of honey. She smiled. If only Peta were here to help her search for it.

The King was speaking. 'Did my son Cormis really try to force himself upon you?'

Amra nodded. She had no reason to protect the prince.

'He is known to many women in Troy. He has an appetite for women. Husbands don't like it, but he is the prince of the land and may do with his subjects as he wishes. I have spoken with him often and he has promised to reform, but nothing seems to change. He has many wives, slaves and prostitutes, yet he would seek to defile a priestess of Mithras.' The King shook his head sadly. 'I banished him to the furthest reaches of my empire, and on condition of his return he promised to change. Yet he has not. I don't understand him.'

Amra dared not say a word. She knew that if she criticised a member of the King's family, especially after she had accused him of trying to violate her, the King would be forced to defend him. Instead she listened attentively.

'I've sent him off as ambassador to tribute monarchs and he has caused me much trouble in their courts by forcing his attentions on their women; I have forced him to the furthest borders of our lands where there are only savage tribesmen and women who perform abominations, but when he returns his wildness still causes a scandal. May the gods protect Troy when I am sent to join them, for his reign will not be good for the wives of those who serve him.'

Suddenly the subdued atmosphere of the throne room was broken by a commotion in the corridor leading to the royal apartments. Cormis stormed in, sword drawn, his face black with fury like a storm about to break. The moment he saw Amra sitting next to his father, the pent-up anger he'd felt since she'd left him emasculated in his room erupted out of his body.

'There!' he screamed, pointing to her, holding his sword high in the air. 'There! That child there. Sitting next to my father like some royal princess!' He spat out the words, as though they tasted foul in his mouth. 'She will die. At my hands. Guards!' he shouted to the Nubians stationed around the room. 'Take her. Now!'

The guards braced their spears and started to move forward.

'Stop!' shouted King Praxis. The guards halted and stared between the King and his son.

The King rose from his chair. 'Nobody will touch this priestess of Mithras.'

Cormis looked at his father in disbelief. 'Majesty, she's not a priestess. She's . . .'

'Silence! She will not be harmed by you. Return to your quarters.'

'But father, she's using tricks and guile to fool you. To fool us all. She's never spoken to Mithras. She got drunk on wine and babbled like an infant. That's all.'

Praxis looked at his son with contempt. 'Did you try to violate this priestess? Did you dare to touch one of the vessels of Mithras? Against the most sacred of our laws?'

Cormis remained silent, looking from his father to Amra. He glanced over towards the other priestesses who were sitting at the further banqueting table.

'Did you?' shouted the King.

'Yes. But she's not a priestess. She's a crude country girl. Look at her painted blue skin. She looks like a slave. Could Mithras have chosen that to be his voice on earth? Ask yourself.'

The courtiers murmured their agreement. Amra turned her attention to the crowd. People were nodding. She was worried.

'This woman is not a child,' said the King. 'She is a priestess of Mithras. She faced the bull and took the golden arrow, something which no-one else has achieved. She heard the voice of the God while she was with the bull in the enclosure. He spoke to her. While she was sleeping the God appeared to her again and warned us that our enemies will come across the sea and enter our city inside giant horses. Is this something which you dare question?'

'Yes,' said Cormis, whose courage had returned. He knew that many people in the room agreed with him. 'Yes, father, I do question it. What proof do we have? Only the stories she tells. And the way in which she calmed the bull. Maybe she used trickery.'

Praxis looked at his son and was overwhelmed by sadness. He had been born with so many hopes, so many opportunities. Yet he spent his life offending the husbands and fathers of Troy and other cities with his constant need for women. But how could Praxis possibly favour a savage girl over his own son, the man who would one day rule in his place? How could he diminish his son further in front of the entire court, all of whom would revel in his disgrace? Praxis stood, silently, thinking what to do next as the court waited in anticipation.

Amra looked at Mithrassa-Urbek; his eyes were wide with horror at what was happening between the two men. She knew things would go badly for her if the King took Cormis's side. She had only one course of action. She turned to the King.

'Majesty, your son wants to possess my body. Yet my body belongs to the Goddess of the Moon: I am her virgin and her voice on earth. Since I have been here your God Mithras has spoken through me. But Cormis believes I am using tricks. Let me prove myself.'

The distracted King turned his attention to her, frowning.

Amra continued. 'I am told by my totem, the bee, who was sent by the Goddess of the Moon, that any man who knows my body will die. The moment he enters me the cold Goddess of the Moon will breathe upon him and freeze his body. And then, when he cannot withdraw himself from my body, she will plunge an arrow into his heart so that when he thaws in the light of the sun he will still be dead. This is how my Goddess will deal with any man who takes me. This is how she will deal with Cormis.

'But Cormis believes that I use tricks. He does not believe I am a priestess. Good. Let him prove it. Let him take my body right here. Then everyone in this room will see whether he is right or whether I am right.'

Amra walked over to Cormis, smiled tauntingly at him and lay down on the floor at his feet. She opened her legs and moved her white robe aside to expose her most private parts. The court exploded in shocked outrage. Even the Nubian guards, impassive at all times, turned their heads to see what was happening.

Cormis stared down at the woman at his feet. She lay there taunting him, offending him, embarrassing him. Her eyes were those of a harlot, a prostitute, knowing she had control and mastery over him. Laughing at him, deriding him, mocking him. He looked away from her to the people sitting and standing at the tables. Then he looked at his father. His stern father. Praxis looked back at him, great sadness in his eyes, knowing that his son was being humiliated, knowing that from this moment onwards nobody would fear Cormis, son of the great King. His son was lost by his own actions and there was nothing the King could do to save him.

'Come on, great Prince Cormis,' said Amra. 'Surely you do not fear a – what was it you called me? A crude savage. Well, prove before your King that I am not a priestess. Kneel down and put yourself into my body. Then we will see.'

Cormis breathed deeply, trying to control the emotions raging in his body. He had no desire for this woman, but he feared her. She was unlike any woman he had ever met. Savages were either wild and vicious or fearful and timorous. But Amra – she was afraid of nothing. She had tamed the bull. And now she was ridiculing him in front of his family, his friends, and those in the court who feared him. He fell to his knees, and moved aside the skirt of his uniform, exposing his flaccid penis. Usually he quickly became erect when he saw a woman's private parts, but now his penis refused to rise. As Amra lay smiling at his drooping manhood, his anger and hatred grew and he knew that he wouldn't be able to perform.

'Come, Cormis. Make your thing rise up and spike me. Shaft me with your penis. Then die at the hands of my Goddess.' Amra's laughter resonated around the silent room.

Cormis stood and turned to the King. 'Father! Help me.'

A look of disgust swept the King's face. 'Help you? Help you bring ruin to Troy? Leave my throne room. Leave this palace. Return when you have learnt some understanding of our gods and of the power of Mithras.'

'But . . .' Cormis looked down at Amra. His anger erupted and he raised his sword above his head, pointing it at her heart. He screamed a bloodcurdling war-cry and prepared to plunge his sword into the object of his hatred. 'Kill her, and you die!' The words stilled Cormis's arm and his sword hung in the air. Cormis looked up. He saw the looks of horror on the faces of his sisters, the priestesses, the queens, the courtiers, his family and friends. But more terrifying, he saw the faces of his many enemies, the husbands of those women he had taken by royal privilege. And he knew at that moment that he was lost.

'Harlot! Whore!' he screamed at Amra. 'You will suffer for what you have done to a prince of the court of Troy. Believe me, I will have my revenge.' Turning on his heels, he ran down the corridor back to his quarters. Although the throne room was utterly silent Cormis could hear voices pursuing him, mocking him, laughing at him, jeering.

Amra lay still, watching his retreating form. Then she stood slowly, knowing that all eyes would be on her. She walked over to the King and kneeled before him, abasing herself to his greater power. Instinct told her to do it. Instinct and an understanding of how any father would be feeling at such a moment. The King had chosen her over his own son. It was only right that now, in her moment of triumph, she should kneel before his greater power.

Besides, she thought, she still had to convince him to give her the secret of making iron and allow her to leave the city before Cormis made good his threat and killed her.

CHAPTER 24

It was late in the evening. The sounds of people laughing as they walked up the hill from the fish restaurant area of Kumkapi back to their hotels in Sultanahmet disturbed the peace of the night. The mosque was dark now, all but one or two lights extinguished. The Imam, high in his office above the school where children learnt the glories of Islam, stared down at the courtyard.

During the day thousands of worshippers had come to kneel on the finely woven carpets, to bow their heads in submission to the one true God. *God is great and Mohammed is His Prophet.* There had been demonstrations throughout the city all day against the woman who had attempted to steal the fragment of stone from the Kaaba. The demonstrations had spread from Ankara, Antalya, Izmir, all over. It was like a forest fire. The dry tinder of Islamic militancy was being set ablaze.

The Imam could see it all quite clearly. It was all over the newspapers. The Minister for Antiquities, a secularist, a woman with no belief in God or understanding of Islam, was being skewered on the deadly lances of the Islamic media.

'It was you who employed this woman.'

'Why are no Islamic experts acceptable to you?'

'Did you know she was a thief?'

'Why did you employ an enemy of Islam?'

It was all that he and his brother clerics had ever wanted during these years of anti-Islamic torment in Turkey. When this secular government had closed down eighty Islamic schools on the flimsy pretext that they were unregistered, it had effectively declared war upon Islam and its mullahs. Now, because of the actions of this

Minister and her American employee, the government was teetering on the brink of collapse. The Iman should be sitting back in his chair and smiling with satisfaction. But doubts were creeping into his mind, sullying the joy in which Islam had been revelling for the past few days.

Why had one of his less worthy junior servants, a man whose morality and faith he had questioned from the moment of his arrival at the mosque, why had he been talking so animatedly with Yussef Barrak? Why had he insisted that the Imam return to his office, telling him that he would attend to everything? The elderly Imam had questioned the young cleric at great length and very angrily after the police left. His answers had all been plausible, the explanations had fitted the facts. The proof was incontrovertible. Yet . . .

In his heart the Imam knew with a burning clarity that all was not right. This was a deception, a lie. The woman had not committed blasphemy. She had been falsely accused, and this contravened the laws of Mohammed, of Moses, of the Ten Commandments. *Thou shalt not bear false witness against thy neighbour.* He could remain quiet. He could watch the government tumble and an Islamic republic take over the reins of power. The future was clear: a nation of God, a true theocracy. Not one like the ungodly Royal Family, the parasites of the nation of Saudi Arabia, nor like that run by the secularists in Syria or Iraq. No! His Turkish Islamic Republic would be built along the model of a theocracy like Iran where Islam was militant, proud and strong. Islam for the people of the people. The pornography merchants, the drug dealers, the mixing of men and women in public places, the bathing beaches of the Turquoise coast and the Aegean, the restaurants where men and women dined together, women openly smoking and flaunting their obscene sexuality – it would all end under an Islamic republic. Decency would return. Women would be dressed in the *chadour*, their faces would be veiled so that men wouldn't be distracted from their prayers, so that the promiscuous acts of temptation which led to adultery would come to an end. Women would remain at home so that family life could return and be strengthened. Every child would grow up to practise modesty and hold it at the epicentre of their lives.

The Iman nodded his head and smiled. A paradise on earth. Turkey would be the shining example to the world of Islamic responsibility, adherence to the Prophet and to the word of God. He took a sip of apple tea, cold since he had been immersed for so long in his reflections.

So much could be gained by him closing his eyes and turning south towards Mecca. So much! And yet . . .

How could a golden mosque rising into the sky be secure if its very foundations were built on the quicksand of lies and deceit? Did the end justify the means? The words of the Old Testament prophets were a searing indictment: *An eye for an eye; a tooth for a tooth.* But what if no eye had been blinded, if no tooth had been broken? What if this woman, this Jewish American secularist, what if she had not stolen the holy relic? What if she had been falsely accused?

He shook his old head slowly and repeated the damning injunction spoken by God to Moses on Mount Sinai: *Thou shalt not bear false witness against thy neighbour.* The words of the Old Testament; it was her Book as well. Was it not Mohammed himself who had demanded that Islam should respect the people of the Book? He closed his eyes and saw the words emblazoned in fire in his darkness: *Thou shalt not bear false witness.*

David Rose woke from a jarring nightmare. He had been deeply asleep and it took several rings of the telephone before he was able to remember where he was and what he was doing. He dragged the receiver off its cradle and mumbled something which sounded vaguely like 'hello'.

'David, sorry to disturb you so early. It's Mustafa Bengazi. Were you asleep?'

In the distance David heard a word which sounded something like 'Yes'.

'So was I until half an hour ago. God, I was tired this morning after working so late with you last night. Anyway, I just got a call from my friend in Ankara. He's managed to trace the whereabouts and description of this chap from Yussef Barrak's diary.'

David mumbled an unintelligible response.

'Wake up, David. It's important. Remember the appointment Barrak had a few days before Sarah was arrested?' Still silence. In irritation, he said, 'The person whose identity we didn't know.'

'Yes,' mumbled David. 'Of course. Who is he?'

'Try to wake up while I remind you. Remember we said that Barrak was too cautious to put incriminating things in his diary and we'd have to be very lucky to find anything? Well, I think we are very lucky with this one. This Ozman Urzak. Remember? We thought he might be a Moslem cleric or a fundamentalist or something, someone linked to the mosque.'

'Uh huh,' said David, sitting up and clearing his throat.

'Well, contrary to what we both thought, he's very much on the other side of the coin.'

'What do you mean?'

'He's about as far from religion as it's possible to get. In the registry of businesses he's listed as an import and export executive. According to the description he deals in spices, farm machinery and agricultural products.'

'Okay,' said David cautiously.

'Now what would somebody like that be wanting with the Head of the Ministry of Antiquities?'

'I don't know,' said David. 'Tell me.'

He could almost see Bengazi smiling at the other end of the line. 'My friend in Ankara checked him out with the police and then, on their advice, went further and checked this gentleman out with the drug squad. They knew him instantly and warned my friend off. He's a Mr Big of drugs. He buys from farmers in the mountains in the east and sells over the Bulgarian border. Instead of being paid in cash, he's paid in arms, which the police are fairly certain he sells on to the Kurds. He makes a fortune on both transactions. He lives in Edirne in the north.'

'Why hasn't he been arrested?'

Bengazi laughed. 'First he has to be caught. And for that you need honest police as well as honest border guards. Let's just say that there are many reasons why the police and customs officials in the area do nothing about him, despite the insistence of the drug squad. I don't know much more, other than that he's got a well-organised network and is suspected to have Mafia connections. Sure, people get arrested now and again, but always at the lowest level.'

'But what's a man like this doing meeting with Yussef Barrak? I don't see Barrak as an arch criminal or drug dealer, regardless of any other complaints I have against him. And what's it all got to do with Sarah?'

'There are possibilities going through my mind, David, but none are enough to begin making accusations. We need to meet to discuss where we go from here.'

'Sure. Coffee in an hour?'

'My office,' said Bengazi.

David replaced the receiver and sat up in bed, hugging his knees. It was more than strange, it was ludicrous. Drugs? Arms-running? The Mafia? What the hell had this got to do with Sarah being falsely accused of stealing a holy relic?

An hour later, David, Bengazi and Satap had mapped out a series of contingencies on a piece of paper. They studied it carefully. They had drawn some very long bows. Sarah was accused of theft and blasphemy. It was certain that Yussef Barrak was behind it in an attempt to discredit her, and most probably his Minister as well. He was trying to bring down an already shaky government. All that was agreed. Then things began to go astray. They had to assume that Barrak had help, probably from the priest in the mosque. Fine so far, but where did a drug-dealing, arms-running criminal called Ozman Urzak fit in? But it was the only lead they had. They needed to find out more before going down the far more dangerous road of bribing Barrak's employees or friends. They worked out three options.

'Okay,' said Bengazi. 'Let's talk about option one. We go to the Minister and inform her of everything, about the meeting between Urzak and the Director of her Ministry. She believes us. She investigates Barrak and has the police put pressure on this Urzak character so he confesses his relationship with Barrak. Sarah is released from prison. The government is saved and everybody congratulates us.'

David nodded. 'I think that's the safest option.'

'Hold on a minute,' said Bengazi. 'The others also have merit. Option two,' he said, reading from the piece of paper, 'sees us going to Barrak. We accuse him, show him the evidence of his meeting with an arch criminal, convince him we're the only ones who can save his backside and get him to confess. The Moslem cleric then is shown to all the world as a liar. Barrak does this because we agree not to publicly implicate him in order to ensure that Sarah is released. The problem with this one is that the government might still fall.'

Satap read out the third option. 'Number three,' he said, his voice higher-pitched than Bengazi's. 'We approach the cleric and tell him we know everything. We threaten him with police action and the hightest Islamic court unless he admits Barrak's complicity. We frighten him into admitting his guilt. He makes a confession and Barrak is arrested for perverting the course of justice. Sarah is freed and everybody is happy because the Minister can fire Barrak and tell the whole of the country it was him after all.'

David shook his head. 'That's the weakest of them all. This cleric has already lied through his teeth. He isn't going to be frightened by us.'

Bengazi interrupted. 'But it's also unlikely that Barrak will confess anything. And the chances of Urzak saying anything are very remote. That type thinks with a gun not a brain.'

David nodded.

'Agreed,' said Satap. 'What about option two?'

Again David shook his head. 'Barrak's gone down a carefully calculated path. The bastard knows exactly what he's doing and he's probably got contingency plans we haven't thought of. He will just say that he didn't know Urzak prior to the meeting, and that he as a loyal servant of the government has an open-door policy and tries to meet with everybody who wants to see him. As soon as he realised Urzak was a crook he kicked him out of his office.'

Again the other two men nodded. 'So, we all agree on option one?'

Bengazi took a deep breath. 'Have you ever been to Ankara, David?' he asked.

David smiled. 'I passed through there on the way to Cappadocia.'

'Well you are about to go again, my friend.'

The Ottoman Empire was still the governing force behind Turkey. Despite attempts by Kemel Atatürk to bring the arthritic and nepotistic administration into line with western standards, Turkey's bureaucratic mechanism still creaked along at a pace to suit its administrators. It was common practice for a western businessman to return to the antechambers of a government office for two or three days, awaiting recognition from somebody more senior than a low-grade assistant.

Being a part of the culture, Mustafa Bengazi knew the ropes. He was duly sycophantic to the administrative secretary at the parliamentary offices of the Minister for Antiquities, begging his pardon for daring to appear in his Ankara office without having written a formal letter or even made a telephone call. It was, said Bengazi, an unforgivable oversight which he promised would never happen again but while here, he continued, would it be possible to talk to an excellency in the more senior echelons of the administration of the Minister's bureaucracy for he had information to pass on which was of the greatest importance to the Minister? Could he perhaps speak with the Minister's personal private secretary, he wondered?

Parliament House was a modern airconditioned building with wings branching off from the central chamber of the deputies. The Minister of Antiquities was well-placed in the wing close to the parliamentary offices occupied by the Prime Minister, having a central role to play in Turkey's income generated through tourism. Apart from which, the Minister was the darling of the middle class which had put the government into power.

After another three hours of waiting in the Minister's antechamber and staring at its walls bedecked with the traditional photographs of the Prime Minister, the President of the Republic and the Minister of Antiquities greeting the famous and the not-so-famous, eventually a tall and striking woman burst into the room.

'You are Dr Bengazi?' she exclaimed. 'We haven't met, but I've heard much about your work.'

Bengazi stood. He was a head shorter than the woman. They shook hands. David noticed him wince at her grip.

'I am Minister Ekerat's personal assistant. How may I help you?'

'Madam,' Bengazi said. 'My business is with the Minister. It is a matter of the gravest importance which can only be told to her.'

The woman nodded. She heard this sort of plea a dozen times a week. The standard reply was called for. 'Regrettably the Minister has appointments throughout today and tomorrow and cannot be interrupted. At the end of the week she leaves for the east of the country for discussions and will be there for at least another week. She will not have an opportunity to see you. However, if you will tell me why you are here, I will make it my business to find the time to tell her between appointments and she will respond to you through me.'

Bengazi shook his head, having anticipated this response. 'Madam, I deeply regret the insult this will no doubt cause you, but the matter is of such sensitivity that it cannot be delivered into any vessel other than the Minister's ear. It concerns the Minister herself, the head of her Ministry, Dr Yussef Barrak, and the very future of her government.'

At the mention of Barrak's name the woman showed a moment of discomfort. Bengazi noticed and drove home his advantage. 'You do not know me personally, madam, but you know of me and my work at the Topkapi Museum. I'm a man in the highest ranks of archaeology in this country. My friend,' he said, pointing to David, 'is an internationally acclaimed cellist. Neither of us is hysterical or given to exaggeration. I would not have said these things had I not been desperately concerned for the plight of this government.'

She looked from Bengazi to David and back again then nodded curtly. 'Follow me,' she said.

The two men followed the Minister's assistant along a procession of carpeted corridors into the private inner sanctum inhabited by the conservatively dressed men and women on whose shoulders weighed the entire edifice of the modern Republic of Turkey. She motioned them to take a seat in her office.

'Before you begin,' she said, 'I fully appreciate who you are, Professor Bengazi. I am a great admirer of your work at the Topkapi. But this gentleman?'

'This is Mr David Rose. He is a musician from America.'

'And how is Mr Rose involved with you?'

'Mr Rose's fiancée has been arrested on a spurious charge of blasphemy and theft.'

The atmosphere in the room suddenly grew colder. The woman's face set as rigidly as one of the Roman statues in the Topkapi. 'You are Sarah Kaplan's fiancé?'

David nodded.

'Then, gentlemen, I am afraid I can be of no assistance to you. The matter is *sub judice*. The Minister cannot intervene nor take any active part in the proceedings.' She pressed a button on the underside of her desk. 'My assistant will see you out.'

'Just a minute,' said David. 'You're wiping your hands of Sarah and that's simply not fair. We have evidence which proves she was framed.'

'Then that evidence must go before the court, Mr Rose.'

'But it should never come to court!' David said angrily. 'The man that should be arrested is Yussef Barrak. He is behind all of this. He is the mastermind. It was he who conspired –'

The woman held up her hand. 'Mr Rose, this is a police matter and must remain so. The Minister cannot and will not get involved in matters such as this.'

'Why not?' David asked calmly, realising it was crucial for him to keep his temper in check. Getting kicked out of the Minister's offices wasn't the way to help Sarah. 'Why is the Minister wiping her hands of Sarah? She hasn't even taken any of my calls.'

For a moment a look of understanding passed between the Minister's assistant and David. Then the hard-edged minder took over again. 'I'm afraid you must leave my office.'

David felt impotent. 'All we want to do is spend ten minutes with the Minister tell her about Barrak and about the association he has with a high-level criminal. It demands investigation –'

Again the woman held up her hand. 'You must leave my office immediately. These are matters that cannot be discussed in Parliament House. Just as matters must follow an official path in your country so it is here, Mr Rose. Any allegations you may have against the Director of the Minister's Department should be made to the police. The Minister cannot and will not intervene. That is absolutely my last word.'

David stood, holding back his instinctive anger. 'Why are you making these decisions about Sarah's future? Sarah was appointed directly by the Minister. Surely she –'

The door burst open and two security men hurried in. They grabbed David's arms and began to pull him towards the door.

'There's no need for that,' said the Minister's assistant. 'But these two gentlemen will be leaving immediately.' She let them leave without a farewell.

Their mood was low when they left the Minister's office, but something occurred to David as they were flying back to Istanbul. It had begun as a niggling thought when Bengazi was describing Urzak and his dealings. David could understand Barrak hatching a plot to overthrow the government, but Mafia connections? It didn't seem to fit with the Barrak they had uncovered in their investigations. Suddenly David realised that there could be a fourth option. He discussed the idea with Bengazi who was horrified. But in the end, he agreed that it was a good option even though it involved terrifying risks. They decided to put it into effect the following morning.

CHAPTER 25

Mithrassa-Urbek was beside himself with joy. He had not felt such elation since his earliest days in the court when, as a young man, he had conspired to win preferment from King Praxis's father. He looked up at the painted ceiling and watched the familiar ochre faces and accusing yellow eyes of the Gods as they acted out the age-old drama which had been captured for eternity by an artist who had died many years previously. The Gods were frozen into immobility, depictions of a moment in time. Their actions were the very antithesis of those of the remarkable child, Amra. He was so incredibly proud of his association with her. It was he who had spotted Amra in the marketplace; it was he who had agreed to allow her to challenge the great bull God, Mithras. He could have laughed in her face and sent her back to her village when she made her ridiculous demands but, for some reason which still mystified him, Mithrassa-Urbek had gone against a lifetime of courtly behaviour and admitted a savage into the presence of the court. And now he, Mithrassa-Urbek, was earning the gratitude of the King.

Amra had managed to do things within the court which nobody else had ever dared. Perhaps because she was a savage, from outside the civilised lands, she recognised no bounds. Those who were born into a system of behaviour and rules, these people were incapable of breaking the barriers around them. Mithrassa-Urbek knew that he could never have done it. It was laughable to think that he could have looked directly at the face of the King, could have fought and defeated Prince Cormis, could have sat beside Praxis on equal terms and made demands on him. The last time someone had shouted at the King he had walked down the length of the table, drawn his sword and cleaved the man's head from his shoulders. The offender's head was carried to the border of his country and stuck on a spike facing the city far into the distance. The war that ensued had dramatically increased Hittite lands and the foolish man's king was now a vassal paying tribute. Yet, this savage girl, Amra, had screamed at him in front of the whole of the court and he had merely sat there, nodding.

But the unsurpassed wonder was the way Cormis had been destroyed in the eyes of everyone who hated him. On the subject of his son King Praxis was all too often deaf. But now, through his terrible disrespect for Mithras, Praxis had finally been forced to confront the truth. Cormis was now licking his wounds in the confines of his room, surrounded by a dozen or so of his sycophants, silly youths who believed their lord and protector prince still had power.

Mithrassa-Urbek's role now was to convince the King to settle the succession on his younger son, a far worthier man. He wasn't like a rampant stag who viewed every woman in the court, including Mithrassa-Urbek's three daughters, as his personal property. The future would be difficult for the young prince if he did succeed his father. In order to secure his reign he would have to banish his older brother Cormis into the far reaches of the Empire or, worse, ensure that he didn't survive for more than a day after the death of King Praxis. But that was something Mithrassa-Urbek would advise the future young monarch about if things went his way.

He looked down from the ceiling and settled his gaze upon Amra. Such a strange girl with her pure white robes and her blue painted skin. She was sitting there, staring at a wine goblet, turning it around in her hands. No thought of drinking what was inside. Just gently turning it over in her hands, admiring its patterns. But was that truly what she was doing? Her thoughts were so deep, so difficult to predict. Before he could ask her, a herald trumpeted the arrival of the King. Mithrassa-Urbek threw himself to the ground; Amra did the same. They heard the King walk towards the throne and the rustle of his gowns as he sat.

'Amra,' the King said, 'stand and walk forward. You as well, Mithrassa-Urbek, friend and counsellor.'

The King snapped his fingers and two seats were brought for them to sit upon. Mithrassa-Urbek gazed at the King's feet. He turned his head fractionally and saw with immense relief that Amra was doing the same. She had come so far in her quest that the last thing she needed to do now was to irritate the majesty of the King.

'So,' the King said, 'let us begin. You are the prophetic voice of Mithras. You have been abused by my son, for which you will intercede on our behalf with Mithras and beg our apologies. In order for Mithras to smile upon this kingdom I am going to admit you into the company of the small body of men who have the secret of the making of iron. I understand your desire to learn this secret. We too know much about these men of iron of whom you have been speaking since your arrival within the walls of mighty Troy. These men come from the north east, beyond the shores of the Eternal Sea. They turn the red rocks which are plentiful in their area into iron, and from this iron, both by the use of moulds and by the force of hammer tools, they make plentiful numbers of strong swords, shields, axes and daggers.

'Many years ago, Amra, in the time of my father's father, iron was found only in very small amounts. It was often said that iron fell from the sky. Sometimes we see the Gods flinging stones to the earth and it is recorded that many generations ago the Gods threw a stone at one of our cities. It flew with a mighty wind and caused fire in the trees and the grasses when it landed. It was made of pure iron. It was black and heavy and glistening, and it could only be cut or marked with great difficulty. Our people kept the iron and revered it. Some said it was the semen of Gods. Others said it was a warning of future disasters. Indeed, a year or so after the iron was thrown from the sky, there was an earthquake which devastated the villages nearby. Many people were killed, but the town which received the stones from the sky was miraculously saved. Look upwards, child, at my finger.'

Amra elevated her gaze from the King's feet to his hands. Praxis held out his ring finger. On it glistened a round black object.

'This is the semen of the Gods, Amra. Maybe even the seed of great Mithras himself. Or the seed of one of his twelve disciples who ate supper with him before he was killed and rose up into the sky. It came from the sky and is more valuable than gold. That is why only I and the priestesses of Mithras are permitted to wear iron, on pain of death.'

He withdrew his hand and Amra lowered her gaze to his feet again.

'Yet these men from the north east, these savage warring tribes of our most distant borders, they take iron from the rocks. We know this because our traders have brought us daggers they have made from it. One day, Amra, I sent a raiding party into their territory. I captured one of their metalworkers and brought him back to the city. I tortured him until he told me the secret and I passed this secret on to my most trusted armourers and metalworkers. My men are now busy searching my lands for similar rocks, but even so, I do not believe that this will be where the course of warfare lies. Still, it is the secret for which you have travelled so far and for which you have endured such torments.'

Amra was breathless with anticipation. She understood enough of what the King was saying to know that the secret was almost within reach. She could feel it. If she learnt the secret today she would still have time to return to tell her people, provided she left the city within the next seven days and nothing impeded her journey home.

'Amra, you have told me why you want this secret for your people. You believe that the iron men are coming from the north to invade your village. Perhaps they are. But this secret could make the difference between a master and a slave. With this secret your people will be able to make weapons of iron. They will be able to build a vast army. Even though I am lord of the world, and my chariots are so numerous that their noise is heard in the homes of the gods themselves, still, I do not wish to see a new and dangerous army on our distant border. Yet I must honour my undertaking to Mithras, despite this danger.'

'But you promised,' cried Amra, all her hopes suddenly dashing to the floor.

'Silence,' said the King, banging his rod of office on the floor. 'No-one may interrupt me. Stupid girl, I would not transgress the demands of Mithras. Of course you will benefit from the secret of making iron, but the secret will not be given to you or your people. It will be taken to your village by three armourers and three metalworkers who will accompany you on your journey home. They will work with the men of your village to make weapons of iron. When the weapons are made these men will return to Troy, their secret intact. Your people will still have their weapons, but the threat to me will be less. Yes, Amra. You will have your weapons but the secret of making iron stays with Troy.'

Amra was silent. Mithrassa-Urbek held his breath, praying that she would accept this sensible compromise which he and the King had determined earlier in the day. A compromise for which Mithrassa-Urbek had been rewarded a purse of gold.

'I am fulfilling my obligations to Mithras,' the King said, a note of exasperation finding its way into his voice. 'I am giving you everything that you requested when you became the voice of Mithras in Troy. More than this I will not do. Now go!'

The King stood, turned and walked back into his royal chambers. Amra continued to stare at the pedestal on which the King's feet had rested. Then she turned slowly to Mithrassa-Urbek. She reached out and took his hand, as she used to hold her father's hand. 'Is this enough?' she asked. 'Is this what I need to save my people? I don't know. Will you help me? You're my friend.'

Slowly Mithrassa-Urbek nodded. 'It is enough. Even if you risk the danger and persist in your demands, you will receive no more. You have already achieved more than anybody could possibly have imagined. Be content, Amra. You now have the ability to beat your enemies and, better, you have made an ally of the greatest king in the world. If ever you are attacked or under threat, you may return to Troy and Praxis will smile favourably upon assisting you. Not even the great kings of the powerful cities on our borders enjoy such a privilege.'

Amra nodded. 'But why won't he just tell me how to do it? How to make iron?'

'For all the reasons he said, Amra. Because knowledge is power, and giving you that knowledge could make you as powerful as him.'

'But these other people, those who want to destroy us, have this knowledge. Therefore they already have power.'

'Their power is halved now, Amra, because Troy knows how to make iron. And it is halved yet again because they have no chariots. They cannot fight the kind of warfare which has made us into the most powerful empire the world has ever known.'

'And do you make iron weapons?'

'A few. We can't see the purpose of making large numbers of weapons. Our power, Amra, comes through our chariots. We have more horses and more chariots than any other kingdom on earth, except for the Egyptians and they are our allies. No army can stand against our chariots, not even an army of ten thousand men armed with all the iron swords in the world.' Amra looked disbelieving. 'These armies, if they ever do march against us, will not come anywhere near our troops. Our archers on the back of the chariots will sting them like bees and they will fall like the pollen in summer.'

Amra nodded and allowed Mithrassa-Urbek to lead her, as a father might lead his daughter, out of the throne room.

Sitting cross-legged in a corridor which led to the throne room, unseen by anybody, was Cormis. He had heard every word of the audience, and now he knew with certainty that his father was mad. He was giving away the greatest secret of Troy. Iron was the most precious of metals, more precious than gold. It was the secret of the Gods. For this blasphemy, Cormis thought, his father must die, for he was leaving Troy unprotected. But first there was somebody else who must suffer Cormis's rage. A girl with blue-painted skin.

The temple of Cybele stood side by side with the temple of Mithras in the centre of the city, one a huge edifice to the God of Gods, the other smaller, dedicated to the Mother of all Goddesses. Sacrifices made to the Goddess Cybele were performed on the roof where the altar was stained with the blood of calves, lambs and pigs. The sacrificial urn beside the altar, into which the blood of the dead animals drained before their flesh was placed on the fires, contained the remnants of a recent ceremony. Flies buzzed drunkenly into and out of the urn, feeding on the rotting blood and entrails.

There was no shade on the temple roof to protect Cormis and his four companions from the blinding sun. Unlike sacrifices to the God Mithras which were conducted during the day under the gaze of the God of the Sun, Cybele's priestesses made sacrifices to the earth mother at the night when the white moon reigned in the skies. This meant that the roof of Cybele's temple was one of the few places in the whole of Troy where Cormis knew he could speak to his friends during the day without the possibility of being overheard. Even his own apartments in the royal palace were insecure. Although he had handpicked his servants carefully, both the King, and certainly Cormis's younger brother were capable of buying a minion's loyalty so that he would report to them everything Cormis did. That was the way of the court. Cormis himself knew everything about the actions of his younger brother and his two sisters through the opportunism of their servants. Even his father's chief bodyguard had been in Cormis's pay since the day he had been appointed.

The five men had been talking for so long now that sweat was dripping from their brows. They had hitched their tunics over their heads to deflect the rays of the sun but soon they would have to remove themselves to the shade or they would faint from its power. They could have left some time ago had it not been for Alses. He was proving difficult. Alses was Cormis's boyhood friend, one of his most trusted companions. They hunted together. They had swum the Channel of the Dardans together.

They had whored together. They had even shared one of the sacred prostitutes on the same night. If Alses believed his plan to be acceptable then Cormis knew with certainty that it would go ahead. The others had agreed readily to his idea but Alses had been more cautious. And still he persisted with his warnings.

'This will turn the Gods against us.'

'Nonsense,' shouted Cormis for the fifth time. 'She is not the voice of Mithras!'

'Your father believes that she is.'

'My father is a fool. He has been deluded by this spawn of the evil gods. And he is a traitor to the city – I told you what he's going to do. How could he contemplate giving our most precious secret to this . . . this *thing*. Surely even you, Alses, can see the dangers.' Alses nodded.

'Then why,' insisted Cormis, 'won't you agree? If the five of us take action there's no chance it can go wrong.'

'There's every chance, Cormis. Your father may find out.'

'Only if one of us tells him. We'll all sign a blood oath to keep this secret to our graves.'

'But even if he doesn't find out, to attack the sanctuary of the priestesses – it is unheard of.'

'Are you worried about killing the Nubian slaves?'

'Of course not,' said Alses. 'I'm worried about . . .'

'I know, I know. You've told me often enough. Nobody else here is worried,' Cormis persisted. 'I, too, hold sacred the priestesses' sanctuary but it has been infested by a plague in the form of this savage. It has lost its purity. It is our job to give it back to Mithras and to cleanse it of this contaminating spirit. Don't you understand that?'

Alses looked at his oldest friend. 'How much of this is driven by what Amra did to you at the feast last night?'

Cormis's face flared with rage. Had anybody else asked such a question he would have reached for his knife and skewered the man through the heart. But Alses was his oldest and closest friend, his brother in all but blood. Cormis knew he would say nothing unless it was for his good. He put his arm around his neck and kissed him on the cheek. 'Alses, for the sake of the Gods, be with us.'

Alses looked carefully at his old friend, his ruler, his master. Despite his severe misgivings, he nodded.

'Thank the Gods,' said Cormis. 'Now we can get away from the anger of the sun.'

They descended into the inner sanctum of the priestesses of the Goddess Cybele and walked surreptitiously along the corridors to emerge into a laneway next to the temple. The guard on the door nodded and Cormis put another coin into his outstretched hands.

Troy was asleep. The God of the Sun had grown old and weary and had fallen into the endless sea. It would be many hours before he was reborn on the other side of the world. The moon, Cybele's vessel and her nightly form, was hidden behind a veil of clouds. It was a dark night. Five men wearing black robes crept along the passageway which led to the sanctum of the priestesses of the God Mithras. Two Nubian guards, tall and impassive, stood before the double door beyond which no man, except for the eunuchs, was allowed to tread. Cormis removed the hood from his cloak to reveal himself in the torchlight of the corridor. The Nubian guards stared at him and his four companions.

Cormis turned and said in a half whisper, 'Brothers, remove your hoods. We are frightening these guards.'

They did as they were told. The Nubians were unsure of what to do. If a man was so reckless, so stupid as to approach the doorway to the priestesses' sanctum they were ordered to kill him before he came within arm's reach of the door. But this was the King's son, Prince Cormis, and he was approaching them slowly and without a weapon, not threatening them in any way. They didn't know what to do. They stood to attention realising that they would have to bar him entry if he asked. A greater power, that of the King, would punish them mercilessly if they let Cormis get beyond them and into the priestesses' sanctum.

Cormis knew what was going through their minds, and his plan had taken their insecurity into account. He stopped and leaned against the wall, a spear's length from the guards. 'This is where the priestesses live,' he said to his friends, as though he were conducting them on a tour of the palace. 'These brave fellows are the guards who stop any man from entering.'

Cormis noticed that both of the huge men relaxed once they perceived that any threat was past. They understood what was going on now. 'Only a fool would try to get beyond these men,' Cormis said, a laugh in his voice. 'Have you seen the size of their arms?' Both men were a head taller than Cormis, even though he himself was tall. Their arms could break the neck of any man who attacked them.

'How strong *are* they?' asked Alses.

'Unbelievably strong,' said Cormis. Both the guards smiled. 'Look, I'll show you,' he said and walked towards one of them. As he did so, he reached behind him and with a swift movement pulled a dagger from his belt. He plunged it through the the first guard's stomach and up into his chest. The second guard, lulled into a false sense of security, looked on in surprise at what was happening, not realising until it was too late that his companion was dead. Before he could react he too was lying slumped on the floor.

Cormis turned his companions. 'Their guard was dropped,' he whispered and laughed. He wiped his blood-stained hands on one of the guard's cloaks and nodded. 'Now,' he said.

They stepped over the bodies of the guards and quietly opened the most private door in the whole of the palace, more private even than the King's. They pulled their hoods low over their heads so their faces were obscured. In the half-light of the room they could see the pool in which the priestesses bathed. The columns and pillars of the room and an altar with the image of the God Mithras behind it were reflected in the water. All around the room were cots draped with sleeping forms. There were no guards in the priestesses' sanctum. Instead eunuchs and maids slept on straw mats at the foot of their priestesses' beds.

Alses whispered into the prince's ear: 'How are we to tell which one is Amra in this light?'

'By her skin,' Cormis reminded him. 'Look for an arm or a face with blue markings on it.'

They crept around the room as quietly as they were able. A woman in the far corner was snoring while others were breathing heavily. One of the eunuchs made a high-pitched whistle as he breathed out. Cormis pointed to a figure sleeping in a far recess. One arm was dangling from the cot; it was covered with blue spirals and lines. They had found Amra!

Cormis and Alses moved over to stand at her head. Two other men stood by her feet and the fifth kept watch, his knife drawn kill any of the eunuchs or maids if necessary. In a swift move – they had been practising all afternoon in Cormis's apartment – the four men covered Amra's face and nose, then lifted her off the bed as though she were a feather. They ran with her across the room, up the steps, through the door, over the bodies of the Nubian guards and out into the corridor. Amra began to struggle the moment she was lifted off her bed, but the men clamped their arms around her so tightly that all she could do was gasp for breath rather than free herself. Three of the maids awoke at the sound of running footsteps and quickly raised the priestesses from their deep slumbers, but it was too late. The raiders had already left. When the priestesses saw the dead Nubian guards, their screams rent the quiet palace.

By the time the screams registered on the sleeping courtiers and the royal family, Cormis and his companions were already back safely in his room, pushing Amra's struggling body down on Cormis's bed and securing her with vicious knots. They forced her mouth open and administered a bitter oily liquid Cormis had got from an old woman who knew the secret ways. Within moments Amra had relaxed into unconsciousness. The five men carried her inert form along the back passages to the servants' entrance of Cormis's apartments; there they placed her on the back of a horse and three of them escorted her to a secret hiding place. Cormis and Alses returned to the royal chambers, took off their cloaks and lay on their beds feigning sleep, waiting for the guards to burst in and for the King to demand their presence.

The following day the entire court of King Praxis was in uproar. It was as though an invading army was camped outside the city walls, waiting to attack. Servants, functionaries, guards and secretaries ran around the palace in confusion. Members of the royal family, as well as their servants, maids, eunuchs, guards and personal priests and priestesses were summoned before the King and asked if they knew of Amra's whereabouts. Nobody had ever seen the King so furious. The captain of the Palace Guard had been executed immediately the breach of security had been discovered. His successor had been given a day in which to discover the whereabouts of the priestess Amra, or he would suffer the same fate.

The King was painfully aware of how devastating the abduction of the priestess could be. He had made an agreement with the God Mithras, and the abuse of the vessel of his voice on earth would surely see the city laid to waste. Had not Amra given warning about what would happen to the city if its people failed to heed the messages of the Gods?

The King gave instructions for guards to be stationed on the shore of the nearby sea. They were to kill any animal, large or small, which emerged. Other guards were dispatched to the distant northern sea at its junction with the land of the Dardans with similar instructions. But more imperative than any defence of the city was the need to find Amra and to make peace with the gods, especially Mithras. And to that end, the King had so far been spectacularly unsuccessful. The entire morning had already gone by and the guards were no nearer to finding Amra than they were when her abduction was first discovered. In desperation Praxis offered a purse of gold to the man who found the priestess.

The gold, however, was not the motivation of the man who sought a private audience with the brother of Prince Cormis. The younger prince, Mesha, was surprised at the secrecy of the request, but these were strange times and the man's urgency him made Mesha agree to admit him to his apartments.

When the room was cleared of servants, Alses removed his hooded cloak. 'My thanks, Prince,' he said, 'for agreeing to the secrecy.'

'But why?' asked Mesha. 'You have been here many times. This sudden need to conceal yourself from my servants —'

'It was very necessary, I assure you. You see, I know where the priestess Amra is being held captive.'

Prince Mesha was stunned.

'And I know who abducted her from the sanctuary. But if I tell you, and you reveal my identity, it will cost me my life. Do I have your word that my name will never be revealed?'

Mesha shook his head. 'No. I cannot give that assurance. If you have blasphemed against the God Mithras, then your actions could destroy the city. If I hide you from his wrath his anger will not abate.'

Alses nodded. 'But if I tell you where the priestess is, and you tell your father, you will be covered in glory. I was an unwilling accomplice and begged him not to do what he did. I was forced to go along with it; had I not agreed, he would have killed me. Once I make this known to Mithras and fast in penance I will be absolved and the city will not be destroyed.'

'Why are you telling this to me, Alses? You are my brother's closest friend. Why betray him now?'

'Because he is mad. Because he will bring destruction to the city. When your father dies and Cormis becomes King, no woman will be safe. The Gods abhor him and everything he does.'

'And are these your only reasons?'

'I also ask to be made the future King's secretary on Praxis's death. Mithrassa–Urbek is old and his decisions recently have failed to take account of the needs of the Trojans. He is too cautious. The new King will need a secretary who is young, with more dynamic ideas, one who understands the ways of the world as much as he understands the ways of the Gods.'

'But if my brother becomes King . . .?'

'Then I would leave Troy forever to journey to the furthest borders of our lands. Because within the year, Troy would be no more.'

Mesha walked closer to Alses and put his hand on the older man's shoulder. 'You shall be my secretary. You have the word of the next king. Now, tell me where the priestess Amra is being held captive.'

Naked, her flesh cut raw by the tight ropes binding her feet and her hands, her head throbbing from the potion she had been forced to drink, Amra lay on the filthy cot listening to the murmur of voices outside the dark room. Her head felt as though evil gods were living inside it, banging their hammers behind her eyes. She had been forced to void water into the mattress and now she was wet and the smell of her urine added to the smell of the fetid straw in the cot.

She could hear her guards cackling outside. The women had come in two or three times to check on her since the three men had dumped her in the room but they showed her no sympathy. Instead they taunted her with what would happen to her when Cormis came later in the day. They made sure that the restraints binding her legs and hands held tight, and sniffed with disgust the urine smell of her body and cot. The last time they came in to check on her, Amra had begged them for a cloth to wipe her face and a drink to slake her thirst. One of them had spat at her, while the other boasted that she had once been Cormis's lover, that she was a sacred prostitute in the Temple and Cormis had been her most ardent admirer. Then they left her alone with her fears.

Amra knew she would die soon. Cormis would storm into the room, threaten her, ridicule her, then kill her. Perhaps he would satisfy himself with her body first. She knew that he was no longer frightened of her. He no longer believed her to be the voice of the Goddess of the Moon and that he would freeze during intercourse with her. That was why he had invaded the priestesses' sanctum and abducted her. Not to pleasure himself but to kill her. Or maybe to kill her after he had pleasured himself. Either way, Amra had spent the last while saying prayers to her totem, the bee, to the Gods who looked after her village, even to Mithras. And when her obligations to the Gods were complete, Amra squeezed her eyes tightly shut to see in her mind the faces of her father and of Peta, so that when she went to join her mother their faces would always be before her. She felt no fear, just an overwhelming regret that her failure would mean death for Peta and the rest of the village.

She had been so close to victory. The King was about to send skilled metalworkers and armourers to make weapons to fight the men from the other side of the mountain. So close, and now it was all over. She lay there, too tired to cry. Her eyes hurt too much to make tears. She heard a voice moaning in the room and gradually realised it was her own.

The Palace Guard, led by its new captain, ran quickly down the main steps and into the large square which housed the weekly market. It was still early in the morning and people were walking to their places of business; shepherds drove their flocks of reluctant sheep and goats in front of them. Geese scampered out of the way, honking loudly as the large contingent of troops ran towards the south gate of the city, towards the megaron where the priests and priestesses held their convocations. Before the south gate, the captain of the Guard turned along the south wall and ran through the narrow alleyways deep into the area of the east wall. Small houses, occupied by impoverished merchants or harlots, were crammed into the quarter. Their inhabitants came out into the bright sunlight to see who was marching through their streets so early in the morning. The guards pushed them aside to get to the home and workplace of Leiei the harlot. A curtain was pulled across her door and the sign of the prostitute, an erect penis, was strung by cord on the left side of the lintel. The captain of the Guard withdrew his sword and struck down the curtain; his men entered the house two abreast. Leiei and her companion screamed as the men walked in.

Before Leiei could ask their purpose the captain struck her viciously across the face with the back of his hand, knocking the former priestess and sacred prostitute to the floor. Her companion and lover tried to run but one of the soldiers grabbed her by the hair and kneed her in the chest. With a grunt, she collapsed onto the floor, too winded to scream. The captain picked up a lamp to illuminate the stinking whorehouse and looked around. There was no sign of the priestess Amra.

He turned to his men. 'Search the place. Everywhere!'

It took them only a few moments to find a red curtain concealed behind a tall wooden cupboard in which Leiei's garish cloaks, dresses and jewellery were hung. The young captain pushed aside the wooden structure; it fell to the floor with a loud crash in a cloud of dust, right on top of the groaning form of Leiei's companion. Ignoring her plight, the captain drew aside the curtain and entered the pitch black room beyond it. The stench of urine, faeces and cheap perfume assailed his nostrils. In the dim light he saw that there were two cots in the room; one occupied by a naked huddled figure, her hands tied behind her back.

The captain strode over and lifted Amra gently from the bed. With a deft flick of his dagger he cut the ties at her hands and feet. She fell naked onto his chest, almost collapsing with relief at being rescued. The captain put his arm around her and turned sharply to his men, ordering them out of the room to prevent them seeing the priestess's nakedness. He continued to hold her, feeling her slight body shaking. She began to sob.

'I thought you were Cormis,' said Amra. 'The noise outside, the fighting . . . I thought Cormis had returned to kill me. I thought I was soon to die.'

'Priestess,' said the young captain, his arm firmly around her shoulders, 'we are your rescuers. The King commands that you return immediately to the palace.'

Amra nodded. 'I am filthy,' she said.

'You will bathe in the priestesses' pool before you appear before the King.'

He took off his own cloak and put it around her shoulders, tightly fixing the clasp and tying the leather cord at the bottom. 'Can you walk, priestess?'

'I don't think so,' Amra said. 'I can't feel my feet or my hands.'

'May I carry you?'

'Yes,' she said gratefully. 'Thank you.'

The strong young man lifted her frail body and carried her gently out of the fetid prison. One of his men held a dagger to the throat of Leiei, who knew not to speak or she would be killed. The captain pointed to Leiei's companion, still lying beneath the cupboard.

One of his guards shook his head. 'She is dead, sire.'

'Good,' said the captain. 'One less for the King to deal with. You,' he said to another guard, 'run back and inform his Majesty that the priestess Amra is safe. We will return immediately.'

Praxis, the king of Troy, sat on his throne before the assembled court. He nodded as Mithrassa-Urbek whispered into his ear. All the royal family were gathered there, as were all the rich and ruling members of Trojan society. The King had commanded their attendance for a special meeting of the city council to say prayers for the safe deliverance of the priestess Amra.

King Praxis stood. All those present immediately

averted their eyes down to the floor. The King crossed the royal bridge which separated his Majesty from the court. 'Cormis,' he said in a low voice. 'Our prayers have been answered. The priestess Amra has been found.' The young prince stood rigid. 'I am sure that you, Cormis, feel a profound sense of gratitude to the God Mithras for having saved his priestess.'

'Yes, father,' said the prince uncertainly. His voice was strained. Suddenly the throne room fell silent. What did his Majesty mean? Why single out Prince Cormis?

'And I think it only fitting, Cormis, that in the middle of the day, when the Sun God is at his height in the sky, you should lead this city's prayers in thanks and gratitude to Mithras for having saved Amra. And for not having brought shame and destruction to this city.'

'Yes, father,' said the prince again.

'Indeed, my son, to show your worthiness as a subject of Troy and as a future King, it is my decree that you will stand before the entire population of the city and pay homage to the bull God.'

The blood drained from Cormis's face and he looked up at his father's face.

'Do not dare to look into my eyes!' shouted Praxis. 'You are a subject of the greatest King in the world. Look at my feet!' In terror, the young man bowed his head to the floor.

Praxis's anger rose to greater heights, his words spat with a venom usually reserved for his enemies. 'You have been given the greatest of gifts this world has to offer. The gift of the Gods themselves. You were to be awarded the city of Troy and the care of all its people. I would have given you the greatest empire the world has ever known. Greater than Egypt. Did not my father, King Muwatalli, humble the great Rameses in the battle of Kadesh? Have not city states in Syria, Palestine and throughout the world thrown off the yoke of obedience to once-great Egypt and turned instead towards me? All of this, my son, would have been yours. But you have abused the God Mithras, just as you have abused me, and the people who surround you here. No more will you abuse the women of this court. No more will you strike terror into the hearts of your brothers and sisters.' The King stepped closer to his son and his voice dropped to a whisper. 'No more will you live.'

Cormis looked up again, hatred marring his fine features. He reached for his sword but before he could withdraw it from its scabbard, two Nubian guards seized his arms in a vicious grip. A third guard thrust a dagger close to the young man's throat. Other guards ran through the frightened crowd and seized three other men, who were already sneaking towards the exits. Only Alses stood free of constraint.

Cormis glared around the room like a cornered stag, his body straining at the constraints of the guards, his face red with the effort. He saw that his companions had also been arrested, but noticed that his life-long friend, Alses, was not being held firm by a Nubian guard. Understanding came upon the prince. 'You!' he screamed at Alses. 'You told them. You will die.' The guard holding the dagger slapped him across the face with his huge black hand and the prince subsided.

'Take him to the priests' dressing chamber,' commanded Praxis. 'Dress him as a priest of Mithras and hold him in chains until midday. At noon he is to be bound hand and foot and tied to a stake in the bull's enclosure. I will give the order for the bull God to be released. This is no competition. This is vengeance by Mithras upon one who has blasphemed against him.'

The three guards dragged Cormis back through the crowd. 'As for the others,' the King said, pointing to his son's three co-conspirators, 'their heads shall be cleaved from their bodies and their corpses shall be thrown on the shores of the sea so that the birds and creatures of the land may tear them to pieces, and at night the tide may take away their bones into the eternity of the sea. They shall be given no religious rites. They shall die lonely and frightened in the view of their families. Go,' said the King.

Guards dragged away the three screaming men. Their families began to cry for mercy but were quickly hurried out of the throne room.

The King hesitated before stepping onto the bridge over the small stream to his throne. 'Come, my son,' he said to the younger prince, Mesha. 'You will be King when I am no longer King. You will be Troy's ruler when I'm away from the city. To you go the spoils of the victor. I command you not to offer any prayers for your brother's soul.'

Praxis turned back to his courtiers, who lowered their heads to the floor as one. 'I command that there will be no mourning or grieving for my son Cormis. His day is over. His memory will be lost to the city. No record shall be kept of him. It shall be as if he never was.'

The King beckoned to Mithrassa-Urbek. 'Where is the priestess Amra?' he whispered.

'She is bathing, Majesty, to remove the dirt from her body. The priestesses are attending to the wounds to her hands and feet.'

'As soon as she is well I want to send her on her way. She will travel back to her land with three of my armourers and three metalworkers. Make sure she has everything she needs for the journey.'

Mithrassa-Urbek bowed and retreated, but the King held up his hand having thought of another matter. 'Before she leaves there are two things I want to do. While she is bathing instruct a priestess to remove this golden amulet she wears around her neck. I will order to be stamped on one side of it the bull symbol of the God Mithras, and on the other side with my own personal symbol of wisdom, the owl of Troy. If ever she or her people need help, all she will have to do is to show the symbol and she will be brought immediately into my presence. If I am dead, my son and his descendants will recognise the sign.'

'Yes, Majesty,' said Mithrassa-Urbek.

'And the second thing I want you to do is to bring her to my side when the God Mithras sends Cormis to his eternal rest. She must see with her own eyes that Mithras has been avenged.'

CHAPTER 26

The drive to Edirne normally took three hours but it took David and Bengazi an hour longer. They deliberately drove slowly, having much to discuss. For the meeting Bengazi had decided to wear a conservative blue suit, while David, whose only formal clothes were the black dinner suit and white bow tie he wore as a concert cellist, dressed in the most conservative thing he had – a shirt and waistcoat with dark pants. Bengazi was nervous that David was there at all.

'I'll just keep quiet,' David promised.

'And you think that will prevent a man like Urzak from noticing your presence?' said Bengazi. 'Anyway, that waistcoat, David. How could you have bought such a thing? You look like a bee.'

'Hey! It's all the rage in New York city. Everybody likes yellow and black. And if I stand out it won't look as if I'm hiding something. It might offset Urzak's curiosity, in a perverse sort of way.'

Bengazi shook his head. 'I still think we should turn back. The very idea of you coming along is crazy.' David chose not to answer.

Bengazi shrugged. He was hot even in the air-conditioned car. He disliked wearing suits at the best of times but he was wired for sound through his jacket sleeves and the front of his shirt and it would have taken a good fifteen minutes to dress again so that the microphone was properly concealed.

The road, which snaked through the ancient province of Thrace northwest to the Bulgarian border, was heavily used by trucks and buses travelling from Asia to Europe. Edirne had been founded in the seventh century by the

Emperor Hadrian who called the city Hadrianopolis. It was the Turks who changed the name to Edirne. When the Ottomans crossed the Dardanelles in 1363, they captured Hardianopolis – by then called Adrianople – and made it their base for their war against Europe. Since then it had been fought over by the Allies and the Greeks, and when Atatürk came to power, the Allies, with the Treaty of Lausanne, gave Edirne and eastern Thrace to Turkey. For a man such as Ozman Urzak, it was an ideal base of operations. Although relatively close to Istanbul, it was largely ignored by tourists who could see no reason for travelling so far north away from the sites of real interest.

They found his home high in the hills outside the city. Being an import/exporter Urzak had no need to hide his legitimate business.

'Let's hope he's there,' said David. He knew Bengazi was thinking the opposite. But regardless of the arguments the Turkish archaeologist had put up, David refused to allow him to make the visit alone.

'What do we do when we get there?' David had already asked the question several times during the journey and Bengazi had answered him. He was nervous.

Bengazi gave the same answer again. 'We do what we've agreed, and we pray. At worst we've wasted a day. At best we get the evidence we read. What else could we do – phone and make an appointment? You know what he would have done.' He patted his left breast, feeling the tape recorder.

The house was surrounded by a huge white wall, breached only by a twelve-foot wrought-iron gate operated by an electronic lock and keypad. Bengazi wound down his window. David felt his heart thumping. If this man truly was Mafia, he would have some seriously heavy guys around to protect him. Not only were the two of them completely unarmed but David didn't fancy either of their chances against a bodyguard. Bengazi pressed a button and a voice squeaked out of the tiny loudspeaker.

Bengazi responded. 'My name is Kemel Arazi. I'm a member of the staff of his Excellency Yussef Barrak of the Ministry of Antiquities. I'm here to see his Excellency Mr Ozman Urzak.'

There was silence. The voice had obviously withdrawn to consult a higher authority. David was scared now. It had been a stupid idea. His presence would only endanger Bengazi in an already dangerous situation.

A few moments later another voice, deeper and more confident, came back on the line. Bengazi repeated his performance.

'No,' he continued, 'I don't have an appointment. I was sent by the Director to speak to Mr Urzak. My employer did not want to use the telephone or put anything in writing. You will, I am sure, understand the need for secrecy.'

'Wait there,' said the voice. The two men sat in their car in the hot sun. They could see the house in the distance. It was a mansion, obviously built for one of Edirne's favourite sons or governors. Three men walked around the side of the house and down the drive. The bulges in their jackets indicated they were armed. The gate opened with a metallic click and Bengazi drove the car forward to meet them. One of the men walked around to Bengazi's window.

'Your identification?' he demanded.

Bengazi handed over plastic card carrying his photograph and his identification as Kemel Arazi, stamped with the official seal of the Ministry of Antiquities, countersigned by Yussef Barrak, Director. The man looked at it and nodded. 'Him?' he said, pointing to David.

David took his plastic identification out of his pocket and handed it over. As the guard studied the card, David suddenly regretted taking the name of Donald Sutherland. It had seemed funny at the time, but now . . . Nonetheless, the face was clearly his own, and the signature that of Dr Barrak. It had only taken the two men an hour to put together the cards using the Museum facilities, yet despite the speed with which they had been created they looked genuine.

'American?' said the guard.

Bengazi nodded. 'I will discuss this with His Excellency, Mr Urzak.'

The guard looked at them both coldly. He wasn't impressed with the car. It was old and dirty, not a Ministry vehicle. He opened the driver's door and ordered both men to step out. His assistant produced a small hand-held metal detector which he ran up and down Bengazi's body. When it drew level with the tape recorder it beeped shrilly. Apologetically, and before the security man could reach into his pocket, Bengazi pulled out a metal cigarette lighter. He laughed at the mistake and replaced it in the same pocket. The guard continued to scan Bengazi then moved on to David. He found nothing. Both men got back into the car while the guard made an intercom call to the house.

After another agonising minute, in which David was certain his heart was going to burst, the guard nodded reluctantly.

'We're through,' said David, almost singing in relief, as they drove up to the house. 'I didn't think we were going to make it.'

'We're not through,' corrected Mustafa. 'All we have gained is entry. If they search us properly we're really stuffed. How am I going to explain a tape recorder?'

'Surely those guys would have searched us properly if anyone was going to?'

'Who knows. At least the cigarette lighter came in

handy. I got the idea from a French movie. Thank God the guard hadn't seen it.'

They got out of their car and walked up the steps to the house. A short portly man dressed in a garish floral shirt and fawn slacks stood in the doorway.

'Who are you?' he demanded.

Bengazi introduced himself and David and both proffered their identity cards a second time.

'What do you want?'

Bengazi stood his ground. 'May I ask who you are, sir?'

'I am Ozman Urzak. You wanted to see me. Why?'

Mustafa bowed and, as he did so, scratched the underside of his arm. He coughed to mask the noise of the tape recorder starting up. 'Forgive me. I wonder if I might impose upon you for a drink. It's been a long journey and the Ministry doesn't allow us expensive cars with air-conditioning.'

'No drink. Just tell me why you're here.'

'Is this the way you talk to the Deputy Under-Secretary of the Department of Antiquities?' said Bengazi arrogantly.

'It's the way I talk to everybody until I know what they want. Now, what the hell *do* you want? I've never heard of any Yussef Barrak.'

'Then I have wasted my journey. I apologise. I have obviously been sent to the wrong house.' Bengazi turned away and began to walk down the steps.

'Wait! What does this man Barrak want?' insisted Urzak.

'His Excellency presents his harmonious greetings and begs to inform you of events subsequent to your meeting.'

'What's happened?' snapped Urzak.

'There have been some developments.'

'Is it bad?'

'It's neither good nor bad, Excellency. Merely information which you should possess.'

The little man nodded. 'Follow me,' he said. He turned on his heel and led them into a high-ceilinged, ornately furnished room with ottomans on the floor, deep black leather sofas and walls covered from ceiling to floor with books. 'Sit,' he said, still treating them like servants.

'Sir!' said Bengazi, raising his voice in indignation. 'I beg that you appreciate my rank. I am assistant to the Director of the Ministry of Antiquities. I am not accustomed to being treated like a dog. I am here on the express orders of his Excellency, the Director.'

'All right, you've made your point. I just don't like people turning up unexpectedly. Why didn't you telephone and say you were coming? And who is your companion? My men said he is American, not Turkish. What is he doing here? I made it very clear to Barrak that there was to be no contact. Your appearance here surprises me. I intend to talk to him about this. It is a breach of our security.'

'First, sir, a drink. It is very hot outside and we have driven directly from Istanbul.' If Bengazi could distract him, his volley of questions would soon be forgotten.

Irritated, Urzak stood and walked over to a drinks cabinet. David glanced at Mustafa with similar irritation. None of this had been planned. He just wanted to get the information and get out. Bengazi's expression, however, assured David that he knew the game and how to play it.

Urzak returned with two glasses of mineral water. 'Now, who is he?' he demanded, pointing aggressively at David.

'Mr Sutherland is with the American CIA. He is currently advising the Director on the international repercussions of what this latest crisis might mean for Turkey.'

Urzak turned puce and his jaw dropped. It was the reaction Bengazi had hoped for. Now, with Urzak offguard, was the time to get him talking. 'There's a strong possibility that the demonstrations currently occurring throughout Turkey as a result of our plot against the American Jewish woman may backfire. This would have drastic implications.'

Urzak frowned. 'What do you mean, backfire?'

'My Director is worried that things are getting out of hand. The backlash against the Kaplan woman may have a more disastrous effect than just bringing down the government. Hence he has employed Mr Sutherland in a private capacity to deal with what is rapidly becoming an international situation.'

'That's impossible. Once the government falls, that's it. The riots will stop when the new government takes power. There was always the risk of upsetting of the Islamic countries. But we knew that.'

'But that's the whole point, Excellency. The riots show no sign of stopping,' insisted Mustafa. 'That's the problem. Dr Barrak is afraid that this incident has started a wave of Islamic fundamentalism —'

'But that's what he wants!'

'It is not,' insisted Mustafa, his voice rising in annoyance. 'Yes, he wants a new government, an Islamic government, but there's a very strong possibility that Iran will seek to intervene. We have this on the best advice of Mr Sutherland and the CIA.'

'Iran!' screeched the little man. 'Tell Barrak he has no need to worry, no matter what this man says. Iran? Nonsense. Maybe there are demonstrations going on in Tehran but so what? They will puff themselves out. Tell Barrak to sit tight. Tell him not to do anything,' he paced to the fireplace, '*anything* to disrupt the present situation. Tell him it's all planned. We know exactly what we're doing. Do you understand me? Never mind what this American thinks. And don't ever bring a CIA man here again. Fool! Now go back and tell your Director this. Tell him immediately.'

Bengazi nodded. 'I will tell him.'

'For God's sake, tell Barrak to sit tight. Anything he says now could be catastrophic. Perhaps I should I phone him.'

'No!' said Bengazi hurriedly. 'You must have no contact with him. None at all. That is why he had sent me to speak with you. He cannot be seen to be involved.'

Urzak looked suspiciously at David. He still couldn't figure the CIA link, but the one thing he wanted was these two men out of his house. 'Okay, I agree. I won't phone him. But for God's sake, keep him calm. And don't ever come to the house again. Everything is progressing to plan. But he will fuck it up if he panics.'

Bengazi translated for David's benefit then both men rose and headed for the door. 'I'll tell my Director everything you have said,' repeated Bengazi. 'I bid you good day. *Salaam alekum.*'

'Yes, yes, yes,' said Urzak, waving them dismissively from the room. But then something caught at him. 'Why call in the CIA? I don't understand. This government is friendly with the Americans. Why would the CIA help Barrak to bring it down?' Urzak's forehead creased as he tried to work out the implications of David's presence.

'Things are never as they seem, Excellency,' said Bengazi. 'Many in this government wish to break away from the American sphere of influence. The CIA believes America will have a closer relationship with a new government, even if it is Islamic.' Urzak nodded, but still looked puzzled.

Bengazi and David quickly took their leave. The guards were nowhere to be seen and their car was allowed to pass through the electronic gate which glided open on their approach.

'Well?' said David when they were on the road again. 'What really happened back there?'

Bengazi withdrew the tape recorder strapped to his vest and handed it to David. As the tinny dialogue filled the car, Bengazi translated for David.

'Great!' he said when the tape had played through. 'Wonderful. Couldn't be better!'

'I still don't understand why you ran the risk of coming along, David. You put us both in great danger. You speak no Turkish and all you could do was to play dumb. And that bullshit story about the CIA – another ten minutes and even an oaf like Urzak would have realised it was implausible. Why didn't you take my advice and stay in Istanbul?'

'It worked out fine though, didn't it?'

'That's not the point, David. The risk was immense.'

David reflected for a moment before answering. Then he said quietly, 'Mustafa, you've made this your fight, and for that Sarah and I are really truly grateful. But it's really my responsibility. I can't put you into a position of danger without being there myself.'

'You must have God on your side, my friend, because the danger was far greater with you there than without.'

They drove along in silence for a time, avoiding the major roads in case Urzak had decided to check out their story. Eventually David asked, 'Why *are* you making this your fight, Mustafa? You could have kept out of this yet you've given your time and endangered yourself trying to help an American woman you barely know. Why?'

'Does there always have to be a reason? Can't you just believe me when I say that I am helping Sarah because it is the right thing to do?'

'I don't know. All I can tell you is that I'm honestly not sure I'd risk my ass to save you if the positions were reversed. Not that I don't like you. But we're screwing around with the Mafia here. That puts it in a whole new league.'

Bengazi laughed then took a deep breath. Softly, he said, 'I am a Professor of the University of Istanbul. To you, that might be a very senior position; indeed, it is. But six years ago the United Nations approached the Department of Antiquities and asked for a submission of names for a very senior post based in New York. I would have killed to get that job. It would have catapulted me to the peak of my profession and given me a lifestyle second to none. I put my name forward, along with a dozen other less qualified men and women. I was the natural choice. I went for an interview to Ankara. Barrak conducted it. All went well for the first half hour. Then he took out a file and began to ask questions about my sexual preferences, whether or not I was homosexual. I told him that it was none of his business but he took great delight in undermining my application from that moment onwards. Naturally I didn't get the job.'

David nodded. 'So you're helping Sarah because of revenge?'

'Partly. But also because of Sarah herself. When I first met her she was warm and friendly towards me. I don't know why, but when we had dinner together for the first time I opened up and told her about my sexuality. She just nodded, as if it were of no importance. Then she smiled and said, "I prefer working with women anyway." I howled and she laughed too. I liked her from that moment onwards. She's a very special young woman. Barrak has no right to harm her.'

'I thought that the Ottomans, and Turkey in general, was tolerant of homosexuality?'

'It was,' said Bengazi, 'until the fundamentalists became powerful. If Barrak succeeds, millions of men and women like me are in for a very frightening time.'

As they drove into Istanbul, both David and Bengazi felt a change in the atmosphere from that morning. There were groups of men gathered on street corners, and the occasional speaker addressed small crowds from the perch of a crate, but generally the streets were far less crowded than usual.

Mustafa took a mobile phone from the glove box and stabbed in a series of numbers with his right thumb. He cuddled the receiver into his shoulder and asked a few terse questions. Switching off the phone, he turned to David. 'There have been demonstrations all day and there was a riot in the Islamic University. The police have been on the streets breaking up crowds. It's the same in other regional cities.'

David had suspected as much. 'I think we ought to go to the police station to check on Sarah,' he said.

It took them only thirty minutes from entering the outskirts of the city to drive to the police station. The road outside was comparatively empty except for police vehicles and groups of officers standing at the doors. They parked the car and walked towards the entrance.

'I'm David Rose, Sarah Kaplan's fiancé. I'd like to see her, please,' David told the sergeant at the desk. He pulled out his driver's licence to prove his identity. The sergeant shook his head. 'She's been moved to an army base on the road to the Black Sea.'

'What?!'

'There was an ugly demonstration here this morning. We had to use tear gas. So we've moved her out there where we can offer her adequate protection. She's safer there.'

'Can we visit her?' Bengazi asked in Turkish.

'I can give you the address but you won't get in. The Minister for Justice has decreed that she is to have no visitors other than her lawyer and authorities from the American consul or the embassy. Nobody else, not even her fiancé.' The sergeant nodded towards David who was desperately trying to understand what was being said.

'She must be terrified,' David said as Bengazi drove him to the hotel. 'That poor girl. Can you imagine what it's like to be in jail one minute, then have some demonstration outside your front door and be carted off to an army camp? My God, she must be going crazy.'

'It's best not to think about it. We're not an uncivilised country. She will be treated with considerable respect in the camp and, let's face it, the reason she's been taken there is for her own protection. I'm afraid we will have to put seeing Sarah aside until we have found enough evidence to get her out.'

David knew that Mustafa was right no matter how much he wanted to argue. Back at the hotel both men collapsed into armchairs, exhausted emotionally and physically. Their elation at getting the tape which could force Barrak to deal with them had drained away the moment they entered the city. Now, everything was as black as it had been the previous day. Despite the evidence against Barrak, they couldn't share it with Sarah, and all they could do was imagine her state of distress. She was cut off from everybody who loved her and had no way of knowing they were doing all they could to save her.

David leafed through the messages he had picked up from the reception desk. There must have been well over thirty. He put them down on the table and closed his eyes.

After a few moments, Bengazi asked, 'Anything important?'

David flicked through them. There were several messages from his parents begging him to call home, a message from Sarah's parents with a similar request, three from Sarah's former law firm in New York, one from the State Department to say that everything possible was being done and he wasn't to worry, one from Sarah herself telling him that she was being moved and he was to contact her before she left the police station at one o'clock that day, then another at five to one begging him to phone if he had any love for her at all. The others were of lesser importance, more friends, more relatives, more people desperate for him to phone to tell them what was going on. And then, towards the end of the pile, a message which he had to read twice to understand it.

He read it aloud to Bengazi: 'Imam Ibrahim Halal wishes David Rose to telephone him at Mehmet Pasha mosque as soon as possible.'

Bengazi looked as though he had been punched in the stomach by a heavyweight boxer. 'The Imam?' he exclaimed.

David shrugged. 'That's what it says.'

'But he's the holy man. He's one of the . . . Let me see.' He snatched the message from David's fingers. 'Good God,' he said. 'You must phone him immediately.'

'Why? He's the boss of the cleric, isn't he? The boss of the lying piece of scum that started all of this.'

'David, don't be silly. Phone him now. I don't know what this means, but it could be extremely important.'

'He probably just wants to gloat. I'm a Jew,' said David. 'There's absolutely no love between Islamic preachers and Jews. None at all.'

'David, think for a minute. This might be some concession. I don't know . . .'

David sat up. 'Yeah, you're right. I'm just tired and

feeling fucked up.' He picked up the phone and punched in the numbers.

'With your permission, will you let me speak to him? We don't know whether he speaks English and anyway, it's probably more appropriate that I talk.'

David handed over the phone. For the next ten minutes he let the Turkish conversation wash over him. Mustafa, for all of his secularism, showed very real deference towards the man on the other end of the line. He spoke profuse thanks as he put down the phone.

'Well?' demanded David.

Bengazi was beaming. 'All isn't well at the mosque, not with the Imam anyway. He wants to see us immediately. He says it's a matter of conscience and wouldn't discuss it over the phone. He wants us to go to his office right now.'

'Jesus, I'm sure it's important but –'

Bengazi put up his hand. 'Don't think for one minute that you can rest until we've seen him. When a man like the Imam wants to talk to you, you go and you listen. These men say little but their words are full of meaning.'

David grinned. 'I've heard Imams before, Mustafa. They say a lot and much of it is venomous.'

'Those sort of Imams are usually from Iran, or Iraq or Egypt, David. They're not holy men. They're terrorists, religious fundamentalists and fanatics. When was the last time you heard an Imam in Saudi Arabia give way to hysteria? An Imam is the intellectual voice as well as the voice of conscience of Islam.'

Within ten minutes, they were sitting in the Imam's office. A cleric gave them apple tea as they waited for the Imam to appear. The walls of his room were lined with bookshelves which were crammed with books, manuscripts, rolls of documents, and photographs of dignitaries. The Imam himself was an old man with a bushy white beard and swathed in black robes. The thing that surprised David was his eyes: they burnt with an intensity which seared into the very being of all he gazed upon. David remembered the eyes of the Ayatollah Khomeni staring contemptuously at the western world from posters, cold black eyes without love, integrity, intellectualism or morality. Hard fundamentalist's eyes. But this man's eyes were the lightest shade of blue, almost milky white, and his face radiant with gentleness.

David stood and the Imam shook his hand. His skin was warm and parchment-like. David felt an immediate and surprising empathy between them which went beyond language, beyond religion. Mustafa bent and kissed the Imam's hand, and the three men sat. The Imam began to speak. His English was hesitant but perfectly understandable. Occasionally he turned to Bengazi for advice on his choice of word.

'Your fiancée came to my mosque as a visitor,' he said to David. 'She was supposed to meet one of my worshippers, Yussef Barrak. It is claimed that she attempted to steal our most sacred relic from the Kaaba and was seen by one of my young priests. Consequently she was arrested and now there is much anger in Turkey at her actions. I am told by my brothers that there is also anger in Arabia, Egypt and Libya.' David nodded.

'But my conscience speaks to me. Turkey is ruled by unbelievers, by men who put money and power before duty to God, by those who seek the way of the west rather than the way of submission of Islam. Without this ungodly government, Islam will rule and Turkey will flourish. What has happened because of Sarah Kaplan's arrest will not be soon forgotten. The anger will continue to rage in the streets and the government will fall. The people will not tolerate this abuse of Islam. Your fiancée, Mr Rose, will be imprisoned or will be sent from my country. This is what should happen. This is good. This is what I am pleased to see.' David knew that he had to remain silent. This repetition of the known facts was not why the Imam had requested their presence.

'I lived in your country for some years when I was a young man, Mr Rose. I was an engineer before I became a priest. I studied at Massachusetts Institute of Technology. There's much about America that I like but there is also much I dislike. I remember one of your expressions: "You can't build a house on quicksand." Very true. How would I feel, Mr Rose, if the Turkish house that rises as a result of your fiancée's theft were on quicksand?

'Lies and deceit cannot be the foundation of God's nation on earth. Many countries have been built on bloodshed, on great sorrow and this has given them great strength. Throughout history we have seen one people being forced to make way for another. My own religion suffered at the hands of the Crusaders nine hundred years ago. Your people, Mr Rose, have suffered throughout history from those who were jealous, who hated them. But no true nation can be built on a foundation which lacks moral strength. Turkey will become a truly Islamic nation with a government for Allah where the priests govern the people. A moral country where immodesty no longer reigns, where the family is important again. But I will not permit an Islamic government to come to power as a result of lies.'

David suddenly realised that he was holding his breath. He released it slowly and took a sip of apple tea. He waited with almost uncontrollable anxiety for the words which he knew would free Sarah.

'I have investigated the claim made by my priest. He says that he saw your fiancée stealing the stone of the Kaaba. I threatened him with great pain and discomfort in ways which you cannot begin to imagine, for I will not have in my mosque a man who does not have alive in his very soul the shining truth of Mohammed and all that he stood for. After searching his conscience, my young priest admitted that Barrak convinced him to steal the stone himself and to place it in Sarah Kaplan's bag when he was searching it in front of the police. He believed that he could bring about an Islamic government this way. But we will not rule by lies, Mr Rose.

'Dr Barrak, I think, wishes to bring down the government. Your fiancée was the tool he chose to use. I will tell my story to the police after you have left which, I believe, should ensure the freedom of your fiancée. I suggest that you leave Turkey then and return only when Islam is again truly in the heart and mind of every Turk.'

The interview was over. For David to express thanks was not only superfluous but gratuitous. The Imam was informing David of a *fait accompli*. Neither David, Bengazi nor Sarah played any role in his decision. It was and it would always be the Imam's action alone. The Imam smiled at David. 'Tell your fiancée that I am deeply sorry and ashamed,' he said.

David nodded. He walked over to the Imam's desk and stood for a moment, looking into the sad old man's kindly eyes. He picked up the Imam's hand, kissed it and followed Bengazi out of the room.

CHAPTER 27

Mithrassa-Urbek held the amulet tentatively towards Amra, as though he were a birthwife giving a mother her newborn baby. He was obviously proud of the new markings engraved into the gold. But Amra was disturbed by them; these were not the patterns her father had etched into the metal, patterns which her bee totem would instantly recognise and act on to protect her. And when he turned the amulet over to show her the other side the heart dropped. This was not the same amulet she had worn when she left her village. Would her totem recognise her wearing these strange new markings?

Mithrassa-Urbek smiled happily and explained the craftsman's work to her. 'This bull is the sacred symbol of the God Mithras. And this,' he turned the amulet over again before placing it in her hands, 'is the symbol of the owls that protect Troy. Although they keep many of us awake at night with their constant hooting in the walls, we are also safe from invaders because of their vigilance. The King has done you the greatest honour imaginable, Amra. You are now protected by royal command. No-one will dare harm you once they see the King's mark.'

Amra nodded. She wasn't happy that her father's beautiful work, his delicate lines and swirls, the impressions he had made to protect her on her journey had been tampered with. But when Mithrassa-Urbek explained that the owl was the personal symbol of the King of Troy and would be recognised throughout the entire length and breadth of the world, she appreciated how much the new markings meant.

Mithrassa-Urbek placed the amulet on a gold chain around her neck and kissed her on the forehead. 'When I first met you outside the city walls and you demanded the right to retrieve the golden arrow, I felt then that you were an unusual, indeed a strange woman. I knew somehow there were things you could teach us. You were from the lands of the savages yet I realised that if you were able to make such a long and dangerous journey there was something we could learn from you.

'I was right. Now Troy has been warned of impending danger from invaders who will come from over the sea. And Troy will be saved, because we will continue to worship Mithras and none will dare turn his head from the God. But more, Amra, much more. We are free of Cormis and his evil ways. When you sit with the King and watch the sacred bull kill Cormis you will be avenged, as will be the many husbands, fathers and sons whose women have been playthings for the prince. It's fitting that he should die at the hands of Mithras. Come child, it is time for us to join the King.'

Amra followed him along the corridors of a palace which no longer held terror or mystery for her. This would be one of the last occasions she would enter the palace. Shortly after Cormis's death, Amra was to ride back to whence she had come. She would ride tall and proud on Wind's back, escorted by Mithrassa-Urbek – who had been ordered by the King to find out what else her savage lands might have to offer the people of Troy – and the three armourers and three metalworkers Praxis had promised her. Also accompanying them would be a contingent of Nubian guards, as befitted a man of Mithrassa-Urbek's rank and Amra's status as priestess and seer. They would travel back along the route she had taken to reach Troy, and once in her village they would make enough iron weapons to arm her people so that they might defend themselves against the armies of iron men.

Amra feasted her eyes for the last time on the paintings which graced the palace walls and ceiling. They were beautiful paintings, but now she recognised them for what they were: equivalent in execution to the images her father made in metal. Similarly the vases and carpets which adorned the corridors no longer struck her dumb with their fineness and delicacy. She still recognised them as extraordinarily beautiful, more beautiful even than the flowers in the fields, but she had seen women weaving the carpets and understood now how they were made. It was not the work of the Gods, as she had first thought, but of skilled women whose nimble fingers wove the bobbin tautly through the exquisitely coloured threads, and she had seen them batten down the pattern and clip the pile to a uniform length with two knives fixed together in the middle. She had also seen the room of the potters where the finest of clay was thrown onto a spinning wheel and, within almost no time, a vase rose up out of it. After drying in the sun the vases were painted in the most beautiful of colours. But, except for the fineness of the work and the beauty of the painting, it was the same process by which her friend's father, the potter of their village, made the villagers' pots and bowls.

Amra had even become used to the material which came from lands far away and looked like the webs of spiders spun into carpets. The material came from the cases of strange caterpillars which were boiled in water then beaten with a brush. Multiple threads adhered to the bristles of the brushes which, when they were pulled out of the hot water, formed a continuous strand. These threads were spun until they were longer than any Amra ever seen before. Then the soft threads were put into vats of dyes until they emerged with exquisite colours. One day she would show her people how to make carpets from this material which the people of Troy called silk.

They walked out into the brilliant sunshine of the middle of the day and were immediately surrounded by a squad of palace guards. Amra felt intensely proud when she reflected that during her first days in the city, the guards would have terrified her. The Nubians escorted Amra and Mithrassa-Urbek to the sacred bull's enclosure to join the King and the rest of the royal family. Even from some distance away they could hear the excitement of the crowd. It sounded as if the whole city was there; and indeed they were! Shops had been shut, potters had put away their wheels, prostitutes had closed their doors; the King had decreed that all should witness his son's execution. The doors of all the houses they passed were firmly closed. Nobody was on the street.

Amra and Mithrassa-Urbek entered the enclosure and climbed up the steps to where the King was sitting under a canopy held in place by four guards. Mithrassa-Urbek bowed and kissed the King's knee. The King motioned Amra towards a seat on a pedestal below his own. She glanced surreptitiously across at him and saw that his face was bleak. For the first time Amra fully realised the momentousness of the occasion; she was about to witness a father watching the death of his son. She thought of her own father, Hasga, and the look of sadness in his face when she had ridden away on Wind. Perhaps he also had thought that he would never see his daughter again, just as Praxis would never again see Cormis once the God Mithras had sent his bull into the enclosure.

But Amra was pleased that Cormis was about to die. He deserved no less and his death would rid the city of a terrible plague. Cormis could never have acted in such a way in her own village, nor in any of the other villages of the valleys of the five rivers. For any chief who behaved like Cormis would have been expelled by the Great Council, or put to death. No, she felt no mercy for

Cormis. But she felt great distress for Praxis. A severe man, he had nonetheless been kind to her. He was a man of his word, but also a father. She wanted to reach over and hold Praxis's hand to comfort him. But she knew she couldn't touch him. Even a priestess could not touch the King. And so she sat still beside him, thinking about how Cormis would soon be dead. She imagined the bull's metal-covered horns spearing him through his heart, ripping vast gashes into Cormis's body. The prince's innards would spill onto the ground and Cormis would view his own destruction for the last few moments before he died a terrible and painful death. She glanced at Praxis again, wondering if this was what he was thinking about too.

Was this truly what Mithras wanted, Amra wondered. Mithrassa-Urbek had told her that Mithras was the God of Justice and Contracts but would he have made this contract? Was Mithras a cruel god? She knew that he was a strange god. She had lied to everybody about hearing his words. She had cheated in order to get her own way. And now Cormis would die because of the lies she had told. Cormis had found her out and she had lied again to save herself. Now he was dying for her. It was right that he should die. He had tried to force her into having sex. But . . .

The crowd's whistling, cheering and laughing interrupted Amra's musings. Cormis was brought in to the enclosure, a loincloth draped over his groin to save his modesty. His arms were strapped to a beam which rested heavily on his neck behind his back. His ankles were chained. Around his neck was a sign which Amra couldn't read. Mithrassa-Urbek saw her frown and leant across to whisper to her, 'The sign reads "Cormis, food for Mithras".'

The crowd laughed uproariously. Amra turned to the King, looking directly at him, not concerned about protocol. Praxis didn't notice. His eyes were fixed upon his son, who was ridiculed as he walked rigidly and with great difficulty into the enclosure. There was no smile on the King's face. His eyes were moist with tears.

The soldiers led Cormis to a vertical stake at the centre of the enclosure. They lifted him off the ground and hooked the crossbeam holding his arms onto a peg holding his arms high on the stake. As it settled into position, Cormis's toes struggled to find support. His feet only just touched the ground, his hands and arms were outstretched on the crossbar, as though he were appealing to the crowd for mercy, and his head hung low. He was sweating profusely and his body jerked for shallow gasps of breath.

The guards left the arena and the crowd slowly came to order. A blast of trumpets heralded the locking of all the doors into the enclosure then a deathly and oppressive silence settled over the proceeding. Suddenly, with a loud click, the door to the bull's quarters slowly swung open. Amra could hear gasps of fear from the crowd as the ground seemed to quiver. There was the sound of hooves, then the huge bull's head slowly, tentatively, appeared in the enclosure.

A huge roar erupted from the crowd. In sudden terror, the bull looked up and panicked, snorting and pawing the ground as it stood in the blistering hot sun, its head weaving from side to side as it tried to understand where it was. It lumbered around the outside of the enclosure, keeping close to the wall, seeking respite from the sun and the crowd's hysteria. It bellowed with fear and its frantic panic goaded the crowd on to even louder catcalls and whistles.

The bull weaved left and right as it loped around the enclosure. It hadn't yet seen Cormis tied to the stake. It was still in a panic, its poor eyesight causing it to shift its head from side to side like an old man affected by the sun. Its nostrils flared ready for attack. The crowd was taut with anticipation, all eyes fixed on the beast that lumbered beneath them. All except Amra's. She was looking into the sky above the bull's enclosure where a bee flew in slow, lazy circles above the bull's head. It wasn't just any bee; it was Amra's totem. She recognised that it was a sign.

Amra looked across at the King. He was looking down at the ground, unable to witness the death of his son. Then Amra stared down at Cormis. The young prince's eyes were open, seeking his enemy who would deliver him to the God Mithras. His head turned frantically one way then the other for a sight of the bull, but the animal was behind him. Amra would see Cormis's lips moving but his prayers were inaudible for the noise of the crowd. Suddenly Cormis saw the bull out of the corner of his eye. It loped around from behind him into full view. Amra saw the fear in his face.

Cormis looked up at his father, his eyes filled with terror, his mouth pleading to be saved. His body shook with despair. Amra looked again into his face, into his eyes and was struck with recognition. She had seen those eyes before, but not in Cormis's face. His eyes had always been cruel whenever he looked at her, lecherous and cruel. But now there was no cruelty there, just fear. The terror which only those on the verge of death can ever know. Amra sat back in horror for she had looked into eyes which had held just this fear before. The memory made her feel ill. They were the eyes of the men who had forced themselves into her beside the river. Not when they had raped her – then their eyes had been full of lust and power – but when she had tracked them down to kill them. One by one she had killed them, waking them first so that they would know she was their killer. In the moment before she had killed them, that fear had come into their eyes. They had stared at her with stark unrelenting terror as she plunged the knife into their hearts. And now, those same eyes were here before her, in Cormis's face. He had not succeeded in forcing himself into her, yet still he was dying because of her. He was an evil man, but this was wrong. It was cruel. She could not let it happen.

Amra quickly stood and walked past the King, down the steps which led to the enclosure. The crowd suddenly fell silent as every eye turned to watch Amra the priestess, Amra the bull tamer, Amra the hunter, pull aside the wooden bar of the door to the enclosure, open it and walk slowly into the bull's domain.

Nobody, not man, woman or child uttered a sound. All held their breath as Amra began to sing her song to the bull. The sudden cessation of noise caused the bull to slow to a walk, then halt completely. It saw the figure in white and began to paw the ground, preparing to charge. It lowered his head, presenting its razor-sharp horns to the young woman before it. But Amra was not afraid. She knew she could control the bull – she was Amra the bull tamer. She continued her song, then when the bull had realised she was no threat, she walked slowly towards it, singing all the while.

The bull was calmed by the song. It let Amra walk up to it and stroke its head. She played with the skin under its neck and scratched behind its ear. Then she grasped its metal-spiked horns and led the huge beast gently out of the enclosure, closing the huge door behind it so it could not return.

But, unlike the first time she had performed this miracle, there was no roar of approval from the crowd. No flowers were thrown at her feet in appreciation of her wonderful skills. Instead, everybody remained silent, their eyes boring into her and into Cormis. King Praxis sat rigid in his seat, his mouth half open in wonder.

Amra walked back to Cormis and laid her hand on his chest. She shouted to the King: 'I am Amra, Priestess of Mithras. I claim the life of Cormis, Prince of Troy.'

The King stood and walked towards the top wall of the enclosure. 'What will you do with his life?' he asked, his voice little more than a whisper.

'Like you, King, Cormis will become a priest of Mithras. Mithras came to me while I was singing to the bull and said that he wishes Cormis to be his servant and his priest. Cormis will no longer have sex with women. Instead he will devote every moment of his life to the service of the God.'

Praxis nodded. 'Tell Mithras that I agree.'

As Amra left the enclosure, Mithrassa-Urbek was there to greet her. It was the second time he had waited for her there. This time Amra didn't faint. 'I want to go home,' she said.

Mithrassa-Urbek nodded. There was nothing else to say.

Wind cantered over as Amra entered his enclosure. Amra saw that his companions were all mares; from his youthful friskiness she could tell that Wind had enjoyed his short stay in Troy. She hoped that now they were about to journey forth together again that he would remember her and offer her the safety and speed of their previous journey. Wind's body had often instinctively protected her as he cantered over rocky ground or through forests. He took curves in a wide arc and slowed on hills or stony ground so that Amra was not endangered. She knew he would have taken far more risks if she had not been sitting on his back.

Wind lowered his head and pushed her in the stomach, forcing her to fall backwards. Amra lay spreadeagled on the floor, looking up at the massive beast who lowered his head to the ground and repeatedly pushed her body, rolling her over and over in the grass. She was sure she heard him laughing. She got up and scratched Wind where she knew he most loved it, between his ears, under his head and all over his neck. His body moved closer to hers and she felt again his warmth and his strength.

'So, Wind, you must say goodbye to your wives. It is time for us to return home.'

Amra put her arms around his neck and sprang onto his back, using the strength in his muscles to haul herself up. Wind lifted his neck and hoisted her back at the same time. She manoeuvred herself into the position she had sat in for so many days on the journey from her village, along the mighty river, over the high mountains, down to the Eternal Sea and into Troy itself.

Wind cantered around the enclosure and the memory of how to ride him instantly returned to Amra, as though she had ridden him every day of her stay in the city. He rode across the paddock to where his mares were gathered in a corner but the strange sight of a human on top of their mate caused them to bolt in fear. Their sudden terror excited Wind and he galloped after them, Amra holding onto his neck and bouncing up and down. She had forgotten how painful riding could be, and prayed that her legs would soon get used to it.

'Wind,' she shouted. 'Wind, slow down. I'm falling off. Wind!' The horse paid no attention. Instead he continued to gallop after the grey and cream-coloured horses, charging from one beast to another, enjoying the chase as though he were a colt again. Amra slid helplessly from one side of his body to the other. Eventually she gained the upper hand, slapping him across the neck and shouting loudly into his ear. She managed to pull his head back using his mane, then used the rope around his neck to turn his head against his neck so that it was not comfortable for him to run. The horse slowed to a canter, snorted then eventually stopped in the middle of the field.

Amra could feel his body heaving for breath, his massive heart beating wildly with freedom and joy. It was a shame to take him back with her, to deprive him of the company of his mares, but without him she would never return in time. And ultimately she had to give him back to the Medicine Man.

'Come Wind,' she said, 'come,' and she pointed his head in the direction of the gate. But the horse turned back to look at his mares who were panting with excitement at the opposite end of the field. Amra could feel him straining to get back to them, but she forced his head around and put her hands across his eyes so that the only things he could see were directly in front of him. Then she turned him to the gate and kicked him in the flanks to impel him forward. Wind walked through the gate and a guard closed it behind him. But when he heard the mares running towards him, not understanding why their stallion was leaving them, Wind broke free of Amra's resistance and forced his head around. He stuck his head over the fence and the four mares touched him, one after the other, with their noses. Amra allowed them their goodbyes for she knew that Wind would never see them again and in the days ahead would miss them. Eventually Wind turned and allowed Amra to lead him to wherever she wanted to go.

She rode Wind along the city walls and down into the metalworking and stables area. The stable master walked over to Wind and stroked his head.

'Do you think he will like it?' asked Amra.

The stablemaster, a fat old man with white hair and a dirty white beard, said, 'He'll get used to it. They all do.

At first they try to spit it out, but once they understand they feel more comfortable with it.'

He forced Wind's reluctant mouth open and placed the bit securely inside, strapping it over his ears and around his neck. Wind opened and closed his mouth, shaking his head. He hated the piece of metal; it was a restriction. The stablemaster took the rope which Amra had used to guide Wind and discarded it disdainfully. Then he threw the reins across the horse's back and placed them in Amra's hands.

'When you want to go this way,' he said, 'pull here. Do it now.'

Amra tugged hard on the left rein, pulling Wind's head around as she did so. The horse whinnied in pain.

'Not like that,' the stablemaster said, irritated. 'Don't hurt the horse or he'll throw you. Do it gently, then he'll get used to it.' He led Amra and Wind out of the stable and onto a road at the foot of the hill leading up to Troy. 'Ride around here and get used to it,' he said.

Amra kicked Wind in the flanks and steered him gently to the left and then to the right. Next she took middle course, then gently stopped him altogether by pulling the two reins back towards herself. She knew he hated the bridle and bit now but he would become accustomed to it. The bit was a miracle. If she'd had this magical device before her journey would have been so much easier. These were an incredible people. They knew so much, much more than she did.

Mithrassa-Urbek came riding towards her on his magnificent grey horse. He led four burly men and, behind them, four more men selected from the Nubian guards of the palace.

'Majesty,' Mithrassa-Urbek said in mock deference, a smile on his face. 'Your escort awaits.'

Amra laughed. How things had turned out! When she

had come to Troy everybody had called her a savage. She had been greeted by Mithrassa-Urbek as an object of suspicion, as a primitive, and now he joked about her being his queen. These were indeed a strange people, she thought.

'Are you ready, Mithrassa-Urbek?' she asked.

'Yes. We have everything we need. Food, arms, protection. You know the way?'

Amra nodded. She felt for her amulet. Her fingers found the new indentations on the front and back. She may never again see the bull or hear the owls but she would carry them with her always. She looked at her friend and told him: 'I found my way here. I can find my way back.'

'Then turn and say goodbye to great Troy.'

Amra pulled gently on the right-hand rein. Wind turned and together they faced Troy for the last time. A huge city, full of more people than there are leaves in a forest, made up of streets crowded with chariots and shops and palaces and temples, baths where the public went to clean themselves, prostitutes who taught the young men the ways of sex and satisfied the needs of the old men, a city full of the most delicate and beautiful paintings and carpets and vases. Amra had imagined Heaven in her dreams. She looked up at the city high on its hill, surrounded by protective walls which could not be breached by even the strongest army and she knew that she was looking at Heaven now. Perhaps, one day, she would leave her village and bring her father and Peta to live here. They would like it.

Amra turned and nodded to Mithrassa-Urbek. Together they began their long journey back to her village in the five valleys.

CHAPTER 28

When Amra first crossed the Dardanelles and journeyed to Troy from the southern bank of the Eternal Sea the trip had taken her three days. And if it were not for the sympathetic fishing villagers who helped her and Wind recover from near death in the sea, and told her the secret of the golden arrow, they might never have reached Troy at all. Amra would have liked to return to tell these kind people of her adventures and thank them for their kindness. But their fishing village was not on the way back to where she needed to go. Now she had to take the most direct route to her village in order to save her sister.

With her new companions the journey from Troy to the crossing of the Dardans took only one day. In no time at all they stood on the headlands overlooking the narrow point which nearly pinched the Sea of Islands from the neck of the Eternal Sea. The crossing was much smaller than Amra remembered. In the far distance, on the other side, she could see boats tied to the pier. She fancied she could even see the same inn where she had drunk beer before she left on that fateful trip which had almost ended in both her and Wind's death.

'Tomorrow,' said Mithrassa-Urbek, 'in the early morning, when the crossing is at its calmest, we will go down to the royal pier and take the King's pontoon across to the other side.'

Amra had never heard of the King's pontoon. Why hadn't the people in the inn mentioned it to her? She nodded. She could hardly wait. She was sick with anxiety over the fate of her little sister. Would she return in time to save her? What if they were held up? What if they were attacked? The questions in her mind were endless.

She walked back to the large fire where the guards were making delicious cooking smells. It was so good to be travelling with other people and to no longer be responsible for making the fire every night or catching the food. Ever since she had become a priestess of Mithras, Amra had never once needed to think about where her next meal was coming from. Whenever she was hungry the food was there before her.

The metalworkers had drawn away to sit on their own some distance away from the fire. Mithrassa-Urbek had warned her that they had strange and mysterious rituals, and were sworn to complete secrecy on pain of death if they ever revealed the ways in which they worked. So used were they to being separated from the rest of the population of Troy that they felt more comfortable if they were able to travel and eat separately. Amra was happy to grant them their privacy but was puzzled by it.

She took a plate from one of the guards and helped herself to the food. It looked wonderful: deer, rabbit, fowl and fruits. Amra ate well. She listened to the stories which the guards began to tell as soon as the meal was finished. She told a few of her own. Even though the guards were servants and protectors, there was no royal personage on this journey and so the formalities were much less rigidly observed than they normally would be. Even Mithrassa-Urbek was talking to a captain of the Nubian guards who laughed in reply. He had a high-pitched laugh, and even though his face was almost invisible in the blackness of the night, his teeth, white and powerful, seemed to flare in the light of the fire.

Amra lay down on her mat, her stomach full. She was tired from the ride and ached again in all the places where she had ached at the beginning of her long journey to Troy. But it was a good ache and it would soon go as her legs became used to gripping Wind's back.

Wind had eaten and was also lying on the ground. Perhaps he was asleep. She had been over and stroked his large head and he had snorted but hardly moved. Amra knew that soon all would be well. This was the last stage of her quest, the best time. The Gods were watching over her, and she was sure that she would return to her village in time to save everybody from the iron men. Before she closed her eyes, she watched sparks from the fire trail upwards into the black night sky. The sparks became stars high in the heavens. What happened to fire when it flew up into the sky, she wondered. But before the answer came she was already asleep.

The following morning Wind was led blindfolded onto the pontoon. It was a much bigger and flatter vessel than the ship on which Amra had first travelled across the Dardanelles. The guards had left their own horses behind, knowing that they would be able to find royal horses on the other side. But Wind had to return with Amra so the guards tied his legs together at the front and the back and told Amra to stroke his nose and his ears constantly during the journey across the water. This would distract his fear, they told her.

A sail was raised on the front and at the back of the pontoon and the royal boatman and his assistants pushed the vessel away from the pier into the fast-flowing tide. Immediately the sails filled and Amra felt as though they were flying across the choppy channel. She sang to Wind, stroking his ears, but the horse knew that he was again on water and he panicked. He tried to kick out but his legs were too securely tied and he stumbled instead. One of the Nubian guards, an expert horseman, came over and grabbed Wind's head, clamping his hands over his ears. The horse seemed to calm down and, although Amra could tell that he was still frightened, he no longer tried to kick.

The journey passed incredibly quickly, as though they were like the birds which flitted across the top of the water, accompanying the vessel. They passed a number of other barges and many ships plying their way on the currents. The sailors stared at them curiously, wondering which royal personage was sailing in the royal barge. All they could see was a huge black horse, some black guards and a slip of a girl. Mithrassa-Urbek was lying flat on the deck, out of sight, doing his best to retain the food of the morning.

And so they arrived safely at the other side. The boatman tied up to the pier and the Nubian guards untied Wind and led him onto dry land, his hooves clopping on the logs. Mithrassa-Urbek looked green, and had to sit on the pier for several moments, waiting for his stomach to calm. Amra had never suffered from sea sickness and looking at her friend, she was glad of it.

A drink of wine helped to settle Mithrassa-Urbek's queasiness and, once the guards had claimed new horses from the King's stables, they were ready to go. But before they set out, Amra looked over towards the inn. She could hear men laughing inside. She thought to herself for several moments then said quietly to Mithrassa-Urbek: 'Please wait here. A man in there stole my father's knife. I'm going to get it back.' Mithrassa-Urbek frowned but before he could object, Amra had turned and walked towards the inn.

As she opened the door the men drinking beer looked up at the newcomer in curiosity. Some had seen the blue-skinned girl before but to others she was a peculiar figure. Amra looked around the room and in a far corner saw the man she needed to talk to. He was drinking a pot of beer. When he put it down he noticed her looking at him. He wiped his mouth, a look of amazement settling on his face. Then he smiled cruelly. Amra walked over to his table.

'I greet the woman-child,' he said. 'You survived the sea. Good. I was sorry when I thought you had drowned.'

Amra looked down at the man contemptuously. 'I want my knife back.'

The man's hand stole into his pocket. Amra knew he had the knife with him. That was good.

'You'll get nothing from me, girl,' he said. 'You nearly capsized my boat. You and that damned horse. Now be on your way.'

'I want my knife back,' she insisted.

The man straightened in his seat and wiped his mouth again with the back of his hand. 'And I said, be on your way. You see these men,' he said, 'they're my friends. I suggest you turn and go right now.'

'Give me my knife and I'll go. You have no right to the payment. You left Wind and me to drown. We nearly died because of you.'

'You nearly died because you insisted on taking your damned horse and then jumped in after him when, by rights, he should never have come. Now be on your way or you'll see the back of my hand. I mean it, girl. I don't waste time on savages like you.'

Amra did not move. The man slowly rose from his bench to face her. There was only one thing she could do and that was to fight him. She slowly withdrew a knife from the sheath in her belt and held the point towards him.

'Give me my knife,' she said again.

The man put his hand into his pocket and slowly withdrew the ornately carved gold and bronze knife which Amra's father had given her for protection and, if necessary, for trade. It was a wonderful knife, the best knife she had ever seen. The man held it menacingly towards her.

'You want your knife – I'll plant it in your guts. Stupid girl. There are men here,' he said cruelly, 'who will cut you to ribbons if you don't leave now. I mean it, savage. Turn and walk away or you'll be dead by the time I've taken two more breaths.'

Amra stood her ground. The ferryman looked at his friends for support but none of them moved. They were keen to see what would happen. Suddenly the door burst open and four huge Nubian guards walked into the inn. They looked around for Amra and saw what was happening. Instantly they withdrew their swords and strode through the nests of tables until they stood beside Amra, two on one side and two on the other. The thieving captain looked in abject horror at the small army which suddenly faced him. He didn't realise the savage had friends like these or he would never have tried to use bravado. In one moment he had gone from strength to weakness and his life was now in danger.

The captain of the guard took the knife gently from the ferryman's hand, turning it around and giving it, handle first, to Amra. She took it from him and smiled. She owed Mithrassa-Urbek a great deal, again! The black captain, who towered over the ferryman by a head and a half, reached down and with one massive hand grabbed him by the throat. He lifted him level with Amra's eyes, the seaman's legs kicking, his face bulging with fear.

'Apologise to the priestess,' said the captain of the guard slowly and deliberately, his voice soft and menacing.

'I'm sorry,' whispered the ferryman hoarsely.

'Next time, never cheat or rob from a passenger,' Amra told him.

'Yes,' gasped the ferryman.

The captain dropped him and he fell to the floor, then backwards onto the upturned bench. The other patrons in the inn watched Amra and her guards leave. No-one spoke or moved a muscle. They were too frightened.

The thieving sea captain lay where he had fallen. Who was this strange woman-child? He had thought she was a savage but she was obviously the priestess of some distant King. Why else would the Royal Trojan guards be protecting her? If only he had known, he would never have taken her dagger!

✷

Peta lay in the long summer grass, trying to ignore the ants crawling over her leg. She winced every time their tiny pincers bit into the tender flesh behind her knee, but still she didn't move. She knew that any movement could scare away her quarry, and she was too tired to chase him further.

All her focus, all her concentration was on the bee. It had been resting on a leaf for some time now. Peta was exhausted from running and was glad of the relief, but she knew that as the Sun God began to sink towards his nightly death into the Eternal Sea, the bee would need to return and tell the hive about the new source of food and drink he had found. Suddenly the insect launched itself into the air. Peta half stood, half crouched, preparing her body for another bout of action. She waited a moment before running in the direction it was flying, following it to a meadow which she had only explored once or twice before. She was a long way from home and was concerned that the distance would be too great for her to return in safety before it was dark. But, joy of joys, when she arrived at another meadow beyond the nearby hill, Peta saw other bees in the air in front of her and knew that she was close to the hive. Another moment and she saw the hive in a tree. Amra would have been so proud of her. So would her mother. Her mother, now long dead, had loved the taste of honey.

Peta flushed the bees out of the hive, just as Amra had shown her. She set alight the pile of brush and wood with

496

the firestones which her father had given her, then piled damp leaves on top to make smoke. When the bees had been reduced to sluggish movement only, Peta took her knife and cut away a large portion of the honeycomb inside the hive. She placed it into the bag she had brought with her, tied it quickly, wrapped it around itself several times and ran back home, laughing as she did so. She wondered what Amra would say if only she could see her now. She knew she would be proud of Peta the honey gatherer.

Amra had been gone for three cycles of the moon and Peta missed her desperately. Her father had become more sad and withdrawn as each day went by. Peta had raised the subject of Amra's return many times but her father didn't want to talk. All he would say was: 'She will return when she returns. We must put our faith in the Gods and in Amra's strength and cunning.'

Peta had slowly come to understand why Amra had to return. The other children had told her. She had asked her father but he had denied it vigorously, telling her not to be silly. But Peta knew that Amra had gone on a long journey because the Headman had dreamt that Amra's sacrifice would stop the iron men coming to the village. Amra had persuaded him to let her journey to the land of the Hittites to find the secret of making iron, instead of sacrificing her. Peta couldn't understand why her father was so morose. Amra would soon return. She would bring back the secret and everything would be all right.

Peta was tired from the long day and alternated her running with walking. She wished she had Amra's strength; Amra could run all the way. But it wouldn't be long now before her body was as big and strong as Amra's. Eventually she came to one of the hills overlooking the river valley. Down in the valley she saw her village; many people were swimming in the river to relieve themselves from the heat of the day. Others brought water to the crops from the river and others drove the oxen in new fields to plough up fresh ground so that her village would have more food in the winter months. She sat down on the top of the hill and rested. She enjoyed this view. She was much higher than the others and that made her feel strong. The thought made her laugh. She would tell Amra when she returned; Amra would enjoy the joke. It was silly because when she went down to the village again she was the same height as the other children. She became a little girl again.

Peta looked into the distance. She could see as far away as two hills. There was a path which snaked up one of the hills and over the other side. She had never been over that road; it was too far away. Travellers used the road, and those from her village who traded with other villages. They came back telling stories of what they had experienced on the road. Peta enjoyed the stories. Amra would be coming back along that road. According to her father, she should be returning soon. In fact her father had said she had to return soon or it would be too late. Too late for what? Peta often couldn't understand her father's words.

She looked up at the sky. The Sun God was almost dying and would soon fall into the Eternal Sea. Opposite him, high in the sky, was the Goddess of the Moon. She had been full a few days ago but now she was beginning to wane. In a few more days she would be just a thin sliver, starving, unloved, cold, uncared for, and then she would give birth again to a new moon and her light would protect travellers at night. That was the best of times, when the moon was full with her child, white and clear. At those times Peta could see the body of the Moon Goddess, could see her breasts and her stomach and the scar that was made by giving birth to other children. When the Moon Goddess was full was when life was at its best. But this time came only after the Moon Goddess died, and that would happen in a few days.

Peta saw that she had allowed the darkness to fall around her. She should return home quickly before her father became anxious. She looked one last time at the long road which wound over the hills. One day she would be standing here and she would see Amra. Then life would be good again.

※

It had been a long and difficult day. Even the Nubian guards were exhausted from travelling over the mountains. They had been riding for so long now, enduring the hardships of life lived without the comfort of a house, that all their initial excitement at the start of the journey had faded away. Amra knew the others still had doubts about her ability to guide them back to her village. They still had a number of days of travelling along the banks of the great river before reaching the tributary which ran into it and which would lead them to the safety of her home.

Night was falling. It was still hot and the insects were buzzing fiercely. Mithrassa-Urbek complained that if he had to eat another fresh river fish he would vomit. The moon was no longer full. It was already losing its body and soon would be a sliver. Amra had to be back in her village before the death of the Moon Goddess. For by the time the moon died, she would have used up all the time the Headman and the Medicine Man had given her to return with the secret of making iron.

They had to keep up the pace or they would arrive too late to save Peta. Every time Mithrassa-Urbek, exhausted, had begged to stop the journey in the middle of the afternoon, Amra had refused, saying that she would continue on her own if necessary. Eventually, after many days, he seemed to have accepted the rhythm of the journey. He stopped complaining and followed the others as they rode silently on their horses.

The Nubian guards were wonderful hunters, used to finding food in the deserts of their own home. Their skills were equal to, perhaps even better than Amra's. They knew how to lay traps. They knew how to stalk an animal and they were experts with bow and arrow. The only thing they didn't know was how to fish. That was something Amra had been able to teach them.

Mithrassa-Urbek's first taste of river fish had come as an unpleasant surprise. 'It's like eating mud,' he complained. She laughed at the way his face grimaced. 'The first time I tasted fish from this river, it was like that. But when you're hungry, you get used to it and it begins to taste good.'

Amra was starving after a day riding Wind. Picking at the bones of her carp with her fingers, her mouth full of flesh and skin, she said to him, 'It's delicious. What's the matter?'

'It's as if the ground is inside my mouth. The fish from the sea is fresh and tastes sweet. But this,' he said, pointing to the carp, 'this,' he shook his head, searching for a word, 'it tastes like mud.'

The captain of the guard ate his fish with obvious relish. 'It tastes different, master, but it tastes good.'

Mithrassa-Urbek scraped the fish from his mouth. 'Have we meat left?'

'We have some venison, and some hare that we caught a few days ago,' said Amra.

'Good. Cut me some of the leg from the deer and I'll roast it over the fire.'

'Tomorrow,' said the guard, standing to obey his master, 'when we come to the end of our day's journey, my men and I will go in search of bear or wild boar. That will be a feast for us.'

Mithrassa-Urbek's eyes lit up. 'Yes,' he said.

'And I,' said Amra, wiping her mouth with a fleshy leaf, 'will find wild roots to cook. We've ridden long and hard and we've made do with food. Tomorrow, Mithrassa-Urbek, I and my cooking pot will make you a meal which even King Praxis would enjoy.'

The guard returned with a large portion of venison which he threw onto the fire. The camp suddenly filled with the smell of roasting meat. Mithrassa-Urbek's mouth watered and the smile on his face assured Amra that tomorrow he would be a much happier man.

The following days brought them closer and closer to Amra's village. Amra knew where she was going, and leading all the horses seemed to give Wind extra spirit; they moved at a fast pace. The company had long since broken up into tribal units. Amra and Mithrassa-Urbek led the group swiftly and confidently through the forests, always keeping sight of the river as they rode. There was no need to ride secretly, as Amra had done on her first journey. There could be no danger to her with Mithrassa-Urbek and the guards by her side, and even when they passed the place where the men had forced their penises inside her, Amra rode by swiftly, feeling taller and more powerful than ever.

Behind Mithrassa-Urbek and Amra came two of the Nubian guards. Their eyes darted from place to place, constantly on the lookout for attackers. Behind the two Nubian guards came the four metalworkers leading a pack horse which bore their heavy metalworking equipment and ores. At the rear were the other two Nubian guards, who occasionally left the party and circled back to ensure that they were not being followed.

They had journeyed over the mountains and down beside the great river. Even Mithrassa-Urbek was amazed at the river's size and power. They travelled upstream until a smaller river branched off, forming a tributary which Amra recognised as it fell into the great river. It was the river which eventually ran through the valley in which her village was situated.

'How far is it now?' Mithrassa-Urbek asked.

'When I was on my own it took me seven days to reach this place. I thought I was travelling quickly but I think we have returned in a much shorter time. It might take us three days, maybe four, before we reach my village.'

'Will we be in time to save your sister?'

Amra nodded. 'Yes. Unless anything happens to us we should arrive a day or two before the birth of the new moon.'

Mithrassa-Urbek could see the excitement growing in Amra's eyes as they came closer and closer to her home. Her pace and her vitality seemed to increase. So did her dreadful jokes – hiding in the forest and jumping out at him, throwing stones at him from behind the foliage, warning him of wild beasts which were close by when there were none. This playful and skittish girl was another Amra. One who was excited to be going home. He thought about how she had changed from a savage to a woman, almost before his eyes. She had entranced the whole of the most powerful city in the world and had saved the life of a prince who had tried to violate her. She had confronted the ugly-looking sea captain in the inn without asking anybody to help her. And she had been strong and brave on a long and difficult journey. Yet now, she was behaving like a child again, more like the savage he had first met that day so long ago just outside the city of Troy. Mithrassa-Urbek had had many children by many wives. Some of them he loved deeply, others had grown to disappoint him. He wondered how it would feel to have a daughter like Amra.

CHAPTER 29

Feyodor had not heard from Natalie for over three weeks and had focused his energy on a relationship with Anna, a whore paid for by Lomonosov. Every time he asked Lomonosov about Natalie, he was told that she was out of Moscow, on a business trip, overseas, indisposed. With profound regret, Feyodor accepted the lies. He had no option but to do so. Natalie had moved out of her apartment and he had no idea where she was living. But whenever he was naked, sweating and forcing his body in and out of Anna's, he closed his eyes to her real and present beauty and instead fantasised about Natalie, that face he loved so much. So when she phoned him out of the blue and asked him to meet her at an address not a kilometre from where his office was situated, he almost tripped over himself to get out of the door.

Her breathy voice had whispered deliciously in his ear. 'There are things I want to do to you. I want you to get over here as quickly as possible.' He had scribbled down the address and now he checked the building number against the crumpled piece of paper. There were twenty apartments in the building; hers was number fourteen. He rang the bell and heard the door click open immediately. It was an expensive building, the type that once would have been occupied by senior Party officials but now was the exclusive preserve of Moscow's wealthy elite. He ran up the stairs and knocked gently on her door.

She was breathtaking, more beautiful than he remembered. Half a head taller than him, she was swathed in a black cocktail dress even though it was only four o'clock in the afternoon. She was wearing high-heeled black shoes, sheer black stockings and was dripping with gold jewellery. But it was her smell that excited him. If he were a dog, he would be panting in anticipation just standing next to her. Natalie's hair was piled up on top of her head, revealing her slender neck. In Paris she could have been a top fashion model but even if she earned ten thousand dollars a day he was sure she was earning more through her Mafia connections. And she had called him. She wanted him.

Natalie took his hand and put her finger over his lips when he began to speak. Like a little boy she led him over to the couch. His drink, whisky and ice, was already poured in a frosted tumbler. God, he loved her. He loved everything about her. He would give up everything else in his life if the next few minutes could last forever. All he wanted to do was to disappear inside the warmth, the tightness, the wetness of her body. He never wanted to be separated from her. She was everything he had fantasised about and now she was his reality.

They sat. He could hardly breathe for the excitement. He wanted to ask her where she had been, why she had suddenly called him now, did she really want him or was it still a part of the pretence? But she would allow no questions. Instead she put her arms around him and pressed her lips to his. Her mouth was so hot and wet and soft. Her tongue entwined with his and he felt her long fingers skilfully undoing his tie and his shirt buttons. His chest was exposed as he lay back and she went down on her knees between his legs. She undid the zip on his trousers.

It was her warmth that did it. That and the wetness of her mouth. He lasted no more than ten seconds. Smiling she stood and looked down at his flaccid form, his whole body deflated and relaxed in the afterglow of orgasm. He didn't hear her leave the room; his eyes and ears were closed to his surroundings. He was breathing deeply, reliving his orgasm, lost in the exploding moments of lust. So he was shocked when he heard Maxim Lomonosov's voice. 'I threw that last one in for good measure, my friend. I thought you deserved it.'

Feyodor opened his eyes and saw his business partner standing opposite him. His hands shot down to his groin and he quickly fastened his zip.

'What are you doing here?' he asked.

'Bad news, I'm afraid. I thought I'd sweeten it with a few minutes with Natalie.'

'What?'

'Bad news from Turkey. The plan has blown up in our faces. I'm afraid the shit is about to hit the fan. It was so close but then this fucking Moslem priest over there blew the whole scheme wide open. Just like Natalie's done to you.'

Feyodor had no idea what Lomonosov was talking about. But once his partner had outlined the details his euphoria quickly subsided. Suddenly the life he had so carefully constructed, with all its glorious potential for the future – the Directorship of the Museum, Natalie and Anna as his joint mistresses, money in the bank, getting rid of his hideous wife – it was all over.

'Is there nothing we can do?'

'We?' said Lomonosov. 'What do you mean, we?'

Feyodor felt a chill seeping through his body. 'You're as involved in this as I am. We're partners.'

'Excuse me?' said Lomonosov.

'You can't get away with this. You can't leave me to face the music on my own. You've made ten times more money than I have. You've got contacts. You can surely get me out of this.'

'The problem isn't mine, my dear friend. The problem is yours.'

'But . . .'

Lomonosov reached into his inside jacket pocket. Feyodor's eyes widened in fear as he expected to see a gun emerge. Instead Lomonosov withdrew a wallet. He opened it and a dozen photographs fell out. He threw them on the glass table. Feyodor picked them up: they were photographs of himself and Natalie. A death sentence. Natalie was wearing jewellery which quite obviously came from the Schliemann collection, ear rings, golden hair ornaments, gold rings. In some shots Feyodor was placing the jewellery on her gorgeous body. He could scream and shout from now until the end of the decade about Lomonosov's involvement but these photographs were evidence that he had stolen the treasure from the Pushkin Museum. His career was over. So was his life.

Natalie came out of the bathroom. She was still wearing her diaphanous clothes but suddenly she didn't look nearly as beautiful as Feyodor remembered.

The next twenty-four hours were among the most harrowing of his life. Suicide again became a real option. His emotions varied between anger, disgust and a morbid sense of reality. When the phone call came from Vardian he knew that it was just a matter of time before he was to die. Obviously Vardian had now got the photographs and would soon hand them over to the police. He drove to the Kremlin.

'Read this,' the Minister said the moment Feyodor entered his office. 'We may have got rid of the Germans but the fucking Turks are at our throats again. I thought their former Minister was bad, but this new Minister for Antiquities is a real bastard. At least the old one was polite in her demands. This new Minister insists — *insists* mind you — that we put the treasure on show immediately so that his officials can come over and examine it. Of all the fucking things! I thought this was dead and buried with the resignation of that bitch Turkish Minister, dead and buried. I was wrong. Too optimistic.'

The Minister scowled at the startled archaeologist. 'I told you to finish it off, you idiot. Now it's raised its ugly head again. I can't stall any longer. You've let me down again, fool! Go back to your office and do a thorough audit of the treasure. Every single piece. Then we'll invite their delegation over so that they can see it. But I want security guards everywhere. They're not getting their hands on it. Knowing fucking Turks they'll try to stuff some of it into their pockets. Well, fuck them. They won't get their hands on our treasure. Zhukov worked his balls off winning Germany in '45. Should we give back the spoils of war just because of the Turks? No, we'll tie them up in the courts for years. By the time they decide on the ownership we'll all be dead and buried and it will be somebody else's problem. Now go! I want a complete audit of Schliemann's treasure by the end of the week.'

The Minister picked up some more papers for signing, leaving Feyodor to replace the Turks' letter on his desk and leave. Ashen-faced, he turned and retraced his steps, past the Minister's secretary, out of the building, back to the car park.

He sat in the car for a long moment before turning on the ignition. He didn't even know what was going through his mind. Thoughts of life and death, of fear, of darkness. He didn't know how he drove home or the route he took. He remembered nothing. It was all so mechanical.

He decided it was a mechanical process and that he needed to end his life. Not slashing his wrists or swallowing pills. Something cold, hard and distant. Something that didn't cause pain. He pulled up outside his apartment block, his mind working on where to get a rubber hose pipe and how to fit it from the exhaust pipe into his car.

❋

David packed up his and Sarah's luggage and checked out of the Hotel Turkoman. The new hotel in Taksin Square had been chosen for its anonimity; there he and Sarah would blend into the sea of tourists. It was the archetype of modern plastic efficiency. Its foyer was an architect's attempt at creating instant Turkish imperial magnificence: the fake chandeliers, the bell-hops dressed as characters out of a production of Mozart's *Abduction from the Seraglio* and the ersatz marble coffee tables all contributed to the effect, a fraud perpetrated on gullible tourists. But it would do.

Ensconced in the new room, David unpacked then looked at his watch. He still had an hour before Sarah was due to arrive. He had asked the army camp commandant if he might pick her up but his request had been refused. Sarah had been released from her cell in the camp the moment the cleric made his admission to the police and had been transferred to VIP quarters normally used by visiting parliamentarians. But because word of her location had been leaked to Moslem fundamentalists it had been decided that, for her own safety, she would be driven in a blacked-out convoy to the north west of Istanbul before being transferred to another car and then taken to the basement of the new hotel. Her final location would be known to only a handful of people.

David paced the room, looked at his watch for the third time in ten minutes, and in desperation went downstairs for coffee. There he read an English newspaper, spoke to a few American tourists about places they should visit and places they should avoid – knowing they would ignore his advice – then returned to his room fifteen minutes before Sarah was due to arrive.

The fifteen minutes stretched into an excruciating half an hour before there was a knock on the door. His heart pounding, David ran and pulled it open. Sarah stood there alone, looking frail and drawn but beaming an enormous smile. He hugged her and half-carried her into the room, closing the door behind them. They kissed and held hands and kissed again. He offered her tea or coffee. She refused both.

'How are you feeling, darling?' he asked.

'Shaken. Depressed. Enormously relieved. Desperate to get out of this fucking country. I just want to go home, David. I just want to go back to New York where I'm safe. Where I'm with my own people. I want to see my mother and father again. I want to see your mum and dad. I want bagels and lox in a delicatessen on 39th street. I want to listen to the sounds of drive-by shootings and hear the police sirens I'm familiar with. I want to watch muggers running down the street being chased by old ladies. I just want to go home.'

He smiled and nodded, wondering if he would have retained his sense of humour if he'd suffered like her. 'I haven't booked a flight for us yet,' he said. 'I didn't know what your feelings would be. Whether you'd be fit enough to travel. I've checked the times though. We can get a plane today, tomorrow, any time. Do you want to leave today?'

Sarah was silent a moment. 'I want to go so badly, I'm almost in tears,' she said finally. 'But I've got something to do before I go.'

She stared at the floor, too embarrassed to look at him.

'I know what you want to do, Sarah.'

'Tell me,' she said.

'You want to confront Barrak.' She nodded. 'I was afraid of that,' David said.

'I have to, David. I have to square off with that son of a bitch.'

'But he might already have been arrested. He could be in prison right now. He'll be suitably punished by the authorities. Why do you have to get involved?'

'He hasn't been arrested yet. I checked it out this morning with the police ministry, who are handling things. They aren't even going near him until they've got all the evidence. He's too senior in the ranks. They want to be certain of their ground. It could take another week before the police knock on his door.'

'I just don't understand why you'd want to continue the nightmare.'

'It would be so easy to let the police have him, but it's beyond that with me. It's not revenge, David, it's – oh shit! I can't explain it. I've just got to face him. Look him in the eye.'

David was concerned. 'No more vendettas, Sarah. No more getting even. You've been through a nightmare. We all have. I've done things no cellist ought to have done. You've been in prison. There have been riots. Your life has been threatened. Now isn't the time to get even, it's time to go home. Know when to withdraw. You can write another OpEd piece for the *New York Times*. You can scream from the rooftops. Just so long as they're American rooftops.'

'Honey,' she said, 'I know what you did for me. Getting that tape recording was the bravest thing a man could ever do. Confronting a Mafia don – I can't even think of the words. Bravery doesn't begin to come into it. But now we've got that tape recording, we have to use it. Let me explain why.'

She did. And he smiled.

David booked seats to America three days after Sarah's release from the army camp. They had planned their remaining time in Turkey meticulously. As long as Sarah remained incognito there should be no hostility towards her from the Islamic groups. The media had reported that Sarah had left the country and was travelling through Europe and at the ensuing press conference, the Minister for Justice had named the cleric from the Mehmet Pasha mosque as deliberately implicating an innocent tourist in order to create social unrest. No mention was made of accusations against the Director of the Ministry for Antiquities, Dr Yussef Barrak. Sarah and David knew why. They wondered what he was thinking right now. Obviously he knew that the cleric had given evidence against him but his best defence would be to deny it, to stonewall. He had no idea that David had a tape recording which irrefutably implicated him in the plot.

Over breakfast Sarah and David discussed their plans for the day. They were interrupted by a knock on the door; the concierge delivered a letter addressed to Sarah. The envelope bore the logo of the Ministry for Antiquities. Sarah ripped it open and read the letter aloud to David:

'My dear Sarah,
I'm so pleased that your innocence has been established and that you have been released from prison. The accusations against you were always baseless. I knew it from the beginning. I hope you appreciate that I was incapable of speaking on your behalf because of my position as a government minister. Nonetheless, I hope that our friendship will not be affected. I wish you luck in your return to life in America, if indeed that is your plan. I hope we will have the opportunity to meet again. I have the highest regard for you and your professional skills. I must also offer my apologies to your fiancé, David Rose, for being unable to see him when he presented himself at my parliamentary offices the other day. I'm sure if you put yourself in my position, you will understand why.
Sincerely . . .'

It was signed by the Minister. David shrugged. 'Just another politician,' he said contemptuously.

Sarah shook her head. 'Oh no, when I first met her she was far more than a politician to me. She held out the hand of friendship when I got here. Then she let me down, big time. And I need to tell her that.'

She went to the writing desk and stayed there for fifteen minutes, thinking, writing and thinking again. She passed the letter across to David and sat back to await his response.

'My dear Minister,'
Your letter coincided with my release from prison. I would like to accept your apologies but I find it difficult. While I recognise that there were professional and legal constraints on your ability to speak publicly on my behalf, I recognise no such constraints on your rights as a human being to speak to me as a friend, or indeed to ensure that privately I received encouragement. I was locked up in prison, desperate for a sign that somebody, apart from my fiancé, David Rose, was fighting for my release.

Justice was abused by your fellow countrymen. I know you knew that this was happening and yet you said and did nothing. I was pilloried, my life was threatened, and you were a willing bystander, happy to see me as the tragic victim of an unfortunate circumstance. There's a saying which I believe is true: Evil will triumph while good people remain silent. I apply this to you. When I first arrived I thought you were a friend. But now I recognise that you were nothing more than a politician using those around you for your own benefit. I reject your offer of friendship, and reject and question the sincerity of your note. I accuse you of the worst form of complicity, of knowing silence. I do not wish to see you again.

In future all my dealings with the Turkish government will be through my lawyers. When I return to the United States

I intend to institute proceedings against your government for wrongful arrest and wrongful imprisonment.

Sarah Kaplan.'

'Jesus!' David hissed.

Sarah shrugged.

'You realise you'll never get another job in Turkey again if you send that note off?'

She laughed and reached over and took his hand. 'David, yesterday I didn't have the energy to thank you properly. A good night's sleep and making love to you last night has recharged my batteries. I owe you my life. I owe you my freedom. More than I'll ever be able to repay you.'

He gripped her hand tightly. 'You owe me nothing more than a wedding ring and the word "yes" to the following question. Will you marry me?'

'I told you before that I would, David.'

'I want to hear you say it again, Sarah. Will you marry me?'

'Yes.'

'You're in Ankara? Why?' Barrak's voice sounded thin and reedy on the telephone.

'We're here to see you.'

'I'm afraid that is impossible. I have appointments throughout the day. You have wasted your journey.'

'You don't understand. You have no option but to see me,' said David.

'Are you threatening me?'

'You *will* see me, Dr Barrak. I'm here with Sarah. We have certain things which you need to hear, a certain tape recording. I repeat that you will see me.'

'Is this a crude attempt at blackmail?'

'Don't be ridiculous, Dr Barrak. We'll be in your office in half an hour.'

'I will not see you,' he shouted in desperation. 'You will be waiting in my secretariat, unattended. I might even have the police remove you.'

'Then you will suffer the consequences,' said David. 'We'll be in your office reception area. If you don't see us, our next move will be to go to the police with this tape recording.'

'The police have already been to see me. Naturally, I have denied the allegations made by this demented cleric. First he blames your fiancée, then me. How much credibility do you think he has now? There is no case against me. I am free and will remain so.'

'They might have no evidence, Dr Barrak, but we do. You will see us.'

David put the phone down and he and Sarah caught a cab from Ankara airport into the city. Thirty minutes later, they were standing in Dr Barrak's reception area. His assistant begged their forgiveness but explained that Dr Barrak was unavailable except by appointment.

Sarah was not so polite. 'Unless you inform Dr Barrak of our presence we will go to the police with evidence against him which will see him in prison by tonight. I strongly suggest you pick up that phone and tell him we're here.'

His assistant nodded and spoke quietly into the receiver. 'Dr Barrak says he can spare you a few moments only.'

Sarah had never been into Barrak's private office. She had been in the building several times before but only for meetings with the group charged by the Minister to reclaim Priam's treasury from the Russians. Barrak's office was large and ornate, exquisitely furnished and meticulous in every detail. She would have expected no less from a man like him, concerned with outward appearance rather than function. His shelves were lined with books and expensive artworks adorned his walls. He was, to all intents and purposes, an Ottoman functionary.

But when they saw him, they were both shocked. This was a different man to the affable controlled gentlemanly bureaucrat who had dined with them just a week earlier. The Yussef Barrak Sarah had first met had been, at different times, imperious, pompous, patronising, sycophantic and ingratiating. But here was a man clearly on the edge of hysteria. There was a wildness in his eyes, the look of the hunted, and Sarah was shocked by his pallor. Under other circumstances, she might have felt sorry for him but this was a man who would quite happily have seen her destroyed for his own personal gain. All she could feel was contempt. She touched her amulet as she sat down.

Barrak waited until his assistant had left the room before speaking, 'Well?' he barked. His voice was hoarse.

David took a cassette out of his pocket. 'This is a recording of a conversation with Ozman Urzak.' Barrak's eyes widened. 'You know the man, don't you?'

Barrak stared at David in disbelief. Urzak had been phoning him for days now but he'd refused his calls. How in the name of everything holy had this American established a link between him and Urzak? How? He fought to maintain self-control. 'Urzak is a well-known functionary. A man who is devoutly Islamic. A follower of the way.'

'He's a Mafia don,' said Sarah. 'He's a drug dealer and he trades drugs for arms. His activities spread from the Iraqi border all the way through to southern Russia.'

Barrak looked at her, his face a mask of incomprehension. 'What?' he said quietly.

'The man you met in your office a week before I was arrested by the police is a notorious criminal. Are you denying you knew that?'

Barrak's mouth dropped. He was staggered. Mafia? He said nothing.

'Did you hear what I said, Dr Barrak?' Sarah had become the prosecuting attorney.

'What?' he said again, his mind grappling with the enormity of what she was saying.

'You conceived a plan using me as a tool to bring down this government. The Mafia boss was the mechanism, the go-between which would ensure its success.'

Barrak shook his head. 'No! No, he came to me as one of the faithful. He told me that he was ... he said nothing about ... the Mafia?'

'You are fully implicated by him on this tape, Dr Barrak. There are copies of it in a safe in a lawyer's office in Istanbul and it will be made available to the police if David and I are unsatisfied with your answers. Do you understand that clearly?'

'This man, Ozman Urzak, is a devout Moslem. He came to me with a wild story, something about this secular government having to be replaced by an Islamic government. He tried to get me involved. I have a full note of our conversation in my files. I warned him I would refer the matter to the police, but I haven't had the time.' Barrak sounded like a bad actor, rehearsing his lines.

'Mafia?' he whispered. He was stunned. Sarah and David had to strain to hear him. 'He told me the way to do it was to create a scandal. When the Minister of Antiquities fell, so would the other government ministers, and then the whole edifice would be brought down. I don't understand what you're saying. The Mafia?'

Sarah was more used to defence than prosecution but she knew a deeply shocked man when she saw one.

'Let me play the tape for you,' said David. From his briefcase he pulled out a tape recorder, slid the cassette into the gate and pressed 'Play'. Bengazi had preset the tape to start at the point where Urzak told his visitors to ensure that Barrak didn't panic and kept his mouth shut.

Barrak recognised the voice. Yet, somehow, hearing the tape strengthened him. 'I will deny this,' he said, the colour beginning to return to his face. 'It is a fabrication. I've met this man once and I have a file note on it. These statements are nonsense. I will deny everything to the police.'

'As you wish,' said Sarah. 'To me it's quite clear, and I'm sure it will be to them. Good day to you, Dr Barrak.'

She stood and David put away the tape recorder.

'Wait,' Barrak said. 'What is your purpose in coming here? What do you want?'

Sarah sat down again. An experienced attorney, she knew at that point she had won. She drove her points home so there would be no chance of a debate. 'Three things. First, a letter from you to the Minister saying I had nothing whatsoever to do with this alleged theft of the stone from the mosque in Istanbul. The letter, which will be made public, will say that you were aware of a scheme but failed to stop it going ahead because of your desire to bring down the government. Second, a letter of resignation to the Minister and an assurance to her that you will retire from public life now and forever. And third, a letter of apology to me to be written to every major newspaper throughout Turkey in which you accept that my role in this affair was absolutely innocent and that the evidence against me was concocted by this cleric.'

Barrak looked at her in astonishment. 'But then I am finished. If I write these letters . . . my career . . .'

'You're finished anyway, Barrak,' said David. 'The cleric from the mosque has told the police all about you and the scheme you cooked up. Sure you've denied it and they haven't got enough evidence to press charges, but with this tape recording they'll be able to link one incident with the other. Then they'll have more than enough evidence to put you in prison and throw away the key. You're looking at charges of treason, sedition, blasphemy, conspiracy to pervert the course of justice and God knows what else.'

'But if I write these letters I'll still be charged.'

'Not without this tape recording, Dr Barrak,' said Sarah. 'It will look as if you were going to do things but decided against it at the last minute. It was this son of a bitch cleric who took it the whole way. Now you're sacrificing him to save yourself from going to jail. You want to make your conscience clear and retreat from public life.'

'May I have a day or two to think this through?'

'You may have until the end of today to write these letters, send them out, and send copies to Dr Mustafa Bengazi at his office in the Topkapi Museum. Of course we'll check with everybody to ensure their receipt. If by nine o'clock tomorrow morning nothing has been received we will go to the police and present them with this tape recording.'

'I don't understand why you're doing this. We are enemies. Surely it suits you to see me imprisoned? This way I will be disgraced, but I will not go to prison.'

Sarah smiled. 'Actually it suits me more to see you humiliated and stripped of your office. That strips you of power which is far preferable to a couple of years in prison. As to the cleric, frankly I don't give a damn.'

'You're a very cruel woman,' he said.

She shook her head. 'I came here as an innocent, a friend of this government. From the very beginning you behaved towards me like an old-fashioned patriarch. You failed to recognise that I am a woman of power, of education. You still think that women should be meek housewives, dressed in a *chadour*, obediently doing whatever it is that you command. Well, maybe some of the poor wretches who live in Turkey or Saudi Arabia or Iran, but not me, mister. Not Sarah Kaplan. I was treated badly by you at the beginning and subsequently I've been treated disgracefully by the Turkish authorities and the government. This country deserves better than you.

'David and I have met some wonderful people, seen some incredible sights. Turkey is an extraordinary place. But you and people like you are a cancer. You have no place in the modern world. Get rid of people like you and Turkey will be one of the greatest countries on earth. That's why I'm going to these lengths. You see, I'm not willing to leave before wrongs are righted. And you, Dr Barrak, are the greatest wrong in my life at the moment.'

Barrak nodded silently. How badly he had misjudged this woman. And now she was his nemesis. What a fool not to have seen through her. She was, to all intents and purposes, a man.

'What about this Ozman Urzak, this person who is the Mafia don?' he asked. 'Are you going to inform the police about him?'

David laughed. 'You don't seriously think the police will move against him, do you? They've been trying to catch him for years. He'll have a whole village full of witnesses to prove he was never here. No,' said David, 'in this regard he's just small fry, a cog in the wheels to bring down the government for reasons we don't yet know. Not like you.'

Barrak took a sip of water and nodded. 'While I still hold my position,' he said coldly, 'I believe I am entitled to give orders. You will leave my office.'

'Of course,' said Sarah, rising. She turned and walked out.

David took one last look at Yussef Barrak. Incredibly he seemed stronger and more in control than when they had first entered. Even the bombshell they had dropped on him had failed to diminish him. David left his office wondering whether this truly would be the finish of the whole thing.

The journey home was euphoric. Sarah read the newspaper stories several times over on the plane. 'HEAD OF MINISTRY RESIGNS AMID SCANDAL.' 'EX-MINISTER RETURNS TO UNIVERSITY TO RIDE OUT SCANDAL FOLLOWING PILLORY BY OPPOSITION.' She felt vindicated, excited. The letters from Barrak to the editors of most Turkish newspapers had chased the Minister from Parliament. While they didn't implicate her, Barrak was her departmental Director and the Opposition had bayed for her blood for the way in which she had run her Ministry. The Prime Minister, desperately trying to keep his government together, had jettisoned her to preserve himself. Well, that's life, that's politics, Sarah thought.

She looked down at the landscape of the Carpathian Mountains far below. A ribbon of silver ran across the green and brown canvas of the ground, the mighty Danube running down to the Black Sea. The earth so far below looked peaceful and uncomplicated. Only a year earlier, she had been in that very region, in Slovakia, and had discovered the depths of her ancestry there, her roots. It was there, amongst the verdant fields and ancient villages, that she had learnt what it meant to truly be a part of her ancient religion, to be a Jew.

She tried to remember the towns and villages that had been so familiar to her only a year back; Novosad, Kosice, the archaeological Bronze Age dig at Nizna Misla. Her hand involuntarily strayed to her breast where she felt the security of her amulet with its strange markings of the bull on one side and the owl on the other. What had been going through the mind of the Bronze Age craftsman all those millennia ago when he carved those designs in the pure gold ingot? Would she ever know why it carried the markings of the ancient city of Troy? Like the identity of woman who had originally owned the wondrous jewellery and headdresses which

Heinrich Schliemann had romantically ascribed to Helen of Troy, the answer to the mystery of Sarah's amulet would remain lost to the mists of human history.

And was it only an hour ago, she mused, that they had farewelled Mustafa Bengazi, promising that they would never lose touch, that they would show him the best time he'd ever had when he visited New York? Promises. So easy to make. There had been a look of loss on his face as they kissed each other goodbye and offered profuse thanks for the umpteenth time. Was it the loss of their friendship, recent yet so deep? Or something far more sinister? Was he hiding from them the fact that nobody could survive as a whistleblower in a country still dominated by an Ottomanic culture? He had gone against the rules and had stood firm as a man of honesty and morality against a culture which still valued nepotism before ability. She would never know. She could write to him and ask but the subtlety of the abuse he would undoubtedly suffer would not be easily defined or put into words. It was an abuse of damaged career opportunities, lack of funding for his work – all too subtle for action to be taken. She prayed not, for his sake. He was a good and honourable man, the very best that Turkey could produce. She hoped all would be well.

She looked over David's shoulder as he read the newspaper. In a left-hand column, buried amid reports of economic collapse, deaths and murders, was a two-paragraph story headed 'PUSHKIN MUSEUM EXECUTIVE FOUND DEAD IN MOSCOW'. Sarah tried to read the details but David folded the newspaper too quickly. She would look at it some other time.

They stopped over in London then flew on to New York. Crossing the coast, Sarah looked down again at the ground far below. The plane wheeled to port and followed the windy Atlantic coastline down to New York

City. Her heart was beating with excitement. Just a few more miles, just a few more minutes, and she would be returning to her parents, to the rest of her family, and to a secure job, if she wanted it.

Did she want to return to Wall Street to work for a middle-ranking law firm? Maurie Friedlander had offered her a partnership, and the finance to support it. It was a golden opportunity. She had discussed it with David the night before they left Turkey and his reaction had stunned her. They had been drinking crisp white wine over a final meal in the hotel's restaurant when she told him that she had phoned Maurie to tell him that she was coming home. That was when he had offered her the partnership and the finance. She had asked David whether she should accept. It was a huge salary increase, the prospect of hundreds of thousands of dollars a year, financial security, stability, status. It was what every young about-to-be-married couple was desperate to achieve.

David had thought for a moment, then: 'I think you should give it a miss,' he had said.

'What!'

'You've gone beyond that, Sarah. You're not a Wall Street lawyer any more. You'd go crazy dealing with corporate restructures and leverage financing and whatever the hell those people do. You're not into black power suits and cold direct language anymore. You're a different woman. You need new challenges. Six months ago you were advising the Czech government about war crimes legislation. Two weeks ago you were advising the Turkish government on how to get their treasure back. Could you really sit with a table of grey-suited men talking about contract law?'

Sarah hadn't even thought about that aspect of the offer. The partnership had come as such a surprise that she hadn't for one moment considered what she would have to do for it – and for the rest of her life. 'Then, what should I do?' she had asked as their meal grew colder.

'Do what the hell you want. You want to work for a human rights group, do it. You want to get a job at the United Nations, great. You want to work for a black activist group, go for it. Just don't lock yourself into crap. You've had more experience in the last couple of years than any lawyer in New York. Use your experience to help other people. Use your training to stand up against the system and beat the shit out of men like Barrak or the equivalent sons of bitches in New York City. Go in for politics. Become a senator. You've got a huge profile. Trade on it. Or have a baby and become a housewife. Whatever happens, Sarah, don't go back to being a part of the system. That's so far behind you; it's just not you anymore.'

Sarah had nodded. She had to think clearly, to use her mind not her emotions.

The chief steward announced that they would soon be landing in New York. David folded up his newspaper. Sarah looked at him. She was so much in love with him, with his gentle ways, his sense of decency. And now there was a new David that she had never seen before – a man who was willing to go all out, regardless of the risks, to save her ass. What a catch!

She reached over and kissed him on the cheek. He turned and smiled. 'Thank you,' he said.

'You're welcome.'

CHAPTER 30

Amra stood at the top of the hill, waiting. Something prevented her from joining the others as they followed the river down the hill towards her village. She knew every tree along its bank, every curve of its path. It was implanted on her memory. She felt that she could almost see the fish which she knew were swimming below its surface.

In her mind, Amra had pictured this scene since the first day she'd left the village on her epic journey to the land of the Hittites. When things were at their worst she had kept herself going by imagining herself returning along the banks of the river and leading Wind down into the valley where her village was situated. She saw the village people running down the slope to greet her, calling her a hero. But not her father, or Peta. They were standing at the top of the hill, alone, proud, with outstretched arms.

That was in her mind. That was what she had imagined when she was away. But the closer she came to her home, the more reluctant she was to finish the journey. She couldn't understand what was wrong with her. And now, when they were only one bend in the river away from where she had caught Old Man Fish all that time ago, she couldn't go on with the others. Only Mithrassa-Urbek had understood. He had told her to take her time before she rushed back to the loving arms of her family. He seemed to understand the turmoil which was racing through her mind, a turmoil which she didn't understand herself.

So Amra stood on the top of the hill looking down at the distant figures of the men and women she knew so well. She couldn't see their faces but she knew by their movements, their gestures, who they were. She searched for her father and for Peta but couldn't see them. She looked for the Medicine Man. Soon he would take back possession of Wind. Amra hoped that he would allow her to ride him from time to time. She couldn't imagine never sitting astride Wind again, feeling his tireless energy, his awesome power beneath her.

It was the middle of the day. There were only a few days left of the old Moon Goddess's life before she died and gave birth to the new moon. Amra shivered in the cold air. She smelt the air, it was the smell of snow. She was just in time. A few more days and Peta would have been sacrificed. Amra knew her father would be worrying about her return and she had no intention of causing him any more concern. She ran back down the hill and smiled in gratitude at Mithrassa-Urbek, an unspoken message which nobody else in the group understood. Now she knew why she had been unable to simply ride into the village – she had needed time to re-orient herself.

Amra looked at the four metalworkers, surly, uncommunicative and resistant to inclusion, even during the long and arduous journey. She wondered how a man like her father, happy and outgoing when her mother was alive, devoted to his friends and family, would react to four such taciturn men. But they were there at the King's command and they would do what they were told or else Mithrassa-Urbek would have something to say.

The group of riders followed the riverbank, and crossed the water where it was shallow. As they left the river and urged their horses up the hill, a villager noticed them. He shouted to his friends and neighbours and people came from their houses to stare at the strangers. They had never seen such a sight before. Too small for an army or for a caravan of traders, the riders presented no threat to the village, but nonetheless the Headman's guards came out to greet them, fully armed with bows, arrows and spears.

But halfway down the hill, they stopped, turned and shouted up to the assembled villagers: 'Amra returns'.

A buzz of excitement coursed through the assembled villagers. Somebody ran to tell Amra's family. Hasga and Peta emerged from their house high on the hill. Amra thought her father seemed smaller than when she had left. But his smile told her that his depression had lifted.

Peta let out a cry of joy, clearly audible even from so far away, and ran down the hill through the crowd of villagers. Amra spurred Wind onwards then jumped down from the huge horse, catching the little girl in mid-flight as she launched herself upwards. They laughed and kissed and Amra swung her sister around and around, suddenly letting her go so that she flew through the air and landed on the ground. Peta rolled and laughed, then stood and ran back to hug Amra again. Her father, Hasga, also ran, outpacing the Headman and the Medicine Man. He hugged his daughter, whispering greetings into her ear, telling her he loved her and that everything would be all right again now that she had returned.

As greetings were exchanged, Mithrassa-Urbek and the metalworkers dismounted. Amra introduced them to her father and then began to introduce the others, but Mithrassa-Urbek stopped her. He was not interested in meeting the leaders of the village just yet. He particularly wanted to speak with Hasga. The Headman, somewhat overawed by the magnificence of Mithrassa-Urbek's cloak and leggings, and considerably intimidated by the four huge black-skinned Nubian guards who stood to attention at the rear of the party, drew back, encouraging Hasga to walk forward. Amra noticed that he was diffident before Mithrassa-Urbek. She couldn't understand why.

'You are the father of this wonderful girl?' asked Mithrassa-Urbek.

Hasga nodded.

Mithrassa-Urbek explained who he was and briefly outlined his relationship with Hasga's daughter. 'Amra, take off your amulet,' Mithrassa-Urbek asked. The girl did and handed it to him. Mithrassa-Urbek held it reverentially in his hands and proffered it to Amra's father, who looked at the amulet he had made with his own hands all those months ago. He had invested it with all the prayers he knew in order to protect Amra on her journey.

'You will see that we of Troy have added our own symbols to this amulet.' Other people close by crowded around to see what Mithrassa-Urbek was describing. 'The bull on this side represents the God Mithras, for whom your daughter Amra is now a priestess. No doubt she will tell you how this happened when she has rested and recovered from her long journey.' He turned the amulet over. 'This symbol may not be familiar to you in lands so far from Troy. It is the sacred owl, a symbol used only by the Royal Family of Troy. This mark was given to Amra by King Praxis himself, Ruler of the World and Lord and Master of All Others. The owl symbol states that Amra is the King's special friend, and that if ever she needs assistance in the future, he and his descendants will render such assistance to her. Do you understand?'

Hasga nodded, although he had only understood parts of what this extraordinary man had said. Mithrassa-Urbek took the amulet back from him, and as though crowning a monarch, placed it in veneration over Amra's head. What he did was designed specifically to be seen and understood by the Headman of the village. And indeed, it seemed to have an effect. The Headman came forward, and looked closely at Amra's amulet, nodding in satisfaction to himself.

Then he looked at Mithrassa-Urbek and said, 'Welcome. This is my village. Amra has done well. You have brought the secrets of making iron and we have much need for you. We know from others in the five valleys that the iron men with their iron weapons are nearby. We have little time.'

Mithrassa-Urbek nodded. 'King Praxis has commanded me to instruct these armourers and metalworkers to make iron weapons for you. They will make swords, lances and spears as well as arrowheads. These will help in your battle with the men with iron weapons. But alone, they are not enough. For what use are such weapons without an army of chariots?'

The Headman had no answer. Instead he said to Mithrassa-Urbek, 'You speak of things which I do not understand. Tonight, when we have food, we will talk.'

There was to be a great feast that night. People were even talking of slaughtering a cow in honour of the metalworkers and the wealthy and powerful man, Mithrassa-Urbek, who had travelled with them. But in truth, the real centre of attention – and amazement – were the four Nubian guards who stood rigidly to attention. The fair-skinned men and women, whose bodies were marked with traceries of blue lines, had never before seen men as tall or as powerful, or with skin as black as coal.

Amra led Mithrassa-Urbek and the guards into the village to show them her home. Her voice was filled with excitement and pride as she pointed out the various buildings. Mithrassa-Urbek found it hard to understand why. This village was a collection of wooden and straw huts, less sophisticated than the primitive rural villages in the land of the Hittites. Some of the houses even seemed to be made of mud. Amra had been privileged to live in one of the greatest buildings in the world. The palace of Troy had more rooms than anybody could count and the temples of Troy were buildings of wonder. People came from all over the entire world just to marvel at the city.

Yet, despite Amra having seen all of what Troy had to offer, she was showing Mithrassa-Urbek these small huts with much pride and joy. Were their positions reversed he would be ashamed of the place from whence he came. But not this strange and unaffected girl.

She showed him the room in her house where he would be sleeping. In Troy, this was the equivalent of a room which would be given to a young servant. Yet because of his fondness for Amra, Mithrassa-Urbek was willing to ignore his surroundings.

Later that night the great meeting of the village was called in honour of Amra and these strange and wonderful people she had brought back with her to save everyone from the onslaught of the men with iron weapons. The fire danced high into the night sky and the beer flowed liberally. The smell of roasting cow and the delicious aroma of cooking tubers and roots such as carrots, turnips and onions filled the air.

Troy seemed so far away, another world. In Troy there were no huge fires in the middle of the city, nor friends and neighbours sitting around laughing, telling stories and drinking beer. There was no Headman dressed in his animal skin of office, nor Medicine Man wearing the skin and the head of a lion, running around pointing his wisdom stick at people. There was no gaiety in Troy like the gaiety Amra was experiencing now.

For the first time in her life Amra was allowed to enter the fire circle as a full adult participant. The law of the village allowed her one request for her initiation: she had asked that Peta, her sister, could sit with her and her father, and that the three members of the family would be feted as one. The request had caused concern for the Medicine Man who believed that Peta was not yet ready for the initiation, but the Headman had overruled him. He had seen Peta develop in the months that Amra had been away, and she had become more confident. Although she was still some years from being recognised as an adult and able to sit in her own right in the circle, for this one special night the Headman decreed that she could be present.

Mithrassa-Urbek and the metalworkers from Troy sat on a raised platform as guests of special significance and honour. Even though Amra had seen the Headman and the Medicine Man sitting on this platform before, for the first time she realised that it was similar to the raised dais which held the King of Troy's throne. She wondered if there were any other similarities which she had failed to notice when she first entered Troy.

The women served the men on the platform meat while all others had to walk to the roasting cow and cut off for themselves delicious strips of its flesh as it turned on the spit. Mithrassa-Urbek in particular enjoyed the meat. Cow flesh wasn't unusual for him – indeed it was a common delicacy in the court of Troy, along with pheasant, ptarmigan, partridge and new-born lamb – but he had been forced to eat such awful food for so many days of the journey, that this meal was delicious. He ate with considerable gusto, much to the pleasure of the Headman.

The metalworkers, on the other hand, ate sparingly, mumbling as they bowed their heads over their plates of food. Hasga watched them carefully. There was a bond between these strange craftsmen that he couldn't understand. They communicated by secret signs and incantations, fingers held in a certain position, hands upturned, eyes narrowed, as though possessors of some secret knowledge. Was this secrecy between them something to do with making iron, he wondered. Would they ever teach him the secret? They had made it very clear that they were being forced to work under the command of this king they all talked about, Praxis, who had told them that they must make iron weapons for the village, but they had been extremely cautious when Hasga asked them *how* to make iron.

He had made iron many times in the past but it was the wrong type of iron. It always broke when he banged the sword or dagger against a rock, shearing into many pieces. And inside it was full of holes; the dark and soft impurities in the iron could easily be seen. The only iron which was good was that which fell from the sky, and it was so rare that he had only ever come across one piece. He had placed it in his kiln and melted it and it had shone a brilliant silver like a fish in the river. If only he could find the source of this iron from the sky. The iron which came from the red rocks, and which he found sometimes on the side of his kiln when he was making bronze, was useless. Hasga could melt the red rock and force it to give up its secrets but its secrets were of no value. Yet these men, and the iron men from beyond the mountains, knew the secret of making strong iron. If only they would teach him he could protect his family and his friends.

A musician began to play a drum, beating out a rhythm which filled the place where everyone was sitting and eating, talking excitedly about the newcomers and especially the return of Amra. What strange people she had brought back with her. Men with black skins! As the drumming intensified, people's conversations came to an end but their excitement remained. The Headman stood and wiped his mouth. He took a draft of beer and held up his hands for silence. The musician stopped his drumming.

'My people, we are often honoured with travellers who bring goods from distant lands for us to trade. Today we welcome important men from Troy, brought here to us by Amra. Amra was called by the Gods to be a sacrifice, but she begged me to listen to the words of the Gods which came to her in a dream. I listened, and now she has returned with Mithrassa-Urbek and men skilled in making iron weapons. I was right to listen to the words of the Gods. These men will make weapons for us so that we can call together the other villagers from the five rivers in the valleys and arm ourselves against the invaders, the men of iron. These men are now on the other side of the mountains, and we know they will soon cross and invade our lands.'

The Headman lifted his stick and pointed into the darkness. All eyes followed but there was no light to see. Everybody knew, however, that the mountains which shielded and protected the village were long longer impassable. The iron men were on the other side of the mountain and would be here in a short while. It was inconceivable that they could climb the mountains – no-one from any of the villages had ever managed to do so – but they could come through the pass which was four days march away. It was guarded by a large army, made up of men from all the villages in all the valleys, but they would need weapons to hold back the iron men.

'Amra is a woman now. Had she not returned, the Gods had commanded that her sister Peta would be sacrificed. Had she returned and not brought the secret of making iron, then Amra would have been sacrificed. But the Gods are pleased, they know that Amra has followed their ways. The Gods have walked with Amra and have returned with her. Usually when we gather here, we listen to the stories of traders. They tell us about their travels and the things that are to be found beyond the mountains. Amra has been beyond other mountains. Now she will tell us what lies beyond and what she has seen.'

He pointed his stick at Amra and sat down. Amra was already light-headed from the beer. She stood and looked down at her father. His look of pride and joy was the most beautiful thing she had ever seen. She knew her mother was also looking down from the seat of the Gods, and that she was smiling. She looked across at Peta. Her face was a mask of wonderment, she was overawed at being at the meeting. Normally she would be lurking in the shadows, trying not to be seen, but now she was with the adults of the village. Amra could feel the pride which was nearly bursting Peta's heart. This was the most wonderful moment of her life.

Amra's legs shook as she stood there looking at her friends, her neighbours, the men and women she had journeyed so far to protect and had returned to save. How could she possibly tell them about the things she had seen? Would they believe her if she described the peacock in Troy? Would they understand its colours and the fan of its tail? If she described taming the bull in Troy would they think she was lying? If she told them about being raped by three men and then cutting off their manhood and wearing it around her neck, would they wince in horror and get angry? She didn't know. What she did know was that she was Amra: Amra the hunter, Amra the bull tamer, Amra who had brought back the secret of making iron. She looked at Mithrassa–Urbek and saw him smiling and nodding gently. He would verify anything she told them and she would tell them everything. She began to speak.

'I am Amra the traveller,' she said. 'Here is my story.'

Amra's head ached. She opened her eyes and her memories flooded back. She could hear again the gasps of shock from the men and women around the fire when she described the horrors and difficulties of her journey. She still felt the warmth of their admiration when she had told of her plight and how she overcame it. She remembered the look of pain in her father's eyes when she described being raped on the river bank, but also the smile of pride on his face when she told how she had avenged herself. Then there were the looks of disbelief when she told people about the bull. She had felt people turning away from her story then, until Mithrassa-Urbek had stood and silenced everybody with his support for every statement that she made.

If only she hadn't drunk so much beer. She opened her eyes wider to try to see the daylight. Peta and her father were no longer in the house. She wondered where they were. She got out of bed but her legs felt like water. She was desperate to drink and slake her thirst. She walked outside and felt the rays of sun shining on her. She smelt the pure mountain air and looked at the thin ribbon of river at the bottom of the valley in the distance. Her river. She had yearned for this sight from the moment she had left her home. The sense of adventure she had felt as she rode Wind into the unknown distance had always been tempered by her need for security. It was this sight, the sight she saw every morning when she left her bed and went outside to gather water and fuel for her parents' breakfast, which was her security. She knew where her home was. She knew where the river was. She knew every blade of grass in-between. When she rose first thing in the morning, she could look down at the river and could tell which tree had dropped its wood in the night for her to gather and use for the fire.

Amra smiled as she looked down at the pot gently simmering on the flames. Peta had taken over her role of making breakfast for her father. The water had herbs steeping in it for a delicious drink. Eggs gathered from nearby nests had been boiled and were waiting for Amra to eat. A pot of honey, covered by a film of linen to keep away insects, was waiting to spread over the bread Peta had got from the baker further down the hill. The last thing Amra wanted was food. She had feasted well last night and was so full she felt sick. But she wanted a drink. She picked up a spoon and scooped up a cupful of liquid from the pot and blew on its surface to cool it. The scent of mint filled her nose; it was delicious. She squatted on the ground and lifted the linen from the pot, scooping a trickle of honey into the cup. As she sipped the drink relief spread through her body. The strains, the fears of the past three months drained away and tears welled in her eyes. She was home. She was safe. She looked up into the Heavens and said, 'Thank you, mother, for protecting me. Thank you, bee totem. Thank you, Gods.'

When she had finished her drink, Amra felt well enough to go in search of her father and Peta. She knew they would be in the forest where her father traditionally made metal, unobserved by the other villagers. In the distance she saw a thin curl of smoke trailing upwards through the trees on the windless day. She ran through the meadow, enjoying the delicious feel of the soft loamy earth beneath her feet, a stark contrast to the dry baked earth of the land of the Hittites. She ran towards the smoke where the four metalworkers were working. To her surprise Hasga and Peta were standing at a distance from the metalworkers, almost out of their sight.

'They won't let me see their secrets,' Hasga said disconsolately.

Amra nodded. 'I know. The King told me that he could not allow so great a secret to be known in case we raised an army against him.'

'Then how will I make weapons?'

'They will make the weapons,' said Amra.

'But they can't make what we need. We need hundreds of swords and many arrowheads for each man in the valley. We have to make enough to supply all of the people who live here and in the other villages. Can these men do that?'

'Yes, father,' said Amra, nodding.

'Are you sure?'

'Yes, father,' she insisted.

'But they have brought so little rock with them. I've seen that rock; the traders bring it from far away. I crush it and make iron from it but the iron is of no use. I need to know how they make the iron which can be used for swords, not the iron which breaks when it gets cold. I've seen them burning wood, not for a fire but to make charcoal. Why? What are they doing with the charcoal? They don't seem to be using it to heat the kiln and the furnace. And the red rock? I must know.'

'I will ask Mithrassa-Urbek,' Amra said.

'I know where to get this rock, Amra. It comes from far away in the direction of the new sun. Many valleys from here. It's in a mountain, or so the travellers say, a red mountain. Often they bring the rock with them. They know how to crush it and I have learnt their ways but I can't make iron which is good.'

'I know father,' Amra said. She could see how worried he was.

She returned to the village, but when she asked him Mithrassa-Urbek shook his head sadly. 'I don't know the secret, Amra, and these men will not tell me. Their lives would be forfeit if they divulged it.'

'But that's why I came to you.'

'The King made it very clear,' he said as gently as he could, 'that the secret would not be given. Instead the metalworkers will spend their time here making as many weapons as you need to equip enough men to fight the army which is facing you. But even so, Amra, no army can win without chariots. That is why you must give up these ideas of making swords and instead do what we do in Troy. You must spend all your efforts in making chariots. That is how Troy became a great nation. It is how we defeated the Egyptians at the battle of Kadesh.

'Let me tell you why chariots make you invincible. At the back of the chariot rides an archer and a spearman. They carry many replacement weapons in the chariot. The horseman rides like the very fury into the face of the attacking army but before he gets too close he slows the chariot and pulls it around. At this point the enemy advances quickly, thinking that the chariot is an easy target and can be simply overwhelmed. But when the enemy gets closer, the archer fires off a volley of arrows into the very face of the oncoming army. Because they are running forward they cannot stop; there are too many behind them. They drop, one after the other, like ants trampled underfoot. The spearman throws his many javelins at the frontrunners, then the charioteer rides his horses away to safety. We have six hundred chariots, Amra. No army can defeat us.'

'Then why won't you give us the secret of making iron?'

Mithrassa-Urbek laughed. 'Because it's the secret of the Gods. Because only the men who are working in the forest yonder can ever know the secret. They, and the King.'

'Will they be able to save my village?'

He stroked her hair and kissed her forehead. 'Yes.'

'You know that if they don't produce enough iron weapons I am to be sacrificed?'

Mithrassa-Urbek nodded.

Amra was relieved. She trusted Mithrassa-Urbek. But she couldn't understand why he kept telling her to make chariots. Didn't he understand that chariots couldn't ride over the ground in the valleys? This was not flat Troy; it was a land of mountains and valleys. Couldn't he see that?

Four days after they had arrived, the metalworkers walked back into the village. They led two horses weighed down by panniers strapped precariously to their sides. The panniers were covered by flax cloths. For the past two days the sound of hammers ringing on anvils had been heard throughout the area. It was the beat of an army, the sound the villagers sometimes heard when Hasga the armourer was working at making a new sword or spear. But these men had been working at a pace which was so furious that it sounded as though the Gods themselves were fighting in the forest. Their hammering never seemed to stop, not even for a moment. The three anvils owned by Hasga were constantly in use and other anvils had been brought in from other metalworkers in the five valleys.

Then the anvils had fallen silent. Now the men walked towards the village and people gathered around them. They looked rough and unkempt and their hands were stained black with the effort of their work. Their clothes were filthy and unwashed and their hair was matted, but there was a look of satisfaction in their eyes as they walked into the centre of the village.

The Headman came out of his house and greeted them. The chief armourer stopped the horses and released the panniers, spilling the accumulated weapons onto the ground. There was a gasp of amazement from those who had gathered around. On the ground where the huge fire had been lit for Amra's return lay an amazing variety of weapons. Each was brilliantly hewn in shining silver, gleaming in the light of day. There were swords as long as a man's arm, daggers the length of his hand, spearheads and arrowheads. The armourer upended the other pannier and more weapons deepened the pile. The other armourers did the same with their two panniers. From a cloth attached to the back of one of the horses, the chief armourer took two shields with leather grips at the back. They were round and blazed like the sun.

The Headman laughed and jumped up and down with joy. 'And these are iron?' he asked.

'These are iron,' said the chief armourer, no longer as taciturn as he had been when he first entered the village.

'And these will fight the men of iron?'

'They are as good as any iron swords which these men will carry.'

'And are there enough?' asked the Headman.

'We have used all of the ore we brought with us. You must find new sources of ore. We have retained a small amount of ore so that you will know what to look for when you hunt. Your armourer of this village tells me that traders bring ore to you. Find the source and send wagons to gather it yourself. You will need much ore if you are to make weapons.'

Hasga walked forward and stood beside the pile on the ground. 'But how am I to make weapons from the ore unless I know your secret?'

'You must discover the secret,' said the armourer.

'How did you discover the secret?' asked Hasga.

'I cannot tell you. We have done what we were commanded to do by Praxis, King of Troy. You have weapons and this girl's debt has been repaid.' He pointed to Amra. 'The King owes you no more.'

The Headman bent down and picked up one of the iron swords. He tried to bend it but it was immovable. He walked over to where a piece of wood lay on the ground, picked it up and told two people to hold it between them. He raised the sword and cleft the wood in two as though he were slicing newly baked bread. He turned and smiled at the Trojan armourers. 'You have done well.'

'I'm sorry we cannot give you the secret,' said the armourer. 'We are forbidden. I don't know how the men from beyond the mountains know the secret of making iron but however they found out, you must now find it from them. I will help you by saying just this. Capture one of their armourers and torture him to give you the secret. Once it is yours, then . . .' He shrugged.

The Medicine Man walked forward and whispered something into the ear of the Headman, who smiled. He turned to the Trojan and said, 'We are many. You are few. If we torture you, we will learn the secret.'

'The secret dies with us,' said the armourer. 'And you forget that we have guards who are invincible.' He nodded to the four Nubian guards who were walking towards the Headman.

The law of the village said that guests had to be treated with respect and hospitality. The Headman knew very well that if he were to imprison any of these people from Troy the Gods would be very angry.

'And further,' said the Trojan armourer, 'if you do kill us, Praxis will send an army to your village which will be unlike any army you have ever seen before. The ground will thunder with their chariots. Not a man, woman or child will be left alive when Praxis's anger has been satisfied. Do not think for one moment, savage, that you can harm me or my fellow metalworkers.'

The Headman knew that the Trojan spoke the truth. He bent and picked up another sword which he handed to one of his own guards. More people bent to the ground and picked up weapons. But even though many people became armed, Amra's joy turned to consternation when she saw that nearly all the weapons the men had made had been picked up. Only her village was equipped. What of the other villages in the valleys? Weren't they also going to need iron weapons when the men of iron descended on them? More ore needed to be found. And they also had to find the secret of turning it into iron.

Amra and Mithrassa-Urbek were sitting by the river, quietly talking. They had been doing this for many days. Their relationship had grown warm, even loving. Mithrassa-Urbek told Amra many of the secrets of Troy, things which, in her short visit to the city, she had not seen. In return, she told Mithrassa-Urbek the secrets of her village.

The armourers and two of the Nubian guards had returned many days ago to Troy. Mithrassa-Urbek had decided not to return with them but instead to stay with Amra and to try to learn more from her of her healing powers. She was pleased to teach him the things that her mother and the older women of the village had taught her. He learnt much about the use of herbs for refreshment and for healing wounds, sores, ulcers and cuts. He learnt which herbs helped a woman in pregnancy, which stopped her from becoming pregnant, which helped a man whose virility was flagging and which were used by mothers when their children's bodies burnt with fever.

In the time he had spent with Amra and her family he had come to know and love the young girl, to look upon her as a daughter. What he admired most about her was the way she cared for her younger sister. She had told him often that she would willingly sacrifice herself for Peta. He did not think his own daughters would promise such a thing, nor had he ever believed similar protestations by loving husbands and parents in Troy. It was often said in propitiation of the Gods, but in his heart Mithrassa-Urbek knew that it was nothing more than rhetoric. But not for Amra. For the first time in his life, he knew with absolute certainty that he had met someone who would willingly lay down her life for those she loved.

Amra was telling him how to make a lotion to treat a sty in the eye when the commotion began. A man ran towards the Headman's house, shouting anxiously. Frowning, Amra stood and began to walk quickly back into the village. Mithrassa–Urbek followed her.

Mithrassa–Urbek found the man's excited babble difficult to follow. 'What is it?' he asked Amra.

'He has just come from cutting wood halfway up the mountain. He says that a man came over the top of the mountain, a man from the other side. I don't understand. Nobody can cross the mountains. They're too high. There are passes in the valleys but they're a long way away. Four days' journey or more. They're only used by travellers and they're guarded by many men.'

'But what is he saying?' asked Mithrassa–Urbek.

Amra listened carefully to the man's explanation. 'He says the man who crossed the mountain told him that his village had been destroyed by men with long swords. There were so many men that nobody could fight them. He said everybody had swords and they were made of iron. He said the iron men are coming, that they will be here soon.'

The Headman forced his way through the crowd and told the man to repeat his story. This time Mithrassa–Urbek could understand a lot more. On hearing the news, the Headman became angry. He pointed up to the top of the distant mountains with his wisdom staff. 'The iron men cannot cross that mountain. They can only cross by the gap in the mountain. That is four days' journey away in the direction of the dying sun. We from the villages in the five valleys have many men there to stop them. That is why they have not come in the past. Now many more will gather and will wait in the valley so that the iron men cannot travel beyond the pass. I will gather together all the men of the villages in the valleys of the rivers and we will march and stop them coming.'

The woodcutter shook his head frantically. 'No. It is too late. The iron men are already there. They're already at the top. The man who told me has gone to warn the other villages. The iron men will be here tomorrow.'

'We must pray to the Gods that bolts of lightning and thunder will be sent against them to turn them away, that rain will make their climb impassable, that wind and storms will kill them when they dare to climb to the seat of the Gods. And if the Gods do not hear our prayers, we have weapons,' said the Headman. But even he had come to realise that the weapons the Trojans had made were too few to stop the hordes of iron men who had done the impossible – they had scaled the mountains. They must be truly powerful.

'I will call a meeting of the Great Council,' he said. 'We will decide what to do.'

Amra looked at Mithrassa–Urbek in despair. His only reaction was to shake his head.

The council met in the afternoon. Hasga participated with great anxiety. The gates of the meeting hall were closed since this was a council of war, a council which could not be disturbed for any reason. But before its conclusion Hasga was seen to storm out of the hall, his face ashen. Amra had heard him shouting. Her father never shouted, but he had been shouting at the Headman, the Medicine Man and the other men of the council. Amra looked at him as he walked angrily towards her. She knew what he was about to say.

'The men of iron are at the top of the mountain. We must beg the Gods to intervene on our behalf to stop them. Despite what I said in the meeting the Headman claims that the Gods have appeared to him.' He could not continue. His face crumpled.

'Is it me?' Amra asked.

Hasga shook his head and the blood drained from Amra's face. 'Peta?'

Hasga nodded. 'You cannot allow this, father.'

'I have threatened to leave the village. I have begged them to take a child from another family. I have told them of all we have been through. But the Headman says that the Gods have spoken. It is decided.'

Mithrassa–Urbek stood beside Amra. 'Is there no other way?'

Hasga shook his head. 'None. It has been decreed.'

Amra's eyes filled with tears. 'You can't. It's not fair. Take me. I have lived a life.'

'There is no way that you can be sacrificed in place of Peta. The Headman has spoken. The whole village will be destroyed unless we propitiate the Gods. He says that you agreed to bring back the secret of making iron, yet we still do not have it. He says that with Peta's sacrifice the Gods will smile again on us.'

'No!' Amra shouted.

Hearing her sister's distress, Peta came running out of the house. She put her arms around Amra, wondering what could be wrong. All Amra could do was to hold her sister tightly and pray for an answer.

Night fell and a huge fire was lit. Amra was too distressed to speak to her father or to Mithrassa–Urbek. She had begged to be alone. She knew there was nothing she could do. She must watch her sister's heart be cut from her body and her young and beautiful life extinguished. Her mind whirled with plans to save Peta – to run away, to offer herself instead – but they all came to nothing. Amra knew her sister would be dead before the fire had grown to its full and awful size.

The guards came for the little girl. Amra sat in her room and wept. Mithrassa–Urbek tried to comfort her but there was nothing he could do to console her. He was desolate for her. She had travelled so far and had been through so much, and now this. These were a cruel people to make Amra suffer so. He suggested that Peta and Amra escape with him and the Nubian guards. The village was doomed anyway and that they should save themselves, as he would save himself, by leaving in the morning. But Amra had refused. She told him that the Gods would find them no matter where they were and would punish them anyway.

Hasga appeared at the entrance to her room. He was wearing his new tunic. 'We must go,' he said.

'I can't,' Amra said, sobbing. 'I can't watch.'

'You must, Amra. You are a woman of the village. You must watch the sacrifice or the Gods will be insulted. Then they will be angry and their anger will be turned against us.'

'I cannot.'

'Amra,' he repeated sternly, 'it is your duty. You owe it to the village.' He reached down and grasped her by the hand. Amra stood stiffly and walked with him out of the house. Mithrassa–Urbek followed them towards the huge fire.

The heat was palpable long before they reached the blaze itself. It was the biggest fire the village had ever made; now it was facing its most desperate threat. Amra looked around for Peta, but realised too late that she would be in the guards hut, waiting to be called by the Headman.

The drummer's beat thumped against Amra's head. The villagers sang and wailed prayers to the Gods. It was an awesome noise. As a child Amra had only ever heard it from the very edge of the village's fortifications; now she was in the middle of it. And it was an overwhelming noise, full of evil, ugliness and terror.

The Headman raised his wisdom staff. The singing stopped and the drummer ceased his rhythm. In the silence a sense of dread filled the village. When the knife plunged into Peta's heart it would be felt by everybody.

When they heard the sudden silence, the guards brought Peta out of the hut. Amra was shocked when she saw her: her face was ashen, her lips white. She knew what was going to happen to her. Tears were coursing down her cheeks. Her hands were tied behind her back and her chest was exposed, her budding breasts glistening in the light of the fire. She screamed out: 'Amra! Amra, help me! Why are they doing this? Stop them. Please!'

But Amra could do nothing except weep for her little sister. The pain was too great, the horror too much to bear. She could feel her consciousness begin to slip away.

Suddenly Mithrassa-Urbek stepped forward. 'Stop!' he cried.

The Headman looked at him in amazement. Nobody had the right to stop a sacrifice. It was an offence punishable by death.

'I am a priest of Mithras,' Mithrassa-Urbek shouted to the Headman and to the villagers. 'This woman Amra is a priestess of the God Mithras. The God Mithras is ruler of all the Gods. He has decreed that this girl Peta shall be spared and that the priestess Amra shall be sacrificed in her place. The God Mithras has spoken to me and demands that Amra is returned to him. This, he says, will make him happy. This will stop the iron men.'

The Headman stared between the Trojan and Amra. He didn't know what to do. Of all the villagers, only he knew that he had not had a dream in which Peta's face came to him. It had been Amra's face all those months ago. But the sacrifice of Peta was the only thing he could conceive of which might prevent the iron men from coming. But now this stranger, this powerful man from a powerful city, was telling him he was wrong. Perhaps the Gods were angry that they had been cheated of their sacrifice all those months ago. Perhaps Amra's death now would appease them.

He shouted to the guards, 'Release Peta. Bring Amra to me.'

The guards cut Peta's ropes and walked towards Amra. Hasga tried to stop them, but when he looked at his older daughter he saw to his amazement that she was smiling. Ignoring her father, Amra walked over to Mithrassa-Urbek and the Headman. She looked into Mithrassa-Urbek's eyes. They were wet with tears. 'Thank you,' she whispered.

'I know it is what you want.'

Amra nodded. 'When I am in Heaven with my mother, I will smile down upon you. Peta will be your daughter now.'

Mithrassa-Urbek tried to speak, but couldn't. He didn't want Amra's last view of him to be of an old man in tears.

She touched his shoulder and said, 'Look up into the sky and you will see me looking down upon you with the love of a daughter.'

The guards grasped Amra by the arms. Mithrassa-Urbek walked back to Hasga and put his arms around him to shield his eyes. The drums began again. Peta screamed hysterically as the Headman thrust the knife into Amra's chest and removed her heart.

Hasga and Mithrassa-Urbek carried Amra's body up the hill to the burial place. They placed her body on its side in the earth, her knees bent, her hands clasped together. Her father kissed her amulet and laid it gently between her breasts, covering the bloody and gaping hole where her heart had once been. Tears coursed down his face as he and two men lifted a heavy flat stone and placed it on the ledge above her. Then they placed stones and rocks over the flat stone and filled in the rest of the grave with earth.

The other villagers threw fresh leaves over the grave then turned to walk down the hill, but Hasga remained with his daughter. Overcome by grief, he knelt by her graveside, then threw himself across the cold earth in the fading light. He lay there sobbing for Amra.

When he eventually stood it was night. The Sun God had died and was sinking into the Eternal Sea. Hasga wiped the tears from his eyes, lamenting his unhappy life, and looked up to the mountains behind the village. There, far away, he saw the last rays of the sun burning on the top of the mountains.

But when he looked more closely, he realised that it wasn't the sun at all. It was a campfire, ablaze. And then he saw another campfire, and another, and another. The whole of the top of the mountain was alight with the fires of the iron men.

EPILOGUE

Ruthenia, 1903

Nussan the farmer felt surrounded by enemies. No matter what the season, Almighty God sent enemies to plague him. Year in, year out. Without respite. He had been working for nine hours since the early morning with only the satisfaction of a drink of beer and a midday schlug of schnapps to relieve the aching tiredness deep in his bones, but he was nowhere near finishing what had to be done.

He straightened his back and wiped his eyes, his neck knotted from the strain of the plough. It came as something of a surprise, but he realised that, despite his aches and pains, he was smiling. He usually managed to smile, even in the worst of adversity, when he was so tired he could barely lead his horse back to the stables.

And who knew more about adversity than Nussan? Sometimes he felt like one of the ancient people he read about in the Torah every shabbos. Like one of the patriarchs. Every time those poor bastards looked up to heaven with their sweat-blinded eyes, there always seemed to be a plague sent by a merciless God to torment them. Nussan felt that he was being tormented just as God had tormented Job. Now why would a merciful God — so the Rabbis called Him — do the sort of things He did to Job? Of course, things were different these days. The plagues which Abraham, Isaac and Jacob suffered were dust storms, insects, plunderers, idol-worshippers and marauders. Today's plagues were vicious landlords, taxes, debts, anti-Semites, pogroms, massacres and drunken madmen from the Christian village who came just to torment his people. But when you boiled it all down, nothing much had changed in three thousand years. God was still as uncaring about his Chosen People as He'd ever been. Still testing them, ensuring they were worthy. Ha! Worthy of what? Of plagues, that's what!

Only the other day, Nussan's horse had been pulling the plough when his foot slipped into a rabbit hole and he went lame. No bones broken, thank God, but Nussan didn't know that. All he knew was that his horse was lying on the ground, whinnying in pain and fear. So Nussan lost his temper with God. He picked up a branch and stormed over to a corner of the field (his only field, the one the landlord allowed him to plough) and he shook the branch at God and threatened Him.

'Look you! You listen to me, I've had enough,' he yelled at the sky. 'You think you've broken me, don't you? You think you've broken my spirit. Well, you haven't. But I'm not going to take this anymore. Now just leave me alone and find some other poor bastard to pick on.' And Nussan had waited, breathing heavily, sweat pouring from his brow, his anger still fermenting, listening to the agonising, contemptuous sound of the Almighty's indifference and silence. He screamed in agony and frustration and threw the stick at the cloud. But the stick just fell ignominiously to earth and Nussan trudged back across the field feeling foolish. He stroked his horse's head and massaged its limb until the animal was able to limp home, leaving the field still unploughed and dangerously close to the time when Nussan would have to plant the corn in order for his family to survive.

The horse recovered. Nussan apologised to God, and together – God, the horse and Nussan – they continued to plough the field as they had done year after year, and as Nussan's father had done for years before that.

Today Nussan was ploughing an area in the upper corner of the field that, in all the time that he had been farming he had never known to be touched. Frankly, that's why the landlord had allowed Nussan's family to farm the field, because at least one-third of it was unusable. Yet the goyishe bastard still charged him the same rent as for a whole field. Nussan and a friend had spent a week at the end of the growing season the previous autumn clearing rocks. Their reward for the backbreaking work was that a large patch of land, which had never been ploughed, was now available for use. Of course the soil had never been turned and so it would be difficult, but he had to make a start somewhere. It had been a terrible job, digging up the rocks, breaking them into manageable pieces and dumping them close to the river. At one stage, Nussan had thought his heart would give out, but between them they had managed to clear a large enough portion of the hill to grow at least another twenty per cent of crops. When they'd finished, the landlord rode out and congratulated Nussan on the work. Arrogant pig. His son had been with him, dressed in velvets and wearing a silk cravat, sneering at Nussan because he was wearing a filthy, torn shirt and patched trousers. What did the young landlord know about work, with his soft, girlish hands?

By the middle of the afternoon, Nussan had managed to uncover and expose most of the new area for the first time. When he was almost at the top of the hill, at the point where the horse was unsure of its footing on the steep incline, Nussan's plough hit a large hidden rock. He sighed. He was only a quarter of the way along the new furrow, but that was typical of his life. One step forward, two back. He looked down and saw what he had already completed that day. He had added considerably to the quality of his holding – it had been a good day's work. He felt satisfied. He looked at the rest of the unploughed ground and was in two minds about giving it away. It would be a hell of a job digging up this hidden rock. After all, it was the last furrow, and he was hot and wanted to get home. But something stopped him from giving in. 'Don't leave things half done, Nussan,' he muttered to himself, remembering his father's words. 'Always finish the job you're doing, Nussan, because if not, it'll only be there in the morning.'

So he got a pick from where he had left his other tools and started to dig out the earth around the stone. It was bigger than he'd thought and he was tempted to leave it, but, eventually, after struggling this way and that, he managed to pry it free of the grasping fingers of the earth. It began a slow roll down the decline, much to Nussan's annoyance. Now he would have to break it up and get rid of it near the river. Looking into the hole, Nussan was surprised to see that it held another stone. But this one looked strange. It was almost flat, as though it had been placed there. He knelt down and further loosened the soil until he had exposed some more of the flat stone. It looked frighteningly like a gravestone, though there were no markings on it.

Nussan said a small prayer for protection and spat over his left shoulder to ward off the evil eye. He worked further into the earth to find the corners of the stone. The hole was now waist deep and sweat was pouring from him. He tapped his pick on the centre of the stone – it sounded as though there was a space underneath. Now he was truly frightened. Shadows were already lengthening and the light in the field was disappearing. There was something other-worldly about this. He could feel his heart beating against his chest and it wasn't just from the hard work. He tried to remember the prayers he had learnt in cheder about evil spirits and God's protection from the demons and the evil eye. 'Make this safe, God,' he mumbled. If only he had been a better Jew, and paid more attention in shul, he'd know what prayers to say, what to do.

Exposing the corner of the stone he worked his pick underneath and, using all his strength, raised the huge slab a fraction, letting light enter a cavity that had been closed to the sun for millennia. Earth ran down from the wall he had dug into the space below as he levered the slab higher and higher until it was almost vertical. Propping it against the wall, Nussan looked down into the cavity and screamed in horror. The dry, broken fingers of a skeletal hand pointed at him, reaching out from deep within the earth.

Panic rose in his chest, and he sprang back from the hideous sight, pressing himself against the earthen wall. He spat over his shoulder three times for protection and mumbled whichever bits of prayers came to his mind. After a few moments the panic began to subside and reason took over from fear. Taking deep breaths, he tentatively bent down and touched the skeleton. It was definitely a human hand, no question about that. But how old was it? Nussan wasn't good at guessing the age of people who were alive, let alone dry bones in the earth. Once, many years ago, he had helped the gravedigger move some ancient graves and had seen the skeleton of an old rabbi who had died a hundred years earlier. But that didn't seem to be anything compared to this. If he had to guess, Nussan thought that it had probably been here far longer than the Jews who had come to the area in the eleventh century. It could even be prehistoric.

And now Nussan began to wonder whether this skeleton could be of value. Maybe to a museum? He'd heard about museums in Prague and London that were interested in these sorts of things. The skeleton wasn't on his land, he was only the farmer, but maybe he could share his find with the owner. Suddenly the skeleton began to take on an entirely different significance.

Slowly he worked the earth to reveal more of the bones. A limb here. Further over, a thigh. Then a skull. And all the while Nussan mumbled half-remembered prayers from the days of his childhood. It was when he was clearing the earth around the ribcage that his eyes lit upon the most exciting thing he had ever seen in his entire life. For there, buried deep in the cavity of the skeleton, was the most beautiful necklace ever made, a work of such beauty that, initially, he forbore touching it out of reverence. It was as beautiful as the gold ornaments he had seen around the necks of rich women in picture books, the heavy necklaces and chains worn by Tsarinas and princesses. Nobody in his stetl, nobody in the main town, wore anything comparable to this. This was large and weighty, and looked wonderfully expensive.

When he finally removed it, it was about the size of a large coin, but thicker and heavier than any coin he had ever held in his pocket. Nussan poured water over it from his flask and even more beauty was revealed. The markings on it were incredibly lovely, carefully carved to form the most intricate of patterns, circles leading into deeper circles until they seemed to disappear into the very centre of the amulet. His hand was shaking. He looked at the amulet carefully. On one side was some sort of symbol, a horse. But then he looked closer and saw horns – it was a bull. He turned it over. On the other side was a fat bird, perhaps an owl. The amulet itself was on a chain of gold which was as heavy as the charm it carried. Nussan spat twice into the ground and mumbled a prayer of thanks to God. But then he recited another half-remembered prayer to protect him from the evil eye because, even at first glance, he could see that there was nothing Jewish about the amulet, nor was there anything

Christian. It held none of the crosses or religious symbols he'd seen outside the churches in the main street of the town. Could it have been made before the Christians? Could it be that old?

If it was, it must be worth a fortune. He was a rich man. He looked up and shouted to the sky, 'God bless you! God bless you for this, dear Lord. You've made me a happy man, a rich man. God bless you for this. God bless you!'

Nussan's wife stared at her beaming husband as he stood there, still covered in sweat and dirt but grinning like a shickerer who had just come home from the inn. Normally when he came in after a day in the fields he was grumpy and ill-tempered until he had washed and eaten. Today he had rushed through the door, screaming her name and telling the entire household that they were rich, rich beyond their wildest dreams.

Serel's eyes widened in amazement as Nussan proffered the amulet towards her, like a doctor handing over a newborn baby. But suddenly he changed his mind and slipped the necklace and amulet over her head, brushing her chestnut curls with his hands.

Serel had never owned a necklace and had no idea what one should weigh. But this one was so heavy it felt as if it was bending her neck. She held her hand to her chest and fingered the amulet. A lightness came over her spirit, a sudden heady moment of excitement, like a first kiss or unexpectedly seeing a man swimming naked in the river.

But then the sun went behind a cloud. 'What do you mean, you found it? Just like that. Punkt! In a field. What am I, a fool? You stole it, didn't you! You found it on the road and picked it up and stole it. Didn't you? Some rich woman dropped it. You're mad. We'll be arrested. We'll all be hanged for theft,' she shouted, her voice rising in anger and panic.

Nussan put his finger to her lips. 'Hush,' he said. 'Look at it. Feel it. This isn't the jewellery of a rich city woman. This isn't what ladies in Prague and Kiev have made specially for them by jewellers in Paris and London. I found it in the ground. See, there's still dirt on it. This is old, Serel. This is really old. This comes from times long past. Maybe a thousand, maybe two thousand years ago, I don't know.'

But Serel shook her head more violently still. Fear began to consume her. She snatched the chain and amulet from around her neck and held it away from her, as though it carried some kind of disease.

'I don't want to keep this, Nussan. There's danger here. If the town gets to hear about it, we could be in trouble. Oh God, what have you done? Please God protect us from your stupidity. Nussan, you have to turn this in to the constable or give it to the landlord. It's his by rights.' She shook her head again, 'I don't want it.' She waved the necklace at him, willing him to take it from her so that she wouldn't be tainted by its danger.

Nussan suddenly became very angry. 'Do you know how hard I work in the field every day?' he shouted. 'I break my back just to grow a few vegetables and then when I've got just enough to feed the family and pay for some meat, the landlord takes half of it just for the privilege of letting me work his land. And now! Now when I have a bit of luck, the first luck I've ever had in all my life, you want me to give it away. Is that it?'

He was shaking with rage. Serel's reaction was so different from what he'd expected. He thought that they'd be celebrating tonight with special shabbos food and maybe some wine and, maybe, when the children were asleep, some loving comfort. But it was all going wrong, as every damn thing went wrong in his life.

Still furious, he shouted at her, 'I'm going to hide it in the barn under the horse shit where the authorities, with their soft, white hands, won't bother to look. And then we're going to find somebody who'll buy it from us so we'll have money to leave this godforsaken hole of a town and go to America.'

Serel was on the verge of tears as Nussan snatched the necklace from her outstretched hands. She loved and respected her husband even when he was wrong. She'd caused him pain and anger, but he was so misguided, so unrealistic. They were stetl Jews. That was all. Not rich and important people. Didn't he understand? Poor people weren't entitled to these sorts of things. He talked about luck. Other people were lucky, not him, not her. Nussan wheeled around and walked out of their tiny house, slamming the door. The sudden noise started baby Eva crying in her crib.

Nussan didn't go back into the house after burying the amulet. Instead he washed himself with what water remained in the horse's pail, dried himself on a rag and stormed up the hill towards the inn where he would get shicker whether there was anybody else there or not.

Two hours later he was still sitting in a corner in the smoke-filled room, and had told his closest friend his deepest secret. And then he told a friend who wasn't so close, and another friend, until even Reb Avram the beggar had heard the news. Just who it was that told the local constable, Nussan would never know, but the following day the constable told the town's burgher that a valuable find had been made in the field which the Jew, Nussan, farmed. The town's burgher informed certain members of the town's council, who in turn told the local Russian Orthodox priest, who in his turn whispered the news to the head of the local group of the Black 100, and so the identity of the informant was lost to history.

As soon as Mikhael Ostrovski, a forty-five-year-old factory superintendent who hated the Jews of the town with a biting vengeance, heard about Nussan the farmer's find, he decided to get the boys together to teach the Jews a lesson or two. Word had come down from Kiev that the authorities would turn a blind eye to a bit of trouble, and that was all the encouragement Ostrovski needed. It took him no more than a day to raise the twenty-three local members of the Black 100.

They prepared to mount their horses three nights after the evening that Nussan the farmer had divulged his secret. The twenty-three men rode cautiously from the Christian part of the town along the single road which led to the Jewish stetl down at the bottom of the hill. As they got closer, the mood of caution left them, they were suddenly charged with excitement. They spurred on their horses until the vibrations from the animals' hooves roused sluggish men and women from their deep slumber to wonder what was happening. As the horses galloped closer to the stetl, the Black 100s began to shout and yell like Cossacks. Their torches joined together as one flaming brand to pierce the dark.

Jewish men, who realised instinctively that they were listening to the start of a pogrom, jumped out of bed and looked through bedroom windows at the advancing spectre. They knew from years of bitter and deadly experience what was happening. They barked orders to their wives, 'Grab the children! Follow me downstairs into the cellar quickly.'

Mothers and fathers ran into their children's rooms, dragged terrified infants from their beds and pushed their hysterical families down stairs and into basements, where heavy iron-banded doors could be shut firmly against the evil eyes of the horsemen of the pogrom. Silent prayers were raised to God in Heaven from the depths of the forty cellars in the town as the horses and riders of the Black 100 thundered around the mud streets of the stetl, terrorising the inhabitants still above ground. The wails of men and the sobbing of women and children were drowned out by the thudding of hooves and the whooping and yelling of the hunters. The men threw their flaming torches up on to straw roofs, or into wooden buildings, which soon exploded with a roar of flames.

The riders drew their swords, waiting to strike down any Jews stupid enough to flee from their houses in fear of the flames. Two people did – an old man and an old woman who were too poor to afford a cellar. The riders wheeled their horses towards the elderly fleeing couple. Ostrovski, the leader, raised his sword high into the air and lunged at the stumbling old woman, who was desperately trying not to plunge headlong as she gathered up the skirt of her old torn nightdress to help her thin legs run faster. He struck her across her back. She pitched forward, the sword severing her spinal cord, and was dead as she tumbled into the gutter. Another rider cantered towards the old man who was trying to escape into a field. He aimed the point of his sword at the centre of the old man's shoulders and drove it easily through his rib cage and into his heart until it pierced all the way through his body.

The horses were wide-eyed with panic at the crackling and roaring of the flames. Pulling his horse to a halt, Ostrovski shouted out, 'Let's find the Jew, Nussan. He lives down here.' He pointed his sword towards a darkened house, whose outlines were barely illuminated by the fires of the town.

Nussan heard the men coming. He had been drinking late at the inn again, celebrating his new riches, and had just arrived back at his house. He took refuge in the bushes. While the riders circled the stetl and burned down the houses of his friends, Nussan could only crouch helplessly and watch them wheeling around like demons from a nightmare. He prayed to God that they wouldn't come this far out of the village. Not to his house! Not to attack his wife and children. Please God, no!

But like the avenging angels of death, the twenty-three men rode swiftly towards him. He should have stayed hidden behind the bushes but in the panic of his drunken state, he ran for the house. Terrified as he was, he had to save his wife and children, but halfway towards the front door, the men arrived, their horses' hooves trampling Serel's vegetable garden.

'Jew! Stand still. Are you Nussan the farmer?' Ostrovski shouted.

Nussan crouched in terror and felt himself pissing in his pants. 'Jew. I asked you a question!' Ostrovski repeated. 'When a Christian asks you a question, you answer. Now, are you Nussan the farmer? Answer me or I'll cut your balls off.'

Nussan nodded.

'This gold that you've found. Where is it? It doesn't belong to you. I want it.'

The other men on horseback roared with laughter.

Nussan shook his head and tried to stand, but he fell into a dead faint. He was awakened moments later, his body soaking. The men had thrown a pail of water over him. He was pinned to a wall by the rough and vicious hands of three of the men, supporting him so that his feet barely touched the ground. The point of a sword was pressing into his throat. Mikhael Ostrovski's face was so close that Nussan could smell his sweat and his foul vodka breath. Mikhael spat in fury, 'Listen, you filthy Jew scum. I want to know where that gold is. I'll give you ten seconds to tell me or we'll tear your place apart, bit by bit.'

He spat in the Jew's face, the spittle hitting him on the cheek.

Nussan shook his head. He was still drunk, trembling with fear. He couldn't focus his mind, couldn't remember where he'd hidden the amulet. Until he heard the words, 'Just kill the bastard and we'll rip the place to pieces.' Then he suddenly remembered. He'd tell them, just to get them to leave him alone, to save his family.

Nussan opened his mouth, but Mikhael laughed cruelly and drove his sword through Nussan's heart with the force of true hatred, pinning him to the wood of his horse's stable. The animal reared up and whinnied in terror. Mikhael tugged and withdrew the sword from the wooden door. Nussan's dead body slumped to the ground.

What the Black 100s didn't see while they were killing her husband was Nussan's wife, Serel, racing across the fields at the back of the house until she reached the river. There she lay with her three children as the madmen killed her family and friends in another of their murderous pogroms, ransacked the house, threw their clothes out of the windows and destroyed their precious furniture – all in their search for the gold amulet. Serel hadn't heard one word of the conversation between Nussan and the murderers, but she knew with every instinct in her body that it was all because of that cursed amulet.

The men continued to ravage the house, drinking bottles of wine and schnapps, until their drunken debauchery became even more violent. When they had pitched everything out of the windows, but still hadn't found the gold amulet, they set fire to the house in retribution. They watched the flames attack the curtains, the wooden beams, the innards of the broken furniture, and roared with laughter when the fire entered the roof and sent up a plume of flames high into the dark night air. Then they mounted their horses and rode away.

But Serel wasn't laughing. She was clasping her terrified children to her body, trying not to increase their fears by wailing to Almighty God.

Only at dawn, when smoke from the village hung like a doomcloud over the valley, did Serel rise up from the riverbank and look at the scene of devastation from the pogrom. Only then did she walk with her three children back to her house, knowing in her heavy heart that her stupid and greedy husband had brought this ruin and destruction upon her house, her family and upon all their neighbours and friends. Nussan's lifeless body lay in the horse shit and filth outside the stables. The children screamed in horror, and Serel hustled them away, instructing them to find the Rebbe and tell him what had happened. She would do her crying later.

She knelt, kissed her husband's cold, white forehead, then looked at the remains of her house, still smouldering, wisps of grey smoke rising into the dark morning clouds. She searched the filthy ground in front of what was once her safe and warm home, finding a dress, some clothes for the children, and a pot which she might be able to use along the way if she could gather some vegetables and herbs. She also found a large cloth, a sheet, into which she placed what little remained to her. It made a pathetic bundle.

Serel stood and walked to the gate. She looked up the road to the village to try and find her children. Men and women were wandering around in a daze, shaking their heads and crying. The old Rebbe was trying to comfort the broken souls. Her children waited dutifully to speak to him. Some men were already saying prayers in the blackened carcass of the shul, while others were picking through the burnt scraps of the holy Torahs to see what, if anything, remained of God.

She walked down the road and gathered up her children before the Rebbe had time to talk to them. Then she returned to her house, biting back tears of anger and fear. Holding her youngest, little Eva, in her arms, the two others following meekly, Serel looked into the carcass of their home. She stopped. Her husband had died for it, the village had been destroyed for it, but much as she hated it, it was her only means of survival. Serel told the children to stay where they were, not to re-enter the house, and walked into the barn.

The horse was quiet now that the noise and fire had died down. It snorted and whinnied when it saw her. It needed to be fed but Serel had more important things to do. Should she take it with her? It was valuable and it would make the journey much easier, but it would also make her prey to robbers along the way. Horses were worth much more than people. Serel looked around the barn and saw the pile of dung where her husband had hidden the treasure. She took a spade and shifted it, uncovering the amulet. She spat on it in disgust, but dropped it into the pail to wash it clean of the dried horse shit.

Outside in the damp early-morning air, Serel stroked her children's hair, whispering to them that everything would be all right. She picked up her baby again and comforted her, as she did her other children, smoothing their hair and tidying their clothes before they began their journey. They all stared at the lifeless eyes, the dead body of their father, her husband. Serel had neither the time nor the strength to bury him. She put the gold amulet inside her bodice and started to walk to America.

REFERENCES

I have consulted many experts to assist me in the writing of this novel and have referred to numerous authoritative texts and other documents.

Readers who are interested in further details of the historical aspects raised by this novel will find much of merit in the following books:

The Lost Treasures of Troy, Caroline Moorehead, Phoenix Giants.

Schliemann of Troy, Treasure and Deceit, David Traill, Penguin.

A History of Civilizations, Fernand Braudel, Penguin.

A History of Warfare, John Keegan, Pimlico.

Technology in the Ancient World, Henry Hodges, Michael O'Mara Books.

Women in Prehistory, Margaret Ehrenberg, British Museum Press.

Fire and Civilization, Johan Goudsblom, Penguin.

Ancient Greece, Utopia and Reality, Pierre Leveque, Thames and Hudson.

The Ancient Mediterranean, Michael Grant, Meridian.

The End of the Bronze Age, Robert Drews, Princeton University Press.

Forbidden Knowledge, Roger Shattuck, St. Martin's Press.

Hall's Dictionary of Subjects & Symbols in Art, John Murray Press.

Sacred Architecture, A. T. Mann, Element.

Strange Landscapes, Christopher Frayling, BBC Books.

Sex in History, Reay Tannahill, Abacus Books.

Writing, The Story of Alphabets and Scripts, Georges Jean, Thames and Hudson.

The Creators, Daniel J. Boorstin, Vintage Books.

Gift of Evil

Book I of Amra's Journey

Alan Gold

An ancient gold amulet with a history of violence and death. A highly organised group of killers who will do anything to keep secret their past identities and their crimes against humanity. A brilliant young New York lawyer with a passion for truth and justice. A Hollywood film director determined to expose the horrors committed in Slovakia under Stalin's regime.

When Josh Krantz wants to reclaim his grandparents' house from the Slovakian government, he has another agenda: to expose the evil crimes committed by Stalin's henchmen against the Krantz family and thousands of others. He engages the services of New York lawyer Sarah Kaplan, and together they travel to Slovakia to begin their fight.

Dr Laco Plastov – an archaeologist who is amazed by the engravings on Sarah's ancient amulet – joins the two Americans on their crusade. Delving into the past, they uncover the Syndicate – an organisation set up to protect the evil killers of thousands of innocent people during Stalin's regime.

Armed with the informationthat will expose these men and bring them to justice, Sarah, Josh and Laco become involved in a deadly and strategic contest – playing for their very lives.

This tale of evil, murder and retribution is international bestselling author Alan Gold at his very best.

ISBN 0 00 651270 4